ADVANCE

Another Must-Read for the Baby Boomer Generation

"I was a big fan of Ed Prence's first novel, *The Last Perfect Summer*. His newest work, *The Last of the Rockland Boys*, is another must-read for the Baby Boomer Generation. The novel grabs readers from the very first sentence and allows you to travel to a better place and time. He interlaces baseball, relationships, and timeless music into a heartwarming story of life and overcoming its obstacles."

~Mark Razz
Program Director
925XTU Philadelphia

A True *Field of Dreams*

"Ed Prence brings his stories to life and makes the written word a true *Field of Dreams!*"

~Rob Pratte
Son of Beaver County
Legendary Pittsburgh Sports Broadcaster

The Last of the Rockland Boys Is a Hit!

~Mike Reuther
Author, *Baseball Dreams*
Williamsport, Pennsylvania

Defines Small Town Values

"*The Last of the Rockland Boys* defines the small town values of a big segment of the Baby Boomer Generation. Ed Prence weaves music, amateur sports, and teenage angst into an inspiring story of overcoming the disappointments of life while navigating the turbulent issues of the 1960s and early 1970s."

~Jeff Potter
Author of *Whatever Happened to Baseball,*
Saving Baseball, and *Far from Being Done*
Odenton, Maryland

Sit Back and Enjoy!

"I've known Ed Prence since we were both teenagers back in Western Pennsylvania. He is bright, insightful, and articulate. If Ed's latest novel is half as good as his initial masterpiece, *The Last Perfect Summer,* then we are all in for a great read. Just sit back and enjoy. Here's to *The Last of the Rockland Boys!*"

~Felix Taverna
Sports Talk Broadcaster
Del Mar, California

THE LAST

— OF THE —

ROCKLAND BOYS

ALSO BY THE AUTHOR

The Last Perfect Summer

Winner of the 2014 Independent Book Publishers Association's
Benjamin Franklin Silver Award for the Best Historical Fiction of 2013,
and also the Pittsburgh Authors' TAZ Award
as the Best General Fiction in the Pittsburgh market

THE LAST

—— OF THE ——

ROCKLAND BOYS

Or The Cripple Creek Index

ED PRENCE

A Novel

The Last of the Rockland Boys
Or The Cripple Creek Index

Windy City Publishers
www.windycitypublishers.com

Published in the United States of America

ISBN:
978-1-953294-28-9

Library of Congress Control Number:
2022913571

WINDY CITY PUBLISHERS
CHICAGO

This novel is dedicated all the kids of Koppel, Pennsylvania ~
past, present, and yet to come.

1

ALL I NEED TO GET BY

I was late for my own party. As always, I had tried to squeeze in one more phone call before leaving the office and, of course, my client was upset about not seeing his TV commercial as frequently as he thought he should. *These car dealers,* I thought, *they watch the news for five minutes, and if they don't see their spot, they're sure we screwed up their schedule.*

I was in television advertising sales in the Pittsburgh market, and every time we started a new campaign, the client was in panic mode for the first two weeks. So, instead of the five-minute "full-speed-ahead" conversation I was hoping for, I ended up spending an hour checking the commercial logs and reviewing the spot in the studio, before calling the car dealer back and telling him what I already knew: The correct commercial had run on time and in the proper break. He had simply *missed* it.

The year was 2003, and I had just broken the million-dollar annual sales barrier for my company. My career was peaking, and I had more than fifty clients on the air every month. The fact that one of them was questioning the validity of his schedule was just part of the job.

This happened almost every week, so I wasn't really upset. But today was my fiftieth birthday and I knew my wife Lynn had invited a few of our closest friends to a dinner party at our favorite restaurant. Even my son, Gene, had flown home from college for the celebration. The party was set for 7:00 and it was already 7:15 when I pulled up to the valet parking booth. *She's going to kill me,* I thought as I swung my Nissan into the lot and tossed my keys to the teenager in the over-sized gold sport coat.

I hustled past the coat check lady and started into the small banquet room just past the main dining room, but I stopped when I heard Larry Gardner taking center stage just inside the door. Larry was a good friend who also happened to be a personal injury attorney and one of my biggest clients. Plus, we played baseball together in a local old-timer's league. He and his wife were two of my favorite people, but Larry loved an audience, and his abrasive humor was his trademark.

"How do you put up with this guy, Lynn?" I could hear him chirping in mock-disgust. "I only have to deal with him a couple times a month, but you're married to him. He must drive you nuts!"

"He has some pretty good attributes," I could hear Lynn saying with a laugh.

"Oh, Jesus," Larry countered. "I don't want to hear about that. Let's keep this G-rated."

"That's not what I meant," smiled Lynn. "He's probably handling some crisis."

"Crisis?" Now my cousin Tony jumped into the conversation. "What kind of crisis can an advertising salesman have? Somebody's commercial doesn't run. Oh, no. Call the Secret Service!"

"You know Ted," Lynn countered. "He watches out for his clients."

Just outside the door, I shook my head and smiled. It had always been the same since the day I met her, Lynn sticking up for me, defending me, never letting anyone get away with even a good-natured slam against my character. Plus, she was practical. With one of my biggest clients in the room, it was good for business for him to hear that I was so conscientious.

We were a team. What was good for either of us was good for the team. It was the reason I loved her. Sure, being sweet and smart and beautiful didn't hurt either, but it was her loyalty that made her stand out above anyone else.

"Let the party begin!" I barked as I entered the dining room full of close friends and well-wishers. Lynn stood back a few steps while the dozen or so guests smothered me in hugs and handshakes. Then she swept in for a big kiss, and hugged me around the neck as she whispered, "Where the hell have you been?" But I could tell from the twinkle in her eye that she was not angry, just relieved to see me.

As my fiftieth birthday bash continued that night, one after another of my old friends toasted me with tongue-in-cheek insults and gag gifts, but I just couldn't keep my eyes off Lynn, so sweet, so supportive, and so proud. How did I luck out like this?

Sure, there had been other girls, other women along the way. They were sweet. They were beautiful. Some of them even loved me, I guess. But somehow, I knew they weren't for me. Something was missing. *Trust?* No, it was more than that, although I certainly trusted Lynn. I knew she always had my back. No one dared make a disparaging comment about me when she was in the room.

Even when I had gone away to college and she was still in high school, I would come home for a weekend and my buddies would tell me about some kid in hallways trying to hit on her by insulting me. "She's like a barracuda, Teddy," Randy Delpino, one of my old high school baseball teammates told me once. "If anyone says you're not worth the wait, she rips them apart."

Now, after all these years, here I was, still married to the girl of my dreams. Lynn was funny and sweet and never let me down. I tossed back another Grey Goose and cranberry as I opened my gag gift from Tony, edible panties, and a can of Redi-Whip. "That's really a gift for Lynn," my brother Nelson cracked from the bar.

"I think he'll look good in those," Lynn countered without skipping a beat.

After the gifts, my cousin Tony stood to offer a toast. "A little quiet, please," he barked in mock formality.

"Everybody, please raise a glass to my cousin Teddy.

"This is called, 'Teddy at Fifty' by Tony DeVito." Tony took a long sip of his Beefeater and tonic.

> *They said that Ted grew old today.*
> *Somehow that don't seem right.*
> *He still plays baseball everyday*
> *And the horses every night.*

Slow-hand applause and chuckles began to fill the room...

Remember when he was a kid,
How he always wore his hat?
And spent all day at the baseball field,
But wait, he still does that!

Now, Lynn nodded, and laughed out loud…

And when it came to basketball,
'I never miss,' he'd say,
'When I bank it off the backboard
While I shoot this fade away.'
Let's see, was that in '68?
No – that was yesterday!

"He's right," I nodded. "It's my signature shot."

And when he was in grade school
He never studied well.
But somehow, when he got his grades,
They always turned-out swell.
Of course, he's more mature now.
He works so hard, they say.
You'll always find him on the road,
If there's not a game that day.

"Usually *my* game," offered my son Gene.

And what about the ladies?
Their faces are a blur.
Like that pretty young Italian girl,
Now what became of her?
I remember back in high school,
How they parked his car and hid.
He said he'd never leave her.
And, you know, he never did.

4

An "Awwww," from the ladies at the party filled the room. "That's right, he didn't," remarked my big sister Sandy. She and her husband Theo had flown out all the way from her home in England just for the occasion.

> *They say that Ted grew old today,*
> *And fifty's what he is.*
> *But every kid in Rockland*
> *Would trade their life for his!*

The whole room exploded into applause and laughter and the kind of family feelings you live your whole life to experience.

"Happy birthday, cousin," Tony smiled in triumph. "A toast to Teddy on his Fiftieth Birthday. It doesn't change the way we feel about Teddy, it changes the way we feel about fifty. *Salute!*"

There were hugs and tears all around, and Lynn kept calling me *the biggest little boy she ever loved.*

As the party started winding down, my son Gene pulled me aside. "Dad," he said, "I'm going to take off. I haven't seen my Lakewood friends since September. But there is something I want to talk to you about. How late will you be up?"

"Anytime is fine," I beamed. Gene was a senior at the University of Miami, and Pittsburgh was a long flight to make during the semester, so we didn't get much time to talk in person. But even in our phone calls, he rarely confided his personal life to me.

"We can talk more when you get home." I smiled, feeling strangely useful. "I'll be awake or you can wake me up. Don't worry about the time."

It wasn't long after Gene left, that the final guests said their goodbyes. Lynn had driven to the restaurant with Tony and his wife, and when she and I got back to my car, I handed her my keys. It was my birthday party, and she knew I'd be drinking, so she had limited herself to one glass of wine. She was the designated driver. I hadn't even mentioned it during the evening. She was just looking out for me—like I knew she would—like she always did. We went back home and put the finishing touches on a wonderful evening. "That's the first time I've ever made love with a fifty-year-old man," Lynn teased, as she drifted off to sleep. "It better be," I laughed as I pulled her close to me and closed my eyes.

That night, I woke up at 2 a.m. to the sound of Gene's keys in the front door. I slipped out from under the sheets, put on some baggy shorts, and walked down the hall to meet him. "Hey, Champ," I beamed as we both headed for the kitchen. "Did you get to see some of your old friends?"

"I saw Alan and JT at Big Dogs, and few other kids I went to school with came into the bar. It was fun. Then we spent three hours talking about women."

"Which women?" I asked, trying not to seem too meddlesome.

"Well, I needed some advice," he said shaking his head in disgust, "But Alan's girlfriend moved out last week and JT is dating some girl he doesn't even like, so I don't think their opinions are worth too much."

"In case you haven't noticed, I've been happily married for 29 years. Maybe I could help. What's going on?"

Gene hesitated for a second. "Well, that's what I wanted to talk to you about," he paused, apparently a little uncomfortable to be discussing women with his father. "The world has changed a lot, dad. Girls now are different."

"Different how?" I asked.

"Well, this one's hard to read and moody and sometimes a little selfish. Her name is Jan, and she's gorgeous. I mean, I'm proud to be seen with her on campus, but she's a little nutty, and not in a nice way. She'll put me down in front of friends and she's always criticizing the things I do, or the music I like or the clothes I wear."

"Well, you can't take that crap, Gene," I groaned. "Get rid of her."

"That's just it; I've tried to get rid of her. I tell her I won't be insulted like that. I tell her I won't put up with it; that we're done. Then she storms out, all upset. And I think, *Okay, I'm going to miss her, but it's better this way.*

"Two hours later, she's back at my door at 2 in the morning, crying to come in and talk. So, we have a heart-to-heart until 4 a.m., and I agree to take her back. Sometimes, I just say 'okay' so I can get some sleep. And then the next day she's at it again; put downs and jokes and sarcasm. I tell her we're done, and two nights later, it starts all over; the crying, the banging at the door. My roommates are getting pissed off, and I'm missing a lot of early classes.

"She always comes back, so I know she cares about me and, like I said, she *is* beautiful. But is this the way it's always going to be? Is love always this crazy?"

"No," I told him. "But I've known plenty of girls like that. It took me a long time to realize it, but that's not the type of woman you want to spend your life with. You want someone who is loyal and devoted; someone who's going to stand by you no matter what, someone with that me-and-you-against-the-world steadfastness.

"Apparently, this Jan loves you in a way, but is she the kind of woman you can team up with for life?"

"And how am I supposed to know that?" Gene just shook his head in frustration.

"Well, when I was at Duquesne, my cousin Tony was one of my roommates, and we had a scale for measuring the loyalty of the girls we dated. We called it *The Cripple Creek Index*."

"What's that mean?" Gene chuckled.

I smiled at the long-forgotten memory. "Well, in the late sixties and early seventies, there was a band that just called themselves *The Band*." They released a song called *Up on Cripple Creek*. Every verse ended with these lines:

> *Up on Cripple Creek she sends me.*
> *If I spring a leak, she mends me.*
> *I don't have to speak, she defends me,*
> *A drunkard's dream if I ever did see one.*

"A drunkard?" Gene smiled. "I'm not sure I want a drunkard's dream girl."

"Well, it applies to all girls. I think the idea is that even when you're at rock bottom, you want a woman who's going to stick by you; who's going to mend you when you're hurting; who's going to defend you when the rest of the world turns against you.

"Tony would bring home some girl that he had been dating for a couple weeks, and I'd say, "What's her Cripple Creek Index?"

He'd say, "About 90; maybe even 95."

"Sounds like a keeper," I'd tell him.

"Actually, Tony always called it *The Cripple Creek Index*. After a few years, I started calling it *The Molly Index*."

"Who's Molly?" Gene leaned forward now, "Did you date her before mom?"

"Way before," I laughed. "She was my first girlfriend, when I was ten years old, but I'll never forget the lessons she taught me."

And we both cracked up. "Okay, maybe I need to explain."

GET IT RIGHT THE FIRST TIME

I was only ten years old and in fourth grade when I first noticed Molly. I was mature for a kid that age, the tallest kid in my class, smart and athletic. For that reason, almost all my close friends were older than me. Most of the social relationships of the kids in my hometown of Rockland, PA, were based on sports, and there was just no challenge in playing baseball or football with the other ten-year-old's, who were a foot smaller than I was.

My cousin Tony DeVito and our buddy Harry Kirkland were my best friends. They were in sixth grade and already had a serious interest in girls. I guess that's why I started noticing them at such a young age. Plus, there were three beautiful little Italian girls in my own tiny neighborhood. I saw them almost every day, and although Stephanie and Connie and Linda were strictly friends, my daily interactions with them gave me a chance to work on my conversation skills with the opposite sex, so I certainly wasn't shy.

Of course, Molly was only ten years old too. Although she was only one month younger than me, she was the smallest girl in my class, but always seemed full of confidence and joy and somehow more mature than the other girls. I loved the way she flung back her soft brown hair every time she saw me. Plus, I could tell by her sweet smile that she considered me something special. I had learned from the neighborhood girls, how to read their moods just by looking at their faces and this smile was an invitation to something, I just wasn't exactly sure what.

I lucked out in one way: my cousin Tony had a girlfriend named Pam Genova, the princess of our Catholic grade school. She was cute and sweet, and her smiles lit up the room everywhere she went. Tony was crazy about her. She was also Molly's cousin, and even though the girls were a year-and-a-half apart, their families were very close and the cousins were constant companions. That was the perfect situation for me. Since I hung out with Tony every day, I had ample opportunity to be near Molly.

I was pretty good at talking to girls, but I often stumbled when approaching Molly. My affection for her made me hesitate, I guess. But, she was willing to meet me more than halfway, and I found out early that to have a conversation with Molly, all I really needed to do was ask her a question, and she would take it from there.

"What did you think of that math test?" I blurted out one day in the hall when she happened to be in front of me in the drinking fountain line.

"It was hard," she sang out with that big smile bursting on her face. "I'm terrible at math. I studied all night and I think I did okay, but I just don't understand long division. And Sister Pious gives us so much other homework. I don't mind the reading and geography. I just have to memorize those. But when there's a math test, we shouldn't have to study spelling words too. That's just too much, don't you think?"

"Uh huh," I nodded.

"Oh, you don't care. You're such a brain when it comes to math. It's just so hard for me."

She was right. Math was my favorite subject, mostly because it didn't require much studying. You either understood it or you didn't, and for some reason, it always came easy to me.

"Maybe you can help me with some of those problems Sister Pious gave us for homework. I mean, we'd have to stay in for recess, but I think she'd let us do that. Oh, I'm sorry. I'm sure you don't want to miss recess."

"I don't mind," I shot back confidently. And just like that I had a study date with Molly.

All I had said was, "What did you think of the math test?" Just eight little words, but now I was on top of the world. She always made it so easy for me.

It was 1964, the height of the Baby Boom and there were forty-two kids in my fourth-grade class at St. Teresa's School. My brother Nelson was in third grade. He had over sixty classmates, all in one room! Our hometown was small, but there were kids everywhere, and the whole world seemed to revolve around us.

Rockland was a small-but-growing steel town in Western Pennsylvania, and our Post-WWII parents were going out of their way to entertain their Baby-Boomer kids. Our little town of 900 even boasted its own roller rink, and in Rockland, the real courting grounds were not the grade school hall-ways or even the playgrounds or soda fountains. The hotspot in Rockland was the Flying Saucer Roller Rink. And every Friday night and Saturday afternoon from September to May, it was the social meeting place for every kid in town. When we were little, say age seven to ten, we went skating on Saturday after-noons. But when we got to be about age ten to fourteen, we skated on Friday nights.

Molly and I were transitioning from Saturday afternoon skaters to Friday night skaters. That's the night when all my older friends went, and of course, that's when her cousin Pam went. Moving up to Friday Night Skating was an important rite of passage, since Rockland was a tiny town and didn't have its own high school. When we reached ninth grade, we headed to nearby Lakewood City, with its school dances and formals and football games. The roller rink in Rockland was the only social setting that prepared us for the world of dating and girlfriends and all the things that go along with high school romance. It was our training ground, I guess.

Maybe that's the reason why the Roller Rink added one more event to their Friday night skating parties, *The Record Hop*. Every Friday from 7 to 9 pm, there was regular skating. Sometimes they'd even lower the lights for a *Couples Skate*. But from 9 to 10 pm, we'd take off our skates, step into our nice cool shoes and head back up to the rink floor for the Friday night dance. It was the event of the week, and if you wanted to court a girl, this was the place.

Although I was only ten, my parents didn't mind me going to the dance on Friday nights. All my best friends were already going, and since I was a pretty big kid, they figured I could take care of myself. Plus, I was a boy. If I had been a daughter, they might have been more protective, just like Molly's parents were. From September to November that year, her parents wouldn't let her go to the dances at all. But she whined and complained and begged them. Then, she got her cousin Pam to intervene. Pam promised that she would watch out for her and never let her out of her sight, and finally, they reached a compromise. Starting in December, Molly would be allowed to attend the dances every-oth-er-week, but only with her cousin. I didn't know it yet, but my life was about to get a lot more interesting.

I'll never forget that Friday afternoon recess in early December when Princess Pam walked up to me...ME...and said, "Can I speak to you alone?" I was playing four-squares with some guys in my fourth-grade class, and every-thing just stopped. My mouth dropped open and all the kids looked at me as if the Publishers Clearing House guy had just handed me one of those big cardboard checks. No one was more confused than I was. What was the prin-cess of the school doing asking me for a private conversation? I figured it was something to do with Tony, and I was hoping she wasn't breaking up with him. I'd have hated to be the bearer of that bad news.

But, as soon as we got out of earshot of my classmates, Pam grabbed my shoulder and spun me around. "Molly's allowed to go to the dance tonight," she beamed. "She wants you to go!"

I don't know what she said next. Her mouth was moving but I couldn't hear a sound. My ears were ringing, the top of my head was tingling, and I could feel a flush of fever burning across my face. I had been chasing Molly for months, counting every smile, calculating every opportunity, and now her angelic cousin was dropping her in my lap like a gift from heaven.

The next words I could hear Pam saying were these: "Can you dance?"

"Uhh, I don't know," I stammered. "I've never tried."

"Well, I suggest you learn." She grinned like the Cheshire cat, then spun around and walked across the playground and back to the world of the sixth graders.

I grabbed Tony on the way home from school and told him everything that had happened. "Hmmm," he said. "She must mean slow dance. That's the only dance we ever do. We better go ask my mom for help."

The next thing I knew, I was in Tony's living room, dancing with my Aunt Betty to Johnny Mathis' *Chances Are*. "Quit looking at your feet," she chided in mock anger. "Look in her eyes." I looked up and immediately stomped down hard on my aunt's foot. "I'm going to need my Epsom salts tonight," she moaned. Tony roared in laughter, first on the couch, then finally, rolling on the floor, grabbing his side and gasping for air.

Oh, great, I thought, *just the reaction I'm looking for.* We practiced for the next hour, but I never improved much. I finally got the steps right, but never really got the connection between the rhythm and my hips and shoulders. "Maybe I'm not ready yet," I sighed during the short walk home.

That night, Tony and Harry and I arrived at the rink right around 7 o'clock. We put on our skates and headed out on the hardwood for a few spins around the floor. Then we rolled back down to the concession stand and grabbed a bottle of Orange Crush with a couple other sixth graders, Will DeLuca and Billy Conti. Billy was Tony's chief rival for Pam's attention, and the two guys never really liked each other much. This competition went on for years, but the 1963-64 school year was all Tony and Pam, so for the time being, Billy just suffered in silence.

Still, rivalry or no rivalry, Tony couldn't help but tell them all the story of my dance lesson in his living room. They roared in laughter and were still giving me the business when Pam and Molly strolled through the front door of the roller rink. Their comments were embarrassing and a little cruel, but Molly ignored them, and instead locked in my gaze. I felt the whole room fade into the background, and I rolled right up to her and held out my soda. "Want some Crush?" I asked.

She handed me her coat to hang up and took a long drink from my bottle. "Thanks," she smiled. "I was hoping you'd be here." When I turned around, everyone else was gone.

The whole night was full of magic, full of feelings and emotions I had never felt before. We held hands during a *Couples Skate*, while the rink's sound system played The Ronettes' *Be My Baby*. The wall of sound filled the air with excitement and enough decibels that I really didn't have to think of anything to say. We just smiled and skated and hung out with our friends all night.

Then at 9 pm, we took off our skates and headed for the darkened rink floor. I started feeling more than a little anxious about the whole idea of dancing with her. Skating together was one thing, but a slow dance was a big step: one-on-one, holding her, talking to her? It was a scary proposition. Plus, I remembered the fiasco at Aunt Betty's house that afternoon.

I spotted Molly near the center pillar of the rink with Pam and a couple other friends, and when I got closer, she came out to meet me. At first, she was her normal bubbly self, but soon we were having a rare awkward moment, watching some of the older kids dancing in one corner of the darkened rink. It was a slow dance. *Don't Let the Sun Catch You Crying* by Gerry & the Pacemakers. We were just standing there. And I couldn't think of a word to say. And for once, neither could she.

"I'm a terrible dancer," I told her finally, just to break the silence.

Immediately, she found her voice. "I don't care if you're any good." She smiled, shaking her head like I was hopeless. "I just want to dance with you." She grabbed my hand, and we were out there.

As bad as I was on the dance floor, Molly acted like I was Fred Astaire. She ignored my sweaty palms and clumsy gait. When I'd look down at my feet to get my steps right, she'd say, "Just look at me. You're doing fine." And before I knew it, I was doing fine. There were some giggles from the older girls and some snide remarks from the older guys. But, by the end of the song their comments faded into the background. It's not that they stopped. I just didn't hear them anymore. All I could see were her eyes. All I could hear was her voice, and the final strains of the Pacemakers fading to silence, "...Don't let the sun catch you crying, oh no, ohhhhhh no."

I lowered my arms, but neither one of us took a step. "What do you think?" I asked her finally.

"I think we better try that again," she whispered. And right on cue, the roller rink sound system floated into the first few bars of *Daddy's Home* by Shep and the Limelites. The next time I looked around, nobody was watching us. And, just like that, we were a couple.

"Do you like, Molly?" Her cousin Pam asked me later that night as we were all putting on our coats to leave. "Sure," I answered. "I like her fine."

"No," Pam persisted, "Do you *like* like her." It was the adolescent way of asking if I considered her my girlfriend.

I could see Molly returning from the girls' room with that big smile on her face and her freshly brushed brown hair lying soft and shiny across her shoulders. "I like her, and I *like* like her." I announced, loud enough for anyone in earshot to hear.

"You better," Molly grinned. And that sealed the deal.

On Monday in school, we were the talk of the class. No one in fourth grade at St. Teresa's had a real boyfriend or girlfriend. "You like Teddy Tresh!" little Mark Minelli teased her. He was a particularly obnoxious punk, and if he wasn't my cousin, I would have pounded him for his comments. But Molly was as cool as a creamsicle.

"So?" was all she said.

"That's right," I agreed. "What's it to you, Minelli?" Although I didn't realize it at the time, I was learning a lesson that day. I was learning that a true girlfriend stays true under fire.

All through that winter we were a couple. I'd carry her books and sit next to her at lunch. I liked the idea that I was so tall, and she was so tiny. Sometimes, when I'd arrive at school and walk into the cloak room, I'd see her book bag lying on the floor. I'd pick it up and place it on the shelf above the coats, right next to mine, just so I could help her get it down when we went out for recess.

Of course, every-other Friday was roller rink dance night, and the anticipation would start building about three days early. I couldn't wait to hold her in my arms. Although to be truthful, she wasn't really *in my arms*. I had my right hand around her waist and held her right hand in my left, but it was enough for now, plenty. She was light and agile and pretty as a rose. And she always seemed so proud to be my girlfriend.

We did have one problem; her mom was not so happy about Molly having a *boyfriend* at age ten. "My mom does like you, Teddy," she confided one night on the dance floor. "But if someone else asks me to dance, I have to say *yes* to at least one song."

This was not good news; my girlfriend on the dance floor with somebody else? "You're kidding?" I dropped my hands to my side and just stood there staring at her as Bobby Vinton's *Blue Velvet* whined through the roller rink's two-speaker sound system.

"It'll just be one dance," she whispered, looking up at me with those big, brown eyes. "My mom says that I really shouldn't hurt anyone's feelings by saying no."

"Should I be worried?" I questioned her again.

"What do *you* think?" she answered, taking my hand, and putting it back around her waist. I just smiled down at her and starting swaying to the music again.

Later that night I was talking to Tony and Harry at the snack bar. "Do you believe this shit?" I shook my head as I recounted my whole conversation with Molly. "It's no big deal," Tony countered. "You know she's nuts about you. Besides, that means you can do the same thing. You can dance with anybody you want."

"But I don't want to dance with anyone else!" I barked.

"What about those weeks when she's not here? You come to the roller rink every Friday. She's only allowed to be here every-other-week."

Hmmm, I thought, *he's right.* I knew plenty of cute girls from my own neighborhood that always came to the dances. And even though they were just friends of mine, dancing would be more fun than just standing around the rink every-other-week watching all the other kids. Little did I know that thinking like this would get me into trouble later.

As expected, I was a bit upset when one night little Craig Harley stepped in front of me and asked Molly to dance. But as I watched them on the floor, I couldn't help but think of all the kids in my class who had picked on Craig mercilessly. He was thin and frail and a foot shorter than me. He even had a slight speech impediment, so he was an easy target for bullies, unless I was around to stop them.

Being the biggest kid in my class, I had unofficially instituted a *no bullying* policy for fourth graders at our school, and Craig was kind of under my protection most of the time. Of course, in those days we didn't call it *bullying*. That was a word from the Forties or Fifties. Everyone knew that picking on little kids was wrong, but there was no real label for it.

I'm not sure what made me adopt this role. I guess it had something to do with my dad. Like almost every father in town, he had served in the Army

16

in World War II, where he learned about sacrifice and honor and defending those who needed it most. And then, he came home and married his teenage sweetheart.

My mom was Catholic and just to make her happy, he had converted to Catholicism. But, like so many converts, he ended up taking his new religion much more seriously than those who were born with it. The philosophies of turn-the-other-cheek and defending-the-defenseless, were more than just words to him. If his over-sized son had started picking on the little kids in class, he would have brought down his own brand of discipline, which usually consisted of a strap across my behind!

I guess that's why I used my strength and size to watch over the easy targets like Craig. Seeing them out there on the dance floor now made me realize how sweet and kind Molly was, and when she looked over at me and smiled, I felt a strange feeling of warmth, admiration, and respect. I was crazy about that girl.

Weeks and months went by, and we grew closer than ever. The Beatles had just done the Ed Sullivan Show in February and their music filled the roller rink with a bigger, livelier sound. The adults were still mourning the assassination of JFK in November 1963, but the kids were ready to be happy again. And nothing made me happier than being with Molly. The world was coming at us with ever-increasing speed. We had more freedom. The local steel mill was booming. Everyone's father was making good money. Televisions were now in color. Motown and the British invasion had set the music industry on its ear. And through it all was Molly, sweet and loyal and as steadfast as any girlfriend could be. I thought every girlfriend would be just like her.

How We Become Who We Are

Gene had made a pot of coffee and was pouring us both a cup. "Geez, Dad, why didn't you just marry *that* girl?"

"Well, for one thing, we were only ten years old!" I laughed. "You don't often end up with your ten-year-old girlfriend. Besides, I hadn't learned any better. I thought they would all be exactly like that. That they would all be loyal and loving and proud to be with me no matter what anyone else said."

"And it didn't work out that way?" Gene knew I was trying to make a point, but he wasn't exactly sure what it was.

"No, Champ. Not by a long shot." I took a sip of coffee but didn't need it. Even though it was nearly 3 a.m., I wasn't really tired. "The thing is I really didn't appreciate how unique Molly was."

"Yeah," he nodded. "If Jan had half the loyalty of little Molly, I'd probably have a ring picked out for her by now."

His comment jolted me for a second. I had no idea that Gene had contemplated *marrying* this girl.

"But, instead," he continued, "I've got this crazy woman, who criticizes me constantly, and then spends hours swearing her eternal love to me. I think, if she wasn't so beautiful, I'd just say get lost.

"My buddies at school used to tell me to just see her when I want to, and not take her seriously. But I can't do that. I have to at least like her. I mean, sometimes I love her, and sometimes I hate her, but mostly, I just feel sorry for her.

"It sounds to me like you're falling for her."

Gene shook his head a little too vigorously. "She's nuts and she's making me nuts. I want to be loyal to her, but lately, I've been thinking that maybe I should start going out with someone else."

"Well, I don't know if she deserves your loyalty, but you probably shouldn't get anyone else involved until you decide what you want to do about Jan. You can't be involved with one girl and playing around with another one.

"That was the first lesson I learned from Molly. She was exactly what I wanted. She was kind and loyal and as wonderful as a girlfriend could be. I was completely happy.

"Then I risked it all for nothing."

A HARD LESSON

I t was late March 1964. Within a couple months, the days would be getting longer, and the roller rink would shut down for the summer and not reopen until September. But for now, we were all enjoying our final few weeks of skating and dancing on Friday nights.

It was an off weekend for Molly. That is, it was one of the every-other-Fridays when she was not allowed to go to the rink, so I was hanging out with a bunch of my buddies. The new 1964 Topps Baseball Cards had just been released a few weeks earlier, and Billy Conti and Will DeLuca had organized a huge card-flipping game in one darkened corner of the skating rink floor.

Kids in those days played three or four different card-flipping games, but they all had one thing in common: they were early forms of gambling. The only reason the roller rink permitted it at all was because they sold baseball cards at their snack shop. So, it was good for business. The most daring game was called *shootsies*. It was also the most rewarding. Basically, you stood about twelve feet from the wall and tossed your card like a Frisbee. If it landed on top of one (and only one) other card, you won the whole pile of cards on the floor. Most "pots" reached about ten to twenty cards before someone would land a winner.

There were eight of us playing shootsies in the corner of the roller rink this Friday night and my cousin Tony had just won a huge pot of about 25 baseball cards. Harry and I both had been big losers to this point, so we skated down to the rink's snack shop to buy a couple more packs of cards to re-load.

I was still paying for my baseball cards when the front door flew open and in walked Gracie Dierdorf from First Avenue with four cute girls I had never seen before. I kind of knew Gracie. She was a year older than me, very friendly

20

and sweet, with piercing blue eyes that were her most outstanding feature. She went to the Rockland public school, not St. Teresa's, so I didn't know her too well, and she wasn't a regular at the Flying Saucer Roller Rink. But she was a Rockland girl, so I wasn't surprised to see her. On any given Friday, you could expect to see almost any kid in town come walking through that door. But out-of-towners were a rare occurrence, and to see four sweet *brand-new* girls come strolling into the rink stopped us dead in our tracks. "Holy shit!" Harry whispered, as we stood there with our mouths opened, watching them taking off their coats and renting their skates.

"Come on," I nudged him. "We gotta tell Tony."

Will DeLuca had just won a pot of about twelve cards and was kneeling over his winnings when Harry and I reached the group. "You gotta see this!" Harry blurted out, and quickly described the scene to all the card flippers in the corner of the rink.

"Game's over!" Billy announced. And he led the whole posse as they skated across the rink and down the three short stairs that divided the upper floor from the snack shop. I hung back from the pack a little. What was I going to say to four new girls I had never seen before? Besides, I had Molly. So, I had no personal stake in this unprecedented social gathering. But I did want to see how the older Rockland boys would handle this unexpected opportunity.

Tony uncharacteristically hung back a bit too and followed along with me. He had already spent some time talking with Pam before the card-flipping session had started, and he could feel her eyes on him as we skated across the rink. "What do they look like?" he whispered to me as we crossed the room.

"Cute!" I replied. "And there's one tall blonde that's gorgeous."

"I'm on the sidelines for this one, cousin," he said, shaking his head gloomily.

"Well sure," I nodded. "You've got Pam."

"And she's *in* the room," Tony chuckled. "But Molly's not here. You're a free man."

"No thanks," I smiled.

"Hey, she dances with other guys. Why shouldn't you dance with one of those girls? You didn't make the rules. She did. But you're crazy if you don't take advantage of them."

I knew this was different. I knew it wasn't the same as Molly not wanting to hurt someone's feelings by saying no. But I just headed down to ground zero without saying another word.

It didn't take long for the Rockland boys to start making asses of themselves. They were all hovering around like a bunch of crows waiting for traffic to let up so they could feed on the dead thing in the middle of the road. They were all talking to Gracie like she was their best friend, and she smiled at the attention.

"Who are your friends, Gracie?" barked out Johnny Hudson from the back of the pack. But, instead of waiting for the answer, he turned his back and ducked away, as if someone else had asked the question. The other guys were just laughing awkwardly and talking to each other. I was embarrassed for them. But, little by little, some information seeped out. One of the girls was Gracie's cousin from New Galilee, a little town about ten miles north of Rockland. And the rest were her cousin's girlfriends. They were all eleven years old, just a year older than me, and a year younger than most of the Rockland boys who had surrounded them.

Eventually, the conversation ground to a halt and one-by-one the new girls headed to the rink floor to do some skating. Tony had already paired off with Pam again and swept her out onto the floor when the DJ popped the Supremes' *Baby Love* on the turntable for a couple's skate.

I was still in the snack shop talking to Mickey Slade, who was showing off his winnings from the *shootsies* game; he had won a Mantle, an Aaron and an Ernie Banks, a pretty good haul for twenty minutes of baseball card flipping. Then he and I rolled up to the counter. "Give me an Orange Crush," I nodded to the owner, Milan Popovic, who was working the snack shop.

"That sounds pretty good," sang a sweet, high-pitched voice from behind me. "Make that two."

When I turned around, there she stood, the sweetest, most striking, blond-haired, blue-eyed girl I had ever seen. She looked like a movie star. "Uhh, hi," I blurted out, trying my best to act smooth. "You're new here, aren't you?"

"I'm Caroline Lash," she smiled, "from New Galilee. I'm here with my girl-friends. We heard there was always a big crowd of kids here on Friday nights, and a *dance* too."

For a moment, I couldn't bring myself to speak. But I was determined not to look as pathetic as the pack of wolves that had just been sniffing around her. She stood there smiling, and I reached into my limited knowledge of adolescent girls for something to say. It was old Milan Popovic who gave me my opening. "We only have one Orange Crush left," he yelled from the cooler, "How about Grape?"

"She can have the orange," I answered in an instant.

"Oh, no," Caroline replied. "You ordered it first."

"That's okay," I said with a nod. "I like grape fine."

"Well, aren't you a gentleman?" Her eyes twinkled like fireflies in July.

"I'm Teddy Tresh," I said, raising my grape soda. "Welcome to Rockland,"

"Cheers!" she answered. And we clinked our bottles. Then I just skated away, but before I hit the stairway to the roller rink floor, I looked back over my shoulder. She was still leaning on the counter watching me. I took it as a good sign.

The guilt didn't hit me until I looked up and saw Tony and Pam just finishing their couples skate. Diana Ross and the Supremes were closing it out in style. "Don't throw our love away…Don't throw our love away."

Shit, I thought. *What am I doing?*

"It's no big deal," Tony advised a few minutes later. "You never even touched her. Just forget about it."

So, that's what I tried to do. But those sparkling blue eyes weren't easy to forget. A few minutes later, Harry and I headed back to the shootsies game that had started up again in the corner, and I decided to concentrate on trying to win back my lost baseball cards. I went bust in fifteen minutes.

It was getting near nine o'clock now, almost time for the dance to start. So, I headed back toward the skate rental counter. I always loved the feeling of taking off my roller skates and stepping back into my nice cool, comfortable street shoes. Then, the DJ's voice boomed across the P.A. system, "This will be our last couples skate of the night. Let's make it a *Ladies' Choice*."

The first few bars of the Beatles' *Love Me Do*, whipped across the roller rink, and a collective "Ahhhhhhhh" went through the crowd like a slow roar of thunder. Everyone who was removing their skates froze for a second, then quickly re-laced them and headed to the floor. Beatles' songs were like magic that spring, and I could feel the music fill the air with energy.

Most couples skates were strictly that, one boy and one girl. But when the couples skate was a Beatles' song, the girls didn't care. They would grab the hand of one of their girlfriends and start skating, anything to be a part of the music. Of course, a guy still wouldn't hold hands with another guy, but we all headed to the floor to watch the ladies flying around the rink.

I was standing along the west wall with Harry and Mickey, and, like everyone else in the place, we were laughing and singing along with John, Paul, and George. "Love, love me do. You know I love you. I'll always be true."

Then I felt someone touch my arm. When I spun around, Caroline Lash was staring me right in the eyes. "Hi," she smiled. "Will you skate with me?" And she put out her hand. Harry and Mickey stood there gaping. Their eyes were big as saucers.

"Sure," I answered. And the thought of Molly never crossed my mind. Out we went into the sea of fanatical kids, singing out loud, and bouncing to the music. I could feel my head pounding with excitement and something like pride as we weaved in and out of room full of skaters. I just watched her smiling and singing, "Someone to love, somebody new; Someone to love, someone like you."

We made a couple more orbits around the rink and it seemed like every eye in the place was on us. I was watching her long, blonde hair floating on the air behind her when, all at once, Tony and Pam came into focus just to our right. *Holy shit,* I thought, *what about Molly?*

There was no way to hide it. Her cousin had just watched me make a spectacle of myself in front of every kid in town. I didn't say another word to Caroline, except, "thank you," when the skate was over.

"Who cares?" Tony chuckled as we took off our skates a few minutes later. "All you did was skate with her. That's kid stuff. All you did was hold hands and take a few spins around the rink. What's wrong with that? Molly dances with other guys every week."

"This is different, and you know it," I stated emphatically.

"That's bull," Tony countered. "Skating doesn't even count. You should dance with her. You have one free dance coming to you. Those are Molly's rules, not yours. You have a free pass!"

"Forget about it," I said defensively. But as the night wore on, I was the one who couldn't forget about it.

The first slow dance of the evening was *Tears on My Pillow,* by Little Anthony & The Imperials, and Harry and I watched in amusement as Rockland's finest took turns asking Caroline to dance, first Mickey, then Johnny Hudson, then Lou Petrella. But she just kept shaking her head *no*. I could hardly believe my eyes. "Next contestant," I muttered to Harry who was standing next to me.

"She's waiting for you," he chuckled, slapping me on the back as he spoke.

"How is that possible?" I wondered out loud. But when the song ended, she looked across the dance floor and directly at me.

"I told you," Harry chided. "Don't be a wuss. Get over there."

"I have a girl," I told him. But all the same, I was pretty excited.

As the night wore on, a steady pack of Rockland boys surrounded Gracie and her friends, and one-by-one the new girls made their way to the dance floor with one or another of my buddies. But Caroline kept refusing every invitation.

Now, both Tony and Harry were on my back. "You've got a free dance coming," Tony kept reminding me. "Those are Molly's rules."

"What a chicken shit," Harry added.

Time was ticking away, 9:30, then 9:40, and now just 10 minutes to ten. I wasn't even sure if the DJ would play another slow song. But, with just 5 minutes left, I heard the speakers rollout the first few bars of the Beach Boys' *Surfer Girl*.

"Now," Harry barked. "Go now."

I took a couple halting steps forward, and then stopped dead in my tracks. *Too late!* Billy was now in Caroline's face and was obviously asking her to dance.

Billy was a sixth grader like Tony, and the two of them were smooth as glass when it came to talking with girls. If there was such a thing as a grade school playboy, it was Billy. I felt some regret and disappointment and even a little shame at my own shyness. Sure, I was crazy about Molly, but I couldn't help but feel that it was fear, not loyalty, that kept me on the sidelines tonight.

I could see Caroline look into Billy's face and hesitate, then she looked across the floor and straight at me. *She's giving me one last chance to move.* The thought shot through my brain, *it's now or never.* And I made a beeline for the tall blonde with the dazzling blue eyes. As I closed in on Caroline, I could see her making her apologies to Billy, but her eyes were on me.

She stepped past him, and I put out my hand. "Would you like to dance?" I asked in a whisper.

"What took you so long?" she answered.

I had danced with Molly plenty of times and even with some of the neighborhood girls, but I had never danced like this. I opened my arms and she moved in so close that our faces were just a couple inches apart. Molly and I usually had a good six inches between us on the dance floor. We were rookies compared to this girl. It threw me off at first and I struggled not to step on her feet. But as the music continued, it started to feel more and more natural.

I wasn't sure what to say but decided to ask her a question. That was always a good conversation starter with Molly. "How do you like Rockland?"

"Well, I wasn't sure at first. But I'm getting to like it more and more," she sighed.

We floated around the floor, and when the final lines came, "Do you love me? Do you, surfer girl?" I was staring straight into those crystal blue eyes.

When I looked up, the entire town of Rockland seemed to be watching us. And Molly's cousin Pam was front and center. "Holy shit," I murmured to myself. "What did I just do?"

Caroline went back to her giggling girlfriends, and I watched her disappear as they surrounded her.

"It's no big deal," Tony reassured me as we put on our coats a few minutes later. "It was just a dance."

"I have one question," Harry added. "Did she stop breathing out there?"

"What are you talking about?"

"For a minute I thought you were going to give her mouth-to-mouth resuscitation," he deadpanned. And we all busted out laughing.

I waved goodbye to Caroline and Gracie and their friends as they made their way to the door. "That was a great night," I whispered to Tony. "But I hope I never see her again."

A Mind of Her Own

"So, did you ever see her again?" Gene was leaning forward with his elbows on the table, taking his last sip of coffee.

"I didn't want to," I smiled. "I had a girlfriend. I had a great girlfriend, one who was sweet and pretty and proud to be with me, who never stopped supporting me. If I won a spelling bee in class, she was proud. If I flunked a test, she'd help me study better. If I hit a home run, she'd be beaming. If I struck out, she'd say, 'You'll get him next time.' She was exactly what a girlfriend should be."

"How old was this girl? Gene laughed.

"She was just ten!" I shook my head, "But the problem was that I was just ten too. She was my first girlfriend, and I thought that every girlfriend would be just like her. I thought they would all be that loyal, that proud, and that supportive."

"Wow," Gene rubbed his hands through his hair. "I'm not sure it was a good thing to find someone like that so young. It kind of sets you up for failure later in life. I mean, it must have been disappointing to find out how unpredictable relationships can be."

"No, I always felt like Molly gave me a guide of what to look for in a relationship. And that when someone fell below that level, a little alarm used to go off in my head, telling me that something wasn't right here."

"What about how you treated her? I mean chasing after some blue-eyed, blond-haired stranger isn't very loyal."

"You're right," I starred him right in the eye. "That was a whole different lesson. But for now, the most important thing on my mind was what would my real girlfriend do when she found out that I had made a mistake, and that I might not be as loyal as she was?"

"So, what did she do?" Gene wondered. "What does a little ten-year-old do when her feelings are hurt?"

"Why don't you pour us another cup of coffee?" I rose from my chair. "This is going to be a long night. I better let your mother know not to wait up."

I walked down the hall and slid into the bedroom to see if Lynn was sleeping soundly. But her snoring stopped as soon as I opened the door.

"How's Gene?" she sighed, as I sat down on the bed beside her.

"He's got a big problem," I whispered.

Now, she sat straight up in bed. "What's going on? Is he okay?"

"Well, his girlfriend is toxic," I said quietly, but deliberately. "And I think he might be in love with her anyway."

"What did you tell him?" Lynn spoke slowly.

"I didn't tell him anything. I just keep recounting stories of how I ended up with you.

"Do you think she's in love with him?" Lynn whispered.

"I'm not sure. I think she likes the attention, and she likes playing games. This girl is mistreating him," I continued, "But, then she begs for forgiveness. And he always takes her back."

"Well, he has to get away from this distraction. Gene needs to concentrate on finishing his education, and getting his degree," Lynn stated, matter-of-factly.

"I agree," I answered, "But I can't just bring my foot down. He's a grown man and he has to make this decision on his own. I'm just trying to help him figure out what he already knows: this is not the right girl for him."

"How are you doing that?"

"By showing him the difference between the kind of love that's good for you, and the kind that's bad for you; by telling him all the stories that led me to you," I smiled.

"Sounds like you've got this well in hand." Lynn sighed, as she rolled back on her side and hugged my pillow.

I could hear her snoring before I got out the door.

6

COOL AS A CREAMSICLE

The next Monday in school, I dreaded seeing Molly. I wondered if she would even talk to me, and, at the very least, I knew I'd have to confront the hurt in her eyes. What would I say to her? What excuse could I possibly come up with? I practiced saying, "It was only one dance" and "You said it was okay to dance with someone else." But it sounded so insincere; I didn't even believe it myself.

There was one thing I was sure of: I didn't want to lose Molly over this selfish, momentary lapse in judgement. But, when I walked into the classroom, she looked up and smiled at me just like she always did. All through math and reading and spelling, she acted like nothing had happened. She giggled with her girlfriends at the blackboard. She raised her hand to read the next paragraph. She was happy and kind and sweet. She was still the same Molly.

Is it possible that no one told her? I wondered. Her cousin was standing right there. Surely, Pam would have said something to her. If my luck has held this long, it certainly won't hold much longer, I figured. I'm going to tell her everything myself. Maybe it won't be so bad coming from me.

"Can I talk to you for a minute?" I muttered, as we put on our coats to go out to recess.

"Sure," she said. "Just wait until we get outside."

Out on the playground, we strolled off by ourselves. The sky was clear except for one big cloud, which momentarily blocked out the sun, and a cold March wind sent a chill down my back. "I've got to tell you something." I looked up into her eyes. They seemed serious, but not angry. "I danced with this New Galilee girl on Friday night." I said softly, "I'm sorry."

30

"Well, I'm glad you told me. But I already knew." She smiled. "And you don't have to apologize. I don't care if you dance with somebody else. It was just one dance, right?"

"Uh, yes," I stammered. I figured there was no need to bring up the couple's skate right now.

"Do you feel guilty about it?"

"Not anymore," I beamed. I was amazed at Molly's reaction. She had ignored the whispers and rumors. She wasn't going to get upset until she heard the story from me directly. How can she be so loyal? I wondered. How can she be so trusting? And right on cue, the sun poked through the sky.

"I heard she was cute," Molly teased.

I shook my head slowly. "Not as cute as you." And just like that, the storm had passed. Little did I know that, just four days later, Hurricane Caroline would blow back into town.

We got to the roller rink at about 7:30 that Friday. Molly and Pam were already skating around upstairs. There was no sight of Caroline or her friends. "See," Tony slapped me on the shoulder. "You were worried for nothing. It was just a one-night thing, a night out with her friends. You'll probably never see that girl again."

"Too bad," Harry shrugged. "I was going to take a shot at her myself."

I didn't say a word. Although, I was certainly glad Caroline wasn't around, I didn't want to jinx my luck by talking about her. I was worried that if I spoke her name out loud, she might just appear out of nowhere.

After we put on our skates, Tony and Harry headed straight for the baseball card-flipping game that was already under way in the corner of the rink, but I stood against the wall waiting for Molly to come off the floor. When she saw me, she broke off her conversation with her girlfriends and rolled right over.

Maybe it was the lighting in the rink that night, or maybe it was the music or maybe it was just that I had come so close to losing her, but I had never seen Molly look as pretty as she did at that moment.

"Hi," I said as she got closer. "Hi, yourself," she answered. And I knew everything was going to be okay.

At that exact moment, the DJ announced, "The next song will be a couples skate." And as The Impressions' It's Alright began echoing across the floor, I took her hand without saying a word and we swung out into the crowd of kids skating and swaying to the music. It was as if the previous Friday had never happened.

She trusted me, I thought. She didn't get rattled by rumors or teasing. She didn't let jealously get the best of her. And I wondered for a moment if I would have been as understanding or trusting if the situation was reversed.

When the song was over, she made her way back to Pam and her friends and I headed for the shootsies game in the corner. Billy was on a hot streak and must have had eighty cards in his hand when I reached the group of flippers.

"Can I get in the game?" I asked as I pulled up. "Me too?" barked Mickey as he made his way up from the snack shop.

"You can get in as soon as I win this pot," chirped Tony, cocky as ever. Tony was a good card flipper, and even though he was behind tonight, he rarely ended up losing in the end. It didn't hurt that his father owned the town drugstore. That meant he got his cards for free, so he always had the firepower to mount a comeback.

There were about a dozen cards on the ground, and Mickey and I waited off to one side while our buddies finished out the hand. "Hey," he smiled at me. "I see your girlfriend's here again tonight."

"I know," I answered, as I counted out the twenty-five or so baseball cards I had taken out of my back pocket. "I just got done skating with her."

"Not that one," he laughed, "The other one."

"What?"

"Yep," he nodded, "I just saw her putting on her skates downstairs."

I felt a buzz of electricity shoot through my whole body. It was like nothing I had ever felt before, a mixture of fear and dread and alarm. I stood there motionless and speechless for I don't know how long. The next thing I heard was Lou saying, "Teddy…Teddy, it's your turn."

When I looked around, I realized that someone had already won the pot on the floor. That a new game had started and that five guys before me had already taken their first shots at the new pot.

I felt sick to the stomach, and I flipped my cards without even watching where they landed. A couple more rounds went by. "You won," Tony was saying.

"What?" I mumbled.

"You won, Teddy. "What's the matter with you?"

When I looked down, I saw about twenty cards on the floor and, sure enough, one of them was lying on top of another card, a winner, but I didn't even recognize it as my card. Everyone was looking at me, so I bent over and started picking up baseball cards.

"I'm done," I muttered. "I quit."

"Quick hit artist!" barked Billy. "Just take your cards and run. The only thing worse than a sore loser is a bad winner." I stuffed the cards in my back pocket and skated away.

"I'm out too," Tony waved, as he followed me off the floor. And when Harry followed him, I could hear a collective moan go up from the card flippers who saw their game breaking up right before their eyes.

"I don't care," yelled Conti, "Go ahead and leave. I'm still up. I'm still ahead!" And he waved his fists full of baseball cards in the air for everyone to see.

I made my way to the top of the three-step staircase that divided the rink from the snack shop. There she was, still lacing up her skates; no Gracie, no Gracie's cousin, just Caroline and one of her girlfriends from New Galilee. They had come on their own, and there was no doubt in my mind that Caroline had come for me.

"What the hell's going on?" Tony barked, as he and Harry rolled up to join me. "I know you didn't get in that game to win one hand and leave."

"Holy shit," Harry whispered, as he followed my gaze towards the benches in the snack shop. "She's here!"

"Don't worry about it, cousin. You can just…." But Tony's reassuring voice trailed off without finishing his thought. "What are you going to do now?" he asked earnestly.

"Well, I'm not going to lose Molly," I shrugged. "I guess I better face this right now." And I skated slowly over to where Caroline and her friend were sitting.

I was still about ten feet away when she spotted me coming towards her. "Hi," she beamed, flashing those baby blues. "Are you going to save me a dance tonight?"

"…Or two or three," chimed in her girlfriend." And they both giggled.

"Um, I can't," I said nervously, and I turned around and looked back at Tony and Harry for moral support. To my horror, the whole group of Rockland boys from the shootsies game was standing together at the top of the stairs staring at us. "Can I talk to you alone?" I asked her, haltingly.

Now Caroline could feel the eyes of the whole room on her. "I don't think so," she replied suspiciously. "I think you better say what you have to say right here."

"Look," I whispered. "My girlfriend's here tonight. So, I won't be dancing with you or skating with you, I'm sorry."

"Girlfriend?" her voice started escalating. "You never mentioned any girlfriend!"

"I'm sorry," I answered, dropping my head.

But sorry wasn't going to cut it. Everyone in the snack shop was looking at us now.

"Why didn't you *say* anything?" She was almost screaming. "Why didn't you *tell* me about her?"

My plan, in the short time I had to formulate one, was to come clean, to get it over with, to apologize and apologize and apologize. But with the whole place watching us, I made the very poor decision to get defensive.

"You never asked," I shrugged.

With my eyes still downcast, I never saw it coming. *Boom!* She slapped me across the face so hard my left ear was ringing.

"Ohhhhhhhh," groaned the entire pack of Rockland boys, followed closely by Billy's high-pitched laughter.

I just stood there in shock. I had never been slapped by a girl before. In my ten-year-old mind, I felt the urge to retaliate, but I could hear my father's voice screaming in the back of my head. "Never raise your hand to a woman, Ted. Men and women are made differently. It's never okay to use your man's strength against a woman."

I looked around the room. Everyone was waiting for my response. I took a deep breath and counted to five. *This is my fault*, I thought. *She's just hurt and embarrassed.*

"I'm sorry," I announced one more time, and then I just rolled away. The Rockland boys at the top of the stairs parted like the Red Sea, and I skated out across the floor to find Molly.

"What happened to you?" Molly wondered as I rolled toward her. Even under the dim lights of the roller rink, she could see the crimson blush on my left cheek.

"Remember that girl I told you about, the one from New Galilee? Well, she's here." I paused for a second.

"Should I be worried?" She smiled coyly.

"Of course not," I shook my head slowly. "I already talked to her. I told her to forget about it."

Now the light went on in Molly's head. "Oh my God!" she gasped. "Did she *hit* you?"

I just stood there with my hands on my hips, looking down at my skates.

"That must have been *some* dance!"

"Maybe it was for *her*," I said defensively. "But I don't care about anybody but you."

"So, I *don't* need to worry?" I was shocked to see a smile coming back to her face. "I mean, you're done with her, right?" Her soft tone and sweet voice were completely unexpected.

Is that it? I wondered. *Am I really in the clear?*

Molly just took my hand and started skating with me. And it wasn't even a couples skate. We had never done that before. The only ones who did that were the hard-core eighth-grade couples who were glued to each other all night long. Every eye in the place was on us.

She wants everyone to know we're together, I thought. *She just wants to be my girl.* And I physically felt lighter, like the weight of the world had just floated off my shoulders. At that very moment I learned a lesson about girls that I would never forget. If you make a mistake, and you're *sincerely* sorry, a *real* girlfriend will give you another chance.

"I can't promise she won't be back to tell me off again," I laughed.

"Don't worry," Molly giggled. "I won't let her hurt you."

I tried to ignore Caroline for the rest of the night. But I couldn't help but notice that she was having a terrible evening. First, Billy Conti was spending all his time with Terri Roberts. Caroline had blown him off last week and was doing her best to get his attention now. But Billy was not so forgiving, and he put on quite a show of affection for Terri.

Not that he needed an excuse for that. Terri was gorgeous. If Pam Genova was the princess of St. Teresa School, Terri was the queen. Where Pam was shy and sweet, Terri was outgoing and flirtatious. Where Pam was cute and angelic, Terri was dazzling and glamorous.

And Caroline had not only burned her bridges with Billy, just a week before she had turned down dance requests from half the eligible guys in Rockland. Plus, her little tantrum with me earlier in the evening was taking its toll now. Eleven- and twelve-year-old boys have enough self-esteem issues without approaching the girl who had just made a spectacle of herself. Pretty or not, most of the guys figured, she was just not worth the risk. I could see she was hurting, and I knew it was mostly my fault. And even though she had smacked me in front of half the town, I actually felt sorry for her.

Molly and I spent the entire evening together, talking and laughing and dancing. I was just milking the last few moments of *Hurt So Bad* by Little Anthony and the Imperials, taking one long look into Molly's eyes as the music died away. And, when we looked up, there was Caroline, standing there with her arms folded and her coat on.

"I want you to know what your so-called boyfriend did!" She shouted at Molly. It was my worst nightmare. "He flirted with me and danced with me all night last week," she squealed.

"It was one dance," I countered, as calmly as I could. "And you did all the flirting. I probably didn't say ten words to you all night." But they both ignored me. Caroline was barking like a town crier, and Molly just stared at her without saying a word.

"And he never even mentioned you to me. That's some boyfriend you have. I hope you two are very happy together!"

The scene had attracted small group of kids, who now hovered around us. "Are you finished?" Molly said evenly. And Caroline nodded. "I have nothing to say to you," Molly continued. And we all stood there in silence for a few moments.

"I called my ride," Caroline seemed to be addressing the whole rink now, and her voice was still escalating, "I'm leaving and I'm *never* coming back to this damn place!"

It was an ugly scene, and I couldn't help but notice that she didn't look half as attractive as she did the week before. She pushed her way through the crowd and took the long walk of shame across the roller rink floor and down the stairway, vanishing into the snack shop. "I'm sorry," I told Molly, as earnestly as I could. And I braced myself for the hurt and anger.

"Let's never talk about this again," she whispered. And right on cue, the rink's speakers rolled out the first bars of *I Will Follow Him* by Little Peggy March. She took my right hand and put it on her waist, and we started swaying to the music.

Where did I find this girl? I wondered. *Are they all this confident and understanding and true?* The music reached out across the room and swallowed us. "There isn't an ocean so deep; A mountain so high it can keep; Keep me away…Away from my love…." I looked into Molly's eyes and the crowd disappeared again.

DIAMONDS AND RHINESTONES

"Well, there aren't too many girls like that around, Dad." Gene shook his head in disbelief.

"Right!" I nodded. "But I didn't know that. She was my very first girlfriend. I had no one to compare her to.

It took me years of disappointing relationships to understand that sometimes, girls, and women too, would rather play hard-to-get. Sometimes, they only show you how they feel when you're popular or when all their friends think you're great. And, even worse, sometimes they put you down in public, just to show everyone that you can't hurt them; that they really don't care that much about you."

"Like Jan, you mean?" Gene got up and poured his third cup of coffee. "I always get the feeling that she's just insecure. That she puts on this show for my friends so that they think that she's on top in the relationship. Then, when I get upset and tell her we're through, all her insecurities come bursting to the surface, and she just falls apart completely. And there she is, beautiful and crying and begging for me to take her back and give her one more chance."

"And you always do?"

"Well, yeah, I guess so. In a way, I feel sorry for her, and I hold her in my arms just to comfort her. But then, it always turns into more, and before I know it, we're back together again. And I wake up in the morning and look at her sleeping, and I think, this time it's going to work out. But..." And his voice just trailed off.

"That just shows that you're part of the problem," I told him. "You're not sure what love is, so you don't know the phonies from the real thing. It's a hard lesson to learn. You can go through a lot of rhinestones before you find a diamond."

"Well, they kind of look alike," he smirked, "to the untrained eye. I guess that's the worst thing that can happen; when you think you've got that precious stone, but all you really have is a cheap chip of glass."

"No," I countered. "The worst part is when you have a diamond in your hand, and you don't even know it."

"Is that what happened with Molly?"

I smiled at my memory of the little ten-year-old girl who was more constant and devoted than women three times her age. "Well, she was one in a million and I didn't appreciate it at the time. But later, she became the one I compared everyone else to. It wasn't even a conscious thing. It's just that when a girl I really cared about would insult me or side with her friends against me or feign indifference when I came in the room, little alarms would start ringing in my head. And I would think, this isn't right, something's wrong here!"

"So, what happened with Molly?" Gene smiled. "What did you do to blow it?"

"Everything was perfect for about six months, but ten-year-old boys aren't very smart, Gene." I told him. "Let's see how much I can remember."

ALL THAT GLITTERS

In the weeks and months that followed, I never strayed again. Molly was exactly what I wanted. No amount of adolescent insecurity could make her doubt me. No peer pressure could ever cause her to turn against me, even for a moment.

When May and June came around, she showed up at all my Little League games, and I could hear her cheering loudly for me every time I got a base hit and encouraging me even when I struck out. She was a ballplayer's dream if I ever saw one.

In July, I was named to the Little League All Star team and, even though I was only ten years old, I won the job as the starting second baseman. She just seemed so proud. Our team went 13–0 that season and won two big western Pennsylvania tournaments. We were treated like heroes all over Rockland, and Molly was there through it all, smiling and supportive and pretty as a rose. It was the greatest summer of my life.

That was also the year I learned that a real girlfriend never embarrasses you in public, never turns on you when you make an error in the infield, never worries about teasing and peer pressure and name-calling. I learned that a real girlfriend is supportive and steadfast. Unfortunately, I had yet to learn to hold myself to those same high standards.

Maybe it was because I spent too much time reading my own news clippings, or maybe it was because older girls (girls my buddies thought were out of my league) started paying attention to me, but most likely, it was because I was just a ten-year-old boy who didn't know any better. But whatever the reason, by October 1964, I had decided I could do better than Molly.

I remember the day I told her that I thought we were too young to be so tied together; that we needed to see what else the world had to offer; that, although she would always be special to me, I no longer thought we should be exclusive.

If she was upset about the breakup, she never showed it. She was all class and dignity. As the years went by, all through fifth, sixth and seventh grades we remained friends, but, of course, it was never the same. I always liked her, always. But, once the damage was done, there was no way to reconcile; no way to go back.

She was my first girlfriend. I was her first boyfriend. We had never broken up with anyone before. We had never felt the loss and emptiness that comes with that. The kind of support I got from Molly was rare, but I didn't know that. That's the last lesson I learned from Molly, the one I remembered the most, that a steadfast, loyal girlfriend was the exception, not the rule. I'm not sure what lesson she learned from me. But it probably had something to do with boys being assholes.

Anyway, I spent the next couple years chasing Rockland's "It" girls, usually older than me, girls who were renowned for their beauty or their style or their popularity. But, when it came to real heartfelt emotions, they just didn't exist.

As for Molly, we had one last flirtation during the summer between seventh and eighth grades. It was a short, six-week period where we hung out with small group of friends every night. The evenings always ended with the whole gang sitting on Molly's porch, laughing, and telling jokes and playing Hearts with an old deck of cards. No one kept score for very long and the game never really ended. It was just a way to have fun and be together. We talked and laughed and enjoyed being close again, but within a couple weeks, it was clear that it was going nowhere.

By then Molly had developed a mild crush on Terry Marino, a ball-playing buddy of mine, who was part of our gang. And I didn't want to stand in their way. They were both great friends of mine, and besides, she had this mistrust of me that she could never shake. And I couldn't really blame her.

Amazingly, it was Pam Genova, Molly's cousin, who caught my eye later that summer, and I guess I caught hers. Pam was a couple years older than us but was part of the crowd on Molly's porch each evening. She had been my Cousin

Tony's girlfriend back in grade school, but that had ended years ago. This fall, she would be going into tenth grade, and I always thought she was gorgeous, but I really didn't think I should approach her. I always considered Tony's old girlfriends to be off limits.

Still, her eyes lit up whenever we were close and, in time, I got up the nerve to walk her home after the streetlights came on each evening. It took five or six tries, but eventually I summoned the confidence to kiss her goodnight; my first kiss, hers too, she said. Imagine that: the former princess of St. Teresa's School was my first kiss.

It was innocent and embarrassing and fun, in a way. We stood there on her doorstep, shivering in the late August evening chill. I gave her my windbreaker to wear. And she wrapped it around her shoulders without putting her arms in the sleeves. She was laughing and smiling like she always did, then suddenly, her face turned deadly serious. And even though I had never kissed a girl before, I knew that that was my cue. She closed her eyes and I closed mine and I felt her soft lips on mine, light and sweet and mystifying. It was over in an instant, and she handed me back my jacket, and flew up the stairs and into her front door. When I saw she was safely inside, I turned and sprinted the three blocks back to my house, pumping my fist and shouting "yes, yes, yes" all the way home. Still, it had happened so fast that I really wasn't sure that it had happened at all.

The next night I walked Pam home again. "Did something ever happen to you," she whispered to me on the way down the darkened streets of Rockland, "And you weren't really sure if it did happen, or if it was just a dream?"

So, I kissed her again. "Are you sure now?" I laughed. It was fun and exciting, and Pam was really beautiful, but it was just a momentary flirtation. Once I went back to grade school in the fall, and she went off to her sophomore year in high school, the whole thing just kind of faded away. I guess, by rights, my first kiss should have been with Molly.

ORNAMENTS

"Sounds like you had an exciting childhood, Dad," Gene smirked. "All these little girlfriends; I wish I had that much fun in grade school!"

"Well, reality came crashing in soon enough," I answered, as the smile on my face twisted into something else. And, although nearly forty years had passed, I felt a little pang of hurt and regret and adolescent pain come creeping back into my gut. It surprised me that it was still there; buried somewhere inside my memory.

"When I was fourteen, I met my Jan," I said. And Gene sat up in his chair and leaned forward, with his elbows on the kitchen table, as he drained the last sip of coffee from his cup. "Her name was Rosie."

"What happened?" he said earnestly. "Did she come banging at your door?"

"No," I told him. "She never even gave me that much. And I know, know that she cared about me as much as I cared about her, maybe more!"

"What the hell happened, Dad?"

"She listened to the crowd, Gene. It's just as simple as that."

"I was in eighth grade," I started, "And the biggest kid in my grade school. I was so big that my father forbade me to fight with any of my classmates. But I went a step further: not only did I not pick on kids half my size, but I didn't let any of the wise guys pick on the little kids either. No one was allowed to yell cooties when they bumped into the poor girl in the ragged dress. No one was allowed to call the kid who walked hunched over from a spinal deformity Big Butt."

"I was the biggest kid in the school, and I didn't bully any of them. And I sure as hell wasn't going to let them bully somebody else.

43

"Sure, it sounds great to the biggest kid in the class but being Big is not all it's cracked up to be. I felt like when any kid hurt some other kid in the school, it was because I let them get hurt. Anything bad that happened, it was because I permitted it to happen. Some children are cruel to the weaker ones. That's just the way it is. But I wouldn't let them be cruel, and they didn't like it a bit.

"It was a tough spot for an eighth-grade kid to be in. I wanted everybody to like me, even the dudes that pushed kids around.

"It wasn't like I was looking to be the sheriff of the class or anything. Initially, I had tried to be friends with all of them. I knew some of the kids liked catching frogs, just like I did, so when I heard them talking about putting on wading boots and going into Damon's Pond to catch newts, I figured I'd check it out.

"I had only seen two or three newts in my life and thought they were cool as hell, and I had to see where this supposed honey hole of fire-orange amphibians was located. Sure enough, when we got to the pond, Joe Novak and my distant cousin Mark Minelli waded out into the reeds with minnow nets and started scooping out the bright orange three-inch water lizards by the hands full. When Joe had all he wanted, he came in and took off his boots, and then passed them to me along with his net. I pulled on the boots and waded out into about 18 inches of water.

"Within five minutes, I had a bait can full of newts. But, in my excitement, I had stepped into some deeper water and drenched my pant leg and sock inside the boot. We were all still laughing and giving each other the business when we got back to Joe's back porch to dry out. Normally, I would have taken my share of the days catch and headed home, but it was a hot day with plenty of sunshine, so I decided to hang out on Novak's back porch until my pant leg and sock dried."

"What does this story have to do with loyalty, dad?" Gene broke his silence.

"I'm trying to show you that people can turn on you in an instant," I snapped. "And that a real girlfriend is always on your side when they do."

"But what does it have to do with newts?" he laughed.

"It starts as newts and ends with people!" I admonished him. "Do you want to hear the story or not?"

There was silence in the room. Then we both start laughing.

"Go ahead," he smiled. "It's too late to turn back now."

"Well, Joe's family had two pine trees in their back yard, right behind the porch. And I could see that he had little strings of dried apricots hanging from each branch of the tree; one string for each slice of fruit. I had never heard of people drying apricots in their backyard, but people in Rockland had lots of strange customs, so I got closer to get a better look. 'What's this?' I asked him.

"Check it out," said Minelli, as he reached into his can of captured newts and sat down at the picnic table under Joe's porch. There was already a spool of thread on the table. He cut off a two-foot-long strand and tied it tightly around the twitching tail of the blazing orange amphibian. And then held out the thread at arms-length and laughed as the three-inch newt squirmed and twisted to get away from the string that held it.

"I smiled at the little lizards twisting and turning at first, but then cold reality smacked me across the face. Those aren't slices of apricot hanging from that tree, those are dried out newts.

"Soon both Joe and Mark had fiery little orange newts twisting at the end of a thread."

"Watch what happens when you hang them up," smirked Novak with a gleam in his eye, as he tied the second end of the thread to a pine limb, like an ornament on a Christmas tree.

"It was a heartless display. And the most horrifying part was that the newts never slowed down. The longer they swung in the hot sunlight, the faster they twitched and jerked and went into spasms. Then within 5 minutes, they were completely dehydrated and stopped moving for good.

"They twist and turn and squirm," laughed Minelli. "Then, bang! They dry out!"

"That's a horrible way to die!" I shouted over their cackling. "You're not getting any of mine."

And I picked up my bait bucket.

"Ohhhh, what a wuss," laughed Novak. "What are you going to do, take them home and build a little town for them?" And they both just kept laughing and laying on the insults.

"You bastards are sick," I shouted. "And for a moment, I was tempted to take their buckets of squirming newts and pour them into my own. There was absolutely nothing they could do to stop me, and I knew it. But, for some reason, I hesitated, and instead I just picked up my bucket and went home.

"'You assholes are murderers,' I shouted as I walked away. 'Maybe next time, I'll hang you by your tails and watch you swing in the sun.' It was an empty threat, of course, but I knew I would have nightmares about those damn newts for months, and I resented that these clowns showed no guilt whatsoever. Instead, I was the one who felt guilty. I was the one who felt responsible. I was the one explaining my sin to Father Fording in the confessional just two weeks later.

"I resented them for that. And they resented me for ruining their fun. That resentment eventually turned to hatred.

"I wasn't even sure what to do about it. Sure, I had to endure some name-calling and razzing from time-to-time, but none of them ever openly challenged me," I told him. "It wasn't even anything I could get a handle on. I just knew there were punks talking about me behind my back.

"That happened in the seventh grade," I nodded at Gene. "Within a year, these jokers had graduated to tormenting human beings.

"I remember the day in eighth grade when one of the neighborhood girls, Connie Pinchotti, came to me at morning recess and told me that her cousin Diane had been walking home from school the day before, and was followed by three of the punks from our class. As soon as she was alone, they started groping her and grabbing her boobs. 'Can you stop them, Teddy, please?' she asked me.

"I was shocked. We were only in eighth grade, and we were in a Catholic school. 'Why doesn't she tell her parents?' I gasped. 'Why doesn't she tell the teachers, the nuns?'

"'She's afraid no one will believe her!' Connie cried. 'Please help her.'

"So, I did. I warned the three bozos that if I heard about it happening again, I'd beat the crap out of all three of them."

"She's lying," screamed Joe Novak, the leader of this pack of hyenas.

"Well, you better hope she doesn't lie again," I warned him, "Because if I hear about it, true or not, you're dead."

"Sometimes I'd hear about comments those punks would make to put me down; my hair was too wavy; my neck was too long; things they would never say to my face. If I heard about it, I would threaten them. But I almost never hit anyone. I was a good six inches taller than anybody else in the school and probably outweighed anybody else by twenty pounds. My father would never tolerate me beating up little kids like that.

"Only once did I really lose my cool. We were out on the playground at recess and one of the troublemakers in the class touched Wendy Lapinski on the shoulder as she walked by. All the punks in class called her, 'Wendy the Witch.' After he touched her, he smacked another kid on the back, yelling, 'You've got the Witch cooties.'

"His name was Jerry Laughlin, and he ran around with a group of about five or six mean-spirited kids who would have tortured our smaller, weaker, less-fortunate classmates if I hadn't been there to stop them. 'Hey, Laughlin,' I barked at him, 'Knock it off!' Then, I went over to where Wendy was standing with her head down. We went to school together for eight years, and I don't think I ever saw her look anyone directly in the eye.

"'I'm sorry,' I told her. 'That won't ever happen again.' She looked up at me and smiled. That's when I noticed that our eighth grade teacher, Sister Mary Alberta, had seen the whole episode, and was making a beeline across the playground to defend Wendy. But, when she saw me standing there, she just nodded her approval and turned her attention back to the girls playing kick-the-can in the parking lot.

"What I didn't realize was that Jerry must have taken a courage pill that day, because, as soon as Sister Alberta turned away, he snuck up behind me and pushed me into Wendy. 'Now, Teddy's got the cooties,' he screamed. 'Teddy has the Witch cooties.'

"I was enraged and when I spun around, he was already running across the playground, 'Take your beating now, Laughlin!' I screamed. 'If you run it will just get worse.' But he just kept running and laughing, so I took off after him, across the grass and out onto the sidewalk. I almost had my hands on him when he cut sharply to the left. I tried to cut with him, but my shoe hit a wet spot on the sidewalk, and I slid to the pavement, tearing the knee out of my good black pants.

"His whole gang was laughing and screaming, 'cooties, cooties,' as I got up slowly from the ground. It was an insurrection, and I knew just how to handle it. I didn't say another word for the last ten minutes of recess, and when the bell rang, I was the first one in line to go back into the school. I could still hear Jerry and his cronies, giggling and chiding me from the back of the pack.

"When we entered the eighth-grade classroom, I stepped out of line and let all the other kids pass, until Jerry and his pack of hyenas strolled in. I took one step forward and they parted like guppies in a fish tank, leaving him alone and exposed. I hit him with one long right to the jaw, and he banged off the black-board and collapsed to the ground. All the girls shrieked, and the other boys just looked on in awe as Jerry's blood formed a little pool on the classroom floor around his open mouth. 'Tag,' I screamed. 'Now you've got the cooties.'

"Sister Alberta, our eighth-grade teacher was standing just a few feet away; she gasped, and tried to help Jerry to his feet, then took him away to wash out his wound. 'We better call your mother,' I heard her saying as she whisked him down the hall.

"All the students just took their seats. No one said a word. You could have heard a pin drop. And I was left alone to contemplate my punishment. I was usually a well-behaved kid, so I figured they wouldn't kick me out of school, but a short suspension certainly wasn't out of the question. My father, who used to spank me with a leather belt for little wrestling matches I had with my brother on a weekly basis, would have a field day with this one. He had spe-cifically told me not to beat up any of those 'little kids' in my class. I was still angry, but the anger was slowly being replaced by fear.

"The worst part was that Jerry, like twenty percent of the people in Rockland, was a distant cousin of mine. When his mother started making angry phone calls to my house, I knew my dad would try to teach me a lesson I would never forget. 'Why didn't I just hit him on the playground?' I thought. 'Hitting him in the classroom is like ten times worse.'

"Fifteen minutes passed, and still I sat there in silence. Finally, the class-room door flew open and in walked Jerry holding a towel to his mouth. His mother stood to one side of him, and Sister Bernadine, the principal, and the toughest, meanest woman I ever knew, walked in behind him, followed by Sister Alberta.

"Jerry slowly walked to his desk, dumped a few books and tablets into his backpack, and then exited the room, while his mother just glared at me. As they went through the classroom door, Sister Bernadine turned to face me. 'Mr. Tresh,' she barked, 'Into my office, right now!'

"I rose slowly from my seat, and the eyes of the entire class were on me. I took a deep breath and started my death march toward the door. But when I got to the front of the room, Sister Alberta caught me by the arm. 'Ted,' she whispered, 'Go back to your seat.' And, instead, she herself followed the principal to her office.

"I went back to my seat and wondered what the hell was going on. Ten minutes later, she came back into the classroom and started teaching science class, like nothing had ever happened."

"What did happen?" Gene said, breaking his long silence.

"There's no way to explain it, but to call it a miracle. Maybe God *had* heard my confession to Father Fording all those months before. Maybe He protected me. Maybe He had opened Sister Alberta's eyes to what was going on.

"I mean, I know she was a nun, and hated any kind of violence," I shook my head. "But I think she was happy that I stopped those guys. I mean, I never knew she was watching the dynamics of her class, but I guess she was a lot more attuned than I realized. I heard she left the order a few years later and married some guy from Indiana."

"What about Jerry's mother?" Gene wondered.

"Nothing from her either," I shrugged. "My dad never even found out what happened. But that doesn't mean it didn't have any effect on my life. That crew of misfits hated me after that. They talked about me all the time, not to my face, mind you. But just the same, they turned a lot of kids against me."

"So, what's this have to do with Rosie?" Gene said looking at the clock. It was now 4:00 in the morning.

"Well, a lot of the girls looked up to me for what I had done. And I guess Rosie heard about it. She was always flirting.

"But she was a year younger than me, and there was a price to pay if she showed me too much affection. She would have to endure the comments of these delinquents too. She would have to be willing to have some of the kids talking behind her back. And Rosie just wasn't made that way.

"Does she remind you of anyone?" I searched Gene's eyes for a flicker of recognition.

"Of course she does," he nodded. "But, if she really cares about you, and you really care about her, isn't that enough?"

"Surprisingly, Champ. It's not enough," I sighed.

SPOOKY

It was just a few months after the first-kiss milestone with Pam Genova that the Rosie Williamson saga began in earnest. And I was about to learn some of the hardest lessons of my life. Like, what do you do with a girlfriend who never stands by you? Whose own insecurities distort everything she says and everything you feel? It was the crazy-love chapter of my life. I guess we all gotta face it sometime.

I was an eighth grader at the time and Rosie was a year younger than me, blond, and sweet, cute as a button. I'm not sure why I hadn't noticed her sooner; maybe because that was the year she was really beginning to mature. We had gone to a few parties and slow danced together, and she had curled right up into my arms. It was body-to-body dancing and all very exciting and I *knew* that this girl liked me.

A few weeks later, we were at it again. It was Rosie's own birthday party in late May, on a Saturday night in her finished basement. We were cheek-to-cheek while the Delfonics sang *La, La Means I Love You.* The music was soft and soulful and, after yet another great night on the dance floor, I couldn't wait to make her my girlfriend. This was going to be a whole new level of relationship for me. Sure, I had done the first-kiss thing with Pam, but when I danced with Rosie, we were *glued* to each other. Summer would be coming soon, and I loved the idea of going to Darlington Lake with her or walking around the New Galilee Carnival grounds with her on my arm, showing her off to all my friends. Plus, I was ready to start developing my newly acquired kissing technique. And I decided that *she* was the one I wanted to help me write those new chapters of my life. All that was left was to make it official.

Rather than ask her directly, I went the juvenile route of asking one of her friends to intervene. He was a longtime buddy of mine named Sammy Bellissimo and, like Rosie, he was in the seventh grade and knew her very well.

He had seen us at the party and, like everyone who had witnessed us together; he figured this girlfriend-boyfriend thing was just a formality. "Check it out for me, Sammy," I had confided on our way to school that morning. "Tell her I really like her and see what she says."

At the noon lunch break, he reported back. "She doesn't like you, Teddy." He shook his head slowly from side to side.

"How is that possible?" I barked back at him. "You saw us together. Sure, it was just a few dances and she had danced with other guys during the party, but *not* like she danced with me. Hell, it wasn't even close. I could taste the sweat on her forehead!"

"I don't know what to tell you." He just kept shaking his head. "But she definitely said *no*."

"I don't believe you," I shot back.

"Rockland boy to Rockland boy," said Sammy, confidently invoking the sacred oath. But I was having none of it.

"You just want her for yourself. You probably didn't even ask her!" Sammy was one of my best buddies. For me to accuse him of treachery was a slap in the face and I knew it. But it was the only thing that made sense. I had been on the dance floor with plenty of girls by this age, but Rosie was *bonded* to me out there. And it wasn't just the physical contact. We were talking and laughing and whispering in each other's ear. We had connected. "You're lying," I concluded. "Either that or you're too stupid to know what she was really saying."

It was harsh, way too harsh. And Sammy just dropped his head and walked away.

After school, I saw Rosie walking home surrounded by her girlfriends. Since the eighth graders were dismissed last, I was about twenty yards behind her. I wanted to approach her, but I wasn't sure what to say. I figured I'd wait until I could find her alone, and go the direct route, tell her myself how I felt about her. It was something I should have done right from the start.

But Sammy spun around from the group of seventh graders and walked straight towards me. "Here," he said, pushing a piece of notebook paper into my hand. And he stood there expectantly. I could see he was still offended by my accusations.

What's this shit? I thought, keeping an eye on Rosie in the distance. I wasn't really interested in some note telling me how pissed off Sammy was. I knew I had offended him, but I was just as sure that somehow, he had gotten it all screwed up. Either he didn't deliver my message accurately or he misunderstood her answer, but there was *no way* this girl wasn't crazy about me.

I unfolded the note without much interest and gazed down at it out of the corner of my eye. Something was written in big block letters, not in Sammy's clumsy hand-lettering, but in a girl's neat and flowery hand. "I DO NOT LIKE TEDDY TRESH!" It proclaimed, and it was signed, "Rosie Williamson."

"What the hell is this?" I barked to no one in particular.

"I told you," Sammy looked me dead in the eyes. "I told you."

I didn't say five words to Rosie for the next two months. But that note sent a flood of emotions rushing through my adolescent mind. Shame, mistrust, betrayal for sure, but strangely my attraction to her was still strong, maybe stronger than before. I had yet to learn about human nature, about how we want the things we can't have, about how our feelings can grow stronger when we're rejected. I was feeling all those things now, but there were also bells and horns and warning buzzers going off in my brain. *This is not how it's supposed to be,* they screamed. *This girl is not 'girlfriend' material.* I wasn't sure how I knew that, but I did.

School ended a few weeks later and when the weather got warmer, a whole group of Rockland kids headed out to Darlington Lake Park. Darlington was a man-made lake created by damming up a small stream just outside of the little town of New Galilee. It was about five-hundred yards across, and the owners had brought in about a hundred tons of sand to form a beautiful white beach about eighty yards wide and two hundred yards long. There were locker rooms and showers and a big concession stand. Out in middle of the lake there was a diving platform, and a big water slide stood about fifty yards from shore.

There were five kids in our carload and Tony's mom, my aunt Betty, dropped us off with instructions that we should call her when we were ready to be picked up. We knew that other Rockland kids would be at the lake that day. So, when we hit the beach, we looked for some friendly faces. We finally spotted an area where eight Rockland girls had already set up their blankets and beach towels, and right in the middle of them sat Rosie, tanned and curvy with sparkling blue eyes, blond hair, and a bright yellow bikini. I dropped my head for a second. This girl was going to be harder to forget than I figured.

And the strangest part was that she was beaming at me, her eyes were dancing. Her smile lit up her face. *She's sorry for what she wrote,* I decided. *She's been missing me for the last four weeks, and now she wants to set things right.*

It was a comforting thought, but I still wasn't sure I could trust her. When we approached the group, Rosie moved her beach towel over to make room for mine. And when I sat down next to her, it was like we had just walked off the dance floor at her birthday party. She was talking and laughing and flirting, and I had to fight hard to keep my eyes on her eyes. I had never seen her in a bathing suit before, and she was just breathtaking in this bright yellow bikini.

It was 1968, the Baby Boomers were coming of age, and the country had suddenly taken a liberal turn. With the Vietnam War in full swing, college kids were questioning the patriotic values of their war-hardened parents. The birth control pill had helped launch a sexual revolution, and even in my small-town community, inhibitions were slowly eroding away. As a fourteen-year-old boy, I was unaware of most of the social changes, but the shrinking size of girls' bathing suits was something that certainly caught my attention.

No reason to hold a grudge, I decided, and I set about enjoying one of the greatest days of my life. "You look fantastic," I told her. "I missed you."

"I didn't go anywhere," she smiled. "I've been here all the time."

I didn't think it was worth re-counting the *I-don't-like-Teddy* episode. Obviously, there had been some miscommunication somewhere. We headed out into the lake with all our friends, but we paired off quickly. At first, we were just talking and joking and splashing in the water, but then she grabbed my hand so I wouldn't splash her, and she didn't let go. I put my hands on her waist and lifted her off the lake bottom. She felt almost weightless, and she let me hold her there in mid-water, finally wrapping her arms around my neck so I wouldn't *dunk* her. She needn't have worried. Dunking her was the last thing on my mind.

The rest of the day is a blur, buying ice cream at the concession stand, tossing Frisbee on the man-made beach, hanging out on blankets with the gang, watching that little yellow bikini and those dancing blue eyes. It was the first time I ever noticed Rosie's beauty mark, just an inch or so above her bust line, and I couldn't take my eyes off it.

When it was time to go home, Rosie and a few other girls needed a ride, and squeezed in with us in Aunt Betty's car. She sat right on my lap and stayed there for the entire twenty-minute ride back to Rockland. When we got back to town, I got out at her house and walked her to her door.

"Will you be my girlfriend?" I asked as the car-full of kids gawked out the windows.

"What do you think?" she teased.

"I'm never sure with you," I smiled.

"Yes," she said finally. "The answer is yes."

I should have grabbed her and kissed her right there. But everyone was watching us, and I didn't want to embarrass her, plus it had been nine months since the Pam Genova kiss, and I wasn't sure I even remembered *how* to do it smoothly. *That's okay*, I thought as I climbed back into the car. *We've got all summer for this.*

Turns out, I was wrong.

The next morning (the very next *frickin* morning), my telephone rang at 9 o'clock. "Hi," she sighed, "It's Rosie."

I could tell by the tone of her voice that something was wrong, but I tried to ignore it. "Hi! How's my girl?"

"That's what I want to talk to you about," her voice was raspy and thin. "I've been up all night. I think we made a mistake."

I knew what was coming, but I decide to play dumb. "What mistake?"

"Well, you're going to Lakewood High in September, and I'll be going to Beaver Falls the year after that."

That was sad but true. Rockland was too small to have its own high school, and for forty years the students from our little town had taken the short bus ride across the county line into nearby Lakewood City, even though officially, we lived in the Beaver Falls School District.

That was about to change. The student body at Beaver Falls High School was about thirty percent black and thirty percent from the city's poor, urban white families, while the remaining forty percent came from affluent suburban towns.

At some point, the politicians in these richer communities decided they no longer wanted to be part of the Beaver Falls District and set about planning to open their own high school, leaving the poorer district behind. And as soon as plans for the new school were approved by the county commissioners, the suburban property values *soared*.

But that left the county commissioners with a new problem; Beaver Falls High School would be underpopulated. That meant less state aid, lower budgets and lower educational standards. What could the commissioners do to raise the enrollment? Then someone remembered Rockland and its two-hundred or so students. The commissioners soon ruled that, because Rockland was a part of the Beaver Falls School District that those students could no longer attend nearby Lakewood High, but would instead be bussed to Beaver Falls. The same thing was happening all over the country in the late sixties and early seventies; students were being bussed into more urban areas. But this time it was reaching right into my own hometown.

Of course, the whole debacle had its basis in the racism of the suburban towns. But then, as now, money talked, and the soaring property values of the suburban communities would line the county's coffers for decades to come. The commissioners mandated that Rockland students must now be schooled in Beaver County and attend Beaver Falls High School.

My class, the class of '72, would be the last Rockland students to attend Lakewood. And since we were starting there, we would be allowed to finish there. But Rosie's class, the class of '73, would start and finish at Beaver Falls High.

It was unfortunate in many ways, but was that *really* the reason for Rosie's sudden change of heart?

"That's bullshit," I said, with a hint of desperation in my voice. "You're just starting eighth grade at St. Teresa's. Beaver Falls is more than a year away."

There was dead silence on her side of the phone. "Listen," I said. "I'm coming up there right now."

"Okay," she whispered.

I threw on some clothes, brushed my teeth, and started the three-block walk across town to Rosie's house. All the way, I kept re-playing the day at Darlington Lake in my mind. Did I miss something? Wasn't she laughing and smiling and holding my hand all day? Wasn't she sitting on my blanket in that cute little bikini, just beaming and talking and flirting with me, like there was no one else on earth?

Maybe I should have kissed her, I thought. I was pretty sure Rosie had never been kissed. *Maybe, even with everyone watching, she wanted me to be more aggressive.* But that didn't really make sense. We had the rest of the summer for first kisses, and with all the contact we had at the lake, she had to know it wouldn't be far off.

No, somebody got to her. Some friend of hers told her to watch out for me or made some disparaging remark about me.

I guess I did flirt with a lot of girls at that age, so maybe she thought I was insincere. And I was kind of cocky about being a ballplayer, so there were certainly kids who didn't like me. *Jealousy,* I thought. *Somebody out there is trying to take me down a peg.*

When I reached Rosie's house, she was sitting on her front steps. I looked up and down the avenue. There were no cars on the streets, no people on the sidewalks. The whole neighborhood was completely deserted. Rosie's eyes were red and watery, and as I approached, she kept them downcast.

I was still pretty sure I could talk her out of this momentary lapse of faith. "Okay," I started, "what happened in the last twelve hours that I should know about?"

"Nothing, really," She just kept staring at her feet. "I just don't think we should be going steady. You're going to Lakewood, and I'll be going to Beaver Falls..." Her voice trailed off into nothingness.

"That's more than a year away!" I tried to lighten the mood. "We probably would never last a year anyway," I laughed. But she wasn't amused.

"Look, Rosie, just tell me what's going on."

She still wouldn't look me in the eyes. "I was talking to some of my friends and to my sister."

Uh oh, Rosie's sister Colleen was a year older than her and in my grade. We never really got along. She was kind of cute and academically smart, but very quiet and I could always tell that she didn't approve of my cockiness. It wasn't that we were openly hostile; mostly she just flashed her disapproving looks whenever I opened my mouth. She was the worst kind of passive-aggressive, so I handled her with complete indifference. I never gave her a second thought.

"So, what did they say?" I asked her finally.

"Well, some of them don't like you. Terri thinks you're sneaky and Colleen says you're egotistical. But that's not why I want to break up. Debby says you're cute and Tammy thinks you're funny."

"And what do you think?"

"You know I like you, Teddy." Now she finally looked me straight in the eyes. "I just don't want to be your girlfriend."

I tried to talk her into giving it a chance. "Let's try it for a few weeks," I coaxed her. "We can always break up later if you really want."

"Oh, great, that's all I need: no sleep for two more weeks. No, I've made up my mind. I'm not going to change it."

"You're making a mistake, Rosie," I was almost whispering. "You're letting other people influence you. What happened to the girl on the beach, the one who only had eyes for me?" But she went back to staring at her feet.

"I still like you," she sighed. "I still want us to be close."

But my 14-year-old pride would have none of that. "I can't do that," I shook my head slowly. "If I go now, I'm gone for good."

And for once, Rosie was completely silent.

I turned and walked down the sidewalk along Third Avenue, across Main Street and headed home. I felt empty and lost and sick to my stomach. But my feelings for Rosie only got stronger as the months went by. She was always *just* out of reach. And anytime I thought we were getting closer, she would abruptly pull away.

I still saw Rosie in Rockland almost every day, all through my high school years. She still flirted and smiled. She still flashed those bright blue eyes, but, for the most part, I kept my feelings to myself. *I never want to be in that situation again*, I vowed. *I'll never give my heart to some girl who won't stick up for me.*

She was a sweet girl, and I know that deep down she really liked me, but she was no Molly. I had already seen what a real girlfriend looked like, and this wasn't it.

I should have learned my lesson from the Rosie episode. I should have learned about the importance of loyalty and steadfastness. I should have learned to avoid girls that were so easily swayed by the opinions of family and friends and outsiders. But two years after our *breakup*, I jumped right back into the fire.

WALK LIKE A MAN

"So, you never dated Rosie again?" Gene asked. It was after 4 a.m. by now, but neither of us showed any sign of fatigue. If anything, the topic of Rosie had pumped some new life into the conversation.

"Nope," I said. "Now, if she had come pounding at my door, like Jan does with you, I probably would have taken her back, but she always played it cool. When she got to high school, she would even introduce me to some of her new girlfriends from Beaver Falls, as if she were setting me up. I even dated two of them. But I could never get a read on Rosie. And I knew I could never depend on her. She hid her feelings for years, and it just wore me down."

"But Rosie was just a kid," Gene interjected. "You kind of expect that from a fourteen year old. It's much worse with Jan. When she's in crisis, she's all over me, but most of the time she pretends she doesn't care at all! I ask her, 'Who are you trying to impress?' But she just turns away and acts like I'm *beneath* her somehow!"

"That girl has problems, Gene," I shook my head slowly. "Do you think you can really ever trust her to stand by you? I mean, if you would flunk out of school or lose a job or even get arrested someday, is this woman someone who would comfort you and fight for you and be willing to take on the world with you? What if you got some horrible disease? Would she be right by your side? You're twenty-one years old now, Gene. That's still young, but you have to start wondering about the future. It's not just kid stuff anymore."

Gene lowered his head. "But she just seems so upset and sad, and she has those big eyes, and she begs me to take her back; to give me one more chance."

"Well, she's afraid of losing you," I said.

"But why? If she doesn't really want me, why does she hang on? Why does she need me sometimes, and then act like I mean nothing to her when other people are around? It doesn't make any sense! I mean, how long does she think I'll let this shit go on?"

"Wow, Champ," I said with an ironic chuckle. "Some women know who they want personally, but they need a crowd pleaser too. They're so worried about what their friends think of you, that they ignore what they're really feeling themselves. My guess is that Jan really loves you, but she needs everyone else to love you too. It's not enough for her that she's found her soul mate. She needs someone that the world adores. She's not strong enough or self-confident enough to look through her own eyes. She needs to think that the whole world sees you as a star. But as soon as one of her friends puts you down, she feels ashamed and immediately throws up her defenses. She'll never really be a true partner."

"Geez, dad, how long will this go on?" Gene tried to take a sip from his coffee cup, but it was completely empty.

"Well," I said, "it can go on for an awful long time, if you let it."

"You sound like you're talking from personal experience," he smiled.

I looked up at the clock on the microwave. The story I wanted to tell him next was a long one, and the sun would be rising in a couple hours. "I better put on another pot of coffee," I shrugged. "We could be here a while."

OUR SONG

My early high-school years were filled with crushes and flirtations, nothing too serious. But about halfway through my sophomore year, I got my driver's license, and things suddenly got a lot more interesting, with dates and parties and dances. It was also about that time that Lorraine Donatelli started to bloom. And once she started, there was no stopping her.

Lorraine was a Lakewood City girl who had been kind of plain and unremarkable during our freshman year. But over the summer of 1969, she had morphed into something else altogether. She had always had a pretty face, but now her short-cropped, dark hair had become soft and slinky and grown to shoulder length. Her once Tom-boyish figure had rounded out in all the right places, and her once very-common legs had grown curvy and seemed to go on forever. Out of nowhere, she had become the *It Girl* of the class of '72.

Like every other guy in school, I noticed the changes. But I really didn't know her well enough to make a big play for her. First, I had grown up in Rockland, and there were still Lakewood kids who weren't ready to share their school with us. And they certainly weren't ready for me to move in on the fastest-rising star in the class. Next of all, I hadn't really paid much attention to Lorraine during our freshman year, so I was starting from scratch.

Still, through the first six months of the school year, we began getting closer. Friendly conversations became long, serious discussions. Mild flirting in the hallways became hour-long study halls, passing notes and swapping phone numbers. I really started to like her. And, when March came around, I began campaigning to take her to the sophomore semi-formal.

At Lakewood High, the underclass semi-formal was sponsored by a girls' club called the Y-Teens. Almost every female in ninth and tenth grade was a member of the club, and because it was a girls' club, it was the girls who invited the boys to escort them.

It was mid-March, and we were coming out of the old gym, after the school's regular Friday night dance, when Lorraine finally brought up the subject of the semi-formal. We had just slow danced to the final song of the night, and the scent of her perfume, the feeling of her soft hair against my cheek and her hand in mine and the way I easily guided her on the floor with gentle pressure on the small of her back, were all still swirling through my brain. The final bars of the Impressions' *I'm So Proud* were still lingering in the air. "That may be the greatest song ever," I whispered as we stepped into the warm spring evening.

As I look back upon it now, the music is what I remember most about those years. It really was the soundtrack to our lives, and almost all my memories are colored by the songs we heard on the radio and on the dance floor.

"I have to ask you something, Teddy" Lorraine said nervously. And I turned to face her. "Will you take me to the Y-Teens Dance?"

I felt a rush of fever surge across my face. It made me pause for a second, which was good. Otherwise, I would have sounded too eager. When my voice finally came back, she was looking up at me with those soft brown eyes, searching for an answer. "Of course, I will," I smiled, as I wrapped my arms around her waist. "It's going to be a great night."

I waited with her until her ride arrived. She was being picked up by her oldest brother, who didn't seem too happy about interrupting his evening to fetch Lorraine. He just honked his horn and motioned for her to come to the car. I started to follow her, to escort her across the street, maybe open the door for her. But she stopped me. "Stay here," she said. "He'll tell my mother. I'm not supposed to be dating anyone, especially not a Rockland boy."

Her comment stung for an instant. *"Especially not a Rockland boy,"* what the hell did that mean? But on the way home, I started romanticizing the whole situation. *We're like Montagues and Capulets,* I thought, *Star-crossed lovers who won't let anything keep us apart.* And for the moment, I pushed the final scene of *Romeo and Juliet* out of my mind.

When the night of the big dance came, my father helped me get ready. He was an accountant for a big steel company, and he wore a suit to work every day. He made sure my new grey suit was meticulously tailored, my white shirt was pressed and cleaned, and my purple tie was in a perfect Windsor knot. I checked my look in the mirror. *Not too shabby*, I thought.

There was one problem. Just two weeks earlier, I had wrecked my father's brand-new silver Thunderbird. He was upset, but it had been a high-speed wreck, and he was mostly just relieved that I didn't get hurt. The problem tonight was that the Thunderbird was still in the shop, so I had to use my grandfather's ten-year-old Plymouth Valiant instead; not exactly perfect for a semi-formal dance, but I was lucky my dad was letting me drive again at all. So, I didn't complain.

It was April of my sophomore year, and only about a third of the guys in my class were driving already, so Lorraine and I were double dating with one of my Rockland buddies Dennis Baldelli and his date Debby Thomas. I picked up Dennis and his date first, and then drove to Lorraine's house.

When her mom came to the door, I saw her check out my shabby Plymouth with a look of disdain. I was about to make a comment about being forced to use my grandfather's car when Lorraine appeared at the top of the stairs. She wore a gorgeous baby-blue dress; cut a couple inches above the knee to show-off her long legs, and a low-cut neckline that featured her shapely bust and real live cleavage! I had never seen cleavage up close before; not in a girl from my class anyway. And before I could stop myself, one word jumped out of my mouth. "Wow!"

"Hmmmpf," her mother shrugged, and didn't say another word. Lorraine's big, almond-skinned Italian father then made his way in from the kitchen, wearing black work pants and a short-sleeved white undershirt. I stepped forward and cleared my throat. "How do you do, Mr. Donatelli?" I spoke clearly and decisively, just the way my father had instructed me. "I'm Ted Tresh." I put out my hand and gave him a good strong-gripped greeting.

He grumbled something I didn't quite hear and just went into the living room to watch television. Lorraine's older sister Angela was right behind her on the steps. Angela had graduated from Lakewood High a couple years before, but she was a legendary beauty whose name was still spoken of with reverence around the halls of the high school.

"Doesn't she look beautiful?" gushed Angela, who had obviously had a hand in her sister's preparations.

"She looks like an angel," I answered. And she really did.

On the way to the dance, we talked like we had been dating for years. There were no awkward silences, and no nervous laughs. We were all just thrilled to be there; thrilled to be teenagers on our way to adulthood. "My sister really likes you!" Lorraine revealed.

"I've never even met her before," I said, a little confused.

"I know," she answered. "But I've told her all about you."

That was good news on two fronts. First, it meant that Lorraine had been singing my praises, and second, it meant that I had at least one ally in the house, because I sure wasn't going to get any support from her mother or father.

The whole night was like a dream. When we walked into the dance, we were surrounded by friends, some were her friends, some were mine, but they all just treated us like a couple. It almost seemed like we had always been a couple, and she never left my side for the entire evening.

"I wish this deejay would play a slow song," she said as I took her hand for the first time.

"*Ooo, Baby, Baby*," I answered. "That's my favorite."

"Or, *Hey There Lonely Girl*," she smiled, taking my other hand, and looking me directly in the eyes.

"Wait here," I said. And I made a beeline for the disc jockey. He was from a Pittsburgh radio station and called himself *Rinky Dink*.

"Hey, Rink," I shouted over the music as I neared his elevated turn tables. "Can you play *Hey There Lonely Girl*?" Up until now he had played nothing but a steady stream of fast songs and rock music and no one was dancing.

"If it'll get these party poopers on the floor, I'll play Beethoven," he snapped back at me.

"I can promise you at least two people on the floor," I said, flashing him a thumbs up.

When the music started, the dance floor filled up in seconds, and Lorraine slipped into my arms and stayed there all night. My song request was about to change the evening for everyone, and I felt almost heroic out there with the prettiest girl in the school in my arms.

Rinky Dink saw the crowd reaction, and for the rest of the evening, it was one slow song after another. I pulled Lorraine in closer and closer, and she never hesitated for a second. I could feel her entire body against mine, and my sixteen-year-old libido was on full tilt. I could smell her cologne; feel the curves of her body against mine. It was like the best dream I ever had.

"This is my favorite song," Lorraine whispered as The Delphonics *La La Means I Love You*, echoed across the gym floor. Then, she said it again during The Miracles' *More Love*. Four straight slow dances and she proclaimed each one to be her favorite. Finally, we took a break.

"Let's be alone for a while," I whispered. And we headed out into the darkened hallway of the high school. I took both her hands in mine as we stood in the dark alone. I moved in for our first kiss. It was soft and tender and natural. Someone opened the door to the gym, and we could hear the first few bars of *Love on a Two-Way Street* by The Moments come leaking out into the hallway.

"Ohhhhhhhhhhh," she sighed excitedly.

"I know; I know," I grinned. "This is your favorite song." And we started dancing again, alone in the dark hallway; nobody else was there, just Lorraine and I, wrapped around each other. The music was faint and far away, and I could hear our shoes shuffling on the floor tiles, and I kissed her again, longer, more meaningful. "Now it's my favorite song too," I whispered. And from that day forward, *Love on a Two-Way Street* was our song.

When the dance ended, we went out to eat at Troggio's Restaurant in New Castle with four other couples. It was the most memorable night of my young life so far. There was never an awkward silence. We chatted excitedly all evening. We laughed and hugged and touched each other all through dinner. She ordered spaghetti and meatballs. I'm sure it was because it was the cheapest thing on the menu. "Get whatever you want," I pleaded, my dad's twenty-dollar bill burning a hole in my pocket.

"I want spaghetti," she smiled, "and we can split a dessert!"

"A chocolate sundae, with whipped cream and a cherry," I told the waitress a half-hour later, as she cleared our dinner table.

"And two spoons," Lorraine added. And the eyes of every couple at the table turned towards us. I was so happy and so proud of her. She looked beautiful and seemed completely absorbed in me.

When we got back to her house, Dennis and Debby were still in the backseat as I walked her to her door. But she stopped just behind a small pine tree, out of sight of the front window. "Let's say goodnight here," she whispered.

And I kissed her again. *This one will seal the deal*, I thought. But after two seconds she pulled away. "Don't," she said. "My mother will see."

I started to protest, but she shook her head. "I really had a good time," she sang, as I turned to walk away. "Will you call me?"

"Of course, I will," I answered, still a little mystified at what had just occurred. I turned back to watch her go through the front door, where her excited sister waited for a report on the evening.

Don't worry about it, Ted, I told myself. *It's just a matter of time!*

When I got back to the car, Dennis and Debby stayed in the back seat as we headed across town to her house. They were strangely silent, and when I glanced up into the rear-view mirror, I could see they were cuddling and kissing. *Good for him*, I thought, and I kind of wished that someone else would have driven, so that Lorraine and I could have had the back seat to ourselves.

Two minutes later, I was watching Dennis walk her to the door to say goodnight. I fiddled with the radio dials for a while, so they wouldn't think I was watching them. When he got back to the car, I said, "Big night, huh?"

Dennis was a longtime grade school buddy. We had attended St. Teresa's Catholic School for eight years. We were altar boys together. And he took his religion very seriously. I had never seen him start a fight or heard him use a profanity or even lie about his homework. And I had certainly never heard him use the name of God in vain. So, I was shocked at his response to my question.

"A big night for *me*?" he screamed. "Jesus Christ, Teddy. The most beautiful girl in the school is in *love* with you!" He was shaking and laughing, and he grabbed me in a bear hug. "Jesus Christ, Jesus Christ," he kept saying, and we both laughed all the way back to Rockland.

THE RIGHT GIRL

Our fourth pot of coffee had just stopped brewing. "So, what did this girl look like, dad?" Gene asked as he got up to pour us a good strong cup.

"Let me grab an old yearbook," I answered, and I started walking toward the bookshelves in the family room.

"That's okay," he laughed. "You don't have to go to all that trouble."

"No, I want you to see her," I told him. On his last trip home, he had shown Lynn and me a couple photos of him and his new girlfriend. And I knew the yearbook pictures of Lorraine would startle him. "Remember," I said, leafing through the pages of my old Lakewoodian, "This was over 30 years ago, so the hair styles and clothes will be different. Here," I said as I handed over the yearbook. "This is Lorraine."

"Holy shit," Gene gasped, "She looks almost exactly like Jan, *my* Jan!"

"I know," I told him, "That's the first thing your mother noticed when you showed us your photos. She said, 'Well, congratulations, your son is dating Lorraine Donatelli!'

"And from what you've told me, she acts a lot like her too, Gene. Not the *put down* part. Lorraine never really insulted me, but she never really supported me either. When I was popular, she openly adored me. But whenever something went wrong, she buried her feelings so deep that it almost seemed like she was ashamed of me."

"What do you mean when *things went wrong?* What kind of things?" Gene wondered.

"Well, I told you that I was a pretty good baseball player."

"Yeah, I know about that, Dad. I've heard all the stories."

"But what you don't know," I continued, "Is that when I first came to Lakewood City High, I was considered a better football player than baseball player.

"When I was in seventh grade, Rockland organized their very first Pop Warner midget football team, and I was the starting quarterback. We weren't great, but we finished with a 3-3-1 record. A .500 team our very first year, and we played against big towns like Beaver Falls and New Brighton and Brighton Township.

"I was supposed to be the quarterback again the next year, but I was a big kid, and the Pop Warner weight maximum was only 110 pounds. When I was in seventh grade, I barely made the weight limit. When I was in eighth grade, I weighed about 125, and there was no way I could get down to the limit. I would have been perfectly happy taking a year off from football, then coming back to play in Junior High the next year. But Nick DeVito, one of our distant relatives, contacted the coach at the Catholic School in Lakewood City to see if they would let me play on their grade school team.

"In those days the school was called Purification of the Blessed Virgin Mary School, or BVM for short, and I got to play with the BVM Blue Angels. I only joined the team about a week before the season started, so naturally, they already had a starting quarterback. His name was Jerry Delpino, and he became my best friend in high school.

"We had a decent season, 3-4, but I really had a standout year. The coaches put me at running back and I led the team in rushing and touchdowns. They even added a halfback option pass to the playbook, and I ended up throwing four touchdown passes that year, one more than our quarterback. A funny side note is that your mom was in seventh grade at BVM that year, and because she was trying out to be a cheerleader for the following year, she went to every game, and saw me play. We never met until a few years later, though.

"My success on the BVM team helped a lot in ninth grade, when I finally got to play for the Lakewood Junior High. Most people in the town already knew who I was, and on opening day, I was the starting quarterback at my brand new junior high school!

"Of course, in Rockland, I was still known as a baseball player. When I was just ten years old, during a perfect summer, I had started at second base for the Little League All Star team that won the tristate tournament in New Castle, and every year since then, I had been the starting shortstop for the Rockland Little League and Pony League."

"So, did you consider yourself a baseball player or football player?" Gene wondered out loud.

"I always considered myself a baseball player first," I admitted. "But the country had started changing around that time. Baseball wasn't seen as glamorous anymore. Football had taken over as the national pastime. Being from Rockland, my first love was baseball, but if being a football star was the key to popularity in Lakewood City, then I was happy to oblige. Plus, I was one of the biggest kids in the Junior High School, so even though I was from Rockland, they had to play me if they wanted to win.

"The truth is, Gene," I continued, "even being a football player was losing some of its glamour. It was the late 1960's, and across the country, there was a youth rebellion going on. Anti-war protests were invading every college campus. Rock bands screamed about free love and social consciousness. College kids couldn't be kids anymore. They had to be young rebellious adults. And that meant that drugs and resistance and political awareness had taken the place of sports as a priority among the student bodies.

"Of course, in Rockland and at Lakewood High, we were still mostly shielded from these influences. But every year the shine on sports stars was growing dimmer and dimmer.

"And then there was the whole Rockland versus Lakewood City thing going on. Rockland had been sending star baseball players to the high school for decades, and the baseball coach was a high-principled man named Bill Sherman. He had been starting Rockland ballplayers on his teams for years and the town had grown accustomed to supporting us as soon as we put on the blue pinstripes of the Lakewood City Wolverines.

"But football was a whole different matter. Rockland had never had a youth football program until two years ago. We had never competed for starting positions on the football team. No one in the administration or the school board

70

wanted to see Rockland boys starting on the gridiron in front of their sons. Even the coaches and, most of all, the other players, seemed to hate us as soon as we entered the locker room."

"I didn't even know you played football," Gene admitted.

"There's a reason for that," I told him. "There wasn't much of a problem with the coaches in Junior High. I was one of the biggest kids on the team, and the fastest. They *had* to play me if they wanted to score. But when I got to tenth grade, they didn't really need me. I just struggled to make the traveling team each week.

"Plus, my teammates were the real difference. In baseball, I had been playing against these guys for years. They got used to getting beat by Rockland; by me and my cousin Tony and Derrick Dawson and Billy Conti and Will DeLuca. We had been beating them for years. They had to admit we were good ballplayers. But in football, Rockland never even had a team until the players my age came along, and those Lakewood guys hated seeing us on *their* football field.

"You know, Gene, I'm telling you this for a reason. I'm telling you this because there will always be people who want to see you fail, people who resent you for no reason. But those people shouldn't be able to influence your girlfriend's opinion. No matter how much I had to struggle with bitter rivals on the football team, I shouldn't have had to worry about the loyalty of my girlfriend."

"So, what kind of struggles did you have with the football team?" Gene wanted to know.

"Practices were the worst. Most guys only play hard in spurts during practice, but when they came heads up with me, they hit as hard as they could. So, I had to go full-tilt on every play, just to stay alive. Not so bad if you're a senior, but when I was a sophomore, there were guys out there who outweighed me by 50 or 60 pounds. I got pretty bruised up every day."

"So, what happened, Dad," Gene looked serious now, as if it was happening right before his eyes. "I'm sure when the coaches saw how hard you battled, they sang your praises. Did you get to play in the games?"

"That's what made it so bad. The coaches *never* gave me credit for anything. I mean, football coaches all act like hard asses anyway. But even they seemed to hate the idea of a Rockland boy invading their space. Like I said, in baseball,

71

Coach Sherman had some integrity, and he wasn't from Lakewood City originally. If you could hit a baseball, you played, period! He didn't care about anything else. That's probably why the Lakewood City High School baseball team had won their section title for five straight years, including two state championship teams, while the football team was lucky to have a .500 season. The football coaches weren't like Coach Sherman. They said I upset the chemistry of their team; that I wasn't a team player. It was all bullshit, and I put up with it as long as I could.

"I got some playing time in JV's. I scored four touchdowns in five games that year. But I never smelled the field in a varsity game. It all came to a boil at a mid-season practice."

"What happened?" Gene was pounding his fist on the table. "Did you get in a fight? Did someone hurt you? Did you hurt somebody else?"

"All of the above," I answered. And I gritted my teeth. The memory was just as fresh now as it was during that fall of 1969.

"I was a sophomore, and we were going to play Aliquippa that Friday night. I was playing halfback for the scouting team against our starters. We were supposed to run the Aliquippa plays that the coaches had seen them running on films from previous games. None of the first and second stringers played on the scouting team, so I was surrounded by a weak cast of players. No problem: that was my job. But, like I said, I had to play at full speed on every play or I would have gotten massacred out there. The exception was when the coaches wanted to dissect a certain play. Then they would call "*dummy*." That meant both teams would go through the play at half speed to see where the holes were forming, and how they needed to match up our defense to stop a certain play.

"One of the assistants, Bob Mason, was calling the plays for the scouting team. Out of all the football coaches, he was my favorite. He was also the Algebra teacher at the high school, and during my freshman year, I was his star pupil, so Rockland boy or not, he kind of liked me. The rest of the staff never had a kind word, no matter what I did.

"Well, he called my number to run a tackle trap play from the Aliquippa play book. Of course, the third team guard who was supposed to pull from the left and block the tackle, never even got a piece of him. I got clobbered by the tackle and both linebackers. When I got up, my chin strap was hanging from one side. The metal snap had come completely dislodged from the helmet, and they sent me off to the equipment manager on the sidelines to get it repaired.

"These metal clasps came unscrewed all the time, and Mr. DeCarbo, the equipment guy, had it fixed in about five minutes. When I trotted back onto the field, Coach Mason told me to line up at fullback and called a power play to the right side of the line. 'You're the lead blocker, Tresh,' he told me. 'Thornridge is lined up in the hole and you need to move him out of there.'

"I glanced up at the line. Sure enough, Wally Thornridge was playing line-backer and was bouncing in and out of the hole I needed to open. Thornridge was no ordinary football player. He was the co-captain of the team and was the only All-American ever to play at Lakewood City High School. He was a monster!

"I tightened up my chinstrap and dug in my cleats. I knew my only chance was to blow out of my stance at top speed and blast him as hard as I could before he really got any leverage on me. When the ball was snapped, I took off like a rocket, and before Thornridge even saw me coming, I rocked him. I hit him so hard that he flew five yards into the secondary. My first thought was *shit that was easy.*

"A huge groan had gone up from the entire team at the moment of impact. Everyone on the field was standing there gaping at us, and for the first time I noticed that there was very little action going on around me. Even the halfback was still standing in the backfield with the ball. Then I heard the words, which would alter my football career forever. 'It's dummy, you Dummy,' barked the head coach from halfway across the field.

"Sometime while I was getting my equipment repaired, Head Coach Fonda had decided to break down the blocking schemes on that play and called *dummy.* I was the only one on the field moving at full speed, every other player was walking through the play.

"The coaches were furious. The players were all giving the business to Wally. 'Oh, that punk pounded you. Are you going to take that?'

"I scrambled to tell my side of the story, 'I was off the field,' I said, pleading my innocence. 'No one told me it was a dummy play.' But the coaches were having none of it 'Give me five laps around the field, right now,' barked Coach Fonda, 'and I don't want to see you break stride.'

"Five laps around a football field? That's over 1200 yards!"

"That's not fair," screamed Gene from across the table. "There was no way you could have known they weren't playing full speed! Surely the coaches knew that."

"They were trying to save face with their players, with their All-American. That's what the main problem was. Most football coaches are just frustrated old jocks themselves. They don't care about fairness. They don't care about a kid who is trying to overcome obstacles. Sure, they scream at their thug football players, but deep down, a lot of them are just thugs themselves. The great coaches command the respect of their players; the mediocre ones just want to be one of the boys."

"So that's it?" Gene smiled. They made you run an extra mile?"

"They made me run." I shook my head, "But that was far from *it*. When I got back to the huddle, I was exhausted, but they put me right back in there running the ball. But now the whole first team defense started pounding on me every time I ran into the line."

"What did you do?" Gene wondered, as he leaned forward into the conversation.

"I did the only thing I could do. I started running harder, accelerating faster. Football is all physics. It's mass times speed. I didn't have much mass, so I had to ramp up the speed and acceleration or get destroyed. But that just pissed off the first team more. They started throwing punches at the bottom of the piles. When that didn't slow me down, they threatened the third-team linemen in front of me; made them intentionally miss their blocks. Made them say where the play was going to go. I was getting pounded, but all I could do was launch myself into them harder and harder."

"You're shitting me," Gene scoffed "The coaches saw the punches; saw the linemen playing dead and they didn't do anything about it?"

"I don't know if they saw the punches or not. They acted like they didn't. But I know they saw me take on their whole team and never back down. I know they heard the banging of the pads; saw the bodies flying, and never a word of praise. It was a Wednesday practice. Every Wednesday, before an away game, they posted the names of the players who made the traveling team for Friday night. No one had worked harder than me that week. No one had run harder; hit harder. But, when I checked the traveling-team list on the bulletin board in the locker room, my name wasn't on it. I put up with this shit for another year or so. I finally quit the football team halfway through my junior year. I should have been starting by then; instead, they actually left me off the traveling team again for an away game my *junior* year. I quit the next day.

"I'll never forget old Assistant Coach Mason, calling me into his office the next day. 'Ted, your time will come,' he told me. 'Next year you'll be the fastest kid on the team. You can catch any ball thrown near you and you run hard with it up the middle or outside. Hell, you can throw a football fifty yards in the air. You'll be our star next year.'

"'I can do all those things now,' I told him, as I headed for the door. Then I stopped and turned around. 'You won't win a game next year.'"

"Wow," Gene shook his head again. "That's a great story. But what does it have to do with me and Jan? In fact, what does it have to do with you and Lorraine?"

"It has to do with loyalty, Gene," I told him. It has to do with who is going to stand by you when you're not on top; when you have a lot of enemies, when things get tough. There were ten or twelve seniors on the football team who hassled me in the hallways every day. I could handle any physical threats, but the constant putdowns were hurting my image, my reputation, around the school. Any girl will love you when you're a star. Who's the one who will still be there when half the school hates you? That's the girl, the woman, that matters."

HOW IS THAT POSSIBLE?

After the big night at the Y-Teens dance, I knew it was just a matter of time before Lorraine would officially be my girlfriend, so I waited for just the right, romantic setting to ask her. And it came just a week after the semi-formal. I had spent that week in school walking her to her classes and sitting next to her in study hall. She was all smiles and flirtations and she lit up like a Christmas tree every time I came into view.

Her closest friend, Margie Ceratti, grabbed me after CP English class on Wednesday. "What did you do to my best friend?" she teased. "Her head has been in the clouds for days, and I'm starting to worry about her."

"I can't help you," I shrugged. "I'm in the clouds myself."

Margie just shook her head. "Seriously, Teddy, she really likes you. I've heard the story of the Y-Teens dance a hundred times already. Lorraine's mother won't let her go on dates yet, but there's a dance at Bell Memorial on Friday, and she's allowed to go. Think you can make it?"

Bell Memorial was the name of a local church, with a big church hall and gymnasium attached to it. Sometimes they held fundraisers at the hall, and teen dances were always an easy way to make a few hundred dollars.

"I didn't even know there was a dance this weekend," I told Margie. "But you can bet your ass I'll be there!"

"Do you think you can bring Jerry along?" she asked cautiously.

Jerry Delpino, my old quarterback rival from BVM and Junior High foot-ball had become my best friend at Lakewood High. He and Margie had an on-again, off-again relationship for years, and she was hoping to re-spark the old romance, I guess.

"I'll ask him," I replied. "But you can tell Lorraine that I'll be there come hell or high water." And I set about planning my strategy.

It was time to make Lorraine my steady girlfriend. It was time I asked her to *go with me*. At Lakewood, and most other high schools in those years I imagine, we didn't say we were *going steady* or even that we were *dating*. When you asked a girl to be your girlfriend, you asked her to *go with you*. That meant you never dated or even flirted with anyone else. If you were a junior or senior, it meant that she would wear your class ring. Of course, we were sophomores, and we didn't even have our class rings yet. But we had already been measured for them, and in September, I envisioned Lorraine walking the halls of the school with my ring on her finger. Just the thought of it made me smile to myself.

On Friday night, I picked up Jerry and a couple of my buddies from Rockland and we all headed for the dance. It wasn't always easy to borrow our dads' cars. So, when I did get the car for the night, it was almost an obligation to take as many other kids as possible. That way, they would owe me a ride. So, if I drove this weekend and Willie drove next weekend and Jerry got his dad's car the week after that, I could parlay one night-out into a month of dances and parties and ball games. Of course, dads' cars or not, we never missed a party. It was 1970, and we had no fear of hitchhiking anywhere we needed to go.

When we got to Bell Memorial Hall, I immediately put my plan into action. Jerry and I made a beeline for Margie and Lorraine. Jerry wasn't really sure he wanted to re-kindle his old flame, but he had agreed to play wing man for me, and immediately swept her out on the dance floor, leaving me alone with the girl I adored.

I sat next to Lorraine on one of the church-hall folding chairs, which were lined against the wall, and took her hands in mine. She was beaming, and her big, soft brown eyes twinkled in the dim lights of the disc jockey's turn table. "Aren't you going to ask me to dance?" she whispered. And a few seconds later she was in my arms, as Tommy James and the Shondells oozed out the refrain from *Crimson and Clover*.

She wrapped herself around me in an instant. It's funny how girls with overly protective parents compensate by pushing the limits of those things they *are* allowed to do. With very few exceptions, like the Y-Teens dance, Lorraine wasn't allowed to go out on dates, or be alone with a guy in his car, or even go for a walk alone with a guy on a summer night. But she *was* allowed to slow dance, and brother, nobody slow danced like she did!

Her head was on my shoulder. Her lips were on my neck. I could feel the entire length of her body swaying slowly against mine. "Crimson and clover, over and over...Crimson and clover, over and over," moaned Tommy James. And those simple words took on a whole new, sensual meaning that I never realized was there.

"He's talking about sex," I said, in surprise. The thought hit me so fast, that I said the words out loud, without the filter that usually kept me from saying anything explicit to a girl, to risk embarrassment or rejection or offense. It just leaped from me. "He's talking about passion." And I cringed to think what this fifteen-year-old angel must think of me.

"Umm hmm," she whispered. And somehow, she nestled onto my shoulder even closer.

Holy shit, I thought. *She knows. She knows what it means, and she feels it too.*

As I walked Lorraine back to her seat after the dance, I realized that the time had come. It was time to make it official. One more thing would make it perfect. "Wait here," I told her. "I'll be right back."

I headed straight for the DJ and pulled him aside. "I want to request a song," I said in a loud whisper. "Can you play *I'm So Proud* by the Impressions?"

"Alright! A Curtis Mayfield fan," He beamed. "I'll play it right after this one."

"And can you dedicate it to Ted and Lorraine?"

"Ted and Lorraine," he repeated. "Sure."

She was still sitting where I left her; still sitting there all alone in the dimly lit church hall. "I'm back," I began, "And I want to ask you something."

Like it or not, the next few moments are etched in time. I took both her hands in mine. The music was loud, so I crouched down in front of her so she could hear me. "I want you to be my girlfriend," I told her. "I want us to be exclusive. I don't want to think about anybody but you. And I don't want you thinking about anybody but me. Will you go with me?"

I fully expected her face to light up. I completely anticipated her leaping into my arms, but instead, she dropped her head. *This can't be good,* I thought. And

I felt like I had just stepped into The Twilight Zone. My face flushed and there was a buzzing in my ear. I had trouble hearing her next words.

"My mother doesn't allow me to date anyone," she was saying.

"We don't have to go out on formal dates," I muttered. "We can meet at dances and parties, just like we do now. But I won't see anyone else, and you won't see anyone else, and I'll call you every night and we'll be together." I was rambling now.

"It's no good, Teddy." She shook her head. "I'm not allowed to go steady with anyone. I'm not allowed to have one, exclusive boyfriend. My mother won't let me. She says I'm too young."

"Then don't tell her," I laughed nervously. "How would she ever know? Why would she ever care? Nothing would change in how we feel. Nothing would change in where we go. And in a year or so, when you are allowed to go steady, you could tell her then!"

"I can't," she said firmly. "She *would* know. She finds out everything! I don't know what she would do; ground me, preach at me. I don't know. It would be bad enough that I defied her, but to go steady with a *Rockland boy?* She'd make my life a living hell."

The full weight of her words hit me like a tornado. I was numb from disappointment and shame and now, anger. Who the hell did this woman, this mother, think she was? She didn't know me, didn't know my family.

"I'm *proud* to be a Rockland boy," I barked. "And if you're too afraid to make up your own mind, then I feel sorry for you." I turned to walk away.

"Teddy, wait," she pleaded. "It's not my fault."

I stopped for a second and looked back at her, and the anger started to wane. She looked so beautiful sitting there. Her eyes still sparkled, and she seemed so helpless, so vulnerable. Then the disc jockey's voice came booming over the sound system, "This one's dedicated to Ted and Lorraine."

"Oh, shit," I thought. "Not now!" And although I knew what was coming, I took her in my arms anyway and started swaying to the music.

"Prettier than all the world," Curtis Mayfield sighed, "And I'm so proud. I'm so proud of you. You're only one fellow's girl. And I'm so proud. I'm so proud of you. I'm so proud of being loved by you."

The words should have meant so much. But now they were a slap in the face. I felt hollow and empty.

"I still like you, Teddy," Lorraine was saying. "I still want you around. I just don't want to be your girlfriend."

I held her in my arms and didn't feel a thing, except the old familiar pain from the whole Rosie Williamson episode. *What a waste,* I thought. *What a waste of time.*

There's a problem with having a wing man. He knows your whole plan for the evening. He knows when you've succeeded, and he knows when you've failed. And it was worse than that, because I had been so confident that Lorraine was going to be my girlfriend that I had told everybody in the car about it. Now, as I was finishing the dance, I saw all their faces, Willie and Dennis and, of course, Jerry.

They heard the dedication. They saw the slow dance. It was Jerry and Margie who got to us first. "Congratulations, you two," he beamed, slapping me on the back, "The best-looking couple at Lakewood High School."

"We're not a couple," I mumbled, as Lorraine dropped her head. "We're just two kids who dance with each other."

Margie knew Lorraine better than I did, and she knew exactly what had happened. "Come on," she said, taking Lorraine by the arm. And I stood there in silence watching them walk away.

"What happened?" said Willie, as he and Dennis joined us on the floor.

"She said no," I responded.

"How is that possible?" Dennis wondered out loud. "Last week at the Y-Teens Dance, she couldn't stop hanging on you. If I ever saw a girl in love, it was her!"

"It's her mother..." I started saying. But I realized how ridiculous that sounded. This wasn't the Dark Ages. In 1970 nobody let their mother control them anymore.

"It's an excuse!" Willie barked out, as he shook his head emphatically. "She doesn't really like you as much as you thought."

"You're wrong," Dennis contradicted. "She likes him plenty. I know what I saw!"

Jerry just stood there, not knowing what to say. He was the only Lakewood kid in the group, and he had gone to BVM Grade School with Margie and Lorraine. "Her mother *is* tough," he sighed, "But I really don't know what to think."

So, there I was in limbo. There was a girl I was crazy about, a girl I thought was crazy about me, but she wouldn't confirm it. I was like a secret that she didn't want anyone to find out about. Maybe it wasn't her mom's fault. Maybe that was just an excuse. How could I know? How could I ever know for sure?

Just for a second, I flashed back to my own childhood days, standing in the school yard with Molly, both of us just 10 years old. "Molly has a boyfriend," Mark Minelli had taunted her. "You like Teddy Tresh."

"So what?" she had responded.

THE WEIGHT

"Let me get this straight," Gene said slowly, as he stood to stretch his legs while the early morning sky began to lighten outside the picture window of our kitchen. "She *wasn't* allowed to be your girlfriend, or she *was* allowed, but didn't want to?"

"Well," I said. "That's the question that I never could get answered for sure. There was her mother laying down the rules. Except for a few school functions, she wasn't allowed to go out on dates until she reached sixteen. I could understand that, I guess. Lorraine was one of the youngest students in the sophomore class. She wouldn't reach sixteen until the following January. That was still seven months away. I was already sixteen, and nearly everyone else in our class would turn sixteen before the end of the year.

"I was willing to wait for the dating. But what didn't make sense was that she wouldn't even *say* she was my girlfriend. How much of that was her mother's doing and how much of it was just this whole Lakewood City vs. Rockland thing? I'm sure they talked about me in that house. Her sister was one of my big allies. So, her mother had certainly weighed in on the *Ted Tresh* situation. And her friends too, there were plenty of them that thought I was too cocky."

"Why did they think that?" Gene questioned.

"I guess because I *was* cocky," I shook my head wearily. "It was part of the Rockland baseball tradition. We didn't go around saying we were better than everyone else. We did our talking on the field. But we acted very confident, almost arrogant, on and off the field. There would always be some Lakewood ball player saying we weren't good enough to compete against them. I'd be walking down the hallways of the high school and some big mouth, like Rob "The Big Baboose" Blaine, this 230-pound fastball pitcher who threw for the Cubs, one of the Lakewood City Colt league teams, would bark out, 'We're going to kill Rockland tonight. And I'll fan you three times!'

"I couldn't just let that go! It was my duty as a ballplayer, as a leader on my hometown team, to show no weakness. Show no fear. If I appear afraid, then my team is compromised.

'We just beat the Cubs two weeks ago,' I'd tell him. 'And win or lose, I *guarantee* you will *never* strike me out!'

"Then he would scream something about meeting him in the parking lot after school. And my response was always the same, 'I do my talking on the field.'

"I didn't mind listening to his threats about beating me up. I didn't mind if he criticized my clothes or my hair or even my hometown. But I would never let him get away with saying he could beat me and my team on a baseball field. That would put us at a disadvantage at game time. I had to act confident. Hell, I had to *BE* confident! And, if the truth be known, I didn't think I was as good a player as these Lakewood City boys. I thought I was *better* than they were. If you don't feel that way, Gene, you can't beat them."

"So, what does all this have to do with Lorraine?" Gene questioned.

"I don't know," I answered, "Maybe nothing, maybe everything. There was a big percentage of the upper classmen who hated us, especially the jocks. They always tore down the Rockland guys. And the things they said got repeated by their girlfriends, and anybody else who wanted to be a part of the popular crowd. We became the villains. We became the braggarts.

"We had a couple great pitchers from Rockland that were almost unhittable. These Lakewood guys weren't going to beat us, not on a regular basis. Let the kings of the school brag all they want in the hallways of Lakewood High, but we weren't about to let them say they were going to *kill* us on a ball field. That was *our* kingdom.

"Anyway, any girl from Lakewood City who dated a Rockland guy was going to have to put up with a lot of shit from her friends and from the *in* crowd. And the more beautiful the girl was, the more pressure there was for her to stay clear of us. Some of them didn't care what their friends said about us. Some of them did."

"I thought you said Lorraine's mother was the problem?" Gene looked a little frustrated, as he tried to understand.

"Oh, she was a problem," I said with a sigh. "But I don't know if she was the *real* problem.

THE BIG LIE

In the days and weeks that followed the Bell Memorial fiasco, my views about Lorraine's situation started to soften. First, her friend Margie told me in no uncertain terms that I was being an ass for holding her mother's restrictions against her. Second, Lorraine was still acting very sweet and flirtatious. But mostly, I just liked her so much, that I decided to stick around and see where all this was going.

It was the spring of 1970, and the high school baseball season had already started. I was a sophomore and the back-up shortstop for the Lakewood City Wolverines. The high school baseball team was always an explosive combination of ball players who kind of hated each other. The Lakewood boys were cocky and dismissive of the talents of the players from Rockland and some of the other small towns.

But the head coach was a different matter. Coach Sherman was a fair man. He was a legend at Lakewood, having won two Western Pennsylvania state championships and was nearing 300 wins for his career. No other coach at the school had ever won even 100 games in any sport. A big part of Coach Sherman's success was that his word was law. He didn't take any shit from his ballplayers, and he didn't take any advice from the townspeople or from school board members. He made the boys from every town play together. There was no favoritism. There was no star treatment. There was only the team, and the only goal was for the team to win.

That didn't change the fact that deep-down the animosity between the Rockland and Lakewood boys was still there. Lakewood had their own ten-team Pony League (13- and 14-year-olds) and five of those teams were made up strictly of Lakewood City ball players, with the other teams from the surrounding small towns, so Rockland was just one team in the Lakewood League.

Colt League (15- and 16-year-olds) was similar. There were seven teams in that league. Three were from Lakewood, and they were made even stronger by the fact that they absorbed some of the smaller town's ballplayers into the Lakewood teams. Some of the best players, like Pete Shaler, the Porter brothers and Big Rob Blaine were from Wurtemburg, Ellicot, and Frisco, and those players were now incorporated into the three Lakewood Colt League teams, so those teams were very strong.

But Rockland kept our independence and kept sending championship team after championship team into the Lakewood City Leagues. Some of those games were absolute wars! And, in the aftermath, there was a deep-seeded animosity between the two towns, and especially among the ballplayers.

That didn't keep Coach Sherman from welding them into a powerhouse high school baseball team. Any Lakewood football or basketball team that finished their season over .500 was hailed as a successful team. But any Lakewood High School baseball team that didn't win the section title was considered a bust. Maybe that's why Coach Sherman had won *twelve* section titles in 18 years, while the football and basketball teams, during that same period, had won zero section titles between them.

That year, there were three Rockland seniors starting for Lakewood High; big Derrick Dawson had been the ace of the pitching staff for three years and had pitched a shutout in the Western Pennsylvania championship game in 1968 as a sophomore, my buddy Billy Conti was a first-year starter at third base and my cousin, Tony DeVito, was the starting center fielder for the second straight year and was leading the team in hitting.

As the backup shortstop for the varsity baseball team, I didn't see a lot of action that year. Sometimes in the non-section games, we would pull ahead by six or seven runs in the late innings and Coach Sherman would send in the whole second team to replace the starters. In many cases our second team was better than the starters of the smaller schools we played. We would enter the game in the fifth inning against Freedom or Rochester or Shenango High School with a 5–1 lead, and by the time the game ended, the score would be 10–1.

I managed to get sixteen official at-bats for the season, and racked up six hits, a .375 average. But I never got even one at-bat during a section game. Our starting shortstop was a senior named Brian Corso. He was a pretty slick fielder, could hit for average and had some power, so I wasn't upset with my limited playing time. I felt like if Brian got hurt, and I had to step in, the team wouldn't have skipped a beat. But I was willing to bide my time on the bench. I was still going to get two full seasons as starting shortstop for Lakewood City, so for now, I was satisfied with my role as backup.

But, backup or not, Lorraine came to every home game and a lot of away games. She always came with her friend Margie, who was there to root for Jerry Delpino, a sophomore like me. Jerry was the backup third baseman, and like me, he was good enough to be a starter. Going to the high school games was something Lorraine's parents actually *allowed* her to do, and she made no secret of the fact that she was there to see me. The few times I did get to play, she would applaud wildly every time I fielded a routine ground ball, and when I got a hit, I could pick out her cheering voice all the way across the diamond.

But, even when I didn't get to play, it was great to have her waiting for me by the dugout after the game. She was so beautiful and always seemed so happy to see me. It was the only time we looked like a real couple, and it allowed me to show her off to my teammates. I'm pretty sure that her being there raised my batting average by a good 25 points!

In school, I still walked her to most of her classes, and we still sat next to each other during study halls in the auditorium. One morning, I missed the school bus from Rockland and had to walk the five miles to the high school. On the way, I passed a house surrounded by a bed of gorgeous spring tulips and snapped off a purple one for Lorraine. I got to school just in time for morning study hall, and when I pulled that flower out on my gym bag and presented it to her; you would have thought it was a diamond bracelet. It blew her away, and she carried it with her for the next five periods.

Still, I wasn't satisfied with the relationship. "So, when you say you can't be my girlfriend, what does that mean exactly?" I questioned her one day. "Does that mean I can still ask out other girls? I'm driving now, you know, and you can't really expect me to sit at home every night when you won't even promise that you're not going to be out there flirting with other guys!"

It was my way of trying to coerce her into an agreement to be exclusive, even if we weren't officially going steady. But she always gave the same answer. "You can do whatever you want to do. I just hope that if you go out with somebody else, you'll tell me about it. As long as you tell me the truth, I won't get angry. And I promise you the same thing. If I ever start to like somebody else, I'll tell you the truth. How's that?"

How's that? I thought. *That's terrible!*

"Oh great," I shook my head. "You won't *go with* me, but I'm supposed to tell you every time I look at somebody else. I don't think that's going to work. I think that kind of loyalty should be reserved for my girlfriend, not for some girl who's hiding behind her mother."

"Why do you say things that are so hurtful?" Lorraine lowered her eyes, "You know I have to wait until I'm sixteen. Why are you making this so hard?"

Now, I felt bad. I wasn't used to these Old-Italian courting rules, if that's what they were. But, I was pretty sure it wasn't her Italian heritage that spawned her mother's rules; it was more about who I was and where I was from. Still, I couldn't hold Lorraine responsible for her misguided parents.

"Alright," I said, "If I go out with anyone else, I promise to tell you."

"And if I get interested in anyone else, I promise to tell you," she proclaimed triumphantly.

It was a bad deal all around, and the more I thought about it the less I liked it. I was walking around the halls of Lakewood High with the queen of the sophomore class on my arm, but I couldn't tell anyone that she was my girl. In fact, I had to tell them just the opposite. "Nope, I have no claim on her," I told my buddy Jerry after practice one night. "Every kid in the school, including juniors and seniors, think they have a shot at her. And I can't even say *stay the hell away from her.* I can't say shit, because she's only too willing to tell anybody that asks that she is *not* going steady with me."

"Come on, Ted Tresh." Jerry always called me by my full name for some reason. "You know she's crazy about you. I saw you two at the dance last Friday. I thought she was going to suck your face off right in the gym!"

"Dances are fine," I answered, "But how can I really trust her? She's free to do whatever she wants."

"You're looking at this all wrong," Jerry laughed. "You're the one who can do whatever you want. You've got the most gorgeous lady in the class hanging on you, and you can still go out with other girls. That's like the best of all possible worlds. And you're driving now. You can even go to New Castle or Beaver Falls to meet girls and she won't know anything about it!"

"I don't want anybody else," I countered. "I just want that girl!"

Jerry just shook his head. "We'll see what happens when the opportunity arrives."

"I'll tell you what's going to happen, *nothing!*" I snapped back.

Turns out, I was wrong.

"Blake Bianchi has been calling me at home in the evenings," Lorraine whispered to me one day in study hall. "I thought you should know."

"What?!!! Why? Why are you even talking to him?" I tried to control my volume, but half the kids in the auditorium spun around and looked our way. Blake Bianchi was in the junior class. There were a lot of guys in that class who were assholes, a lot of them I really hated. But Blake wasn't one of them. I didn't know him very well, but we were both on the football team. He was friendly with everybody. I certainly had no grudge against the kid, but what the hell was he doing sniffing around my girl?

"He's nice," Lorraine sighed. "And I'm allowed to get phone calls at home, you know. You almost never call me."

"So now I have to compete with Blake Bianchi?" I growled. "You can forget that shit. If you want to be with someone else, then be with him. I'm not going to compete with him over how much phone time I get with Your Majesty."

The truth was that I hated to call Lorraine at home because, no matter how many times I'd call, her mother would always answer "Ted who?" and if her father answered the phone, he would say "hello" and never say another word. I'd ask for her, and he would just put the phone down and yell, "Lorraine" and then walk away. And if she wasn't home, neither of them would take a message. It was embarrassing to put up with that treatment, so I rarely called. It was easier just to talk to her in school every day.

"And what does your mother say about some 17-year-old trying to court her 15-year-old daughter?" I barked, thinking that maybe this kid was getting the same *unwanted guest* treatment that I was getting.

"Oh," Lorraine countered, "My mother *likes* him!"

Now the pieces started to fall into place. Blake's dad was a local attorney, and his uncle was one of a handful of family doctors in Lakewood City. Lorraine's old lady was *encouraging* her to pursue this kid. No wonder she acted disgusted every time she heard my voice on the phone.

"Are you shitting me?" I was livid. "Do you really think I'm going to sit around waiting for you while you're mooning on the phone over Blake Bianchi?"

"I'm not mooning. I don't feel about him the way I feel about you. You should *know* that. But my mom doesn't want me going steady with anyone. And she thinks I should be willing to talk on the phone with a boy if he calls, that is, if he's a nice boy."

"And what do you expect me to do, while you're sweet talking with him every night?" Lorraine just lowered her head.

"I can drive now!" I roared. "I can go out with anyone I please, but I don't. Do you know why?" I paused for effect, "Because I only want to be with YOU; because I'm only interested in YOU. I want *you* to be my girlfriend, Lorraine. What the hell do you want?"

"I'm not allowed to date until I'm sixteen," Lorraine stammered. "And I'm not allowed to have a boyfriend until then either."

"I didn't ask what you were allowed to do," I sneered. "I asked what *you want*." Lorraine just sat there with her head down for the next five minutes until the bell rang.

"I'm not waiting anymore," I informed her, as I got up to leave the auditorium. "I can't promise you anything. If there's a girl I want to take out, I'm going to do it. This is ridiculous."

"Teddy," I heard her say as I started to walk away. "You can go out with anyone you want. I can't stop you. I don't have a right to. I'm not your girlfriend. Just promise me that if you do, you'll tell me about it."

"Why do you get to make the rules?" I countered. "I promise you nothing."

The blow-up with Lorraine only lasted a couple days. By Friday night, we were back at the high school dance, face-to-face and body-to-body. I guess I was just crazy about that girl, and she certainly seemed crazy about me. Every slow dance was like a dream, and when the music stopped, it would take us both a good thirty seconds before the trance would be broken. She would still be in my arms swaying to the music that was no longer there. I was sixteen and had never really felt like this. She was fifteen and was falling in love. But her situation and my ego were headed for a massive collision, and it was just a matter of time.

"Blake Bianchi asked me to dance," Lorraine blurted out one Friday night as I walked her back towards a group of her girlfriends.

"And what did you *say*?" I was glaring at her.

"I said I would," Lorraine whispered, "But I told him that I wanted to talk to you first."

"What bullshit!" I countered. "Why are you doing this?" But now, for the first time all night, I noticed that Lorraine's group of friends was not her normal gang at all. It included four or five junior girls, all popular and all friends of Blake. "Damn it," I said, "So the queens of the junior class are all out here singing that kid's praises. Why don't you ever think for yourself?"

"I am thinking for myself," Lorraine countered. "It's just a dance. And I came to you first."

"For what: to ask my permission? Then the answer is no. No, I don't want you dancing with him, rubbing your body against him. Hell, no!"

"I'm not asking your permission," she sighed. "I'm just trying to be honest with you. I am going to dance with him and there's nothing you can do about it."

"Oh, that's where you're wrong," I barked. "You can dance with him all night long for all I care, but I'm not going to stick around to watch this circus." And with that I stormed out of the gym, grabbed a couple buddies in the hallway, who had come with me to the dance, and headed straight for my dad's car.

"Teddy, wait," I heard her say over my shoulder as I walked away. "It won't be like it is for us. I don't feel the same about him as I do about you." But I just kept walking.

It was time to make a stand.

"Hello, Teddy?" a sweet voice sang out on my telephone just two nights later. It was familiar, but I couldn't quite place it. "This is Sherry Sanders, you know, from Beaver Falls."

"Oh, hi, Sherry," My brain swirled and tried to bring up a face to match the name, finally locking in on a little cherub-faced blond that my cousin Nancy from Beaver Falls had fixed me up with a couple years before. She was my age, cute, and I remember thinking at the time, that she was a little aggressive for a fourteen-year-old girl.

Our *set-up date* was with a small group of friends at the annual New Galilee Carnival back in July of 1968, when I was just coming out of eighth grade and just after the one-day romance with Rosie Williamson. I remembered that we had walked the carnival grounds together, hand-in-hand, went on a few rides, and kissed during the fireworks display. There was some kid at the carnival that she had just broken up with, a former boyfriend I guess, and every time he came into view, she wrapped her arms around me and laughed really loudly as if I had just told some wonderful joke. We had a nice time, but I never called her again and we hadn't even spoken since that night.

"Are you just calling to say hello?" I asked expectantly.

"Well, no," she answered. "I'm not sure if you know it, but I'm a majorette at Beaver Falls High School, and well, the band has a semi-formal dinner dance coming up next Friday night, and I was hoping you could take me?"

My first instinct was to say *no, I have a girlfriend*. But I was still furious about the Blake Bianchi fiasco, and I thought this might be the perfect solution to my problem; something to jolt Lorraine into dropping her flirtation with this Junior-class interloper.

"What time should I pick you up?"

Back in study hall the next day, Lorraine was all apologies and flirtations. "Why did you leave the dance?" She sounded so hurt and worried. "I waited all week to be with you and then you just left me there alone."

"Hardly alone," I countered. "Did you have a nice evening with Blake?"

"I danced with him one time, just like I said I would. And I didn't even enjoy that, because I was worried about you. Were you trying to hurt me?"

"I was trying to wake you up," I shook my head. "We can't *officially* go steady. I get it. But if you think I can just watch you with somebody else, you're crazy. How can you just turn it off and on like that? He calls you at home. He waits for you at the dance. He has all his little friends from the *in crowd* telling you how wonderful he is. And what do you do? You *take* his calls. You chat for hours. You dance with him. And you never even tell him about us!"

"I told him I have feelings for you."

"Well, he's not listening, is he? And I can't tell him to back off. You won't back me up on it. You'll say I have no claim on you. Where's the loyalty? I'm in this all alone."

"You're not alone!" Lorraine began to tear up. "If we're just truthful with each other nothing can keep us apart. January is just seven months away. I'll be sixteen then. Can't we just be friends for seven more months?"

"Friends?" I screamed. "Now we're supposed to be friends?"

"That's not what I mean," she sobbed. "You know how I feel about you, don't you...*don't you?*"

It was my cue to tell her about the Beaver Falls Band Formal; to show her how the truth doesn't keep you from feeling jealous and abandoned and alone; to show her that this whole charade was hurting us. I had the perfect weapon ready to prove my point. All I had to do was pull the sword from its sheath and show her how much the truth can hurt.

I looked into her huge brown eyes, still moist from frustration and disappointment, still looking for reassurance, and I couldn't do it. I couldn't tell her. It was obvious how much she cared about me, about us, but she was afraid to stand up to her mother. If I told her about the date now, it would trivialize our relationship. This wasn't some guy on the phone. This was a girl I had dated before. This was a big semi-formal dinner dance, with gowns and flowers and slow dances. Just like the Y-Teens Dance; just like the dance where we started falling in love. *Maybe she'll never find out,* I thought. *There's no use hurting her feelings. Really, I'm just lying for her sake.*

I was standing at a crossroads and didn't even know it. Whatever happened from now on would be my fault.

That whole week I wrestled with the question. *Should I tell her? Shouldn't I tell her?* I kept putting it off. And the worst part was that Lorraine was extremely affectionate that week; passing love notes in class, taking my hand in the hallways, whispering in my ear in study hall. I knew she was trying to re-assure me that the dance with Blake was meaningless.

On Thursday, she really put me on the spot. "I'm available tomorrow night if you want to see me," she smiled. "I'm allowed to go out with Margie. We might go to Ewing Park, or Dairy Queen, or maybe just walk around town. Can you meet us somewhere?"

The trouble with a lie is all the additional lies you have to tell to hide it. If I had told Lorraine about the dinner dance to start with, she probably would have been upset, but maybe she would have understood that our *halfway* romance couldn't work in the long run. That's what I really wanted, to teach her a lesson, to show her what it felt like to be jealous and hurt and full of doubt. Instead, I got cold feet. I decided our relationship couldn't take anymore jealousy. I decided to hide it. The date would be over in a couple days. No one would ever know about it. And soon enough, it wouldn't matter.

"Uhm, I can't get out tomorrow night," I told her. "I have to go to a sports banquet in Beaver Falls. It's only for Beaver County ball players." Since Rockland was in Beaver County, and Lakewood City was in Lawrence County, this seemed like a plausible excuse, a banquet that she wouldn't know about. But the story was full of holes.

Oh great, I thought, *now I'm creating a whole event that doesn't exist. How am I ever going to pull this off?* The only person I had confided in was my Rockland buddy, Willie. He had met Sherry a couple years earlier when I took her to the carnival, and was with me at the dance when Lorraine blew off my first attempt to make her my girlfriend. He thought the whole *my-mom-won't-let-me* excuse was a lie. And I knew he was happy that I wasn't going to sit around waiting for Lorraine.

He's the only one that knows, I thought. *He'll keep the secret and she'll never find out.*

I picked up Sherry at about 6 o'clock the next night. The dinner started at 6:30 with the dance to follow. She looked great, blonde hair, big blue eyes and all decked out in a pink, lace gown.

There still weren't many sophomores who had their driver's license, so Sherry had asked me if we could double date with another couple, who were friends of hers. I remember almost zero about the couple, except that they were all over each other from the moment we picked them up. The good news was that I didn't have to make small talk with them, because they always had their tongues in each other's mouths.

The dinner was uneventful, and I saw nobody else I knew all night. On the dance floor, Sherry was pretty aggressive, and I kissed her a couple times, when I could tell she really wanted to be kissed, but I was holding back, and she knew it. "What's the matter?" she asked, looking up at me with those big sad eyes. She was beautiful and sweet, and she had her heart set on making this a date to remember. But all I could think about was Lorraine.

The DJ was playing *Traces* by The Classics IV, and Sherry was wrapped around me like batter on a corndog, when I decided to tell her the truth.

"Look," I said, "There's this girl."

"Is she your girlfriend?" Sherry blurted out.

"No," I answered, "But she's going to be. It's kind of hard to explain." This was the damn problem with the whole Lorraine issue. I didn't really know what she was. "I guess I just really like her," I nodded. "I thought you should know."

"Okay," she smiled. "You've done your duty. You warned me. Now, how about giving a girl a chance?"

I looked down at her sweet round face, her big, beautiful eyes, her puffy little lips, and I kissed her again.

As we walked off the dance floor, Sherry leaned over and whispered in my ear, "How about if we get out of here?"

I was a little stunned. It wasn't even 9 o'clock; the dance wasn't over until 11. This girl was only fifteen years old. *Where* did she want to go?

"Let's go," I responded. And off we went, into the great unknown.

It wasn't hard to convince the other couple to leave, Elvis and Priscilla had been pawing at each other since we picked them up, and they started rolling around in the back seat as soon as I put the car in drive. They guided me down a couple Lovers Lanes on the outskirts of Beaver Falls, but I just kept driving. Sherry was pretty and sweet, and the music on the radio was Motown, but all I could think about was the lie I told Lorraine, and how I hoped she'd never find out.

"Are you going to stop this car or what?" moaned Elvis from the backseat.

That's all I needed, some trumpet player from the marching band advising me on my love life. "Shut up, kid," I barked. "Let's get some ice cream first."

"I could go for some ice cream," laughed Sherry. "Where do you want to go?"

They had been leading me around on Beaver Falls' streets and backroads that I had never seen before. I decided to get them into my territory. "We're going to J&T Custard," I proclaimed. "That's a Lakewood City hang out!"

It was about a 15-minute drive to the custard stand, and Sherry had moved all the way to my side of the Thunderbird's front seat. The car had just come back from the body shop a week earlier, and it felt good to be free and back at the wheel. I put my arm around her and drove left-handed north on Route 65, until the big J&T sign came into view. A little sign below the big one announced the flavor of the week, Pistachio. *Great*, I thought, *I love Pistachio.*

I started to swing the car into the long horizontal parking lot, when my headlights flashed upon two familiar faces. It was Lorraine and Margie with big ice cream cones in their hands and shocked looks on their faces. I felt like I had been struck by lightning. A jolt of electricity shot through my body, and without even thinking, I swung the Thunderbird back out onto Route 65 and slammed the gas pedal to the floor.

"What the hell are you doing?" screamed Elvis from the backseat.

"That was her, wasn't it?" whispered Sherry.

I kind of felt bad for Sherry. She hadn't done anything wrong, and now her night was about to be ruined.

"This is bull shit," screamed the prone trumpet player. "Where are we going now?"

"I'm not sure where *I'm* going," I growled. "But *your* ass is going home."

We didn't say ten words to each other the rest of the drive. I kept thinking maybe, just maybe, Lorraine and Margie hadn't seen me. My headlights were in their eyes, how could I be sure? I dropped the lovers off at his house, and then pulled up to Sherry's front door. It was 9:45. The dance wasn't even over until 11:00. "I'm sorry," she said. "I'm sorry if I screwed things up for you and your girlfriend."

"No," I shook my head slowly. "This is entirely my fault. You were perfect. I'm the one who screwed up."

"You don't have to leave you know?" Sherry was glowing like a painting by Raphael.

"I'm sorry," I told her. "My head's spinning. It's all I can do to breathe in and breathe out."

I gave her an uninspired kiss goodnight. Then turned the Thunderbird back onto Route 65 and prayed for a miracle.

It took me fifteen minutes to get back to J&T, but Lorraine and Margie were long gone. I got out of my car and walked the length of the parking lot, hoping somewhere in the sea of faces I would spot Lorraine; not knowing what I would say if I did. Then, I hopped back in the car and flew the last ten minutes into Lakewood City.

I passed Lorraine's house, looking for *what*? I didn't even know. The lights were on, but I didn't see any other activity. I couldn't really knock at the door. She might not be home yet, and I would just panic her family needlessly. Plus, her old lady probably would call the cops on me.

I made two more right turns and pulled up outside Margie's house. She and her parents were just getting out of the family car. Her mother still carried the remnants of a marshmallow sundae in a plastic bowl. I shielded my eyes to look inside their station wagon hoping for some kind of reprieve, but Lorraine wasn't with them.

I got the picture now: bored on a Friday night, they had decided to go for custard with Margie's family. I jumped out of my car and headed straight towards Margie. I could hear her making excuses to her mom and dad, and then she turned towards me and stepped out under the streetlight alone.

My brain was still buzzing from the shock of seeing their faces. I kept thinking *this can't be happening*. I wished I had the last hour back, to just keep driving the backroads of Beaver Falls; or the last day back, so I could have told Lorraine the truth; or the last week back, so I could have said *no* to this stupid date in the first place.

97

I desperately clung to the faint hope that they hadn't seen me, that my head-lights had blinded them, that my car didn't look familiar. But one look at Margie's eyes, and I knew that this nightmare was only too real.

"Ted, what the hell?" Margie whispered when I got close enough. "Who was that and why did you pull away? How stupid are you?"

"I panicked," I groaned. "I was just so shocked to see her."

"She knew all along," Margie shook her head in disgust. "All night long she had a feeling you were out with someone else. And I kept saying, 'No, he wouldn't do that. He's crazy about you. He wouldn't lie to you like that.' But I was wrong. You're just another asshole.

"She kept calling it her ESP. But it was more than that, Ted. She *knew*. Somebody had told her you were on a date. She wouldn't admit it, but I'm sure she knew. But, I just kept saying 'Trust him. No matter what you've heard, just trust him.' And then, there you were, right in our faces! She'll never trust you again!"

On the long ride home to Rockland, my head was pounding. The streets and roads were all familiar, but they looked foreign now, dark and foreboding with broken dreams at the end of each one of them.

When I reached my door, I went straight to bed, hardly saying a word to my parents. I laid my head on the pillow and tried to close my eyes, but the scene kept flashing through my mind. The headlights illuminating Lorraine's face, the shock, the hurt in her eyes. I started composing a goodbye letter in my head. "With school almost over for the summer, and things being as they are between us, I probably won't be seeing much of you anymore."

I got up, grabbed a pencil and piece of notebook paper off my desk and wrote that sentence down, then another and another. "I want you to know that the last three months have been, by far, the best three months of my life. I'm sorry I lied to you. If I could take it back, I would. None of this is your fault, so please don't change a thing about yourself, especially your principles, which I respect so much. Love, Ted"

I stuffed the note into my wallet, laid my head back on my pillow and dove into the nightmares I knew were waiting for me.

Monday was the start of the last week of school, and I sought out Lorraine for a face-to-face, but she would have none of it. If she said anything at all, it was filled with sarcasm and disdain. "Do unto others as they do unto you!" she said mockingly.

"That's from the Bible," I said as she turned to walk away. "And the real quote is 'Do unto others as you would *have them* do unto you.'"

But she didn't look back. I never even got a chance to give her the note. My last opportunity would be Friday night, when the school held a farewell dance in the gym.

I arrived with my posse at about 10 o'clock. Jerry, Willie and Dennis, the same troops from the Bell Memorial fiasco, were all there for moral support. Jerry had just had a heart-to-heart with Margie a few days earlier and let her know that things between them weren't going anywhere. In fact, he had started dating someone new, by some wild coincidence it was Rosie Williamson's older sister, Colleen, who was in our class at Lakewood. Small world.

I had a funny feeling about Willie too. He was the only one I had told about the dinner dance date with Sherry. It didn't make any sense, but I couldn't shake the feeling that he was the source of Lorraine's so-called ESP.

When we entered the darkened gym, I could see Lorraine front and center with Blake Bianchi draped all over her on the dance floor. When she saw me walk in, she dropped his left hand from hers and wrapped both arms around his neck. *This is my fault,* I thought to myself; *just find a way to get her alone.*

But Lorraine wasn't going to let that happen, she clung to that kid all night. I don't know how she really felt about him, but she was certainly putting on a show of affection. Finally, I approached them both. "Look," I said. "I'm not asking for forgiveness. I'm just trying to say goodbye." And I slipped the note into her hand, and turned to walk away, but she held on to my hand for an instant. I turned and looked straight into her eyes. She was holding onto something, a dream maybe, and she wasn't sure she wanted to let go. But she did let go, then watched me walk away.

This thing with Bianchi can't last long, I told myself. *In a couple months, he'll be a senior. There is no way he's going to wait around until January to go on a date with her, and by that time, she'll realize the mistake she made.*

Even though school was out for the year, our high school baseball team was still playing. It was the following Tuesday, and we were in the third round of the

Western Pennsylvania high school championship playoffs. One more victory and we would be headed for Forbes Field, the home of the Pittsburgh Pirates, to play for the title. Coach Sherman had called this 1970 team his best team ever, even better than the two that had won the championship in 1962 and 1968. And even if I was just the backup shortstop, I took some pride in being part of the legacy.

Lorraine had always come to my games. And even though this game was played at a neutral field, almost two hours from Lakewood City, I kept poking my head out of the dugout to see if she was in the crowd. Two busloads of students had made the trip, but I just wasn't sure if she would be one of them. Then I spotted her, high in the bleachers, barely paying attention to the game. Sitting to her right was Blake Bianchi, holding both her hands in his, staring into her eyes. It made me sick to watch them.

We ended up getting upset by a Bethel Park team that had no business on the field with us. And even though their pitcher looked very hittable, none of our usual sluggers hit the ball. We lost 3–0.

I'm not sure if I was sicker about the game or about the big display of affection Lorraine was putting on in front of my teammates. All season long, they had watched me meet her near the bleachers, saw us talking, flirting, saw her put my baseball hat on her head and pretend to catch fly balls with my glove.

Now, there was zero recognition. And, if my teammates weren't so sick about losing the game, I know they would have been giving me the business about blowing my chance with the sweetest girl in the sophomore class.

I decided I wasn't going to let her see my pain. There was another girl in my class I had had my eye on for a while; nothing serious: a smile in the hallway, a brief conversation here and there. Her name was Robin Samson, from Ellicot. She was cute and blond and had some great curves. *And* she was a baseball fan. Robin had come to almost every game that season, and I'm sure she had seen me with Lorraine a hundred times. I'm also sure that she noticed that Lorraine was with somebody else today.

"I'm sorry about the game," she said to me as both the team and the fans walked back towards the waiting school buses. It was hard not to look over my shoulder at Lorraine and Blake, but I forced myself to focus hard on Robin. *Damn, she's sweet,* I thought. *I wish I wasn't so hung up on someone else.*

We walked and talked about nothing in particular, all the way across the parking lot and I dropped her off at the door of the student bus. I could feel the eyes of the entire busload of kids watching us. *They think we're together;* I shook my head and felt something resembling pride returning to my psyche. As I walked away, I passed Lorraine and Blake, but just stared straight ahead.

I was the last ball player to climb aboard the player bus and sat down next to my buddy Jerry.

"Robin Samson?" he laughed, "Jesus, Ted Tresh, you don't stay down for long, do you?"

The comment felt good. After ten days of pain, it was the first time I laughed, a good, deep, down-to-the-soul laugh. I had never been the playboy type, but it felt good for someone to think I was. *I can be that guy anytime I want,* I thought, *anytime I want.*

It was the first official day of summer, a full three weeks later, when I finally saw Lorraine again. She and Margie were at a summer-league baseball game at Lakewood City's Ewing Park. They were sitting in the bleachers, and I walked over to the concession stand to grab a Coke and a pack of sunflower seeds. I waited in line for a few minutes, and when I turned around, Margie was standing right behind me.

"Well, Ted Tresh," she announced, "I see you're still alive!"

"Why wouldn't I be?" I shrugged. "Where's your friend? Is she still not talking to me?"

"Do you blame her?" Margie countered. "She's trying to forget you."

"*Trying?*" Now she had my interest.

"I thought she was done with you," Margie shook her head slowly. "But that goodbye note? It really got to her. Who knew you could be so mature? And the ending, 'Especially your principles which I respect so much,' it blew her away."

"So, you're saying there's still a chance?" I whispered.

"Look, Teddy, there's something I have to tell you."

"Not right now." I could feel the excitement buzzing through my brain. "Right now, I have to talk to her!" I made a beeline to the bleachers, where Lorraine sat alone.

When she saw me coming, she stood up and walked towards me, slow and emotionless. I was just two feet away from her now. "Listen," I said, lowering my eyes. "I know we have problems, but I want to know if there's still a chance. I want to know if I'm wasting…"

And then I saw it, a sight that crushed the words before they could get out of my mouth. A wave of shock and disbelief took my breath away. A feeling of betrayal and disappointment and pain hit me like a tidal wave. "What the hell is that?" I screamed.

There on Lorraine's fourth finger, left hand was a boy's class ring, gold with a blue stone and gold "L" on its face. "You're *going steady* with him? Are you fucking kidding me!!!?"

Lorraine had never heard me use that kind of language. Hell, I never *did* use that kind of language. She took a step back. Her eyes were as big as saucers. "Well, you…you lied to me," she stammered.

"I lied to *you?*" I was losing my mind now. "*This* is the *big* lie." I grabbed her left hand and waved the ring in front of her eyes. "You couldn't go out on a date, you said. You couldn't go steady until you were sixteen! What a bunch of bullshit. *You're* the liar. What I did is *nothing* compared to this. You make me sick!"

I turned around and headed straight towards the Thunderbird. "Teddy, wait," I heard her say over my shoulder. But I just kept walking. When I got to the car, I jumped in, slammed the pedal to the floor and peeled out down the road, driving away from the stadium lights, heading into the darkness and feeling more alone than I could ever remember.

THE NEXT VOICE YOU HEAR

"Oh my God!" Gene was saying, as the first rays of sunlight flickered through the oak trees and into the living room. Our coffee cups had long since gone empty, and I was loading them into the upper rack of the dishwasher. "You mean she made it all up? She *was* allowed to date, but didn't want to? She *was* allowed to go steady, but she lied to you?"

"No, that's not exactly what happened," I told him with a shake of my head. "But that's the way it seemed to all our friends. It was painful and infuriating and humiliating. All this time, I had been telling my buddies that she and I were some kind of star-crossed-lovers; that we had these deep feelings, but her parents were standing in our way. But now it was just an excuse, an excuse that *I* seemed to be making up. As if I was the one lying, as if I was trying to deceive people into thinking she cared about me, when she really didn't.

"I should have hated her for it. I should have never talked to her again. But I was too young to realize what losing someone does to your head, to your heart. It makes you want them even more! It's human nature, I guess. I could feel the loss everywhere I went. I thought about her all the time. And then, she had her girlfriend call me, and I wasn't even sure that she *had* lied to me at all."

"Why," Gene looked at me with surprise. "What could her girlfriend possibly say that would change your mind?"

"Margie said that Lorraine hadn't lied. She said that, although Lorraine liked the Bianchi kid, she didn't like him nearly as much as *he* liked *her*. She said that when Blake asked her to be his girlfriend, she told him the same thing she had told me, that she wasn't allowed to date until she was sixteen, that her parents didn't allow her to go steady until then either."

"So, what happened?" Gene shook his head. "What changed her mind?"

"The damn kid had more guts than I thought he did," I sighed. "He drove straight to her house that night and confronted her mother at the door. He said he really cared about Lorraine and asked her permission to date her daughter right now. The old lady said *yes* before he even got his foot in the door."

"What?" Gene could hardly believe his ears. "What happened to being over-protective, and traditional and cautious?"

"At first, I wasn't even sure I believed Margie's story," I told him. "But, as the weeks and months went by, it became pretty clear that this was the old lady's end game all along. She *wanted* her daughter to be with this kid. His family was a big deal in Lakewood City. It was her dream to marry off Lorraine to somebody exactly like him!"

"So, you don't think that if *you* would have asked her mother's permission…."

"Hell no," I barked. "I was the one she was trying to keep away from Lorraine! I was probably the *reason* for the restrictions in the first place. No, Gene, if I had gone to her front porch with a request like that, she would have called out the National Guard."

"Okay," Gene replied, "So Lorraine's mom approved of the courtship, but what about Lorraine? If she had feelings for you, why would she agree to date someone else exclusively?"

"That's the question, isn't it?" I stated emphatically. "I tried to find out. Summer had started, and I wasn't going to see her in study hall anymore. So, I tried calling her house three nights in a row. The first two, her mother answered and said she would pass along my message to Lorraine, but I knew she wouldn't. In fact, I was pretty sure Lorraine *was* in the damn house when I called.

"Finally, on the third night, her sister Angela answered. 'Can I speak to Lorraine?' I asked.

'Is this Blake?' she said brightly.

'No, it's Ted Tresh.'

'Oh,' she replied, suddenly whispering, 'Hold on, Teddy. I'll go get her.'

"I felt good that I still had one partial ally in the house.

"When Lorraine came to the phone, she too was whispering. 'I can't talk much,' she murmured. 'My mom's right in the kitchen.' She sounded like a damn refugee.

"'Listen, I talked to Margie,' I told her finally. 'I know about Blake asking for your mom's blessing and all that, but I still have one question. Why did *you* say yes? I mean, it's obvious that this kid is your mother's choice, but what about *your* choice?'

'I don't know,' she started slowly. 'I'm not sure what I want. I mean he came all the way over here. And he confronted her, and she just thinks he's the most wonderful thing. And after he left, she came up to my room to give me the *good news*, and I wasn't excited or anything. In fact, I was kind of scared. But she told me that he was special and that I should give him a chance.

'Then, I talked to my sister. And she's already dating some guy that my mother doesn't approve of. And she said that I should follow my heart, and not let my mother make these decisions for me. So, now I don't know who to listen to.'

"The guy she was talking about was Mr. Donofrio, a young History teacher at Lakewood. Teachers didn't earn much in those days, and I guess Lorraine's mother thought her gorgeous sister could get someone more successful than that.

"The whole conversation made me a little sick to the stomach. This girl didn't need a boyfriend. She needed to love herself first. 'You need to listen to your heart, Lorraine,' I whispered sadly.

"I could feel some kind of depression taking over my thoughts. It was this floating pain that I couldn't quite pin down. But, over the next two years, it would become way too familiar.

'I better go now,' I told her, feeling empty and alone. 'But do me a favor. Don't ask your mother about it. Don't ask your sister about it. Just ask yourself—what do you really want?'"

"There was a full minute of silence on the phone. Neither of us wanted to end the conversation. Neither of us knew what to say next. 'Listen,' I told her at last, 'I'm going to hang up now. You know how I feel. Let me know when you want to take on the world.'"

"Wow, Dad," Gene gasped. "I know I have my *problems* with Jan and her put-downs, but your situation was even worse. I mean, that girl really cared about you. She *wanted* to be with you, but she was afraid of what someone else was going to say?"

"It's *not* really different, Gene," I proclaimed with a shake of my head. "I mean, Lorraine was just a teenager, so I couldn't expect her to as independent as a grown woman. But, Jan should know better. She wants to be with you. She *loves* you. But, just like Lorraine, she's afraid that people will think less of her. She's afraid of what they're going to say!"

"Are all women that confusing?" Gene asked with a grin.

"No," I said. "All women are *not* that confusing. There are some that will stand by you no matter what people say about you. Those are the kind of women you really need, but human nature puts up a battle. Human nature makes you think that the pain a girl causes you is actually some weird kind of *love*. That only love can cause those feelings of abandonment and loss. But the truth is, *it's not love!* And it takes years and years to learn that lesson."

"So, how long did it take you, Dad?" Gene was smiling now.

"A long time," I answered. "Just thinking about her made me sad. And I thought about her all the time. Finally, I came to a decision, a bad one as it turned out.

"There was only one other girl who had ever weighed on my mind like that. Only one other girl I had ever had really strong feelings for. And in my mind, there was only one other girl who could make me forget Lorraine."

"Oh, no!" Gene shook his head in mock disgust. "Don't tell me!"

"Yep," I said. "I went back out looking for Rosie Williamson."

18

IMPENETRABLE

Chasing after Rosie one more time was probably a lousy idea. Over the years she had developed a habit of putting me down in front of the neighborhood kids. It was just her defense mechanism, I guess. But how many disappointments would I be willing to endure from this cute little Rockland girl?

Just like with Lorraine, I couldn't shake the feeling that deep down Rosie really, really liked me. Hadn't she clung to me a hundred times on the dance floor? Hadn't she slipped into my arms in Darlington Lake and wrapped her hands around the back of my neck? And, right there in the water, clung to me so tight, that I thought she'd never let go? And, my God, that little yellow bikini was the only thing between us? Surely that meant something!

Anyway, the background pain from the Lorraine episode was always on my mind, making it hard for me to get through the day. The thought of her was always waiting, just beyond my conscious thoughts. Waiting there, so that every enjoyable moment was followed by the reality that something was lost. Only Rosie could cure that. *Only Rosie can make me forget about Lorraine*, I thought. *She's my only chance!*

Of course, Rosie was going to Beaver Falls High School by now. Just as promised, my class, the class of 1972, was the last one from Rockland to go to Lakewood High. From that point on, Rockland students were used to balance out the racial disparity at Beaver Falls. But it was summer now, and I'd catch a glimpse of Rosie, two or three times a week, just walking through the neighborhood. So, where she went to school didn't really matter as much.

Besides, I had an ace in the hole, and his name was Jerry Delpino. Yes, by some miracle, my buddy Jerry was now dating Rosie's sister, Colleen. He spent hours visiting her at her house three or four times a week. All I had to do was call him, find out if Rosie was going to be there, then ask him to pick me up on his way to their house.

It worked like a charm. Sure, sometimes Rosie and her friends wouldn't stick around long, but there were always a few of Colleen's friends hanging out too. So even if Rosie left the house, I didn't have to worry about being an unwanted guest. The place was full of unwanted guests, so Jerry and Colleen weren't going to be alone anyway.

On one Thursday night, about a dozen kids were hanging out on the Williamsons' back porch. Rosie's mom was serving us Kool-Aid and hot dogs that she grilled on the backyard grill, when somebody got the idea that we should all head out to Moraine State Park on Saturday and have a real picnic on the lake.

It didn't take long for the idea to snowball, and soon we had all made phone calls and invited nearly twenty kids to the big event. Moraine was on Lake Arthur, a beautiful, manmade body of water, surrounded by a beach made from several thousand tons of sand that had been shipped in from western Pennsylvania stone quarries. It would be the perfect setting for courting Rosie and forgetting about Lorraine. In fact, the excitement of the plan was already making me feel better.

The only thing I needed to do now was to ask Rosie to go *as my date!*

"I'll bring chips and pop," Rosie laughed, as her sister started making a list. "Who can bring the hamburgers?"

"I can," Jerry responded, "My father owns a restaurant, remember? I can grab a couple boxes of quarter-pound burgers, and he won't even care."

"What are you going to bring?" Rosie smiled, poking me in the ribs.

It felt good just to have her touch me again. And for the moment, the thought of Lorraine never crossed my mind. "Hmmm," I whispered, "Maybe I'll just bring a blanket and a couple towels for us, you know, to wrap up in!"

She was beaming, and her eyes sparkled like sapphires. *This is it,* I thought, *It's finally going to work out this time.*

"Uh, oh," chirped Colleen from across the porch. "I heard that. The rest of us are going to be cooking out, while you two are cooking something up under a blanket in the sand!"

"What's wrong with that?" I laughed.

But Rosie's defense mechanism was already kicking into high gear. "That will be the day!" she smirked. "I'm not going anywhere near a blanket if you're on it. You're dreaming!"

Ten years later, long after we both were married, I would meet Rosie at a downtown coffee shop and she would tell me how much she regretted those words.

But now, at age fifteen, her defenses were impenetrable. I tried again, "Well, I guess I'll bring hot dogs then," I joked. But she didn't laugh.

"Look," I said finally. "Can I talk to you alone for a second?"

"Why?" she stammered in mock outrage. "I don't want to be alone with you. Whatever you want to say, you can say right here!"

I got that old, sick feeling of embarrassment and disappointment. Her eyes were still dancing; still sparkling with emotion. But her words, as always, had been so hurtful, so caustic.

"Alright," I sighed with one last flicker of hope. "Here it is: I want you to go on this picnic *as my date*. I want to pick you up in my car. I want you to be practically sitting in my lap on the front seat. I want you on my blanket. I want to take you out on the lake in a rowboat and come back sunburned and humming something from Motown. That's what I want. That's what I have to say. Now, what do you have to say?"

"You're crazy!" she laughed, looking into the eyes of her astonished friends. "You think, after all this time, you can just pop up here and ask me out? You think I'm going to just jump into your car and go out with you on two days' notice?"

I looked at her in stunned silence. "That's an insult," she rambled on, "to ask me out on two days' notice, just because you can't find anybody else to go out with you."

"Whoa," I said. "Who said I can't find somebody else? I could call a hundred girls, but you're the one I want to go with."

"Oh, sure," she teased. "You could call a *hundred* girls? Well, hold on a second." And she vanished into the house.

Jerry grabbed me by the sleeve. "This is bad, Ted Tresh," he whispered. "Why is she doing this?" I just shook my head slowly.

"Here," barked Rosie, roaring back through the kitchen door and holding out the Lakewood City phone book. "Now's your chance, Romeo. Let's see you get a date for Saturday."

At that moment, something replaced the emptiness and hurt. And that something was anger! "Give me that damned book," I growled, as I started flipping through the pages.

But Rosie was at her antagonistic best. "Come on, hot shot," she mocked. "I thought there were a hundred girls you could call!"

I was so mad, I could barely see straight, but just then my eyes caught a glimpse of the listings for *Samson*. There were four or five of them in the phone book, but only one had an Ellicot address. I stepped into the kitchen followed by the entire gang of kids and started dialing the number.

"Hello," came a woman's voice from the other side.

"Hi," I answered, "Is Robin there?"

There was a rumbling through the kitchen now. Except for Jerry, I could tell that no one in the place had any idea who *Robin* was (maybe because I hardly knew the girl myself). All I had going for me was the brief chat we had on the way back to the bus after the Bethel Park game. I was staking my reputation on a two-minute conversation. And why? I didn't even want to date her, but that damn Rosie had pushed me to this. I had to make it work.

"Hi, Robin," I said with as much charm as I could muster in a crowded kitchen full of laughing teenagers. "It's Ted...Ted Tresh."

There was a moment of silence from the other side of the line as Robin tried to process this unexpected information. "She doesn't even know who he is," laughed Rosie in the background.

"Listen," I continued. "A bunch of us are going to Moraine on Saturday for a picnic, and I was wondering if you'd like to go." I hesitated for a second, and then pronounced the next phrase very slowly and distinctly, "*as my date!*"

The room had gone completely silent now, as Robin asked a few more questions.

"Uh, huh," I spoke calmly and directly, "You know most of them, Jerry Delpino, Colleen Williamson, Patty Milo."

Again, there was silence on the other side of the line. "She's asking her mother," I told the roomful of onlookers.

"Who's *Robin?*" Colleen asked Jerry, sincerely.

"I guarantee you one thing," Rosie laughed nervously, as the sparkle vanished from her eyes. "She's not really asking her mother, and her answer will be *no way.*"

When Robin finally got back on the phone, everyone in the room strained to hear what she was saying, but only my side of the conversation was audible in the room.

"Great!" I barked triumphantly into the mouthpiece. "It starts at ten o'clock. I'll pick you up at nine." I looked over at Rosie, but her eyes were on the floor. "I'm really looking forward to it too." And I hung up the phone.

"Okay," snapped Colleen. "Who the hell is Robin?"

"It's Robin Samson," Jerry laughed. "I saw them talking after the Bethel Park game."

"Oh, that's great," Colleen smiled. "I like Robin!"

"So do I," her friend Patty agreed. "She's really sweet."

"I'll say," laughed Jerry. "Jesus, Ted Tresh, Robin Samson is gorgeous!"

I watched Rosie go through the door and back out onto the porch all alone. It was partly my fault, I guess. I had really put her on the spot. But, I was too young and inexperienced to see things from her viewpoint. My ego was still too fragile to recognize the highs and lows of youthful romance.

"I really loved you," she would say years later. "Why didn't you fight for me?"

"That was some defense mechanism you had, Rosie," I told her then. "It was impenetrable!"

19

FLAVOR OF THE SUMMER

"Geez, Dad," Gene looked up at me from the La-Z-Boy recliner in our living room. "Did you date every girl in your class?"

"I really wasn't a playboy at heart," I told him. "I was always motivated by just one girl or another. But I started getting the reputation for being a player. It was just an act, but I was good at it. And it was a lot better than being thought of as somebody's clown.

"Anyway, the whole idea of dating Rosie had blown up in my face. The bad news was that she was gone for good. I saw her hundreds of times after that, but never asked her out again. She was *not* going to be the solution to my problem. And she was not going to make me forget Lorraine.

"The *good* news, on the other hand, was that I had earned the admiration of every kid in that kitchen. I had been openly challenged by Rosie and came through. About half the guys in my class were sixteen and driving by then, but it was still unusual to actually pick up a phone and ask a girl out on a date. Their admiring looks brought me back a little pride, and for the moment, the pain of losing Lorraine vanished. It was a pattern I would repeat for the next year and a half.

"Here's the thing, Gene," I told him with an air of finality. "Some girls just won't take a chance on you. They always hold something back. They want you, but the idea of eventually losing you, is more than their fragile egos can take. So, what do they do? They give you just enough attention to keep you around, just enough affection to *hold* you. But they never want to put themselves in a position where they can be hurt *by* you."

"And that's *exactly* what Jan is doing with me," Gene shouted, jumping to his feet. "I know she loves me. I *know* it! But she keeps testing me. She keeps trying to prove to herself that I'll stay no matter what she does to me."

"And that's what eventually will drive you away," I nodded.

"So, what do I do? Do I leave her? Do I find somebody else? The problem is that I don't really want anyone else. Do I just go out with the next girl that comes along, and hope I forget about Jan?"

"Well, that has its drawbacks too," I shrugged. What about the new girl? What about her feelings? What happens if she really falls for you while you're just trying to forget Jan?

"So, what happened with this Robin Samson? Did you date her for a long time? Did it turn into anything real?"

"Hmmm," I closed my eyes and tried to picture her face, her smile. "Well, she was sweet, and we were both so inexperienced. The picnic was a fantastic start, but when you're hung up on the wrong girl, you don't even see the right girl under your nose."

"When I picked her up at her house, she came out on the porch wearing a frilly pink halter top with white shorts. She looked like a dream. All my friends were so nice to her. And she loved the attention.

It was a wonderful first date for both of us, enough so that we didn't want it to end. When we got back from Moraine State Park, we went out with Jerry and Colleen for frozen custard, and then we all played miniature golf. The date lasted over twelve hours!"

"Her parents weren't too thrilled when we got back home. She had called them from Colleen's house at about 5 o'clock when we got back from the picnic, but when we didn't get home until after 10 p.m., they were pretty pissed off. I went inside with her and spent the next half hour trying to assure her parents that I was a wonderful, trustworthy kid, and that their daughter was safe with me.

"By the time I left, we had their blessing, and we promised we would never stay out that late again without phoning home every hour. I kissed her good-night under her porchlight, and promised I'd call the next day.

"On my drive home, I felt so grown up, so proud of the fact that I had just called this girl on the phone, and taken her out on a tremendous date, and faced down her parents, and kissed her goodnight. 'That was a perfect day,' I thought, 'And a perfect night. So, this is what it's like to be an adult.'

"But, as I weaved my way back home through the dark streets of Ellicot, I couldn't keep one thought from pushing its way back into my mind, *She's not really Lorraine, is she?*"

"Oh, come on Dad," Gene cupped his head in his hands. "Don't tell me you blew it with this sweet girl, just to mourn over Lorraine? Did you at least take her out again?"

"Oh yeah," I answered. "We dated all that summer. But something was missing. I guess we just didn't have the right chemistry. There wasn't the same attraction I had for Lorraine or even for Rosie.

"We had a lot of fun over the next few months. We went to movies and drive-ins and carnivals. We went to friends' houses together and had become a real couple.

"In mid-July, my buddy, Jerry suffered a horrific injury playing baseball. Normally a third baseman, he was out of position, playing second base for the Lakewood American Legion team. Even though he was only sixteen years old and played for one of the Lakewood Colt League teams, the Legion coach was short-handed that weekend and had asked Jerry to fill in for them. He was trying to turn a double play at second base, when a big New Castle runner slid hard into his planted left leg. Both the fibula and tibia were shattered, and the bones ripped through the skin and his high stirrup socks. Blood was everywhere!

"Jerry was hospitalized for two weeks and had major surgery on the damaged leg. And even though we had only been dating for a few weeks, Robin and I seemed like an old married couple, visiting him at least five times during his recuperation.

"Even though we weren't *in love* by any means, it seemed like my relationship with Robin might last a long time. Unfortunately, as soon as we had our first fight, it was over.

"As I remember it, she was mad that I kept dropping by her house unannounced. One night I showed up and she was visiting one of her girlfriends in the neighborhood. Her mother called her on the phone and told her I was there. But she said I hadn't called first and that she was not coming home.

"I drove away from Robin's house and never looked back. I don't think I ever had another real conversation with her. One day, we were dating and the next day, poof! It was like it had never happened."

"What?" Gene could hardly believe his ears. "You walked away for that? Geez, Dad, you were a real jerk. Why would I take advice from you?"

"I'm just trying to show you how you can piss your life away waiting for someone who will never stand by your side."

"But you hurt someone else, Dad. Didn't that bother you?"

"It should have. But I wasn't thinking about it that way. I wasn't even upset about it," I confided. "I mean, she wasn't really Lorraine, was she?"

Just then, Gene's cell phone interrupted the conversation, blasting out the intro to Pearl Jam's "I'm Still Alive."

"That's Jan," he shrugged, looking up at the clock on the wall. "That's *her* ring."

I followed his gaze. It was 5:30 a.m. "Wow! She's getting an early start today," I proclaimed. "Do you need some privacy?"

"No, I'm not going to answer it," he told me. "We had a fight on the phone last night. She's calling this early just to piss me off. She thinks she's waking me up. I'll wait until she calls five or six more times. I'm just not ready to deal with her right now.

"Finish your story," he nodded. "Weren't you upset about ending things with Robin?"

"Actually, I was a little relieved," I answered. "Summer was coming to an end, and I had been formulating my plan to get Lorraine back for weeks. School was starting soon, and I was ready for a showdown with Blake. It was all I thought about!"

"Wow," Gene shook his head. "You really had it bad for that girl."

LONG ROAD TO NOWHERE

The start of my junior year was full of promise. For the first time, Lorraine was in my homeroom, so we had ample opportunity for conversations. But she was Blake's girl now, and the entire school knew it. If I kept pursuing her, *I* would be the one they considered the bad guy.

Still, I knew she had feelings for me. Her eyes gave her away. I'd look up from my desk and catch her staring at me. And when I did *catch* her, she would wait a full five seconds before looking away. What was she searching for? I thought I knew, but we just couldn't talk about it.

Whenever there was a conversation, it was filled with regrets and sarcasm. "Look, Lorraine," I whispered across the aisle one morning before first period. "I'm sorry I lied to you, but you *can't* be serious about this guy. I *know* you still care about me!"

"I got along without you before I met you," she smiled, finally shifting her gaze. "I can get along without you now."

I recognized her words as lyrics to an obscure old pop song. "Really?" I snapped, shaking my head, "Now, you're quoting Skeeter Davis?"

We both laughed, and her eyes danced like sunshine off a waterfall.

It was enough to let me know the feelings were still there. But any actual, meaningful dialogue was still months away. "What's that?" I asked when I spotted some sort of mimeographed form laying on her desk.

"Junior class elections are coming up soon," she stated without looking up from her paperwork. "I'm running for Prom Co-Chairman."

From freshman year through senior year, Lakewood City High School had the same class officers as any other school: President, Vice President, Treasurer and Secretary. But, during the junior year, they added two more officers, the prom co-chairmen. One had to be a boy and one had to be a girl. They were in charge of all the arrangements for the Junior/Senior prom, which took place late in May.

These chairmen had a lot of power compared to the rest of the class officers, who were largely ceremonial. The prom co-chairmen actually controlled the special prom budget, which was huge.

When we were sophomores, the previous spring, our class had conducted a fundraising candy sale. Every student was given a *goal* of thirty boxes of candy, with weekly prizes for everyone who met their quota. *All* the money from the candy sale was earmarked to be used exclusively for the prom. And we had pocketed over $9,000 from our sale! That's like having 30 grand today, and it all had to be spent on the prom decorations and arrangements.

"Well, good luck with that," I told her. "I'll vote for you!

"You know," she answered, finally looking me straight in the eyes, "There are no boys running yet."

I had never even considered running for class officer, but now the thought wouldn't leave me. And the fact that Lorraine had suggested it, made it even more intriguing. After lunch I stopped by the principal's office and filled out an application form. All it needed was my name, home room number and the name of the office, *Prom Co-Chairman*.

I waited out the rest of the week to see if anyone else would apply to run. It was now 1970 and, as that rebellious decade drew to a close, the values of our generation had been going through constant fluctuation. Aspiring to be a star athlete was starting to be considered shallow. Running for class officer, once a sign of status and honor, was now viewed as somewhat vain. The job of prom chairman would be a lot of work and, for many of my classmates, working hard was no longer considered *cool,* so I figured that anyone from the *in* crowd would pass on it. Plus, if the prom decorations didn't meet everyone's high expectations, the chairmen would get blamed, and most of the cool kids weren't about to put their celebrity status on the line.

The biggest problem was that no one from Rockland had ever won a popularity contest like class officer. This was still the Lakewood kids' school, and they weren't about to hand out any accolades to an outsider. I was pretty sure that no one would run against Lorraine for the female chairman's spot. She was the *It Girl*, and no one really had a chance to beat her. I just hoped no one else wanted the male chairman's spot. Working in close quarters with Lorraine for the next seven months would put me in the perfect position to get her back.

When the ballots were announced on Monday, I felt pretty good. There were multiple nominees for every office except one, Lorraine would go in unchallenged. And there was only one other nominee who had applied for the boy co-chairman's office, my Rockland buddy, Willie Gacik.

I had just told the damn kid on Wednesday that I was running. He had to know I'd be pissed off! What was he trying to do? It made me wonder, more than a little, about his supposedly earnest friendship. It also made me wonder again if maybe *he* had been the source of Lorraine's so-called *ESP*. Did he *tell* her about my date with the Beaver Falls Majorette?

The good news, of course, was that, like me, he was a Rockland kid. He would have no advantage in the election. He did pick up the support of the hippie element of our class. These were kids who smoked cigarettes and sometimes pot. They spouted anti-war slogans but couldn't have named the Secretary of State if their lives depended on it. The concert at Woodstock had taken place just fourteen months earlier, and they thought that music would save the planet. They called themselves *The Freak Party* and had nominated and endorsed a full slate of candidates, Willie was one of them.

This was a new kind of *cool*, and the traditionally *popular* kids weren't quite ready to admit them into their circle of honor. The entire Freak Party slate lost, including Willie, who had pledged that, if he were elected, *Woodstock, A Celebration of Peace and Love*, would be the prom theme. I won the election almost by default.

On Tuesday morning, Lorraine and I both got memos from the junior class sponsor, Mr. Maluka. He was a biology teacher and a pretty serious type. "Report to my office during third period," the memo read, "To discuss a theme for this year's prom." My plan was beginning to take shape.

"What ideas do you have for this year?" the class sponsor asked as we took our seats at his desk.

"Well, I've talked to a lot of kids," Lorraine began. "I think the best ideas, so far, are *Camelot* and *Tropical Paradise*. You know, for Tropical Paradise, we could bring in palm trees and sand and straw huts. For Camelot, we could construct a paper-machete castle and have Maypoles and maybe a jousting ring."

"What do you think, Ted?" Mr. Maluka now turned to me.

Truth be known, I'd hadn't spent one minute thinking about the theme of the dance, and I certainly hadn't polled my classmates for ideas. My whole reason for being there was to be close to Lorraine, and I scrambled for a reasonable concept to toss in the ring. My eyes darted around the room.

On the top level of Mr. Maluka's wall-anchored bookshelves I spied a title, "The Lost Continent of Atlantis," it read.

"Ummm, how about *The Undersea World of Atlantis?*" I stammered. "We could use some of the same tropical-paradise props like palm trees and sand, but then have the kids go through an underwater cave to the lost continent." I started getting excited now, "And we could have a live band in a giant clam shell and statues of sea gods, and mermaids and fish hanging from the ceiling of the gym."

Maluka's mouth fell open and he stared across at Lorraine. "I love it," he gasped finally.

"So do I," nodded Lorraine, "And I thought I'd have to plan this all by myself?"

She wasn't far from wrong. Coming up with a theme was the biggest contribution I would make as Prom Co-Chairman. After that, she just took the ball and ran with it; organizing committees, setting budgets, planning trips to the party-supply store in nearby Youngstown, Ohio, to buy props and decorations.

Lorraine was on a mission to make this the best prom ever at Lakewood High, and I was just along for the ride. Still, she bounced every idea off me. I had to sign off on every artificial palm tree, every black light for the underwater cave, and every grain of sand for the makeshift beach.

We were together buying supplies or meeting with the previous year's chairmen or running the prom committee meetings at least once a week, and we were on the phone together every-other-night. Things were going exactly as I had planned.

It was the height of our *non-relationship*, as Lorraine would call it months later, but it was no substitute for the real thing. She was still Blake's girlfriend, and every flirtatious comment I'd make was met by a *let's-get-back-to-business* sigh from Lorraine. This was going to take longer than I thought.

I decided I needed a diversion, someone I could date in the meantime, and someone who wouldn't be hurt if I broke things off suddenly. The perfect candidate was sitting right in my homeroom. Her name was Amy Maroni.

Amy had been another late bloomer, sweet and fun and pretty in an Italian kind of way. She had been sort of plain until tenth grade, but all of a sudden her figure had filled-out and she had let her short dark hair grow long and flowing. She was turning heads all over the school. Enough so, that in the final months of our sophomore year, she had started dating a pretty good-looking senior boy named Jeff Morris.

But Jeff was off at college now. And I had overheard her in study hall telling one of her friends that she and her boyfriend had an *understanding*, that he didn't want her to miss out on all the fun of high school, the dances, the parties, and the dates. Amy was saying that, although he was still her boyfriend, she was going to enjoy her high school years, and she wanted him to enjoy college.

Perfect, I thought, *this girl is just what I need!* I didn't waste any time either. Before September was even over, I asked her if she wanted to go out for a movie and a hamburger, and just like that, we were dating. "You know I have a boyfriend!" she warned me. "This can't turn serious."

"No problem," I advised her. "I'm kind of hung up on someone else myself."

"Lorraine?" she smiled.

"How did you know that?" I questioned.

"Oh, Teddy," she laughed. "Everybody knows."

"Oh, great," I moaned. "Just what I want to be known for…"

"I don't care," she continued. "I really don't. I just want to have fun this year. That's what you want too isn't it…to have fun?"

The relationship with Amy turned out better than I ever thought it could. We danced every Friday night in the gym. We hung out with friends. I stopped at her house a couple times a week and we would just sit around her kitchen table and talk for hours. Her little brother Theo who was later diagnosed with some mental issues would always hang out at the table with us. I just figured he was a pain-in-ass eight-year-old, and although he was irritating as hell, out of respect for Amy, I would patiently sit and talk with the kid for hours. That was no easy task.

Theo had a way of zeroing in on any weakness, any flaw I might be trying to hide. "That's some pimple on your nose," he remarked one day as we sat around their kitchen table.

"Thanks for noticing," I smiled sarcastically.

"I see you're covering it with makeup," he went on.

"That's Clearasil," I laughed. "It's medicine."

"It sure looks like makeup to me," replied Theo. "I thought only girls wore makeup."

"Maybe we should change the subject," Amy offered. It was obvious that she was embarrassed by her brother's annoying behavior, but it was just as obvious that she would do anything to protect him. "Ted is our guest, Theo," she smiled, "And you're insulting him."

"Why is he here?" the kid went on. "Don't you already have a boyfriend?"

"I do have a boyfriend," she answered patiently, "But he's far away at college. You wouldn't want me to miss high school football games and dances and parties, would you? Ted and I go on dates sometimes. That doesn't bother you does it?"

"It doesn't bother me," he replied flatly. "I like him better than Jeff anyway."

"Oh, Theo," she laughed. "Now you're embarrassing me."

"I just wanted to know about the pimple. Will it go away by itself?" he prattled on.

"That's what the Clearasil is for." I answered patiently. "It helps the pimples go away."

"Why is it pink?" Theo wanted to know.

"Well, that helps hide the pimple until it's gone," I answered calmly.

"So, it *is* makeup," said Theo triumphantly. And we all busted out laughing.

"Yes, it's makeup," I laughed. "You got me."

Talking with Amy's obsessive/compulsive brother was always a challenge. But, I did my best to treat him with patience and respect. I think she really liked me for that. We dated two or three times a month, sometimes with friends, sometimes just the two of us. We never had any long *make-out* sessions, but I always kissed her goodnight.

She was the perfect non-girlfriend, but deep down, I always thought that if I ever gave up on Lorraine, that, boyfriend or no boyfriend, I could easily start-up a real relationship with Amy. Maybe that was true. Maybe it wasn't. But I always *thought* that it was.

Lorraine, for her part, seemed a little unnerved by my involvement with Amy. On our way back from one of our trips to Youngstown to buy prom supplies, she abruptly broke off a conversation about the price of black lights and crepe paper to express her disapproval. "Teddy," she began, "Is it okay if I ask you a personal question?"

"Uh, sure. I guess so."

"Just what are you doing with Amy Maroni?"

The question caught me off guard. "We're having fun, that's all."

"Aren't you afraid you'll hurt her? I mean, I know she has a boyfriend in college, but I've seen the way she looks at you; the way you two dance together in the gym. What happens if she really falls for you?"

"I don't know," I shrugged. "What if I really fall for her? Besides, it's our business."

"Well, somebody is going to get hurt," Lorraine pronounced.

I just shook my head. "What do *you* care anyway?"

"C'mon, Teddy, open your eyes. You *know* I care!"

We were still a half hour from home; driving back along the dark country road, but neither one of us spoke again. I just let the sound of her last statement linger in the air, and the echo of her voice bounce back and forth across the interior of my dad's silver Thunderbird.

When I pulled up in front of her house, she opened the door and started to get out. "Lorraine, wait," I called to her. And she turned to face me. "I care too," I whispered.

She didn't say a word. She just danced across the sidewalk, floated up the steps, and disappeared into her house.

A LITTLE MORE TIME

"So, you had everything going your way," Gene surmised. "You had a cute girl to date. You were seeing your *true love* two or three times a week. Surely you made some progress with her? I mean, if she really cared like she said she did, it was just a matter of time before you were together?"

"It's funny that you say that, Gene," I said, rising from the sofa to get a better look at the slowly brightening sky. Gray clouds had started rolling in from the west end of town, and only small patches of blue sky were still visible. "She was like a tennis ball bobbing in a swimming pool. She'd get close, then closer, and then just when I'd reach out for her, some little ripple would push her just out of reach.

"One day she'd be laughing at everything I said, she'd be playful and flirtatious. But, the very next day, she'd act disgusted if I made any type of suggestive remark, especially if it was made in front of witnesses. It was like, she wanted *me* to care about *her*, but she didn't want anyone to think that she cared about me."

"That's *exactly* what Jan does!" Gene exclaimed, as he leaped to his feet. "Privately, she's as loving and caring as a woman can be. But, whenever she has an audience, it's one putdown after another. She puts on this show of indifference, like I mean nothing to her.

"But when I call her on it, when I say, 'You can't treat me like that, we're done,' she starts crying and sobbing and banging on my door in the middle of the night."

And, right on cue, Gene's cell phone blasted out the first few bars of Pearl Jam's *I'm Still Alive*. "It's her again," he looked down at the phone and shook his head in disgust. "It's been forty-five minutes since her last call. I'll wait until she gets down to five or ten minutes between calls. Maybe she'll be ready to listen by then."

I had to laugh. "Well, it's not exactly like Lorraine. She wouldn't even open up to me in private. But she did *flirt* in private, and she was sweet and caring. But get her in a crowd, and she was nothing like that. She became sarcastic and insulting, like she wanted everyone to think she didn't care. Meanwhile, everybody *knew* I cared about her.

"I could understand it in a way," I continued. "I mean, officially, she *had* a boyfriend. And he was someone that all her friends admired, a Lakewood boy, the son of a lawyer, the nephew of a doctor, the perfect match her mother wanted for her.

"That wasn't something she was going to throw away easily, and I think her feelings for me just got in the way of her well-planned life. But it was the Seventies now, for Chrissakes! And she was only fifteen years old. This wasn't Napoli in the Eighteenth Century! This was Lakewood City, Pennsylvania, in the decade of rebellion and independence and women's rights. Surely, she would wake up soon. Surely, she would eventually defy her mother's wishes and make her own decision. Surely, in the end, she would listen to her heart!"

"So, did it ever happen?" Gene wondered out loud. "Did she ever just throw caution to the wind and tell you how she really felt?"

"Only when she saw me slipping away," I turned away from the window and shook my head; "Only when I started to care for somebody else."

"That sounds bad, Dad," Gene frowned, as he sunk back into the couch. "It also sounds pretty damn familiar."

NOTHING TO SAY

Our whole junior year of high school went by that way: fun, but fairly meaningless dates with Amy, followed by frustrating evenings with Lorraine, where we debated and argued over plans for the prom, but never really got down to discussing *us*.

So, we would argue over the number of black lights to put in the Paper Mache cave, or which way the band-on-the-half-shell should be facing, but the real, underlying tension, the *800 pound gorilla* in the room, we would never discuss.

The only time Lorraine ever seemed concerned was when I showed an interest in somebody else. By November, she was pretty used to the idea of me dating Amy. It was obvious that no serious relationship was going to come out of that situation. But just a month before my seventeenth birthday, I met a girl at a wedding who Lorraine saw as a real threat.

Her name was Winnie Tyler and she was already nineteen years old! My buddy Willie was dating her cousin, Belinda. That's why we were invited to the wedding. Of course, I didn't realize her age when I asked her to dance. She was just sweet and funny and sexy. And I was just passing time on the dance floor. When I walked her back to her table, I asked her what high school she attended.

"Oh, Sweetie," she said, "I went to Freedom High School, but I *graduated last year*, the class of 1969."

Whoa, I thought. I wasn't going to graduate until 1972, and although I really didn't want to get serious with anybody who wasn't Lorraine, this girl might be worth taking a chance on. Besides, her name was *Winnie*. What sixteen-year-old boy could resist a temptation like that?

The first time I asked her out, she giggled, "Aren't you afraid of me?" But I guess we both decided it was worth a chance. I was still *sixteen* the first time we went out; burgers at Jerry's Curb Service, and then just cruising on a Saturday night. "We have to be in by midnight," I warned her. "I still have my junior license, plus, I have to get up for mass tomorrow."

"Mass?" she sputtered. "Are you Catholic?"

"I sure am," I grinned. "I go to church every Sunday."

"Were you ever an altar boy?" She was laughing at me now.

"*I still am!*" I shot back. "The nuns asked me to stay on after grade school, and I agreed."

"But aren't you *taller* than the priest?"

"I am," I laughed. "But no one seems to mind. I've done it for ten years now. So, I figure I might as well finish high school as an altar boy."

"But aren't you embarrassed?" she smiled.

"Sure," I nodded, "That's what makes it a sacrifice."

"What am I getting myself into?" She slid across the seat, took my left hand and kissed my index finger. And I guess I was wondering the exact same thing.

We dated throughout November and December and into January, including Christmas Eve and New Year's Eve. It was time to start growing up, and new personal milestones fell every week: First time making out with a girl, first time parking, first time…well, a lot of firsts. It was the most physical I had ever been with a girl, because she was no girl, she was a woman. And she definitely had my attention.

Right in the middle of all these events fell the December Y-Teens dance at Lakewood High. It was the same dance that I had taken Lorraine to just a year before. But now, we were juniors, and not eligible to attend this semi-formal; *except* for the girls who had been selected for the Y-Teens Court the year before. Those girls were invited back to pass on the crown and accolades to the new queen and her court.

Lorraine had been on that court, of course, but when she asked Blake to escort her, he told her that he was a senior and he didn't want to go to the dance with a bunch of little kids. So, she needed to find somebody else, and fast. Asking me was out of the question. Blake would never have stood for that. So, she asked a friend of hers named Dave Lutz to be her escort.

I didn't think much about the sophomore dance until one of my old Rockland neighborhood friends, Stephanie Bellissimo, asked me to escort her. She had been on the Y-Teens Court the previous year too. It was just going to be "eight junior girls and eight junior guys out for a fun night," she explained to me. Of course, they were eight of the sweetest girls in our class, and one of them was Lorraine, so I figured, *why not?*

Winnie didn't seem to mind. After all, we weren't dating exclusively, and Stephanie was just a childhood friend. It seemed like the night would be harmless enough. But it didn't turn out that way.

The dance fell on a Friday night in mid-December, and Stephanie and I were double dating with her best friend Connie and my buddy Willie, who was still dating Winnie's cousin. Connie and Willie were just friends too. In fact we had all grown up in the same neighborhood in Rockland and lived about a hundred yards from each other. None of us had any romantic notions about the dance. It was just a big group of friends going to a party and enjoying the night out.

The plan was to stay at the Y-Teens Dance just until the new court was introduced and the new queen was crowned, then all eight of the junior girls and their dates would drive out to a nice restaurant in Pittsburgh to round out the evening. It was a great plan. We seemed so mature and experienced compared to the sophomore and freshman couples. And we relished our roles as the relaxed, outgoing, cool-as-hell junior class.

As it turned out, every one of the eight junior girls had asked a guy that they considered *just a friend,* so that we were all just joking around and having a good time. There were none of the usual relationship problems. No one was jealous, or mad, or worried that their date was looking at someone else. Stephanie could have jumped up and kissed every guy at the dance, and I wouldn't have cared. We were all just friends, out on the town, having fun.

Right after the crowning of a new sophomore queen, we jumped into four cars and headed out to the Glass Tower Restaurant near the Pittsburgh Airport, where I had reserved a table for sixteen. It was a small restaurant that held about fifty patrons, but it was now nearly 9 pm, and most of the tables were empty, so our group made up about half the diners in the place.

"Looks like we've got the place to ourselves," I mentioned to the hostess, as she showed us to our table. "I see you've got a juke box in the corner. Do you mind if we play a few songs?"

"Well, we don't usually allow it to be played during dinner hours," she responded, looking around the half-empty room, "But I guess it will be okay this late at night; just don't play anything too loud or wild."

I headed directly for the machine and popped in a dollar. In those days, that bought us twelve songs, and I proceeded to pick out four or five of my favorite Motown tunes. Stephanie and Connie had followed me there. "The rest are up to you," I told them.

"Can I pick one out?" said a voice from behind me. It was Lorraine. We hadn't spoken much during the entire evening. Although at the dance we had exchanged glances a few times, my whole infatuation with her seemed, finally, to be winding down. There was always a kind of bittersweet, underlying pain when I spoke to Lorraine. But on this night, I really was just enjoying the evening, and that pain seemed far away.

Besides, I was dating Winnie now, a seriously hot, older girl, and was the envy of every guy in the junior class. Plus, tonight I was out with a bunch of good friends at a big-city restaurant, where I had made all the arrangements. I took some pride in that. And I was beginning to see that there just may be life after Lorraine after all.

"Save one pick for Lorraine," I told Stephanie and Connie, as they made their selections.

The music played all through dinner, and we all laughed and told jokes and zinged each other with teenage one-liners. The food was great, the girls all looked beautiful, and the staff at the Glass Tower treated us like celebrities, not a bunch of high school kids. There weren't many other diners in the room, but eight of the most beautiful girls in the junior class of Lakewood High were seated at our long, banquet-style table. And the eyes of every male guest or staff member were glued on them.

Just as the waitress was coming around to take our dessert orders, the juke box whirred and dropped a 45 rpm record on the vertical turntable. It was the last of the twelve songs we had selected, the one Lorraine had chosen.

"*I found love on a two-way street,*" the first bar of the Moments' big romantic hit swirled through the table conversation and drowned out the waitress' voice reciting the dessert menu. "*...And lost it on a lonely highway.*"

It was *our song,* mine and Lorraine's, and I looked up to see her staring right at me. Then she got up, and slowly walked around the table to where I was sitting. She bent over and whispered in my ear. "Can I have this dance?"

I felt an unexpected jolt of emotion, a thrill, an explosion. Just when I had started to give up on her, here she was, holding out her hand to me. "I mean, if your date doesn't mind?" Lorraine continued.

Stephanie didn't even answer. She just put her hand in the middle of my back and pushed me to my feet. Every eye at the table was on us. "You realize there's no dance floor?" I laughed, as I led her out between the tables of the half-empty restaurant.

My mind raced for a topic to break the ice, but it wasn't really necessary. "So," I pronounced, as we made it to an open spot of the floor, and I wrapped my arms around her waist, "How's my Prom Co-chairman?"

Lorraine looked up at me and shook her head in mock disgust. "You're really clueless, aren't you?" It had been months since I had danced with Lorraine, but it immediately became clear that this girl meant business from the very first note. She wrapped her arms around my neck and pulled my lips down next to her ear. I could feel the length of her body against mine, and we swayed slowly to the music, then slower, then slower still, as each word, each note of *our song* burst to life with a whole new meaning.

"What is this, Lorraine?" I asked finally.

"What do you mean?" she sighed.

"What about your boyfriend?" I whispered. "There are fourteen witnesses sitting over there. Aren't you worried he'll find out?"

"No," was all she said.

"So, what happens when..."

She raised her hand up and put a finger to my mouth. "Shhhh," she breathed, "Shhhhhh."

And we never spoke another word. The song was sweet and slow and romantic.

"With music softly playing, her lips were gently saying, Honey, I love you." The Motown sound echoed off the walls and the tables and the long gold draperies.

It had been seven months since I held Lorraine like that. I could feel her body against my chest, her raven hair against my cheek. I could smell her perfume and taste the little beads of perspiration on her neck. All those months of growing apart; all those exciting dates with Winnie; was I going to throw all that away just because Lorraine was back in my arms? *Yes*—that's exactly what I was going to do.

"Shit," I said out loud. "I must be crazy."

She lifted her fingertip up to my lips again. "Shhhh," was all she said.

When we returned to the table, Stephanie had moved to another seat and was chatting with Dave Lutz, Lorraine's date. The waitress was serving desserts to everyone at the table, and she looked up at me expectantly. "Chocolate Sundae," I called out, "With whipped cream, a cherry and two spoons."

Lorraine sat down next to me. "You just took my breath away," she whispered. "I can't believe you remembered me ordering that ice cream with two spoons."

"I remember everything," I said, nodding my head, "Don't you?"

When the waitress brought our dessert, Lorraine reached over and took the spoon from my hand. "We really only need one spoon," she teased, as she leaned over, pushed her spoon through the toppings, and then fed me a bite of pure whipped cream with a cherry on it.

"Now you took *my* breath away," I whispered. "But, Lorraine, what happens next?"

"What do you mean?" She taunted me.

"I mean, if this was a perfect world, what would you want to happen next?"

"Well, if this was a perfect world, the next thing to happen would be you'd kiss me."

So, I swallowed my bite of whipped cream, wiped my mouth on my napkin, and swept in for a long, soft kiss. It was sweet and romantic, and the rest of the room just disappeared. When I opened my eyes, the entire table was staring at us.

"Hey, that's my date," laughed Dave, who by now had Stephanie sitting on his lap. Everyone else was ooo-ing and ahh-ing.

"Get a room, you two," chirped Willie.

We separated slowly, still looking into each other's eyes. "I actually meant what would you want to happen in the future." I whispered to Lorraine. "What about your boyfriend?

"What about him?"

"Are you serious?" I said out loud. "Are you going to act like this doesn't mean anything?"

"Of course, it *means* something," she sighed "But do we have to talk about it now? Can't we just have tonight without worrying about what's going to happen next? I mean, it was *just* a dance!"

So, this is how it's going to go? I thought. *In spite of all these witnesses, in spite of re-igniting all these emotions, she is going to play it cool; just a friendly dance, just a meaningless kiss?*

"*Just a dance?*" I whispered the words, but it was an angry whisper. "You can sell that shit to your girlfriends, if you want to, but don't try to pedal it to me. I know what just happened."

"See," she sighed. "That's why I didn't want to talk about it. I knew you'd get mad."

"Listen, Lorraine," I was staring her right in the eyes, "For future reference, when you dance with me, it's *never* just a dance."

I called for our tab, and ten minutes later, Stephanie and I, with Willie and Connie in the back seat, were on the expressway heading for home. "Wow," laughed Stephanie. "I didn't see that coming. What's she going to do about Blake?"

"She's not going to do anything about him," I shook my head in disgust. "Apparently it was *just a dance.*"

"And the kiss?" scoffed Willie from the back seat.

"I guess that was *just a kiss.*"

"Oh, Teddy," groaned Stephanie, "I'm sorry. I knew you liked her, but it wasn't until tonight that I realized how much she likes you. What are you going to do?"

"It's like her mind is not her own," I sighed.

"I've known you since we were five years old," Shrugged Connie from the back seat. "Do you want some advice?"

"Sure."

"Run!" she offered.

But the memory of that night would haunt me for months. For some reason, my mind drifted back to the playground at St. Teresa School, back to Molly, sweet and constant. "You like Teddy Tresh," Mark Minelli had tried to tease her.

"So?" was all she said.

The bells and whistles and alarms inside my head were all ringing at once, but I just wasn't listening.

THE JOKE'S ON YOU

The incessant opening bars to Pearl Jam's *I'm Still Alive* bleated out of Gene's cell phone to announce yet another call from Jan. It was now about 6am, and Gene had already ignored at least five calls from her in the last hour. "I better grab this one, Dad," he grimaced. "Excuse me."

I stayed in the living room watching the sun peek through the oak trees in our front yard, while Gene walked into the kitchen for some privacy. "Hello," I could hear him saying as he vanished from sight, but not quite out of earshot. "No," he sighed into the phone, "I wasn't avoiding you. I just woke up."

I could only hear bits and pieces of the conversation, but it sounded like Gene wasn't getting much chance to respond. "No, I *don't* think you're serious, now that you mention it," he said sharply. "And just *where* are you going to go?"

There was a silence in the house, and for a few seconds I grew aware of the singing of the last few cardinals of the season, chirping away in the miniature cherry tree outside in our front yard. It was December 6, and the winter cold was late arriving this year, but change was in the air.

"You really expect me to believe that you're going to move back to your mother's house? That's ridiculous! That's in L.A. What about school? What about your internship? What about us?"

Now I could hear Jan's shrill voice all the way in the next room. "How dare you! How dare you!" she screeched. And with the added volume, Gene stepped out the back door and into the cool December morning air, to regain his privacy.

He came back into the house after about five minutes. "She hung up on me," he said, shaking his head as he slunk back into the living room. "I was mid-sentence and she hung up!"

"What did she say?" I wondered out loud.

"It's a big argument," he said. "But with her, they're all big. Anyway, she said if I loved her, I'd go back there right now." He shook his head in disbelief. "She *knows* I'm flying back tomorrow. She *knows* there is no way in hell I'm moving my flight to tonight. She just wants to argue and pout and make me *prove* that I love her.

"That's what I spend ninety-five percent of my life doing these days, *proving* that I love her, no matter how much of a shithead she is!"

"Why don't you just cut her loose, Gene?" The question was in the air, I had to ask it.

"I *do* cut her loose," he sighed. "But she keeps coming back and crying and pouting and telling me how much she loves me."

"And you take her back?"

Gene looked up at me slowly. He knew this was more of an accusation than a question. And he dropped his eyes to the floor. "And she *knows* I will."

"Whoa," I sighed, rocking back in my recliner, as the seriousness of Gene's situation smacked me in the head for the second time. He was in love with this girl.

"It's just when she *comes* back," Gene swallowed hard, and looked me in the eye, "And she curls up on my chest, and she holds on so tight, and she begs me to never leave her, well, it feels like love. I mean a *kind* of love. And she's so beautiful that sometimes I think she might be worth the trouble."

I looked down at the floor myself now and tried to process all this new information. "What did I hear you saying about L.A.?" I asked finally.

"Well, she said she phoned her mother to complain about the way I treat her, and her mother said if she wanted to leave Miami right now, she could live with her and have a job in her fashion design company in L.A. I guess her mom is this big-deal fashion designer.

"But it's stupid. In one more year, she'll have her degree and be worth twice as much to the company. I'm sure her mother just said that to call her bluff. Like, *if you hate it so much in Miami, then come home.* Her mother is no fan of mine. I mean, I've never met her in person, but I've heard them on the phone. They both blame me for everything!

"But now Jan's saying that if I don't get back there fast, she may be gone to California when I get back."

"That sounds like a good solution," I chuckled, but Gene didn't seem amused.

"She's not serious," he groaned. "She just wants me to call her and plead with her and tell her how important she is. This is nothing new, Dad. This is my life every day."

"First of all, Gene," I began. "You're not in school to court women. You have other things that should be taking up your time first, like graduating. This girl has forced her way into every portion of your life. That's fine if she's the right kind of girl, a partner, a teammate. But if she's going to distract you, well she's more trouble than she's worth right now. You're a college student. You have real life to worry about!

"I understand that relationship problems are hard to ignore, especially when you think you might be in love. But the truth is, Gene, a real partner is never part of the problem. She's part of the solution."

"Why do I feel a story coming on?" he joked.

"It's okay," I replied. "If you want to get some sleep, we can finish tomorrow."

"No," he protested. "I want to know. What's the lesson from the Lorraine story? How did you handle a girl who knows she can get you back anytime she wants?"

"Not well," I conceded. "I made a few mistakes along the way."

JUST A DREAM

On Monday morning, Lorraine came strolling into home room with her arms full of prom supplies, boxes of streamers, black lights and poster paint. "Help me with this, Teddy," she moaned, as she struggled to load everything into a storage closet in the back of the room.

I swooped in to hold the boxes as she unloaded the supplies. "How are you feeling today?" I asked warily.

"Fine," she said, "How are you."

"I'm not inquiring about your health," I laughed. "I mean how are you feeling about Friday night?"

"What about Friday night?" she said without looking away from the shelves and the boxes.

"Are you shitting me, Lorraine?" I just stood there in stunned silence.

She finally looked up into my eyes. "What?"

I dropped the last box at her feet. "I'm sorry," my words were now cold and distant. "I must have you mistaken for *somebody who was THERE!*"

"Look, Ted, it was a very nice night with some very nice moments, but it doesn't change anything." Now, she inadvertently started twirling Blake's class ring between her right thumb and her index finger.

"You might be fooling yourself," I said, as I turned to walk away. "But you're not fooling me!"

I felt hurt and a little bewildered by the whole episode. And, over the next few weeks, it would be a feeling that just grew worse and worse.

I decided that I should concentrate on my relationship with Winnie; that I should put my efforts into someone who appreciated me. And, although my heart wasn't completely into it, my pride certainly needed a boost.

Winnie knew nothing about the night at the Y-Teens Dance, and nothing about the slow dance at the Glass Tower, but she knew that *something* was wrong. When I went to pick her up for a date the next Friday night, there was a certain tension in the air. I even hesitated to kiss her when she opened the door, and that never happened. We went to see a movie at the Mall Theater, about forty-five minutes from her house. It was the new Jack Nicholson film, *Five Easy Pieces,* and it took the pressure off by giving us something to talk about for the rest of the night.

Finally, on the way home, I asked her if she wanted to stop by the county airport. It was a small suburban airfield which serviced about ten private prop-plane flights a day. At this time of night, there would be no flights at all, just ten-thousand or so square feet of blue runway lights and a sky full of stars. Whenever I asked, "Do you want to stop at the county airport?" She knew that meant, *"Do you want to go parking?"*

It was our favorite place for necking, just the soft blue runway lights, and the moonlit sky and Motown music on the car radio. But when I shut off the engine, and pulled her against my chest, she hesitated. "Are you going to tell me what's wrong?" she said finally. "I've never seen you so quiet."

I tried to assure her that I was fine, but she wasn't buying it. "You're usually so sure of yourself," she whispered. "That's what I love about you. That's why I'm dating a guy three years younger than me; because you're cocky, because you're confident. But tonight, something's up. Are you going to tell me what it is?"

"Did you just say you loved me?" I teased.

"Don't change the subject," she sighed. "Tell me what's wrong."

And so, I did. I told her all about me and Lorraine. I told her about our first big dance last spring, and how I was sure she was going to be my girlfriend. I told her about Lorraine's mother and about how she said "no" when I wanted to date her. I told her about the Beaver Falls majorette and how I had lied. I told her about Blake and Lorraine, and how I was sure that that mismatch would never work out. Then, I told her about the previous Friday at the Glass Tower. I even mentioned how Lorraine had played *Love on a Two-Way Street* to get my attention.

Poor Winnie didn't know how to respond. "Are you saying you *love* this girl?" She pulled away from me now and put her back against the passenger-side door. The Thunderbird had just one long front seat, but she had always sat right up against me. It seemed strange to see her so far away.

"No, that's not what I saying at all," I responded. "I'm saying that I'm a little hung up on her; that I'm doing my best to forget her."

"Oh, I could *make* you forget her!" Winnie laughed. "I'm just not sure I want to date a guy who's on the rebound. I have to give this some thought." She put her hand to her chin, like that sculpture by Rodin. "Okay," She sighed, "I guess you're worth a shot." And she leaped into my arms, and finally initiated a long, passionate kiss.

"That's a pretty good start," I chuckled. But something had changed. Although Winnie and I had never gotten really intimate, I was shocked when she wouldn't even let me slide my hand up under her blouse. We had passed that milestone weeks ago.

"Maybe we had better slow down," she sighed.

"The rewards of honesty," I mumbled. And we both laughed, although neither of us was truly amused.

A few weeks later, the Christmas season was on us. I took Winnie to Midnight Mass on Christmas Eve, and afterwards, to a party at Aunt Betty and Uncle Joe's house, where I introduced her to my extended family. My dad and uncles all loved her. My mom was not so sure. "What does she want with a kid like you?" my mother complained. But my dad just kept smiling at me all night.

When New Year's came around, Winnie agreed to go to a New Year's Eve party being hosted by one of my classmates. This was no small concession. She would be among a group of kids three years younger than her, and I knew she would be a little uncomfortable. I'm pretty sure the only reason she wanted to go was to check out Lorraine for herself.

The party was actually at my friend Connie's house in Rockland. So, I would be on my home turf. And when we got to the party, things couldn't have started out better. All my buddies were blown away by Winnie, and she seemed to love all the attention. When we walked over to the punchbowl, she leaned in and gave me a big, wet kiss. I was so proud of her; so proud to be *with* her.

Finally, she whispered in my ear, "Okay, where is she?"

The party was being held on two floors of the house. Upstairs, on the ground floor, where music was being played on an old 45 rpm turntable and being piped through speakers throughout the house, and downstairs in the finished basement, where the snacks and most of the party guests were gathered.

For some reason, Lorraine had stayed upstairs with Blake. I knew they were hanging out by the turntable, picking out the music.

"She's upstairs," I told Winnie. "Do you really want to meet her?"

"I wouldn't miss it for the world," she replied. And at that moment I was pretty certain coming to this party was a mistake. Still, there was no way to avoid this.

"Come on," I said with a shrug, "Let's get this over with." I led Winnie up the stairs and into the kitchen, where Loraine and Blake were looking through a stack of Connie's forty-fives. "Hi," I called out to them as we approached the turntable. I hadn't spoken to Blake since the end of football season, and Lorraine just shook her head slowly. Just like me, she knew that this confrontation couldn't end well.

"This is my date, Winnie," I started. "And this is Blake and Lorraine. Lorraine and I are prom co-chairmen." As soon as the words left my mouth, I knew it was a mistake. First of all, Winnie knew about *me* being prom chairman, but had no idea that the girl I was meeting with every week was Lorraine. Now, she knew that the two of us *had* to work together. Second, we all knew that my mention of the prom was a cop out. It was like I was trying to downplay any feelings I had for Lorraine by acting like it was just prom-planning that linked us. Both ladies just rolled their eyes, and Blake nodded a greeting, then got up and walked away.

But Winnie wasn't done by a long shot. "So, if you have a boyfriend, why can't you keep your hands off my Teddy?" she smirked.

Out of the corner of my eye, I could see Blake stop dead in his tracks and look back over his shoulder. He hesitated for a moment, then thought better of it, and walked down the stairs.

"Maybe *your Teddy* likes having my hands on him." Lorraine smiled. It was obvious that she wasn't worried about Blake overhearing what she was saying. "Besides, if he ever told me to stay away from him I would. But, guess what, he never has."

The whole thing was getting out of hand, and I stepped between them and tried to lead Winnie back down the stairs. "Come on," I said. "This isn't helping anything."

"I'm not done," Winnie demanded, "Why are you protecting her?"

"I'm not protecting her," I argued. "I just want to celebrate the New Year with a little Peace on Earth. Let's get back down to the party."

Over Winnie's protests, I finally got her halfway down the steps, and for a moment, I thought that the worst was over. But, as one song ended, I could hear the sound of the record changer drop the next record into place. *I found love on a two-way street,* the singer intoned, and just as it had at the Glass Tower, our song (mine and Lorraine's) filled the air.

Except, Winnie *knew* about the song. She knew about the slow dance at the Glass Tower. She knew that Lorraine was sending me a message.

"Goddamn it," she said, stopping at the bottom of the stairs. Then she spun around and tried to push her way past me to get back to Lorraine.

"Forget about it," I pleaded. "Coming here was a bad idea. Let's go."

"Go where?" she demanded.

"You know what? My mom and dad are out for the evening, why don't we just go back to my house where we can be alone?"

"I think being alone might be a great idea," she shrugged. "I think we need to talk."

And somehow, I knew that this wasn't going to be the kind of evening I had envisioned.

My house was only a minute away by car, but when we walked into the darkened living room, there was no kissing and hugging. This was a moment of truth.

"Why did you protect her from me?" Winnie challenged.

"I just wanted to avoid a scene."

"A scene? A scene?" she screamed. "So, now you're ashamed of me?"

"I'm not ashamed of you. I'm proud of you!" I told her.

"Sure," she countered, "You want all your little friends to see me. You want them to think you're all grown up. But I don't play second fiddle to anyone!"

"You're playing *first fiddle*," I smiled, trying to lighten the mood, but she was having none of it.

"I saw how she looked at you," Winnie was furious now. "She *loves* you. And she wants me to know that she can get you back!"

"That's ridiculous," I shot back. "You're the only one I want!"

But Winnie just kept screaming. "And you tried to protect her. You love *her*!"

"I don't," I answered. "You're wrong. You're just wrong!"

"Okay," she said. "Then promise me something, altar boy. Promise me you don't love her. Promise me that even if we break up, that you'll never date her again. I want to hear you promise me!"

I took a step back and surveyed Winnie from head to toe. Her long, dark hair fell like silk, in ringlets across her shoulders. Her tiny 22-inch waist abruptly swelled into her round, 34-inch hips. Under her blouse, her braless breasts, though not big, were firm and high. I looked at her sweet face, her big brown eyes and pouty lips.

I swallowed hard. "I can't," I said. "I can't promise you that."

"I *knew* it," she cried, pulling her coat back on her shoulders. "You're a chump. She's just using you, and you're too stupid to realize it. Now, take me home. Take me home right now."

There was really nothing left to say. I put on my coat and gloves and drove her home. *How many times am I going to let this happen?* I thought to myself. *How many wonderful girls am I going to give up for this pointless dream?*

I never saw Winnie again. I heard she joined the Navy a few months later. Imagine that.

MORE IMPORTANT THINGS TO DO

Gene's phone was at it again. It was no wonder he had picked *I'm Still Alive* as the personal ring tone for Jan. It must have been his way of re-assuring himself that things could always get better.

"Are you going to answer that?" Lynn was awake now, and walked into the living room, wondering why the phone kept ringing, but nobody was answering it.

"That's Jan," Gene replied. "But I don't feel like talking to her."

"Well, I don't feel like listening to *Pearl Jam* anymore. It woke me up a half hour ago. She's not going to stop. Just answer it and get it over with."

"Hello," Gene sighed into his cell phone.

I could hear Jan's wailing voice from across the room.

"Man, that girl has a piercing tone," I chuckled to Lynn.

"No, I'm not ignoring you," I could hear Gene stumbling through his excuses. "I went out for a jog. Didn't take my phone."

Jan's cries of outrage were unintelligible from across the room, but I was pretty sure she wasn't buying Gene's excuses. "Don't you have to be at your internship at 8:00?" Gene interrupted. "When do you finish? I'll call you then.

"No," he continued. "You don't want to call off. It's important that you go. If you're done at noon, I'll call you at 12:30. No, I *promise* I will."

After another five minutes of haggling, he finally hung up the phone, then shook his head and walked back into the living room, looking up at the wall clock as he entered. "Well, I bought myself five hours of peace," he laughed.

Lynn just shrugged her disapproval and walked out of the room.

"How long are you going to put yourself through this?" I asked finally.

"I know. I know," he dropped his head and sat back down on the couch, "I should get away from her."

"You *should* get away from her," Lynn barked, as she took a bath towel from the hall closet and headed for the shower off the master bedroom. "And it should be soon."

"I know this relationship's not healthy," he shrugged, as he sat down across the room from me again. "I guess that, deep down, I just really want this to work out."

"Look," I told him. "If you're not ready to give up on her, then keep trying to work things out. But you can't let it affect your schoolwork. Miami's costing us thirty grand a year. Your priority has to be earning that degree. You can't spend all your time agonizing over this girl. You need other interests.

"You work at the campus radio station, right? Well maybe you need to spend your spare time there, learning the industry. You're in college to learn, Gene. You can't let this girl distract you. Besides, if you really dive into something else, you'll begin to see that the sun doesn't rise and set on Jan."

"Oh, is that what *you* did to forget Lorraine?" he smirked. "Did you *dive* into your school work?"

"Better than that," I smiled. "I'm a Rockland boy. Spring was coming, and the thing I dove into was baseball!"

A Good Season

I was sick of girls. I was tired of the dating game. I needed something real. And to a Rockland boy, there was nothing more real than baseball! The second half of winter was extremely warm for western Pennsylvania, and the high school team, which always started practicing in the gym in mid-February, was already practicing outdoors before the month had ended.

I thought we had a pretty good team, although we only had one starter returning from 1970. That team had won the section title and lost in the semi-finals of the WPIAL championship. Coach Sherman was a legend at Lakewood City High School with over 275 victories, and he had called that 1970 team the best he ever coached.

He wasn't saying anything like that about this 1971 team, but we, the players, knew we were good. Anytime, that 1970 team had gotten way ahead in a game, Coach Sherman would put in the second team players, and we always, *always* extended the lead. So, we knew that even our second team was better than most of our opponents' first teams. We were just waiting for our chance.

Sure, Lorraine and I still had prom committee meetings, and private planning sessions and car trips to Youngstown to pick up supplies. But, as I immersed myself in that baseball season, I could feel my old pride and cockiness returning. I was back in my element, back at shortstop, back on a baseball diamond. And, for once, I was putting Lorraine on the back burner. Her refusal to admit her feelings for me seemed like a small problem compared to a bad session in the batting cages. Her sickening obedience to her mother's match-making choice of Blake Bianchi paled in comparison to the embarrassment of dropping an infield pop-up.

Every day, I dove more and more into that team, that season, and everything else had to take a back seat. The team jelled quickly, and with the section games still a month away, Coach Sherman took advantage of the mild spring weather and started scheduling games with every high school team within a 30-mile radius of Lakewood City. We opened with a 2–1 victory over cross-town rival Riverside, then ran off five more wins in a row.

On the Monday after Easter (a school holiday), Coach Sherman scheduled *two double-headers* on the same day. These weren't cupcake teams, either. They were both playoff contenders. We had a morning-afternoon double header with the Beaver Bobcats in Beaver, followed by a twi-night double-header at home under the lights against the Butler Golden Tornadoes, a school with more than twice the enrollment of Lakewood High. We won all four games! Even when we got down to our third, fourth and fifth best pitchers, we just kept winning. And before March had ended, we were already 10–0.

I was hitting pretty well, and our infield just kept getting better and better. Sure, we had lost my buddy Jerry Delpino, who still had not fully recovered from that horrific leg injury ten months earlier. But, Coach Sherman moved our starting center fielder, Phil Lombardo, to third base to replace Jerry. We were loaded with good outfielders, but Phil was the only one who was right-handed and had some experience in the infield. He got better and better at the position, and our outfield never skipped a beat. Most high school teams had played only two or three games by the time April rolled around. We had already played ten, and the more we played, the better we got.

Of course, the Rockland-boys-versus-Lakewood-boys rivalry was always there, just below the surface, but it didn't seem to hurt the chemistry of the team, and everyone seemed to put it aside as the win totals kept mounting.

The only teammate/former opponent I still needed to deal with was a big right-handed pitcher named Rob "Baboose" Blaine. He and I had played against each other (and despised each other) for years. It all started at a Little League All-Star game when we were 12 years old. I was pitching for Rockland against

The Lakewood City All-Stars when Blaine lined a shot right back at my head. The ball knocked me off the mound, but I managed to get my glove up first and caught the liner before it hit me in the face. "You're lucky, punk," screamed Baboose as he trotted back towards the dugout.

Blaine was big as a house, and out on the street, under normal circumstances, I would have avoided antagonizing him anymore. But this was a baseball game. I could never show any type of weakness on the field. My weakness would indicate fear. And fear could weaken the whole team. "Go sit down," I barked with a wave of my hand. "Your ass is out!"

He started back towards the mound before his coaches grabbed him and pulled him into the dugout. *He can be rattled,* I thought, as I watched his teammates try to settle him down. I stored that information away for future use.

My next run-in with Baboose was just a year later. We were both thirteen and in our first year of Pony League. Rockland was playing at home against a team called Wur-Ell. It was a combination of two nearby towns, Wurtemberg and Ellicot, but to me it was just another Lakewood City team.

They had started a huge 14-year-old kid named Jim Porter against us. He was regularly a catcher but threw so hard that it was downright scary facing him, especially since he was pretty wild. Wur-Ell was ahead 2–1, when we came to bat in the bottom of the seventh, and last, inning. Porter got the first two batters out, but his wildness finally caught up with him, and he proceeded to walk the next three hitters. That loaded the bases for me with two outs.

The Wur-Ell coach couldn't tolerate Porter's wildness anymore. He came to the mound and called in his stopper, the Big Baboose! I stepped into the box and promptly lined his first pitch into the left-centerfield gap scoring Billy Conti from third and my cousin Tony from second. Rockland had an incredible, two-out, come-from-behind victory, and the 150 or so fans in the bleachers streamed out onto the field. It was the biggest hit of my life to that point, and I relished every second of the celebration.

But Baboose just stood on the mound glaring. He had already thrown his glove and hat into the stands, and now he gave a tremendous roar as he bent over and pulled the pitching rubber itself, anchored by two 10-inch spikes, out of the ground with one heave and tossed it into the outfield.

"This ain't over!" he screamed at me.

"Maybe you better take a look at the scoreboard," I chuckled.

He started toward me but was again restrained by four or five of his team-mates. "I mean between you and me," he barked. "This ain't over by a long shot!"

A couple years later, we were both attending Lakewood High, and when spring came around, I was playing shortstop for the Rockland Colt League team, while Blaine was playing for the Lakewood City Cubs, one of three Lakewood teams in the league.

"I'm pitching against you guys tonight," he barked at me as we passed each other in the hallways of the school.

"That'll be an easy win," I countered, as a crowd of students started gathering around us.

"You cocky son of a bitch," he growled. "I'm going to drill you with the very first pitch."

"Go ahead," I smiled. "Then I'll steal second and third and score on the first fly ball."

"When I hit you, you won't *get* up." Baboose laughed, while the pack of hyenas that cruised the hallways with him chimed in their own special insults.

"I'm from Rockland," I smirked. "Do you think I'm afraid of getting hit by a baseball? Hell, in Rockland we count those as base hits. You hit me. I get a base. We win. You lose. You play for yourselves. We play for our team. That's why these Lakewood teams are so easy to beat."

"Then I'll strike you out!" screamed Baboose.

"That's one thing you'll never do," I said shaking my head. "I *never* strike out!"

"We'll see about that!" he said, his voice growing fainter, as I hustled off to class. "You cocky bastard, we'll see about that."

Although I never really hit him consistently, in five years of playing organized ball against each other, Rob "The Big Baboose" Blaine never struck me out even once.

Now, Blaine was a senior and I was a junior, and we were trying to play as teammates. I was willing to let go of the past for the good of the team. But Baboose? Not so much.

The high school team's top pitcher in 1971 was a fire-balling left-hander named Joe Porter, the younger brother of Jim Porter, the big catcher who had pitched against us in Rockland all those years earlier. Joe was always a tough, crafty pitcher, but over the previous three years, he had shot up from 5'7" to over 6'1" and his fast ball was off the charts. He was our ace, but Blaine was a close second. It gave us one of the best pitching staffs in the state.

As we piled up win after win, the comradery between the Lakewood boys and Rockland boys grew deeper and deeper, except for Blaine. He still hated me, and to be truthful, I still despised him. It's so hard to put behind you all those years of rivalries and heated competition. For the most part, we both kept our mouths shut, but the hostility was always in the air.

Finally, in our fifteenth game of the season, all that changed. It was a Saturday, and we were playing a double header against our cross-town rivals, Riverside. We had won the first game 3 – 1, behind Joe Porter. But when Coach Sherman announced the line-up for the second game, he had replaced me at shortstop with a senior named Nick Martini. It wasn't unusual for Coach to rest a few players in the second game of a double-header, but I knew that he had been getting some flak from school board members and townspeople who thought he was playing too many Rockland boys. Besides me, our starting first baseman, Johnny Hudson, was also from Rockland.

In the previous season of 1970, Coach Sherman had started *three* Rockland boys, my cousin Tony DeVito, who led the team in hitting, big Derrick Dawson, who had already been drafted by the Detroit Tigers, as well as hard-hitting Billy Conti at third base. He caught a lot of criticism for that line up and this year there was more pressure than ever to play as many Lakewood City boys as possible.

I tried to ignore the sinking feeling that I was being targeted, but when I checked the lineup card, I could see that the only players getting *rested* were me and Johnny Hudson. With Blaine on the mound, Coach had moved Porter to centerfield and Don Hicks, another left-handed outfielder to first base.

My hope was that this was just a move to shut up his critics, and not a permanent lineup change. To be fair, Nick was a pretty good fielding shortstop, with good hands, good range and a decent arm. Based solely on his defense, Coach Sherman would surely have played the Lakewood boy. Nick's only problem was that he couldn't hit high-school-level pitching. *He'll hit himself out of the lineup,* I figured. *No use getting myself all worked up.*

The game was a pitching duel from the first inning on. Riverside started their ace, Darrius Montana, III. From the first pitch, everyone on our bench started ragging the kid about his name, but he shut us up by striking-out our first three batters, and then added five more shutout innings. No matter, Baboose was up to the task, he blew through the tough Riverside lineup without surrendering even one hit. When we came to bat in the bottom of the seventh and final inning, the game was still scoreless, and Blaine was sitting on an as-yet uncompleted no-hitter.

Finally, Montana began to show some weakness. He walked the first batter, Joe Porter. Then, after Donny Hicks popped out to third, he walked our catcher Rick Theisman. That brought Nick Martini to the plate with one out and runners on first and second. Nick had already struck out twice in the game, and without a second's hesitation, Coach Sherman summoned me from the bench to pinch hit for him.

Nick had been batting eighth in the lineup and Blaine, who was pitching and batting ninth, was in the on deck circle. As I swung a couple bats before entering the batter's box, he glared at me. "You better get a hit, Tresh," he barked. "Don't leave this up to me!"

"Put your bat away, Baboose," I smirked with bravado. "This game is over."

The truth was I was scared shitless to be forced into this crucial situation. But, this cockiness, this *show* I was putting on, was my defense mechanism against the haters. Now the only way out was to succeed.

Just as I stepped into the box, a tiny tornado-like dust storm began swirling between the mound and home plate, *dust devils* we used to call them, and before I could back out of the box, Montana hurried his wind-up to take advantage of the distraction. I knew it was too late to ask for a time out, so instead, I bore down my concentration and just tried to pick up the ball as he released it. I could barely see the pitcher through the dust storm, but the ball kind of popped out into the open, and for a moment, it just seemed suspended there, big as a honeydew melon. I lined it up the middle for a base hit, and Joe Porter flew around third and easily beat the throw to home.

149

THE LAST OF THE ROCKLAND BOYS

Half my teammates bounded onto the field and lifted me to their shoulders, while the other half of the team mobbed Rob Blaine in the on-deck circle, congratulating him on his no-hitter. When the two piles of humanity finally met in front of home plate, the Big Baboose just reached out his hand and rubbed my head. "You said you were going to do it," he laughed. "You said you were going to do it and you did!"

We were 15–0 after the victory. And with the all-important section games just a week away, the team seemed to be in harmony at last. Poor Nick Martini never played another game at shortstop, and Baboose and I, although never good friends, buried the hatchet that day, and got down to the business of winning a section championship.

DON'T LOOK NOW

"Okay, Dad," Gene interrupted my story with an uncharacteristic display of boredom. "Okay, so you dove into baseball to forget about the girl. You became this big star and you both went your separate ways. I get it. But, what if I'm not ready to forget about Jan? What if I don't want to just go our separate ways?"

"I didn't forget about her," I countered. "I just didn't make her the focus of my life. I didn't live and die with every word out of her mouth. I found something just as important, and I moved on to that."

"But I don't want to move on to something else," Gene implored. "If I don't focus on her, I'll lose her. She can't be ignored. I know you don't think that's important, but it's important to me. If I go about my business with classwork and the campus radio station, she'll just take up with someone else. That's what happened with your Lorraine, isn't it? You both moved on."

"Actually," I smiled, "That's exactly the opposite of what happened. Do you want to hear the story, or not?"

"I wouldn't miss it for the world," yawned Gene. "But don't be surprised if I rest my eyes for a little while.

"So, tell me about your *Glory Days*. Did they impress your dream girl? Did you keep chasing her around?"

"Of course, we were still being thrown together as prom co-chairmen," I shrugged, "But, as the baseball season wore on, she started getting more flirtatious again. There was a new sparkle in her eye, a new appreciation of our time together. Every time she looked me in the eyes, her gaze would linger. Every time our hands would touch, there was a five-second delay before we'd let go. Something was happening. I just wasn't sure what. But I'll tell you this for sure: My devotion to baseball didn't push us apart. If anything, it drew us together."

"Well, how do you explain that?" Gene wondered out loud. "You showed her less attention, so she showed you more attention? That doesn't make sense."

"Nothing about relationships makes sense," I laughed. "When I was chasing her, she concentrated on how she might lose Blake. But when I turned away, she started concentrating on how she might lose me."

"It helped that the baseball team was rolling along toward a section championship, and that I was having the best season of my life. My name was in the newspaper almost every day and the whole school started getting excited about the team. Somehow, her mother's suggestion that a Rockland boy was too far beneath her, made less and less sense to her. Here I was getting pats on the back from the guys in the hallways, and sweet smiles from the girls. Maybe she just started to realize what she was throwing away.

"At any rate, Lorraine started coming to my games again. She would even drag her friend Margie along to avoid any suspicion that she might be there for me, but it was pretty obvious that she was *my* fan and not just a Lakewood City fan."

"Was baseball really that important?" Gene wanted to know.

"To some of us it was," I nodded my head slowly. "But baseball, like all sports, was beginning to lose its glamour for the Baby Boomer generation. Even at the age of 16 or 17, we were already getting dragged into political debates about drugs and race relations, and the military draft. Hell, if the Vietnam War were to continue another two years, they would start pulling my graduating classmates and me out of school and sending us to Southeast Asia to die. That's pretty hardcore stuff for a teenager whose biggest problems had been getting a prom date or fielding a bad-hop ground ball.

"But I was a Rockland boy. For the first seventeen years of my life, I had lived and died with what I accomplished on the diamond. In Rockland, who you were on a baseball field was who you were! The whole world might be changing, but my values were ingrained in me. The better I hit, the more self-assured I became. Maybe, that's what attracted Lorraine, the self-esteem, or maybe it was just the little bit of fame I was beginning to enjoy. But, whatever the reason, we grew closer and closer as the season went on."

"You keep mentioning her mother's distaste for Rockland boys. Where did that come from?" Gene pondered.

"I think it was at least a generation old, Gene." I told him. The kids in my class didn't really look down their noses at Rockland boys. Sometimes they hated us, sure. But that was because of rivalries and hard-fought games and competition for playing time in high school sports. I don't really think the Lakewood students thought they were better than us. But some of their parents did.

"Their parents?" Gene looked surprised. "Where would their parents get ideas like that?"

"It was the politics of the Depression, Gene. Back in the Thirties, unemployment was over 40%. People didn't blame their leaders. They didn't blame the rich. They blamed each other. The politicians always play people off against each other. It wasn't that there weren't enough jobs. It was that someone else had *your* job. It wasn't that there wasn't enough food. It was that someone else was eating *your* food. And the suspicion and hatred wasn't directed at those who had everything. It was directed at those who had almost nothing, like the Italian immigrants in Rockland. They had come to the U.S. with nothing, stonecutters looking for work in the quarries in western Pennsylvania. But now the quarries were shut down, and the newly-poor were seen as parasites on the economy.

"Even the low-income Italians in Lakewood City needed somebody else to blame, and many of them blamed the little immigrant town of Rockland. That's the kind of poison that carries over from one generation to the next: *disdain for the poor*. Imagine that!

"But, by the time my generation came along, all those one-time immigrants were now war heroes. There were plenty of steel mill jobs for anyone who wanted one, but the need to look down their noses at someone else was deep-rooted in them, and that's the prejudice that some of them were passing along to their children.

"I'm not really sure how widespread that sentiment was in the town of Lakewood City, but for this particular woman, it was enough to blackball me from her daughter's life."

Gene got up now and went into the kitchen. It was nearly 11am. "Do you want me to make another pot of coffee?" he hollered.

"I'm all coffeed-out." I nodded. "Better pour me a screwdriver!"

"I'll make it two," he smiled.

"So, what happened next?" Gene said finally in mock displeasure.

"To the team or to Lorraine?"

"What does one have to do with the other?" he smiled.

"I guess that's the million-dollar question," I answered.

THE TROUBLE WITH HEROES

Our winning streak finally came to an end with a non-section loss to New Brighton on April 20, but we bounced back with two more wins and entered Section 5 play with a 17–1 record. The school was buzzing with anticipation.

In most high schools in Western Pennsylvania, baseball took a back seat to the football and basketball programs, but not in Lakewood City. The basketball team had 25 boys try out for the varsity squad. The football team had 54 prospects to choose from. But the baseball team had 85 ballplayers trying to make the 25-man roster. That meant 60 boys were cut from the team before the season even started.

Not coincidently then, the varsity football team finished their season at 4–6. The varsity basketball team was 6–11, while the baseball team was off to their best start in school history at 17–1.

Still, Section 5 was the toughest section in the State, as it included Beaver Falls, Hopewell, Aliquippa, Ambridge, Beaver, New Castle, and of course Lakewood City. And, unlike football and basketball, there were no class divisions in baseball, no A, AA, AAA, and AAAA. All 120 high schools in Western Pennsylvania (no matter how big their enrollment was) vied for *one* WPIAL Baseball title. Lakewood City had won the title in 1968 and reached the semi-finals in both 1969 and 1970. But we all knew that winning this section title would be a war, and most students treated us like war heroes in the midst of battle.

Lorraine was no different. She noticed every encouraging comment I got as I walked through the hallways of Lakewood High, every cheer that went up in the bleachers when I knocked in a run or made a play behind second base and threw out the runner. She had become my number one fan, and every day, I was sure, she got a little closer to dumping Blake and giving me a second chance.

The prom was drawing closer now too. It wasn't just planning meetings and trips to the party supply store now. It was work meetings and decorating committees and, two nights a week, we had to direct the entire junior class as they constructed giant 20-foot-high clam shells out of chicken wire and crepe paper, and painted Papier Mache caves and hung starfish from the ceilings in the gym. We were in charge of it all.

Of course, it was Lorraine who did most of the planning. She was much more artistically inclined than I was, and she was a much harder worker. But, for some reason, she let me run all the meetings. She'd hand me an agenda or a work schedule or the plans for turning the old gym into the Kingdom of Atlantis, and I would present the plan to our classmates. It was the old story of the woman behind the scenes doing all the real work, while the man takes all the glory.

"You can present this week's work detail," she'd say before every meeting. "And make sure they spend time actually working and not just flirting with each other. Remember, you're the boss."

"Why don't you run tonight's meeting?" I'd offer her. "These are your ideas. You should get the credit."

"They won't listen to a girl," she'd shake her head. "They respect you more. Besides you're tougher than me."

Of course, nothing could have been further from the truth. Lorraine was as tough as they came. But she was right, when she spoke, they practically ignored her. When I called a meeting to order, they begrudgingly came to attention.

Still, it was embarrassing for me to take credit for Lorraine's work. That's why I ended every meeting by saying, "Be sure to thank Lorraine. She's doing 80 percent of the planning and 90 percent of the work."

Certainly, I wanted to give credit where credit was due. But I also had an ulterior motive for being so humble. Every time I reminded the class of Lorraine's contributions, she would smile at me from across the room, and her gaze would linger for a full 30 seconds. *This girl's in love with me*, I would tell myself. *It won't be long now.*

We opened the section schedule against Hopewell, one of the toughest teams in the state. And although we trailed 1–0 going into the bottom of the last inning, our big catcher Rick Theisman came through with a two-out bases-loaded single to rally us to victory. Joe Porter got the win, surrendering just three hits to the powerful Hopewell squad.

After an embarrassing 9–2 loss to Beaver in the next game, we reeled off wins against Ambridge, Aliquippa, Beaver Falls and New Castle to finish the first half of the section schedule at 5–1 and sitting in first place.

The New Castle game was a real thriller. We led by just one run when they loaded the bases with two outs in the last inning. Up to that point, Rob Blaine had shut out New Castle, but now they had the tying run at third and the winning run at second. Coach Sherman signaled Baboose to throw from the stretch to keep the runner at second from getting too much of a lead off the base.

But the runner, who desperately wanted to make sure he could score on a single, took a huge lead anyway. From my shortstop position, I flashed Blaine the pick-off signal, fingers-to-the-cap, and he whirled and fired a perfectly timed pick-off throw to second to end the game. The team went crazy! I ran to the mound to celebrate, and the Big Baboose lifted me off my feet, losing his balance as he did. We both tumbled to the ground and were buried by our teammates, who jumped on top of the pile in celebration. You could feel the pride building. This was Phil Sherman's team. It was Lakewood *and* Rockland. The best of the best! We began to feel invincible.

The local newspaper, *The Lakewood City Ledger,* ran a photo of the celebration on page one, under the banner headline, *"Lakewood Grabs Section 5 Lead."* In the story that followed, they referred to me only as "Lakewood Shortstop Ted Tresh." It was the first time they did not add "*of Rockland*" to my name. We were finally being recognized, not as a group of all-stars from neighboring towns, but as a solid, harmonious team. Nothing could stop us now.

Back at school, the momentum of a successful season and possible championship rolled through the halls and into the classrooms. Even the teachers would congratulate us as we took our seats in class. Every kid seemed to slap me on the back. Every girl seemed to smile and wave. And Lorraine? She was like my Juliet, my forbidden fruit, my secret admirer. Every look in her eyes seemed to say, *we've got a secret, just we two.*

The second half of the section schedule started with an easy 8–0 victory over Aliquippa, pushing our section record to 6–1 (23–2 overall). We had played 25 games (while most of our opponents had only played about a dozen), and we just outclassed every team we faced, with a solid defense, heads-up base running and timely hitting. Then we travelled to Ambridge and completely fell apart.

The Ambridge game had been scheduled for Wednesday afternoon, but rain forced it to be postponed until Friday. Joe Porter took the mound for us again that day, and his curveball was off the charts. So much so, that our catcher was having a tough time handling it. We led 3–2 in the sixth inning, when a slow-rolling grounder slipped under the glove of our star second baseman Kerry Rolley, allowing the tying run to score.

Then in the bottom of the seventh inning, Joe gave up a leadoff single. The next batter was a left-hander, and Porter threw three big curveballs by him for the first out. But our catcher Rick couldn't handle the last breaking ball, which bounced off his glove and then his chest protector and lay on home plate in front of him. The batter took off for first base, while the runner from first took off for second and, with Rick's strong arm, should have been an easy out at second base. Instead, incredibly, he picked up the ball and threw to first base!

For Coach Sherman, this was the worst kind of error, a mental error. With first base occupied and less than two outs, the batter who was running to first was already out. There was no need to make a play on him. The throw should have gone to second. But now, the winning run was in scoring position.

Porter struck out the next batter, but Theisman again dropped the third strike. This time, with first base unoccupied, he did have to throw to first to retire the batter, letting the runner advance to third base with two outs.

Joe was furious but settled down enough to get his first two pitches by the next batter. With the count 0–2 he reached back and fired a high fast ball, hoping to get the batter to chase it out of the strike zone. If Theisman had been standing up, the pitch would have hit him right in the facemask, but in his catcher's crouch, he had to reach up for the ball. It nicked off the top of his glove and rolled all the way to the backstop, while the runner at third streaked home for the victory.

We all just froze in our positions. No one could believe what had just happened. Ambridge was a decent team, but they were no match for us at our best. We had played 25 games together. We were polished and slick. We took advantage of our opponents' mistakes. They didn't take advantage of ours. Now, here we were, shocked into silence. We had just given the game away. The loss dropped our section record to 6–2, tied with Hopewell for first place.

Coach Sherman was furious, and the confidence of the whole team was shaken. We filed back onto our bus and didn't say a word on the long ride home.

As we sat there lost in our own thoughts, I couldn't help thinking that this had actually been a pretty good game for me. I had two base hits and drove in two of our three runs. Before the game, I had been worried about a mild slump I was going through, getting only three hits over the previous five games. But today the ball looked big as a melon. I was comfortable at the plate and, Rockland boy or not, I felt ready to start taking a leadership role on this Lakewood City team.

Since the Ambridge game had been postponed until Friday due to rain, we had little time to brood. We had to face a tough New Castle Red Hurricanes team at our home field at 10 am the very next morning.

When I got to the field on Saturday, I could see that New Castle was starting their ace, Bobby Blackmon. He was a big fire-balling right hander, and although we had beaten him 2–1 earlier in the season, he had held me hitless. But that's when I was struggling. I was seeing the ball much better now, and I was looking forward to a big day at the plate.

We started "Baboose" in what was certain to be another pitchers' duel. Our team was still a little shaken from the shocking loss to Ambridge, and the usual confidence and cockiness was strangely missing from the dugout banter.

Our co-captains were senior second baseman Kerry Rolley, who for the moment was leading the team in hitting, and senior left fielder Gino Petrella, our clean-up hitter. But Rolley was still rattled by the ground ball that went through his legs at Ambridge, and Petrella was mired in his worst slump of the season. After infield practice, I decided to assert myself a little more. I had spent the last six years of my life being one of the leaders on the Rockland Little League, Pony League and Colt League teams and, outsider or not, it was time for me to show some leadership on this team.

"Come on, guys," I barked. "Let's get our heads into this game. We're still in first place, and dammit we're better than these guys – *we're better.*"

But Baboose walked the leadoff man, and their second batter, Larry Gardner (yes, the same Larry Gardner who would one-day become a personal injury attorney and one of my biggest advertising clients), singled to right field. The New Castle coach had signaled for a hit-and-run and their leadoff man streaked all the way to third base, leaving them with first and third and nobody out. It was way too early to worry about a single run, so we played with our infield back. The next batter was their 6'4" first baseman Dom Rossi who smashed a hard ground ball to me at short. I flipped it to Kerry, who turned a smooth, crisp double play, as the first run crossed the plate.

Blaine struck out their clean-up hitter on three fastballs to end the inning. Then the Big Baboose proceeded to shut down the Red Hurricanes for the next six innings, surrendering only three hits and no more runs the rest of the way.

It didn't matter. We couldn't get anything started against Bobby Blackmon. No matter how much I barked and clapped and prodded, I just couldn't get the team out of the funk from Friday night's humiliating loss. I singled in the second inning; doubled in the fourth; and singled again in the seventh. But all to no avail. Blackmon shut us out in convincing fashion. We managed only five hits, and I had had three of them. Our section record was now 6–3, a full game behind Hopewell, and our winning streak at the beginning of the season was a distant memory.

Back at the high school, we showered and got dressed in silence, and were just about to leave the locker room when Coach Sherman barked out, "Porter, Tresh, I want to see you in my office."

The office was a glass enclosure right inside the locker room, and Joe and I sat at the coach's desk as the rest of the team filed out. Besides our catcher, Rick Theisman, we two were the only juniors in the starting line-up, the rest were all seniors, and I couldn't imagine why the coach was singling us out.

"I need you two boys to come through for us," he began, as he closed the door behind him. "Joe, I know you just pitched yesterday, but we've got Hopewell on Monday, and we have to win that game. Do you think you can go on just two days rest?"

Porter hesitated for just a second, then nodded, "Yes, coach. If that's what it takes, then give me the ball."

"Teddy," he said, turning his attention to me. "You've been batting eighth in our line up all season long, and you know I hate to change a winning formula. But we're struggling to score. I'm moving you up to sixth in the order. It will give you more chances to drive in runs, but there's going to be more pressure too. Are you ready for it?"

"Yes, sir," I replied. "I've never been so ready in my life."

It had been a season of such promise; a season that started with a school record-setting 15-game winning streak and now Coach Sherman was placing the responsibility for the team's success squarely on the shoulders of two of his junior starters.

My dad had been at the game and was waiting outside in the parking lot to drive me home. "What took you so long?" he asked, as I stepped into the car.

"Sherman wanted to talk to me," I explained, then proceeded to tell him about Joe being asked to start on two days' rest, and me being moved up in the lineup.

"He should have moved you up in the batting order weeks ago," my father nodded. "You're the only one hitting the ball."

"You don't know this guy, Dad. He's very superstitious. He would never have made this change during the winning streak."

"Well, then I guess you'll have to start a new winning streak," my dad laughed.

On Monday, the disappointment of the weekend losses was evident in every hall and classroom in Lakewood High. Guys who, just a few days earlier, had been slapping me on the back, now averted their eyes when I walked by. Girls, who had been flashing smiles at me for weeks, now huddled and whispered when I came in the room. I'm sure the whole team was getting similar reactions all over the school. But, for a Rockland boy like me, whose very acceptance and popularity was tied directly to baseball, the change in the students' attitudes was even more devastating.

It's not really fair, I thought, *I'm playing the best baseball of my life. But, if the team keeps sinking, I'm the one who goes down with the ship.*

The only kids who seemed unaffected were the hippies, the *freaks* we used to call them. They always downplayed anything the athletes did anyway. There was an unorganized movement among the student body in Lakewood City to reject sports and popularity as a way of determining success. I'm sure that in the major urban markets and on college campuses this movement had been taking place since the mid-sixties, but here in Lakewood City, where traditional values died hard, it was still something new in 1971.

I was friends, or at least on a friendly basis, with most of the freaks. Their attitudes seemed more real and lasting than those of the frivolous student body at large. And they readily accepted the Rockland students without reservations.

I used to divide the hippies into two groups; the *bums,* who were ready to adopt any anti-social behavior and who were basically in it for the drugs and the escapism, and the *social activists,* who actually wanted to improve the country by advocating for an end to the war in Vietnam, reducing the voting age to 18, equal rights for women and minorities, and lots of other social causes. While there were extremes among the freaks, most of them were somewhere in the middle of these two sub-groups.

I wonder who my friends really are, I whispered to myself, as I walked the halls of Lakewood High on that fateful Monday. But I didn't really want to find out. I just wanted to start winning again.

"Joe, how do you feel?" I questioned our star pitcher, as I sat down beside him in home room.

"I feel like a win," he barked. "I feel like a damn shutout! How do you feel?"

"Like about five RBI's," I trumpeted in mock confidence. And, just like that, we were back in our comfort zone, back to our denial of any weakness, back into the cockiness that masked our fears. "Bring on Hopewell," I sang. "Tonight, we rise again!"

That afternoon, Joe Porter threw his best game of the season, striking out ten Hopewell Vikings, spearing a hot line-drive to the mound, and picking the lead runner off third base with two outs in the fifth inning. The game was scoreless until the sixth inning, when Porter smacked a bases-loaded single to give us a 2–0 lead. We only got two hits (I had the other one) off the Hopewell ace Tom Rogan. But no one was scoring on Porter today. We trotted off the field with a 2–0 victory and tied for first place at 7–3.

On Wednesday, we sent the Baboose to the mound against winless Aliquippa, and he recorded his third shutout of the section schedule. Meanwhile, the Beaver Falls Tigers did us a huge favor, knocking off Hopewell again. We went into the final game of the section season with an 8–3 record, while Hopewell had fallen to 7–4.

A win on Saturday against Beaver Falls would lock up Lakewood's fourth straight section title, while Hopewell would finish with a tough game at New Castle.

It was the most topsy-turvy week of my life; within just three days we had gone from second place to tied-for-first place and now, to first place alone. But baseball wasn't the only thing on our minds, because the Lakewood City Junior-Senior Prom was scheduled for Friday night. That was a big deal for nearly every student and every ballplayer, but especially for me, because I was the damn Prom Co-Chairman.

We had committee and decorating meetings every night that week. On Monday, after the big win at Hopewell, we didn't get out of the Art Club studios until after 10 pm. And, on Wednesday, after the victory at Aliquippa that put us in first place alone, the decorating committees didn't break up until almost midnight. Lorraine and I were alone at the school until 12:30 planning the final strategy for turning the Lakewood High School gym into the *Kingdom of Atlantis*.

"I don't know how we're going to get it all done," Lorraine looked up at me tearfully, as I drove her home in the wee hours of the night.

"We're going to do it," I smiled, as we crossed the Fifth Street Bridge and turned up Maple Avenue towards her house. "We've got a great committee.

Almost every kid in the Junior Class is obsessed with this prom, and they'll stay all night to finish the job if we need them to."

She looked up at me and shook her head in doubt. "I don't know if we can get it done in time. What if they don't take it seriously? What if they start goofing off?"

"Look," I answered. "You're the one who had the vision for this whole concept. You're the one who organized the committees. You laid out the work plans. You've created this whole Kingdom of Atlantis."

"But I don't think they respect me," she sobbed. "I don't think they take me seriously."

It was the problem women had faced throughout the ages. She had done all the work, faced all the challenges, had all the vision and ideas, but now she was at the mercy of students, both male and female, who could destroy everything, just because they might resent taking orders from a girl.

"We'll bring it home together," I assured her, as we pulled up in front of her house. "You just take charge of the committees, and I'll make sure they give you the respect you deserve. You've done 90% of the work up until now. But I promise to support you 100% the rest of the way."

We were seated in the long front seat of my dad's silver Thunderbird. And when I turned to look at Lorraine, she was already moving towards me. A few seconds later, we were wrapped in a long embrace, which morphed into an even longer kiss, sweet and wet and passionate. I was shocked at her boldness, shocked and delighted. *This is it,* I thought, *the time for us is right now.*

We came up for air for a second, and I was just about to lose myself in her arms again, when Lorraine looked over my shoulder and blurted, "Oh shit!"

When I spun around to see where she was looking, her mother's glaring eyes were burning a hole through me. "Shit," Lorraine cried out again. "What's she doing on the porch at 1 o'clock in the morning?"

"Big deal," I chuckled. "She'll get used to it."

"You don't understand," she brooded. "She's not ready for this. She's not ready for *you.*" And she leaped from the car and headed straight for the figure on the porch, never even bothering to look back."

"What was that?" I shouted to no one in particular, as I headed down the road towards Rockland. "What the hell was that?"

The next day in school, she acted like nothing had ever happened. It was vintage Lorraine behavior, and I had had just about enough of it.

"The decorating committee is pulling an all-nighter," she announced, as she met me in the Commons Area before classes the next morning, "Can you skip baseball practice tonight, so we can start right after school?"

"That's it?" I shook my head in disbelief. "*That's* what you want to talk about?"

"We have to get this done," she announced in a formal, business-like manner. "You said you would support me 100%. I hope you meant it."

"Don't worry," I answered. "I'll do my job, but not until *after* baseball practice."

She turned and walked away without uttering another word, and I just watched her disappear down the hallway.

This girl is not good for me, I thought as I made my way to my first class of the day. *I'm under all this pressure already. I've got to convince everybody in the Junior Class to pull an all-night work session tonight. Then get ready to take Amy to the prom tomorrow night. And then be ready to play Beaver Falls for the section championship on Saturday. But instead of concentrating on what needs to be done, I'm walking through the halls worrying and wondering if Queen Lorraine gives a shit about me.*

"I'm too busy for this!" I screamed at no one in particular. And I did my best to block out any thoughts of her for the rest of the day.

Respect

"So, remind me again why I should take advice from you," Gene joked. "You were in a worse mess than I am. Here, you were at the top of your game, practically a star. You were the prom co-chairman, so everybody in the class was taking orders from you. You had other girls interested in you. And you had this gorgeous girl who liked you, maybe even loved you. But she didn't treat you with, with…"

"Respect?" I added, finishing his thought.

"Yes!" Gene nodded. "That's the perfect word for it. She liked you, but she didn't respect you."

"That's exactly right," I nodded. "That's exactly what it was. I knew she had feelings for me, deep feelings. But how could she think that I would stand for that type of treatment? Sure, I blamed her mother, and I blamed the whole Rockland-Lakewood thing. I thought she was afraid to commit to me, because of what her family would say, because of what her friends would say. But, to string me along? That's just a lack of respect.

"The problem is that, for a long time, I didn't see it that way. I just thought there were problems that we could work out. I didn't understand that the family pressure and the peer pressure were just symptoms of a bigger obstacle. She didn't respect my feelings. She didn't respect me. And why should she? Whenever she beckoned, I was there. Whenever she apologized, I forgave her. Because she always seemed just out of reach. It was like her love was just a day away."

"Wow," Gene dropped his head. "That's what Jan is doing to me. It *is* a lack of respect."

"That's a hard thing to realize," I told him solemnly. "But that's why I told you about *The Cripple Creek Index*, remember? It's a way to take stock of your relationship, a way to decide if you really have a future together."

"I was wondering when we'd get back to that," Gene smiled. "What were those lyrics again?"

"Up on Cripple Creek she sends me. If I spring a leak, she mends me. I don't have to speak, she defends me. A drunkard's dream if I ever did see one," I said with a grin.

"Incredible," Gene nodded.

"Doesn't seem like such a mindless song after all. Does it?" I put my hand on his shoulder.

"I think I'll pour us another Screwdriver," he smiled, heading for the refrigerator. "So, what happened next?"

FACE YOUR FEARS

A t the baseball field that afternoon, I was bubbling with confidence. Infield practice was ten rounds of smooth fielding, crisp throws, and effortless hustle. I was in the best shape of my life, and I glided around the diamond like I was born there.

When I got up to the plate for batting practice, the ball looked as big as a cantaloupe. I was always a good line drive hitter, but now I was also driving the ball deep into the outfield gaps, and even pounded one long fly over 350 feet to dead centerfield. The whole team looked sharp, and I felt confident we could handle Beaver Falls on Saturday.

When I arrived back at the school later that night, the prom decorating was at a fever pitch. We had a delivery of two tons of sand poured out across the entrance to the Commons Area. And with giant sheets of plastic covering the tile floor, members of the junior class were shoveling it out until the entire Commons Area was four inches deep in sand.

To the left was the entrance to the school's main hallway and, above the entrance, a full-sized waterfall had been fabricated. It looked so real! Water poured down into a pool beneath and was pumped back to the top. The waterfall was angled in such a way that it would allow prom-goers to walk behind it and into the hallway, which was covered by long crumpled sheets of coarse, gray construction paper, molded and highlighted with touches of white paint, so that it looked just like the inside of a real cave. You couldn't even tell the school walls were behind there. "This is amazing," I nodded as I headed down the darkened hallway.

"You really have no idea what this is going to look like, do you?" I could hear Lorraine's voice behind me. She had seen me come through the door and was ready to pounce. "Come on," she commanded. "You need to take charge of the giant clam shell bandstand. It's way behind schedule, and I need those people to start painting fluorescent fish in the underwater cave."

As she got closer, I could see she had a streak of blue poster paint on the side of her nose and halfway across her face. "Come here," I laughed, as I pulled a clean handkerchief from my back pocket and started dabbing at the dried paint. "It won't come off," I said in mock disgust.

I took a step back and looked into her smiling eyes. "Here," I whispered. "Let me make it better." Then I dabbed the handkerchief to my tongue, and started wiping away the blue streak, little-by-little.

Her smile turned into something deeper. "You just took my breath away, again" she sighed. And then immediately spun away, barking, "Come on. Come on. We've got hours and hours of work to do before we can get out of here tonight."

Just for a moment I got a flashback, back to my grade school days, back to Molly, my little ten-year-old girlfriend. Lorraine had the same smile, the same sigh, and the same big brown eyes. Of course, Molly never had Lorraine's hips or her bust line or her sex appeal. But she did have something Lorraine didn't have: steadfastness, commitment, and pride in us as a couple. *Imagine what the world would be like if Lorraine felt like that?* I wondered.

"Teddy, let's go!" She chirped out again, and I followed her into the old gym.

When I looked up, it seemed like the entire ceiling of the gym had vanished, and all I could see were giant parachutes hung from the rafters, pulled and tucked in such a way that it seemed we were looking up at the waves from underneath the sea. "Holy shit," I gasped. "This is beautiful!"

"Yeah," she said, shaking her head again. "But the bandstand's not so beautiful. Get those people to work on that giant clam shell."

It was a simple task. The round frame of the arched clam shell had already been wrapped in chicken wire and all the committee members had to do was twist a wad of crepe paper into each hole. Each wad looked amazingly like a carnation, and the whole shell looked like a giant bouquet. Pink crepe paper outlined the edges of the shell with white paper wads covering the rest. I could see that it was going to look great, but only about a third of the clam was finished. It didn't require much creativity, but there were still about ten thousand chicken-wire holes to fill, and a lot of our classmates were just goofing off, while two or three volunteers were doing all the work.

"Alright, let's go." I shouted. "We don't have all night for this damn shell. Let's get it done." And everyone snapped to attention. With ten dedicated workers, we completed the project in less than an hour. *I'm not really like a chairman,* I thought, as we hoisted the top of the huge shell into its open-mouth position. *I'm more like a foreman.*

We placed the large wooden bandstand inside the "mouth" of the clam, and then focused the floor lights onto the stage. *This is going to look fantastic,* I said to myself shaking my head in disbelief. *How did she figure all this stuff out?*

The decorating took all night, installing black lights in the caves and positioning fake palm trees on the fake beach. The Art Club members had painted fish and octopi and underwater scenes in fluorescent colors throughout the gym and cave walls, and a giant Papier Mache statue of Poseidon graced the great underwater pillars and coliseums.

By 7 a.m. the sun was shining on a bright Friday morning, as the last of the junior class volunteers made their way back home. The school had given both juniors and seniors the day off to prepare for the prom. After a few hours' sleep, the guys would be washing and vacuuming out their cars and picking up their date's corsages. The girls would be getting their hair and nails done and slipping into their prom gowns.

Lorraine and I were the last ones to leave. We took one last walk through the entire kingdom we had created. The caves with their florescent fish and their black lights looked like the inside of a gigantic aquarium. The walls and ceilings of the old gym were completely transformed by the underwater scenes of ancient buildings and giant clams, and you couldn't even tell you were *in* the gym.

"I can't believe this," I wondered. "It doesn't even look like a school. It really looks like an underwater kingdom. You did it!"

"*We* did it," she corrected me. "You're the one who got things done."

"But you had the vision," I told her. "None of this happens without you." And while I was still looking at the handmade beach and the flowing waterfall, I felt her kiss, wet and warm on my cheek. But, when I turned to return the favor, she slipped away from me.

"You better go home and get some sleep," she winked. "You've got a big night tonight and a big game tomorrow."

We stepped out into the bright morning air together, and it felt like the dawn of a new day for us too. "See you tonight," she smiled. "Maybe next year, we can do this together."

I drove home in a daze, set the alarm for noon, got into bed, and closed my eyes. But sleep was the last thing on my mind.

I dozed, off and on, for about four hours. I have no idea how much actual sleep I got. And then, I got up and headed across town to pick up the purple Plymouth Duster I was borrowing for the big dance. It's funny, my dad's silver Thunderbird was a much nicer car, but for some reason we all borrowed someone else's car for the prom. It was kind of an unofficial tradition, which added some glamour to the big night. I had asked one of the great former Rockland shortstops, Eddie Danza, if I could borrow his Plymouth Duster. I had often seen him cruising around town in the car, and I knew it would perfectly match Amy's purple prom gown. "If you wash it and wax it, you can borrow it for the night," the local legend said.

A few hours later, I was pulling up to Amy's house in my brown crushed-velvet tux and my sparkling purple Duster. She looked like a dream when she stepped through her front door, all lace and fineness, with her hair done up in ringlets and just the right amount of that blue eye shadow that makes beautiful young girls look like beautiful young women.

But, two seconds later, the spell was broken when her boyfriend, now back from college for the summer, stepped out onto the porch to take our pictures, posing us on the front steps and then near the fireplace inside the house. He even took my hand and placed it on her waist for a shot next to the purple Duster. "I'm sorry," Amy whispered between shots. "He just showed up with his camera. What could I say?"

"It's okay," I told her. *What did you expect?* I thought to myself. *You never took her seriously because you wanted to be available for Lorraine. That's why you dated a girl with a college boyfriend. So, no one would get hurt.*

But we had a great night anyway. Dancing in the darkened gym with about 200 other couples, we were cheek-to-cheek most of the night. At ten o'clock, we left the gym and rode across town to the Sons of Italy Hall for the "After Prom." As each couple arrived, the sophomore emcee introduced us. "The next couple is Amy Maroni, escorted by Prom Co-Chairman Ted Tresh."

We got a huge round of applause from all the parents and well-wishers who had gathered on the sidewalk at the entrance to the hall. "Best prom decorations ever!" yelled somebody's mom from the crowd. And there were shouts and nods all around. In fact, all night long, classmates had been showering me with compliments and congratulations. "It was ninety percent Lorraine's doing," I had tried to explain. But everyone passed it off as modesty.

The After Prom was scheduled to start at 10 p.m. and end at 5 a.m. It was the wildest party I had ever seen. Amy looked gorgeous and couldn't have been sweeter to me. But, of course, I kept getting distracted by Lorraine and Blake. She was the Belle-of-the-Ball in her baby-blue, low-cut gown, and he kept his right hand planted on the small of her back all night long.

Around midnight, the Lakewood City Ledger's photographer arrived and called for a shot of all the adults who had served on the After Prom Committee. "Now, let's get one with the prom co-chairmen," he shouted.

Lorraine and I stepped up on stage with the adult committee members, who ushered us to the front and center of the group photo. It was the first chance I had to talk to Lorraine without Blake hanging on her. "Pretty romantic night, isn't it?" I teased her.

She shot me a quick smile, looked around for witnesses, and then grabbed my ass just as the photographer snapped our picture. "You're pretty daring in the dark," I laughed. "But you shouldn't bring out those hands unless you're ready to use them." We parted with our customary long and longing gaze, but went our separate ways for the rest of the night.

I went back to my table to join Amy. We were sitting with my buddy Jerry and his date Colleen. Jerry was still on crutches. His broken leg had now been in a cast for nearly a year. "You better not stay too late, Ted Tresh," Jerry warned. "You've got to beat Beaver Falls tomorrow."

"Sorry you're not with us, buddy." I lamented. "It should be me and you on the left side of the infield." Ever since Jerry and I had made the varsity squad as freshmen, we had dreamed about being starters in our junior year. We even called ourselves *The Left Side of the Infield.* But while I was living our dream this season, Jerry was quietly sulking in the bleachers. Luckily, he had found Colleen, who worshipped him and made his life on the living room sofa a lot more bearable.

"So, you go out and win the section title tomorrow and we'll all go to Idora Park for a picnic on Sunday," he smiled bravely. It was a tradition in Lakewood City that prom couples went on picnics and excursions on the day after the big dance. But, with the Beaver Falls game looming, Jerry and Colleen and Amy had all agreed to postpone the date until Sunday.

"If you lose the game, you still have to take me to Idora," Amy smiled. "And you have to act happy!"

"If I'm with you, I'll *be* happy," I flirted, almost reflexively. "Just make sure your boyfriend doesn't come along to take our pictures." And although we had consumed no alcohol, we all laughed that drunken laugh you get when fatigue is starting to distort your brain.

"Are you coming to the game?" I asked Amy, who was never much of a baseball fan.

"Hell, no," she answered, "I need my beauty sleep. If you guys win the section, and win the playoffs, and go all the way to the championship game at Three Rivers Stadium, I promise I'll go to the game."

"Three Rivers," moaned Jerry. "I might have been playing at Three Rivers Stadium."

The WPIAL Championship game was always held at the home of the Pittsburgh Pirates, but this year that was more important than ever, because in July of the 1970 season the Pirates had moved from their ancient home at Forbes Field in the Oakland section of Pittsburgh to their brand-new multiplex stadium on the North Side. Three Rivers was huge and bright and sported a 100-foot scoreboard and artificial turf. I had never even seen artificial turf, and in 1971, the thought of playing on it was every high school ballplayer's dream.

As the dance finally neared its end and Amy and I completed one last waltz around the room, we were nearly sleeping in each other's arms. Finally, we all exited the SOI hall, as the sun came peeking over the rolling hills of Western Pennsylvania. I drove Amy home and kissed her goodbye. "Good luck today," she smiled. "But you're so good, you won't need it."

I made my way back to the purple Duster alone. *This whole year could have been different*, I thought to myself, *if I could just have gotten over Lorraine.*

I drove the Duster back to Eddie Danza's house in Rockland, and then walked the three blocks back home. It was 9 a.m. and the game was scheduled for 3 o'clock. I set my alarm for four hours sleep, but never closed my eyes.

At the game that afternoon, some of the senior baseball players looked worn out. Most of the underclassmen had headed home in the early morning to grab a few hours' sleep, but many of the seniors didn't want to miss any part of their last prom date. Some had snuck flasks of booze into the after-prom. Some had gone straight to their Saturday picnics with their dates and hadn't slept in over thirty hours!

It was 85 degrees that afternoon, and just before game time, I walked over to where Joe Porter, our starting pitcher, was warming up with our junior catcher Rick Theisman. "We've got to play well today, boys," I chirped. "Most of the seniors look hung over.

"How's the arm feel, Lefty?" I said, out of habit.

"It frickin' hurts," Porter moaned.

Now I was alarmed for real. "What do you mean, it hurts?" I screamed, remembering that just five days earlier, he had pitched us into first place on only two days' rest.

"It's been sore since Monday." Joe confided.

"He's struggling, Teddy," barked Rick from 60 feet 6 inches away. "But he's still throwing hard and he's still hitting his spots."

"Can you go, Joe?" I whispered, as I stood beside him near the warm-up rubber.

"What choice do I have?" shrugged Joe.

"Let coach know," I suggested. "Maybe Blaine should throw today?"

"If you say anything to Coach Sherman, I'll kill you," he glared back.

He's just like a Rockland boy, I thought, as I turned to head back into the dugout. *He doesn't care about personal injuries; he just cares about winning.*

I decided to hit the men's room once more before the game, but when I walked through the door, I could hear someone in the stalls vomiting violently. A quick peak through the door frame confirmed my worst fears. Our senior right fielder Jay Farroni had been out all night and was now paying the price. *Shit,* I thought. *This could be bad.*

In the top of the first inning, Porter already showed signs of weakness. He walked the first two Beaver Falls batters. Then their number three hitter lofted a routine fly ball to right field, where Farroni should have been planted under it. But the hung-over outfielder charged the ball instead, and then watched helplessly as it fell to the ground behind him for a bases-clearing double.

Coach Sherman was furious. He could see Farroni was in no shape to play baseball, and he immediately walked out to the mound and pulled the senior right fielder from the game, sending largely untested junior outfielder Curt Fairmont in to replace him. To make matters worse, Jay batted third in our line-up. So, Curt wasn't only playing, he was right near the top of the order.

We all congregated at the mound as we watched Fairmont jog out to his position. "We have to end this threat right now, men," Coach Sherman confided. "If we get any further behind, we may not be able to come back."

But Beaver Falls wasn't done. After a strikeout, they managed another base hit, and then another walk to load the bases. That brought up the Tigers' hard-hitting sophomore right fielder Sammy Bellissimo.

Sammy was a familiar face. He was a Rockland boy, just a year younger than me. While my age group was the last Rockland class to go to Lakewood High, Sammy's age group was the first Rockland class to go to Beaver Falls. It was a changing-of-the-guard of sorts. The baseball talent from my hometown had always impacted the Lakewood City teams; but from now on, they would be impacting the Beaver Falls teams instead, all because of the bussing and anti-segregation issues that were spreading across the United States.

Someday, Rockland boys will be fighting for section titles for Beaver Falls, I thought. *Someday, all of Rockland will be behind them instead of behind us.*

Sammy stepped up to the plate and smashed Porter's first offering right up the middle. But Joe speared the line drive as it passed the mound, and then whirled around and fired to third base to nab the runner, who had broken for home on the crack of the bat. The unlikely double-play saved us from anymore damage.

As we came up to bat in the bottom of the first inning a busload of unfamiliar baseball players pulled into the parking lot and started filing into the stands. It was the entire Hopewell Vikings baseball team. Their noon contest at New Castle had ended in victory when the Vikings' fire balling senior Ed Bondel threw a no-hitter against the Red Hurricanes for a big 2–0 decision. That left them with an 8–4 section record, just a half game behind us at 8–3.

Now, we knew we needed to win. And, we knew we'd have to come back from a two-run deficit with the entire Hopewell team trying to rattle us from the bleachers.

In the bottom of the first, we scored one run on an error, a walk, and an infield single. I was batting sixth in the lineup and came to the plate with two outs and runners on second and third. I battled to a 3–2 count, while players from both teams, as well as the Hopewell squad in the stands, taunted and cheered and moaned with every pitch.

Beaver Falls was throwing a kid named Tommy Serkovitch. His older brother had been a major league pitching prospect and had led the Tiger baseball team to a WPIAL Championship game in 1966. But Tommy was *not* as good as his brother. He grooved the 3–2 pitch belt-high and right down the middle. I lined it into center field for a two-run single to grab the lead. We added one more run and ended the inning up 4–2.

In the second inning, we scored two more runs on a bases-loaded, two-out single by our senior first baseman, John Hudson. Like me, Johnny was a Rockland boy. He batted ninth in our lineup but was about to go on the hottest hitting streak of his life. Along with senior base-running specialist Skip Bruno, Johnny and I were the last three Rockland boys to ever play for Lakewood High.

In the stands, half of the Rockland fans at the game were rooting for Beaver Falls. *I hate to see things change,* I thought to myself. *Someday all the Rockland fans will be Beaver Falls Tigers' fans.* "But not today," I said to Skip, as we watched Johnny take his lead off first. "Not today!"

By the fifth inning, we had a 9–3 lead, and we watched the Hopewell team file back onto their bus and drive away. I managed another single in the sixth inning and was bouncing all over the infield making plays.

It was as near to a perfect game as I would ever play. In the third inning with one out, Beaver Falls had tried the old first-and-third-double-steal. We had practiced defending against that play all season long, so no one was surprised that I cut off Rick's throw to second base and fired to home to cut down the runner trying to score from third. I also fielded two ground balls that appeared to be headed for base hits up the middle and fired out the runners at first base. By the time the sixth inning rolled around, a frustrated Beaver Falls Head Coach Joe Shantz was actually shouting in frustration, "Stop hitting the ball to shortstop," to his batters.

And by the time the game ended, I had two hits, three RBIs, and had made every defensive play I could reach, including an over-the-head catch of a pop-up down the left field line. The next day, the Lakewood City Ledger ran a photo of me grabbing that pop-up behind third base. "Tresh aided Porter greatly with seven assists and three putouts," the cutline beneath the photo read.

Since there are only twenty-one defensive outs to be had in a seven-inning game, the fact that I had played a part in *ten* of them, was probably more important than anything I had done at the plate.

We ended up beating Beaver Falls 9–4 and grabbed the section title with a 9–3 record, a full game ahead of Hopewell's 8–4.

For the season, we were now 26–5, and to top it off, the victory was the 300th of Coach Sherman's storied career. No other Lakewood City coach in any sport had won even 100 games.

We were ready for the playoffs. We knew it, and so did every other school in the WPIAL.

The next morning, I picked up Amy around 9 a.m., and shuddered when I saw her boyfriend once again waiting there with his camera in hand. We let him take a few pictures of us, and then hopped into the Thunderbird and drove away. Amy was wearing white shorts and a light blue blouse. As soon as we lost sight of Jeff in the rear-view-mirror, she proceeded to pull out the shirt-tales from under her beltline, and tie them in a knot in front, revealing her well-tanned abs. I tried not to stare, but I ran straight through the stop sign at the end of her block.

"Watch where you're going," she laughed.

"Okay," I answered. "But how did you get a tan like that in May in Western Pennsylvania."

"I've been laying out in my back yard for four weeks," she smiled. "Sometimes it was only forty degrees out there."

"I guess you have to suffer to be beautiful," I smiled.

Amy was quiet for over a minute. "Do you think I'm beautiful?" she asked finally.

"You *know* I do," I answered. "It's just that…that…" I hesitated.

"That I'm not Lorraine?" Amy smirked.

"I didn't say that. Don't put words in my mouth."

"But it's true, right?" Amy kept smiling, but it didn't seem to fit the rest of her face. "*She's* the love of your life, right?"

"What about Jeff," I argued, "isn't he the love of *your* life?"

She only hesitated a second. "No," she answered. "I don't think he is." And she didn't say another word until we reached Rockland, where Jerry and Colleen were waiting to leave for our double-date to Idora Park.

It was a magical date. I was still flying high from the section champion-ship game, while Jerry and Colleen had this *lovers' euphoria* that made every joke seem hilarious and every comment seem meaningful. Amy, of course, looked gorgeous, just like a 17-year-old Italian beauty should. Still, I couldn't get Lorraine off my mind. She had been with Blake for 24-straight hours. She had been at almost every game all year long, but she was missing-in-action for the section championship.

I wonder what they did all night. I tortured myself with the thought. *And all day Saturday?*

Amy and I rode dozens of rides that day. In spite of her fear of roller coasters, I talked her into going on *The Jack Rabbit,* the smaller of Idora's two coasters, and she hung on to me for dear life, just as I was hoping she would.

Finally, all four of us got in line for the park's tunnel-of-love ride, *The Rapids.* It was called that because after cruising through a dark tunnel for about 3 minutes, the boat would latch onto a chain which pulled it into the light of day and up the tracks of a 50-foot-high hill before it plunged back into the water and floated to a stop, usually soaking the riders along the way.

As we boarded the boat, which held four couples, Jerry and Colleen slid into the seat right in front of us. The ticket-taker gave Amy a quick head-to-toe glance as we passed him, and then shook his head slowly and winked at me as I followed her into our seats.

He's right, I thought, *she's a living doll.* But I just didn't see any future in it. I had kissed Amy a hundred times before, but they were mostly good-night kisses, never anything meaningful. I put my arm around her as I took my seat, but only kissed her once during the entire trip through the tunnel. It didn't help anything that Jerry and Colleen were in the seat in front of us, flopping around like two dolphins trying to mate on the beach.

She has a boyfriend, I figured. *She might just slap my face if I come on too strong.* But deep down inside I knew it was me, not Amy, who was shying away from commitment. When I left her off at her house later that evening, I kissed her goodbye one more time. We never dated again.

I didn't dwell on it long though. I was a Rockland boy, living a Rockland boy's dream. There were sixteen teams in the WPIAL baseball playoffs, sixteen section champions, and we were just three wins away from a trip to Three Rivers, and four wins away from a league championship. There was no time to think about girls right now. *Win this championship and everything else will work itself out,* I thought.

Plus, I was one of the last three Rockland boys to play for Lakewood City, and a year from now; I would be *the* last Rockland boy to wear the Blue and White of the Lakewood City Wolverines. *Wouldn't that be a dream come true?* I wondered. *Wouldn't that be a great way to say goodbye?*

We started the playoffs the next Wednesday, against a familiar opponent, New Brighton. They had ended our 15-game winning streak at the start of the season, and then went on to win their own section championship a month later. But this was no meaningless non-section game. This was the WPIAL playoffs, and we sent our stopper, Joe Porter out against their best pitcher, Randy Lane.

The game was close for a while, but we had played thirty-three games to that point in the season, while New Brighton had only played about twenty. And by the fourth inning, our class and experience started to shine through. With one out in the bottom of the fourth, New Brighton had runners on first and second, when Lane came to the plate and smashed a hard ground ball between third base and shortstop. It looked like a sure base hit. But I lunged at the ball and made a spectacular back-hand play. Everyone thought I would flip the ball to our third baseman, to get the lead runner at third, but the ball had been hit so hard that I figured *we can get two.* I spun around a fired a strike to our second baseman, who stepped on second and whipped the ball to first to complete the inning-ending double play.

"Good play short," sighed Lane as I passed him on the way to the dugout. *He's a good sport,* I thought, *but that play had to shake him. He's got to be wondering what the hell they have to do to score a run.*

As happens so often in baseball, the guy who makes a great play in the field inevitably leads off the next inning. A shaken Randy Lane went back out to the mound, and I lined his first pitch up the middle for a base hit. The single started us on a three-run rally. And, although New Brighton finally managed a run in the bottom of the sixth, we added two more in the top of the seventh and finished with a solid 5–1 win.

As we boarded the team bus for the ride home, I saw Lorraine walking towards the student bus. Blake apparently had better things to do that day. "Great game, Teddy," she was beaming, and we locked eyes until she disappeared from my sight.

"It won't be long now," I thought, as I sat on the team bus, celebrating our victory. *"It's been over a year since I lied to her about that dinner-dance date. Surely, she knows I deserve another chance by now. She wants to get back together. It was written all over her face."*

Three days later in the quarter-final game, we threw the Big Baboose in the second round of the WPIAL Playoffs and came away with a 6–2 victory. I stayed hot with a single and triple, and fellow Rockland boy, Johnny Hudson, our first baseman, smacked two hits and had three RBIs. We were cruising toward the title game, but our toughest test of the season was just four days away.

All season long, the biggest newspaper in Western Pennsylvania, *The Pittsburgh Press,* had been publishing a coaches' poll of the top ten high school baseball teams in the WPIAL. When we opened 15–0 back at the start of the season, Lakewood City had moved up all the way to #4 in the poll. There were 120 baseball teams in the league, and it was a big honor to be listed among the top ten teams, but after we took six loses during the season, we had dropped off the newspaper's radar.

I never thought that was fair. We played in the toughest section in the state. Hopewell, Beaver Falls, New Castle, Ambridge, and Beaver, any of them could have made the playoffs. And any of them could have competed for the title. Plus, we played more games than any other school in the league. Hell, we once played *two* double-headers in *one* day and eight games in one week. *Of course* we had more losses than those other teams. Some weeks we got down to our fourth or fifth or sixth best pitcher. What other team could win with their sixth-best pitcher on the mound?

But Coach Sherman wasn't trying to go undefeated. He was trying to get us to play together as a team. "The only way to prepare for baseball is to *play* baseball," he would say to anyone who ever questioned our huge schedule. And we were always the most prepared team on the field, if not the most talented. Anyway, our playoff run had us back near the top of the poll.

There were only four teams left in the WPIAL playoffs now, and we drew the #1 seed, West Mifflin North as our next opponent. The Press poll had the top four listed this way: #1 West Mifflin North, 24–0; #2 Penn Hills, 19–1; #3 Highlands, 16–1; #4 Lakewood City 29–6.

The day of our semi-final game with West Mifflin North was a Monday, and it was also graduation day at Lakewood High School. It seemed strange not to see the seniors in the hallways. Actual classes for the rest of us didn't end until Friday, so I had a whole week to court Lorraine without Blake around.

The entire school was buzzing about the baseball team. One more win and we would be one of the first two high school teams ever to play at Three Rivers Stadium; that was our goal from the first day of practice in February, and now it was just one more win away. All we had to do was beat the team that *The Pittsburgh Press* had called, "The best Pennsylvania high school baseball team of the last decade."

Who could argue? Their pitching ace was a kid named Kurt Dewey. He had thrown *two* no-hitters during the season and had a bus full of college and pro scouts following him everywhere he went. I was playing the best baseball of my life, but deep down I had to wonder whether that would be good enough against this kid. Plus, their lineup was packed with .400 hitters. Nobody in our lineup had hit .400. I was the closest at .388.

We lucked out in one respect; the location of the game was in our favor. The WPIAL playoff games were always played at a neutral field, but high-quality facilities were hard to find. The infield grass had to be plush, and the base paths had to be lined with red clay. The field had to be completely surrounded by a fence, so that the WPIAL could charge admission to the game, and no fans could see the game for free.

The stadium they choose for the semi-final game was the fine sports complex at Hopewell High School. That was a gift for us. Hopewell was in our section. We played on this field at least once per season. We knew to what degree the infield grass would slow down a ground ball. We knew the angles that the sun and shadows could take. We knew how much space we had to catch pop fouls before running into the bleachers. We were in our comfort zone, while West Mifflin North would be playing on a field they had never seen before. That was important to a team like us, a team that won with defense and mistake-free execution, not always the most talented team, but always the best prepared.

Our players' bus arrived at the Hopewell field at 3 o'clock, an hour before game time, but most of the West Mifflin North fans were already there. So were a handful of major league scouts, setting up in the stands directly behind home plate. One wore a Baltimore Orioles hat. One had a Dodgers hat, and one wore a Polo shirt with the Yankees logo on the pocket. Michigan State was represented. So were Auburn and the University of Arizona.

"I guess they heard about me," joked our co-captain and clean-up hitter Gino Petrella. But we all knew they were here to watch Dewey.

While we warmed up before the game, I noticed that all the scouts carried what looked like police bull horns on their laps. "What are they doing with those megaphones?" I asked Rick as we headed back to the dugout after infield practice.

"Those are radar guns," he chuckled. "Haven't you ever seen one before?"

"Sure," I replied, "When the state cops caught me doing 65 miles an hour on Route 18."

"Get used to it, Rockland boy," he smiled. "You're in the big leagues now."

Our student buses had arrived by then, and so had four or five hundred Lakewood fans who had driven themselves to the game. I watched Lorraine and Blake take their seats among the student body. The stands were a sea of our school colors, blue and white, up and down the baselines as far as you could see.

But, because of their early arrival, the West Mifflin North fans had the best seats, right behind the dugouts. They held banners and homemade signs. "24–0" flashed one sign, bragging about their undefeated record.

One fan held a sign saying. "Where the hell is Lakewood City?" That one kind of pissed me off.

"Check out that sign," I nodded to Kerry Rolley, our senior second baseman and co-captain.

"Where the hell is Lakewood City?" he repeated. "They should know where we are. We've won two of the last seven WPIAL Baseball Championships and been in the playoffs for the last six years in a row. Where the hell is West Mifflin?" he screamed into the stands.

"Kerry, get in here," barked Coach Sherman, as the team huddled together for his pre-game pep talk. "Get your head in the game."

"Sorry, Coach," the co-captain shrugged. But I was happy to see his confidence and determination, as we prepared to meet the best high school baseball team in the state.

"This is the big one, boys," started Coach Sherman, as we all found our seats on the bench. "Win this one at you'll be the first high school team ever to play at Three Rivers Stadium. But we need Joe to pitch the best game of his lifetime, and we need to play errorless ball behind him. See that sign out there," he nodded towards the West Mifflin cheering section. "24 and 0," he continued. "What's that tell you?"

"Umm, they're undefeated?" offered Rick timidly.

"Here's what it tells *me*," Coach Sherman continued. "It tells me that we're 29–6. It tells me that we've played *forty percent more games than they have!* It tells me that there's nothing they can show us that we haven't already seen before. There's no situation we haven't already been in. There's no jam that Joe can't pitch out of. There's no pitcher that can intimidate us. You've seen it all. You've been through it all. You have nothing to be afraid of.

"They're supposed to be the best team in the state," He continued. "That means the pressure is on *them*. You just go out and play your best game, and I guarantee you that *we'll* be the one's playing in Pittsburgh, not them! Now, get in there, Phil, and get us started."

Lombardo, our senior third baseman, grabbed two bats and a batting ring and headed for the on-deck circle as West Mifflin North took the field to a thunderous roar from their student section. There were about 2500 people in the stands as Dewey took his warmup throws. I had never played before a crowd so large, and the sheer volume of their voices sent a charge through my body.

Dewey was huge, about six foot four, and the sound of his fastball smacking into the catcher's glove actually overpowered the crowd noise. *Pop, pop, pop!* The damn pitches seemed to explode into the mitt.

Phil stepped in and took the first pitch, as he almost always did; an outside corner fastball. "Strike," screamed the umpire, like it was the seventh game of the World Series. And I watched as half a dozen scouts looked down at their radar guns and nodded in satisfaction.

Phil tried to drop down a bunt on the second pitch, but the ball rolled foul along the third base line. Then Dewey threw a pitch that dipped and swirled but didn't spin at all. Phil swung wildly, but he was nowhere near making contact. "Strike three," barked the ump. But the darting, swirling pitch moved around so much that it smacked right off the catcher's mask and rolled over near the on-deck circle, as Phil streaked toward first base. The catcher recovered, but his throw was too late. "Safe," shouted the first base ump.

"Was that a *Knuckle Ball?*" I moaned to Skip, who was sitting next to me on the bench. Skip was a reserve outfielder and base-stealing expert. Besides me and Johnny, he was the only other Rockland boy on the team.

"That's the greatest pitch I've ever seen," he shook his head in disbelief. "But the good news is the catcher can't handle it. He'll never throw that pitch with men on base."

I smiled to myself and felt a surge of boyhood pride. Skip was a backup player on this team, but like every kid from Rockland, he knew the game of baseball like the back of his hand.

Kerry stepped in and bunted Dewey's first pitch down the first base line, where the big right-handed pitcher fielded it cleanly and threw him out at first, but the sacrifice put our leadoff man in scoring position.

Dewey struck out the next batter with two pin-point fastballs and a curve that must have broken a foot-and-a-half. But with two outs and a man at second base our cleanup batter, Gino Petrella, who had been hitless throughout the playoffs, smashed a sinking line drive to left, where their slick-fielding out-fielder raced in to make a shoestring catch.

A roar went up from the West Mifflin student section, but as we took the field for the bottom of the first inning, I felt a wave of confidence come over our team. *This* is what we have to do to win the game; just scrape and scrounge for every base runner. Move him around the bases with bunts and steals and ground balls. If Petrella's rocket to left field had hit the ground just six inches sooner, we would already have the lead.

We're going to score on this guy, I thought to myself. *If Porter can just throw the kind of game he's capable of, we can beat this team.*

Then, Joe went out and did just that. Our left-hander didn't have his precise control that day, but he was what Coach Sherman called "effectively wild." He was throwing hard, almost as hard as Dewey, but never came right down the middle of the plate. Inside corner, outside corner, high strikes, he was picking their lineup apart. When he got ahead in the count, he'd bounce his curveball in front of the plate, and more times than not, the aggressive West Mifflin hitters would chase the pitch out of the strike zone.

The game was scoreless into the fourth inning, when their leadoff man finally singled with a soft liner to left. They bunted him over to second base, before Porter bore down and got their number three hitter on strikes. Now, with two out and a man at second, their cleanup hitter came to the plate. Joe made his only mistake of the game and hung a curveball to the big right-handed hitter.

Crack! The kid crushed a line drive to centerfield for a base hit. Our center-fielder Don Hicks charged hard and caught the ball cleanly on one hop, while their third-base coach waved wildly for the runner to score from second. But Don fired a rocket from 250 feet away that never even touched the ground. Theisman dropped to his knees and applied the tag without an inch to spare. "Out!" screamed the home plate umpire over the roar of the crowd. And the game remained scoreless.

In the top of the fifth, Dewey got two quick strike outs. But with two outs, Porter came to the plate and bounced a ball deep into the hole between short and third. The West Mifflin shortstop made a terrific back-handed play to cut the ball off, but Joe was safe at first, our very first hit of the game. That brought me to the plate. I was hitting sixth in the lineup and had hit a hard ground ball to shortstop in my first at bat.

I took the first pitch for a ball, but Dewey's second pitch caught the outside corner to even the count at one-and-one. What happened on the next pitch, I still can't believe to this day. Dewey cut loose with what looked to me like an inside fastball that was streaking right for my head. I twisted out of the way and dove backwards to avoid the pitch and lay on my stomach facing the ground. "*Strike two,*" screamed the ump.

What? How could that pitch have possibly been a strike? But there was the catcher, the ball still in his mitt on the inside corner. It wasn't a fastball at all. The damn thing was a curve ball. *No one can throw a curveball that hard.* I thought to myself. *That pitch must have broken two feet at ninety miles an hour. That's impossible!*

I glanced up at the pro scouts behind home plate. They were all busy scribbling onto their clipboards. A gasp went up from the Lakewood City fans, while the West Mifflin student section broke into delirious laughter and cat-calls. "This is the big league, kid," hooted someone from their bench. "Go back to Lakewood City," screamed a thick old man standing next to the West Mifflin dugout.

I looked to our bench for comfort but found none. Kerry held his hand over his mouth and bobbed his shoulders up and down, simulating an exaggerated laugh. It was just good-natured ribbing from a teammate, but deep down I could see the whole team was shaken up. I had come into the game as our leading hitter. What's more, I had been on a tear, raising my average over fifty points in the last two weeks. If Dewey could do this to me, what chance did the rest of them have? *Outclassed,* the thought popped into my head, and I could read it on the faces of every Lakewood City ballplayer sitting on our bench.

But, through my embarrassment and doubt, I could hear one voice in my head over and over. It was my Uncle Joe, who had coached me in Rockland for the last ten years. "When a pitcher fools you that bad, he's going to come right back with the same pitch," he had preached. "You can bet the house on it."

I dusted myself off, but before I could step back in the batter's box, Coach Sherman called time out and walked towards me from the third base coaches' box. He thought I knew what pitch was coming, after all I was a Rockland boy, but he wasn't 100% sure. I met him halfway down the line. He covered his mouth and whispered, "You know what's coming?" Not so much a question as a declaration.

"Same pitch," I murmured.

"Stay in there," he added firmly.

I looked up into the stands once more as I walked back towards home plate. There was Uncle Joe in the bleachers down the first base line. *Jiggy,* everyone called him, and even from 150 feet away, I could see him mouthing the words, *Stay in there.*

The count was one-and-two as I stepped back into the batter's box, and as Dewey delivered the pitch, I could see Joe Porter break for second base.

Again, the damn pitch was thrown hard and seemed to be aimed right at my head. *Get out!* I could feel my instinct for self-survival screaming from some deep, primitive portion of my brain. But some other force had taken over my will. *You're a Rockland boy,* it demanded. *You can't step out. If it hits you in the face, then it hits you in the face.*

And, in that split second, I saw the pitch start to roll over. It broke sharply, across the inside corner, and I lined it past Dewey's ear and into centerfield for a base hit. Porter hit second and headed for third base, as the outfielder threw high and wide. If Dewey hadn't been backing up the throw, it might have gone into their dugout. I scampered into second base, as something approaching euphoria flooded through my veins.

I got him! The thought shot through my mind like a bolt of lightning. *I got the bastard!*

The Lakewood cheering section let out a roar, but, nowhere more than in our dugout. "That's Teddy Tresh," bellowed our backup second baseman Randy Delpino. "He doesn't care who you are!"

"Let's go," I barked into our dugout. "We're Lakewood City, goddamn it. We're better," I screamed, pounding my chest out at second base. "*We're* better!"

I looked over at Coach Sherman at third base, grinning from ear to ear. Then, I pointed at him, to tell everyone that he had called the pitch.

"No," he shook his head slowly and pointed twice back at me. It was the proudest moment of my season, a season full of proud moments. Dewey glanced up at me as he walked back to the mound, and then tipped his hat. I touched the brim of my cap in response. *He knows he's in a ballgame now,* I nodded to myself. *And all that fame isn't going to help him one bit.*

But the game was still scoreless, as Don Hicks stepped into the batter's box with two outs and runners at second and third. Don was a tall, lanky left-hander, who had driven a fly ball deep to centerfield in his first at bat.

The West Mifflin North coach called for the intentional walk to load the bases. It was a smart play. With the bases loaded, they would have a force out at any base, and with our catcher Rick Theisman on deck, they would get the right-hander verses right-hander match-up they wanted. But our team saw it as weakness. "He's afraid of you, Donnie," shouted Jay Farroni from the bench. "The star is afraid of you!"

Now, Theisman walked toward the batter's box, but only paused for a second to ask for time out, then proceeded directly towards Coach Sherman in the coach's box. From second base, I couldn't read Rick's lips, but I knew what he was saying. He wanted permission to swing at the first pitch.

He's smart, I thought to myself. *He knows that with the bases loaded, this kid doesn't want to get behind in the count. If Dewey gets ahead, he can throw that unhittable curve ball and maybe even that uncatchable knuckle ball. But he's going to start with a fastball and Rick knows it.*

Theisman returned to the box and Dewey reached back and fired. You could hear the sound of the ball as it sizzled toward home. *Sssssssssssssst... Crack!* Rick had guessed right. He turned on the belt-high fastball and smashed it deep and high toward the left field wall. Porter trotted toward home, glancing back over his shoulder to see if the ball would leave the park.

I lowered my head and ran hard toward third base, hit the sack then turned toward home. *Bang,* I heard the ball slam against the left field wall and turned to see it bound away from the outfielder. Porter scored. I scored, and now Don Hicks was trying to score all the way from first. He slid into the plate a half second before the throw arrived. And, when the dust had cleared, there was Theisman, standing at second base with his hands on his hips, while the team and the entire student cheering section shook the stadium.

We jumped and hugged and screamed in disbelief. We had been hitless until the fifth inning. We had two outs and nobody on base against the best pitcher in Pennsylvania. Then, bang, bang, bang...we had grabbed a nice lead.

The chants from the Lakewood cheering section started almost immediately. "Three Rivers...Three Rivers...Three Rivers!" Our impossible dream didn't seem nearly as impossible now. Johnny Hudson popped out to end the inning, but nobody cared.

Porter mowed through the tough West Mifflin lineup in the fifth and sixth innings, and our defense was everywhere. Gino ran down a long fly to left in the bottom of the fifth and Kerry made an unbelievable backhanded play on a ground ball up the middle to end the sixth.

We never scored again, but Kerry singled in the sixth and Joe got his second hit of the game in the seventh, pushing our hit total to five. Porter actually tried to steal second after his base hit but was thrown out by the West Mifflin catcher.

It was hot and humid that day, and when Joe returned to the mound, he seemed winded after running the bases. He went 3–0 to the first West Mifflin batter in the seventh and final inning, then battled back to make the count 3–2.

Finally, the kid smacked a hard ground ball towards the hole between short-stop and third. I got over there in time, but the ball took a weird hop and bounced up off my chest.

"Here we come, short," barked their on-deck hitter, with a good measure of disdain. "You can feel it, can't you? You can even hear it. That's the sound of an undefeated season closing in on you. We're coming like a runaway train!"

I walked the ball into Joe. "Sorry, Lefty," I shrugged.

"Don't worry about it," he whispered, putting his hand on my shoulder. "Shake it off. That's in the past. We need you right now."

I nodded my head and jogged back towards my position, but before I could even get comfortable, the next hitter smacked a bouncer towards the middle. Rolley went for the ball, and I moved in to back him up. But Joe cleanly stabbed the ground ball as it passed the mound. Kerry immediately dove to the ground to get out of the way. Porter fired the throw to me at second base, and we turned a clutch 1–6–3 double play.

The Lakewood fans were delirious, while the West Mifflin bench fell silent. Their dream season had just turned into a nightmare. Their left-handed first baseman came to the plate and swung hopelessly at three Porter curve balls.

We mobbed Joe on the mound, as the players and the students and what seemed like the entire town of Lakewood City started chanting again. "Three Rivers…Three Rivers…Three Rivers…"

PLAYING HERO

"Y ou always told me you were a pretty good ballplayer," Gene nodded, as he swirled the tiny remnants of ice cubes around in his otherwise empty cocktail glass. "How good were you?"

"I was a better-than-average ballplayer," I agreed, "Who happened to have some *great* seasons. And this one was the best of those. I was flying high."

"Well, that's great for you," Gene laughed. "But I'm not sure what I can learn from that. I'm struggling with this girl, Dad. You were on top of the world. I mean, it's kind of hard to identify with that right now.

"I know you didn't get the girl you wanted right away, but *boo hoo*. You don't sound like you're suffering much?"

"Well, I'm just trying to give you the perspective from when everything's going right," I explained, "Because it can be a hell of a lot different than when everything's going wrong.

"Sure, for the next week, we were the heroes of the town. Everything was wonderful, but being on top doesn't last long. You have to be careful to find someone who's with you win-or-lose. I mean if you're serious about the girl, you want someone who will go through hell with you, not just take this little stroll through heaven."

"So, what happened?" Gene laughed. "Did Lorraine come to her senses?"

"No, she *still* wouldn't admit her feelings. But she was getting close." I smiled.

"What was she waiting for?" Gene baited me.

"What's *Jan* waiting for, Gene?" I shot back. "When will it finally be okay for her to throw in with you? When will she finally decide that you're not the enemy?"

"What do you mean?" Gene replied defensively.

"I mean, when will she finally understand that what's good for you is good for her, for the team?"

"We're not really a *team*, Dad." Gene spoke quickly without really listening to his own words, so I paused to let them hang in the air for a second or two.

"You just said a mouthful, Champ." I spoke slowly and deliberately. "If you're not a team yet, when will you be? Is this relationship real at all?"

Now, Gene started pushing back. "Was your relationship with Lorraine real? It seems all one-sided to me. Was it ever real for her?"

"Well, I wasn't sure. But I was a star that week. And the seniors had just graduated. The underclassmen would have the halls of Lakewood High School all to ourselves, and that meant I would have Lorraine all to myself. It seemed like the perfect time to find out just how real she could be. Of course, that week wasn't really a good indication of anything. Don't get me wrong, it was one of the best weeks of my life, but you can't get a clear view of a girl's feelings when you're sitting on top of the world."

32

You Can't Have It All

Back in school on Tuesday, I was in paradise. All the seniors were gone, having graduated the night before, just hours after our big semi-final victory. That meant that the junior class now ruled the school, especially me, Porter and Theisman. With the championship game set for the following Monday, we walked the halls of Lakewood like kings. Everyone we saw sang our praises, or slapped us on the back, or shouted out words of encouragement.

For a Rockland boy to be so accepted at Lakewood City High School was unheard of. And I felt a small pang of loss that my brother and sister and so many of the kids I grew up with, were not there to see it; that they, instead, had been bussed off to Beaver Falls.

"It's a shame," I told Willie, as we walked from our second period CP English class to our third period Study Hall, "All this tradition and no one to pass it on to."

"You can't worry about that," he scolded with a straight face. "This is your time, right now. Besides, we're not really Rockland boys anymore. We're Lakewood City boys."

I stopped and stared at him in stunned silence for a moment, and then we both burst out laughing. "That's one thing we'll never be," I chuckled.

"Rockland boys for life," he nodded, holding out the palm of his hand. I obligingly *slapped him five.* And he responded with the Rockland-boy trademark, slapping my open palm with the back of his hand instead of the traditional palm-on-palm greeting. "Too cool for *this* school," he added.

When we got to the auditorium for study hall, I made a bee line for Lorraine. During the school year, she always sat with Blake during third period, but now that the seniors were gone, I coasted down the aisle and plopped right down next to her.

"I'm glad you're here," she smiled. Her eyes were twinkling, and there was an excitement in her voice I hadn't heard in many months. "The yearbooks are being handed out in homeroom after lunch. And I want you to be the first one to sign mine."

What could be more perfect? I thought.

Lorraine and I were in the same Home Room that year and, when we got back after lunch, several Lakewoodian staff members were proudly handing out the new 1971 yearbooks to everyone who had pre-paid. I'll have to admit, they were pretty slick: a black silhouette of a student, casting a long shadow down one of the hallways of Lakewood High.

"It makes me think of how time passes," Lorraine lamented, as we exchanged the heavy yearbooks with the white-on-black, leather-look covers.

"Faster every day, doesn't it?" Normally a common response I guess, but today it seemed all full of extra meaning. "Do you want me to sign this right here?"

"No," she answered emphatically. "No, take your time with it. How about if I see you at my locker after next period?"

"That's perfect," I nodded. "It's a date."

Normally, Lorraine would have corrected me, "It's a meeting, not a date." That had been her mantra for the last eight months, as long as we had been prom co-chairmen. She said it without even thinking about it. But this time she just smiled. "Take your time signing it," she said with a twinkle in her eye.

I knew what that meant. She wanted something real, something from the heart. Just a year earlier, I had written her a breakup letter, even though she was never officially my girlfriend.

"That letter took her breath away," her best friend Margie, had told me in confidence one day last summer. It was one of the things that made me think I still had a chance with Lorraine.

Just before the bell, an announcement rang out over the school's public address system: "The WPIAL has announced Lakewood City's opponent for

Monday's championship at Three Rivers Stadium. The Wolverines will be facing the Highlands Rams, who defeated Penn Hills 5–4 in extra innings yesterday."

I knew about Highlands. They were one of those new super schools that had just been put together by combining three other school districts. Like West Mifflin North, they were twice the size of Lakewood City High School. A few years later, the WPIAL would start assigning classifications to the baseball leagues, just like they did for football and basketball, Class A, Class AA, AAA, Quad A and so forth. But for now, there was only one high school baseball classification, and you had to beat them all. *I wouldn't have it any other way,* I thought. *Bring 'em on!* I was a Rockland boy. *And Rockland boys are used to slaying giants.*

I took Lorraine's yearbook with me into my C.P. English class. The instructor was handing out our graded final term papers, and she reviewed them for about fifteen minutes. "Take the rest of the class to study on your own," said Mrs. Byers, even though there was nothing left to study for. The final tests were over. So, almost everyone in the class was exchanging Lakewoodians, and writing their goodbyes to each other.

I opened her yearbook to the Junior Class Officers page, where Lorraine and I had posed for our Prom Co-Chairmen photo together in a jail cell in the municipal building. It was a funny picture, and it set a good mood for all the things I wanted to tell her.

"Remember when…," I started writing. And then listed all the good times and not-so-good times we had been through. I reminded her of our first date at the Y-Teens Dance, our first slow dance, our first kiss. I wrote about the day I missed my bus and had to walk to school from Rockland. Along the way I had stopped to pick a purple tulip out of somebody's flower garden and gave it to her in study hall, "because it looks like you," I had told her.

I reminisced about all our trips to Youngstown to order prom decorations, about our cheek-to-cheek dance at the Glass Tower, about meeting her outside the dugout after every game our sophomore year. And, finally, I reminded her about ordering the flowers for prom decorations, and how I secretly snapped off a daffodil on the way out of the flower shop and presented it to her when we got back to my car.

All-in-all it was an emotional tribute to our time together, exactly what Lorraine was hoping for when she told me to take my time writing it. I knew it would blow her away. I sat up straight in my seat and re-read it a few times, and I guess I looked pretty satisfied with myself.

"Is that Lorraine's yearbook?" I looked across the aisle to see Margie, who sat next to me in C.P. English. "Can I read what you wrote?" she asked.

"Ummmm…I think I better let her see it first," I laughed. "I'm sure she's going to show it to you anyway."

"Teddy," Margie whispered. "Something's happening that I think you should know about."

In that instant, a million questions shot through my mind. *Does Lorraine want me to leave her alone?* I wondered, *or is she finally going to give me another chance? Is she sending me a message? Or is Margie just making her own observations?*

"Well, what is it?" I said in a voice that was neither a whisper nor an exclamation. "You have my undivided attention."

"You can't repeat this," Margie cautioned. "She'd kill me if she knew I was talking to you about it."

"Jesus, Margie. What is it?" I shot a quick glance up at Mrs. Byers' desk to make sure she hadn't heard me raise my voice. "What the hell is going on?"

"Well, she really likes Blake," Margie continued, "But she really likes you too." Margie took a long pause to decide exactly what to say next.

So far, this was good news, I figured. If she really cared as much about me as she did about Blake while she was wearing his class ring, then I was in pretty good shape.

"She's just not ready for what he wants," Margie said finally. "I mean… physically."

I felt a little sick to my stomach. This was a topic that I tried *never* to think about. *How physical were they being?* Now I pictured him with his hands all over her, under her blouse, under her skirt. *My frickin' girl with this bastard on top of her?*

But wait. Margie had just said that Lorraine "wasn't ready."

"Well, does she tell him to stop?" This comment was a little too loud. And, Mrs. Byers gave me a quick, hard glance, then went right back to writing in her grade book.

"Shhhh," Margie cautioned, and then whispered again. "She does. But ten minutes later, he tries again."

Okay, I thought. *So, he's persistent, but not out of control. She can handle this guy for a few more weeks until I can come in and rescue her.*

Hell, who was I to judge? Winnie was a lot more experienced than Lorraine, but she had told me "no" plenty of times. This was just part of growing up.

"Maybe she should tell her mother about it," I chuckled, remembering how strict her parents had been about her dating before sixteen or going steady with a guy. Of course, this was 1971, and I figured that no teenage girl was going to take a problem like this to her mother, not unless the situation was getting out of hand.

"She did," Margie hissed. "Her mom said that's just the way boys are!"

"What?" I barked out, way too loudly.

Now, the teacher couldn't ignore me any longer. "Ted, I said 'study quietly,' not shout at the top of your lungs. I know you're a big hero this week, but that doesn't give you the right to disrupt my class."

"I'm sorry," I muttered. And I tried to keep quiet for a few minutes, but it didn't last long. "What about her old man?" I asked Margie as quietly as I could.

"Her mother *forbids* her to tell her dad."

When the class ended, I walked out into the hallway in a daze. This situation was so much worse than I ever thought it could be. If it were me pawing at her, her mother would have called out the FBI. Her father would have skinned me alive. But, this lawyer's kid, this *pillar of society* gets a pass? And if Lorraine was upset enough to go to her mom in the first place, then she was asking for help.

I resolved then and there to rededicate myself to getting her back; to make one final supreme effort. A few minutes later, I was reading her inscription in my Lakewoodian, and I knew that *now* was the perfect time to make my charge.

"Teddy," it said, "The two flowers you gave me were nearly a year apart. But they reconnected me to all those old feelings, and I realize that those feelings never really went away. If we had just stayed together, everything would have worked out for us. All those arguments we pretended to have, when our eyes were anything but angry. All those prom-decorating trips to Youngstown that we both knew we really didn't need to take. All the feelings I still had inside me, and I could see were still inside of you."

Whoa, I thought. *This is it. She's coming back to me, right here, right now.*

"We had our problem (my mother)," the inscription continued. "I knew I was mature, but she knew I wasn't mature enough. If we could just have stayed together, if you could just have waited a little longer, I know we could both have said, 'I love you' and really meant it."

Now I had an uneasy feeling. She was using the past tense, instead of looking to the future; that couldn't be good. And she was pushing the blame for failure onto me, as if it was too late, as if our whole lives weren't still lying ahead of us.

"But I want you to know, that the flowers will always grow in my heart, and will always be welcomed there."

And that's where it ended. It was vintage Lorraine; leaving the door open, while being completely non-committal, enough to entice me, but leaving her an escape hatch.

Damn her, I thought to myself. *She's drawing me back into this Twilight Zone.* There was no mention of her part in it. No admission that two weeks after telling me she was forbidden to date or go steady with anybody, that she was dating *and* going steady with Blake Bianchi. And the future, where was any mention of the future?

"What am I supposed to do with this?" I said out loud. She had basically said that she was in love with me, or did she really say that she *could have* been in love with me. And this crap about the flowers always growing in her heart, was that a promise or a lament? I took some comfort in the fact that she never even mentioned Blake in the whole monologue, as if he were a non-factor in our lives. But the whole thing left me with more questions than answers.

Later that day, I showed the inscription to my best buddy, Jerry. "Jesus Christ, Ted Tresh," he shook his head in disgust. "I can't tell whether she's saying hello or goodbye.

"But I'll tell you one thing, you've got the biggest baseball game of your life coming up in six days, and you can't be letting this girl get in your head and screw everything up. You've got all summer to deal with Lorraine; right now you better get ready to deal with Highlands High School."

Leave it to Jerry to talk some sense into me, I smiled to myself. And I went about the rest of the week strutting around the halls of Lakewood High School like I owned the world; practicing baseball with my troops every afternoon and basking in the role of hero that would soon be mine with just one more victory.

Friday was the last day of classes before the summer break, and I had a weird sensation as I took my last look around the halls of Lakewood High. Somehow, I had a feeling that the next time I saw them, they would look completely different. I strolled into my fourth period Journalism class, where Mr. Ionelli, the journalism teacher and the staff sponsor of the Lakewood ECHO, was passing out old copies of the school newspaper. This year's Journalism 101 class would become the staff of the ECHO in the 1971-72 school year, and he was describing the regular beats that staffers usually covered, Student Council, Sports, Class Officers, ten different beats in all, and showing us examples of stories from this year's staff.

"We also need to elect an editor and assistant editor," the teacher paused here and looked around the room. "Is there anyone who would like to run for editor?"

"I'll run for assistant editor," chimed Debbie Palumbo from the back of the class. Debbie was a sophomore, who would be a junior in September. She was a real organizer, smart and hard-working. I was a little surprised that she didn't want the top job.

"First things first," Mr. Ionelli chuckled. "Who would like to be the editor?"

Nobody raised their hand, and I knew why. The job of editor was a hard, time-consuming position. You would have to be very organized, plus you would have to be willing to make assignments for the entire staff and run herd over everyone to make sure the assignments were completed on time, and that the stories were coherent and entertaining. Then you'd have to work with the printer to edit them to fit the eight-page format of the monthly student paper.

It was a tough, thankless job. Staffers were always complaining that their stories had been cut or shortened or buried on page eight.

I considered it for a second. It would be an honor to be the editor of the ECHO, but was it really worth the time and the hassles? I sat there with my hands on my desk, just like everyone else. Finally, one hand went up in the back of the class. "Yes, Lynn," the journalism instructor breathed a sigh of relief. "Would you like to run for editor?"

It was Lynn Batista, another soon-to-be junior classman. Lynn was super sweet, with a gorgeous face with long dark-brown hair and eyes that sparkled every time she smiled, which was almost all the time. And she was sharp, acing every journalism test and assignment we had had all year.

"I suggest that we don't have just one editor next year," she offered. "It's too much work and responsibility for one person. How about if we have page editors? So, one issue, Ted would be page-one editor, and Debbie could be the page-two editor, and I'd be the page-three editor. And then, for the next issue we would all switch around."

"Who would write the headlines?" Mr. Ionelli questioned thoughtfully.

"Well, the page editors would each write the headlines, make the assignments and edit the stories for their own page."

"That's great," chimed in our sports specialist John Cicero. "Then on our college applications, we could all claim to be *Co-editor of the school paper.*"

Everyone in the class loved the idea, and our sponsor agreed to give it a try. I took one long look at Lynn. She was the daughter of one of the school's History teachers, Gene Batista. I kind of had a crush on her from the first day of class, but she was going steady with Denny Nowitzki, one of the senior boys, and they were *always* together.

"I loved your idea about the page editors," I congratulated Lynn on the way out of class. "But as smart as you are, I would have voted for you to run the whole show."

"Thanks, but that job is way too tough for one person," she smiled. "Hey, good luck at Three Rivers Stadium on Monday. My parents are actually letting me go to the game, so this will be my first chance to see you play."

"I didn't know your mom and dad were so protective."

"Well, it's mostly my mother," she answered with a shake of her head. "I'm not allowed to go to dances unless my father is chaperoning. And I'm not allowed to go on dates at all until my junior year."

Now, I was confused. "Aren't you going steady with Denny," I asked, looking down at the class ring on her finger.

"Sure," she said, "They can't stop me from liking whoever I want to like. I guess that's why we're always together in school. I mean, I can meet him at the park if we're both out with a group of friends, and we can slip away for a walk on our own for a while. But I've never been on an official *date* with him."

"Well, you'll be a junior in three more months," I teased.

"That's right," she declared, as she turned to walk down the hallway to her next class. "And I can date whoever I want to date."

Whoa, I thought, as I turned toward the stairs to the cafeteria. *Was she flirting with me?*

I stopped dead in my tracks. But Lynn just kept walking for about ten more steps, finally glancing back over her shoulder to see if I was watching her.

"What do you think of Lynn Batista?" I asked Willie Gacik, as we sat in the lunchroom munching down slices of pizza and slurping on our chocolate milks.

"Absolutely beautiful," he pronounced. "But she's taken. She's going with Denny Nowitzki, and they are *in love*."

"Are you sure?"

"Don't even think about it, Teddy," he chided me. "Denny is a great kid. Everybody loves that guy. The hippies love him. The jocks love him. Even the greasers love him. He's just a nice guy. He's kind of a freak and his girlfriend is kind of straight. But you know he's one of those guys that are cool in every group, and when he's around, even the straights and the freaks seem to get along better.

"If you tried to break them up, everyone in the school would hate you. Plus, it wouldn't work. He's devoted to Lynn and she's completely loyal to him."

"Hmmm," I sighed. "I wish I could find a girl like that."

We were sitting at a cafeteria table made up mostly of Rockland kids. With the seniors already gone, there were only about twenty-five of us left in the school, and even though we had all adapted to our other classmates by now, we still clung to each other for acceptance and support. Molly Belinsky, my old grade school girlfriend, was sitting next to Willie, and she rolled her eyes sarcastically. "You're such a bird," she admonished me. "You can't have everything, Teddy.

"Everyone knows you're hung up on Lorraine. Why would you want to involve someone else?"

I was a little stunned by her comment. How did she know that? Over the years, Molly and I had grown to be good friends. She never seemed bitter about the breakup from when we were kids. But that didn't mean she wouldn't put me in my place if she thought I needed it.

"Lorraine *has* a boyfriend," I said with some disdain.

"She's bragging to everyone about what you wrote in her yearbook," she whispered across the table. "If you still like her, you have to let her know."

"But I don't know what *she* wants," I snapped back. "I can't read her mind!"

"Girls don't always show how they feel," Molly shook her head slowly.

"You did," I laughed.

"Stop your barking, Toto," she smiled. "You're not in Rockland anymore."

Truer words were never spoken, I thought. *I'm in the Land of Oz now. And nothing is the way it seems.*

"There's no place like home," I sighed, as I rose to head off to my afternoon classes.

At noon on Saturday, the baseball team held our final practice before the WPIAL Championship game at Three Rivers Stadium. I hit first in batting practice with the same bat I had used the entire season, a thin-handled, 34-inch Hank Aaron "Flame Fused" model. I loved that bat, and today it felt particularly balanced and steady in my hands. I whipped it through the strike-zone, generating a sharp *crack, crack, crack,* that echoed across the field. I was playing the best baseball of my life at just the right time. It was the first week of June, but the mild spring weather was rolling right into an even milder summer. As practice came to an end, the thermometer outside the dugout read 80 degrees.

Our star second baseman and co-captain, Kerry Rolley, had an in-ground swimming pool in his backyard, and he had invited the entire team over for a pool party after practice. I was on top of the world, as I strolled through Kerry's living room, being greeted by teammates, classmates and friends. Kerry's twin sister, Katy, met us on the patio in a gorgeous two-piece hot-pink bathing suit. And she and her boyfriend Joey Colombo *both* hugged me like a long-lost brother.

Katy was in the middle of a conversation with her dad and two uncles, who considered themselves baseball experts. "We were lucky to beat that West Mifflin team," her dad was saying. "That Dewey kid was the best high school pitcher I ever saw. Most of our hitters were overmatched. I don't know how we won that game."

"Well, Porter shut them down," his uncle countered. "You have to score to win. But I'll tell you who's carrying that offense. It's that Tresh kid!"

"That's him right there," Kerry's dad barked, sticking his finger in my chest. It was one of the proudest moments of my life.

"Oh, Jesus," Kerry moaned in mock disgust, "As if your head isn't big enough."

We all laughed and hugged each other. The entire team was loose and confident, and we couldn't wait for Monday afternoon.

I drove home with Johnny Hudson and Skip Bruno. Together we would be the last three Rockland boys to ever wear a Lakewood City uniform. "Just think of it," Huddy was saying, "All those years, all those great Rockland ball players."

"Like Johnny and Karl Gallo and Trippy and Bobby Wyeth," Skip added.

"Hell, Trippy was the best player on that 1962 WPIAL Championship team," I chimed in; "He was their leading hitter and started at shortstop for four straight years.

"He's been a legend in Rockland ever since," Skip sighed. "And then he went off and started at Notre Dame for four years. He became bigger than life."

"At St. Teresa's School, we just called him Pope Trippy I," I laughed.

"And Lakewood City doesn't win that 1968 Championship if Dawson doesn't shut out Waynesburg."

"When he was a *sophomore*," Huddy laughed. "And look at last year's team, Tony DeVito and Dawson and Billy Conti, where would Lakewood City have been without those guys?"

We sat in silence for about a mile or so, thinking of all those legendary Rockland names, all those guys who had been our inspiration, our role-models for as long as we could remember.

"Do you really think we could be remembered like that?" Huddy sighed.

"I don't have much chance, coming off the bench," Skip chuckled, "But you guys, you could do something at Three Rivers Stadium that Lakewood City could never forget."

"So could you," Huddy encouraged him. "It's just one game. You could pinch run and steal a base or track down a long fly ball or score the winning run. Anyone can be the hero when it comes down to one final game."

"And anyone can be the washout," I added. "Anyone can be the bum."

The car fell silent again. *That's the other side of glory, isn't it?* I thought to myself. *That's the problem with the big showcase game in the major league stadium, what if you screw it up?*

"Well, let's not think about that," Huddy said, reassuringly. "This is our time. This is our opportunity. The town of Rockland will be backing Beaver Falls soon enough. Let's close out this Lakewood City era in style. Teddy, the way you've been playing, they could end up calling you Pope Trippy II."

Huddy was a special ballplayer. Just being around him, always kept us positive. He constantly looked for the bright side and brought out the best in his teammates. That's just who the kid was, and just the kind of man he would someday become.

"I hear it might rain on Monday," he added, trying to change the subject. "If we get postponed, I wonder if the Pirates would let us come back. They're on the coast now, but they're hosting the Mets on Wednesday. We might have to make up the championship game at some college field."

The trip to Three Rivers Stadium was something every team in the WPIAL had been hoping and striving for all year long. "I'd rather lose at Three Rivers, than get postponed and win somewhere else," Skip groaned.

"Well," I countered, "I wouldn't go that far." And we all laughed nervously.

THICK AND THIN

"Well, you finally met Mom," Gene smiled. "Was it love-at-first-sight? Did you finally give up on Lorraine and come to your senses?"

"No, buddy," I laughed. "I thought your mom was beautiful, and I thought she was sweet, but she was somebody else's girlfriend and besides, I had unfinished business. I had to let this Lorraine thing come to some sort of conclusion. I still had to make one final effort to find out if that relationship was real."

"How does anybody ever know what's real?" Gene shook his head thoughtfully. "Is *Jan* real? Only time can tell me that."

I felt old feelings of confusion and fear and insecurity wash over me; feelings that were once so familiar, but now nearly forgotten. I reached out and put my hand on my son's shoulder. "No, Champ," I told him. "You *can* be sure. But sometimes you have to hit rock bottom to find out what's real and what isn't. I didn't know what Lorraine was looking for, somebody her parents would approve of? Somebody that all her friends respected? A hero? I didn't know if that would matter.

"But, for some reason, I felt like it all depended on that damn baseball game. I felt like my whole future depended on that game. And, in a way, it did."

It was exactly 12:30 p.m., and neither of us had slept in over twenty-four hours, but Gene was sitting on the edge of his kitchen chair, and I was still wide awake. I got up to mix us another Screwdriver just as his cell phone started singing out again.

"Well, she's done with her internship," he groaned. "He we go again.

"Hey," he grunted into the phone, coming to his feet and heading for the front door. "No, I *was* going to call you." Gene stepped out into the cool afternoon sunshine and closed the door behind him.

"Haven't you two had enough of those?" chirped Lynn, nodding at the cocktail glasses as she walked up the steps from the family room.

"I'm not sure," I replied. "Is it too early or too late to be drinking?"

"You two better get some sleep. What the heck have you been talking about all night?"

"Women problems," I sighed. "The kid has gotten sucked into the middle of a big mess."

"How big?"

"I think he's at a crossroads. I think he might be falling in love with this Jan, and she might even be in love with him. But she doesn't respect him. She just wants to keep her claws in him and make sure he doesn't get away."

"Did you tell him that?" I could see the concern growing in Lynn's eyes.

"Sure I did," I smiled. "Then I just keep telling him stories and hoping he can see the truth for himself."

"Well, he better not let this girl affect his schoolwork. We're not paying for him to star in a soap opera; we're paying for him to get an education."

"No one wants to hear his parents preach to him," I shook my head slowly. "But I think he's starting to get the idea. I think he's beginning to understand that a woman needs to be more than somebody to hold onto at night. That she needs to be a teammate. She needs to be on your side *all* the time. He just needs to *see* the light."

"Well, if anyone can convince him, you can." Lynn kissed me softly on the cheek. "After all, *you* saw it." She sat down on my lap for a few minutes, talking to me. I don't remember what she said. I just remember how sweet it sounded.

"Yeah, and what happens *next* time you decide to threaten me?" Gene's voice came booming up the stairway, as he swept back into the house. "Look, I'd rather deal with it right now too. But, it's my dad's birthday, and I'm *not* flying back until tomorrow."

Lynn and I glanced at each other. "Well, if you're not there, you're not there," Gene barked. "I'll be back tomorrow night. That's it!" And he stuffed the phone into his hip pocket.

"Looks like you're making some progress," Lynn whispered. "I'll leave you two alone."

"Jesus," Gene shook his head as he picked up the vodka and orange juice I had just poured for him. "What does she want from me?"

My first impulse was to say, *she wants too damn much, Gene.* But instead, I asked a question.

"Do you consider her your girlfriend, buddy?"

"Umm, sure, I guess so."

"Well," I continued. "Do you think this girl will be there for you through thick and thin?"

Gene laughed a disgusted kind of laugh. "No," he said, "Not even close."

"The real girlfriend is the one who loves you when you're on the top and even when you hit rock bottom."

"What do you mean by *rock bottom*?" Gene sat down at the table and leaned forward.

"I guess I mean that tons of women will love you when you're cocky and confident. Most women love confidence. But, how about when you lose that confidence?"

"What's confidence got to do with love?" Gene looked confused.

"It has everything to do with *everything*," I barked. "You just don't realize how your reality can change. Especially when you're young and you haven't already seen it happen again and again and again. You lose your confidence, and you think that the world has changed. You don't even realize that eventually it's going to change back.

"And here you have this girl, this woman, who tries to shake your confidence every chance she gets."

"You're not just talking about me and Jan anymore, are you?" Gene mused. "Why do I feel another story coming on?"

"It's not just another story," I told him. "It's *the* story."

THE BALANCE

On the night before the championship game, Jerry and I were just cruising down Lawrence Avenue in my dad's silver Thunderbird. Jerry's family had long been grocery store and butcher shop owners in Lakewood City, and they had recently added a fast-food burger joint to their modest empire. It sat right in the middle of the town's main drag, and quickly became a hangout for Lakewood and Riverside high-school students, especially the jocks. In fact, any Lakewood football player who scored a touchdown, or basketball player who scored ten-or-more points in a game, or baseball player who recorded an extra-base hit, got a gift certificate for a free burger. I was sitting on a couple free quarter-pound steak burgers right now.

"It's my treat," I told Jerry.

"I don't have to pay, Ted Tresh," Jerry laughed. "We own the place."

It always cracked me up how Jerry called me by my full name. We were best buddies, but it was always *Ted Tresh*, never Ted or Teddy.

"That's okay," I told him. "I want to show off my gift certificates."

"Maybe Lorraine will be there," he nodded, "If she can pry herself away from Blake Bianchi for a couple hours. Honestly, Ted Tresh, I don't know why you put up with that. You're a frickin' star and you're wasting your time chasing somebody else's girlfriend around."

"I just like her," I shrugged. "But this crap *is* getting kind of old."

"I wouldn't give her too much more time." Jerry shifted uneasily in the passenger seat. It had been nearly a year since he had had his gruesome leg injury, but the huge plaster cast had just come off a couple weeks earlier, and he was still getting around on crutches and trying to regain full movement in his left leg.

We walked into the restaurant to a chorus of cheers and mock cheers from the twenty-or-so high-school students gathered in the restaurant. The Lakewood kids were loud and boisterous, while the Riverside jocks were more subdued. Riverside's baseball team had also had a fine season, and won their section title, but they were eliminated in the first round of the playoffs.

We had handled the team who beat them pretty easily in round two, so I chalked up any of their catcalls and taunts to competitive envy.

I did feel a little uneasy when one booth of recent Lakewood grads completely ignored us. Two of them were facing us, Vince DiMuccio and his girl-friend Debbie. Vince was a senior running back for Lakewood last fall, and there was no love lost between us. But our school was about to play for the WPIAL Baseball Championship. I expected at least an encouraging word or two.

Then I saw who was sitting across the table and it all made sense. "Umm, good luck tomorrow," intoned Lorraine obligingly. She was holding hands with Blake, who never even looked up from the menu, while Vince and Debbie just stared at Blake. Lorraine glanced at me one more time, but was careful not to let it linger for more than a second or two.

"Yeah, thanks," I muttered as we walked past their booth and into the arms of our more enthusiastic classmates.

"You can't worry about that, Ted Tresh," admonished Jerry as we approached the counter and ordered our free steak burgers and a couple chocolate shakes.

"Listen," he said as we finally took our order to the booth. "You have to concentrate on that game. She's just some *girl*."

I raised an eyebrow in mock surprise.

"Okay, okay, she's a *beautiful* girl with a gorgeous smile and a knockout figure, but she's still just a girl," he laughed. "And she has nothing to do with the real world of baseball."

Suddenly the smile left his face and he leaned across the table, serious as a heart attack. "Do you know what I'd give to be in your place tomorrow?"

Ever since we both made the varsity baseball team as freshmen, it had been our dream to be the left-side of the Lakewood City infield. And now, here I was, heading to Three Rivers Stadium as the starting shortstop, while Jerry was still limping around on crutches, his spot at third base filled by Phil Lombardo.

Phil had been a star outfielder, who could play a little infield, but he wasn't the slick, experienced third baseman that Jerry was.

"I had a dream last night," whispered Jerry as his eyes began to cloud-up. "Lombardo kept kicking the ball around the infield, and finally Sherman came out of the dugout and called me out of the stands to replace him. The crowd went wild, and the very first hitter bounced one into the hole. I dove and got it and turned it into a round-the-horn double play, and you were hugging me, and you said, 'Where the hell have you been?' And the fans were screaming, and we were laughing."

"Then what happened?" I asked as I took a big slurp of my chocolate shake.

"I woke up," he said in disgust.

And I laughed so hard a mouthful of milkshake sputtered all over the table.

"So, forget about the girl," Jerry grinned. "You're living *my* dream. Just go out and win the goddamn game. Then, next year, we'll go out and win the whole frickin' thing again."

I didn't sleep well that night. I could hear thunder in the distance, and a slow, steady rain was sighing across the roof of our old two-story, red asphalt house in Rockland. I kept getting up and looking out the window, as the street-lights reflected off the wet grass of our big backyard.

After all this time, I thought, *we're not going to get to play at Three Rivers. We're going to get postponed and have to make up at some college field.*

I tried to get back to sleep, but every time I closed my eyes, I remembered our February practices in the gym, running the bleacher steps, pushing our-selves to get stronger, better. "Three Rivers, Three Rivers, Three Rivers," we would chant.

We didn't care that it was a long shot. We didn't care that there were 120 high school baseball teams in the WPIAL. We held onto the dream, and with every victory we got closer. When we opened the non-section schedule with fifteen straight wins, we knew we could contend with anybody. When we won the section 6 title, we started to believe. When we took out West Mifflin North, we could almost see the giant scoreboard and feel the artificial turf. And now rain, a frickin' spring rain, was going to wash it all away.

It's the championship that matters, I told myself, *not the stupid stadium.* But deep down inside, I was heartbroken. I fell into a half-sleep, and when my alarm went off at 9 a.m., I was groggy and moody, and it was still raining outside.

Coach Sherman had identical twin daughters, Bonnie and Betsy, who were in my class. I had even taken Bonnie to the first Y-Teens Dance my freshman year, but I still couldn't tell the two girls apart. "Teddy, there's a call for you," my mom shouted up the stairwell.

"Ted, it's Betsy Sherman," came the voice from the earpiece. And I held my breath. "My dad says that the game has *not* been cancelled. The team bus leaves the gym at 11 o'clock. Bring your uniform and equipment and wear a jacket and tie."

On the ride over to Lakewood City High School gym, the rain was still falling. "Don't worry," my father tried to comfort me. "They have a tarp on the field. If it stops soon, you'll still get to play today."

On the car's A.M. radio, The Carpenters were just breaking into *Rainy Days and Mondays.*

"Hanging around," sang Karen, "Nothing to do but frown. Rainy days and Mondays always get me down."

"Oh, great," I sighed, as a feeling of doom and gloom swept through the car.

"I think it's slowing down," my dad said encouragingly. And by the time we got to the school parking lot, all that was left was a slow drizzle.

"Get your heads in the game," barked Coach Sherman as we boarded the team bus. "If it rains, it rains. But, if it stops, you have to be ready to go."

On the hour-long drive to Pittsburgh, the sun began to peek through the clouds. And although there were puddles and wet pavement throughout the drive, the rain had stopped altogether. *We're going to play this thing,* I thought to myself. *And it's perfect timing. I'm playing the best baseball of my life, and I'm about to step out onto the biggest stage. This is exactly what I've always wanted.* Yet, somehow, I still had a hollow feeling inside.

We were the home team for the game, and when we got to Three Rivers Stadium, a security guard led us into the Pirates locker room. There were the names of all our boyhood heroes hanging over each locker, Clemente, Stargell, Blass, Oliver. I made a beeline for Bill Mazeroski's stall. Maz had been my favorite Pirate since I played second base in Little League, and although he was no longer a starter in the Pittsburgh lineup, he was a future Hall-of-Famer and the hero of the 1960 World Series. Maybe some of his gutsy, clutch playing style would rub off on me. I tossed my gym bag into the locker and started pulling off my tie and sports jacket.

As we made our way out onto the artificial surface of Three Rivers Stadium, we could see some Pittsburgh Steelers' players running the stadium steps behind home plate, completing a morning workout.

"Is that Bradshaw?" gasped Johnny Hudson, grabbing me by the sleeve. The Steelers had drafted quarterback Terry Bradshaw number one, overall, just before the 1970 season, and he had yet to demonstrate the kind of talent that would lead them to four Super Bowls in the next decade. But his Herculean physique and flowing blonde hair were already recognizable to any true Steeler fan.

"Damn," I responded. "We're here, Huddy. We're really here."

The ground crew had just finished rolling up the tarp and the infield was dry and ready for play, as the sun began peeking from behind the clouds. The outfield, on the other hand, was still soaking wet, but the artificial surface kept it from being soft and muddy, and it quickly became apparent that this game would not be cancelled.

I was shocked to see that the artificial *turf* was really nothing but a green indoor/outdoor carpet. It was nothing like grass. It was flat and hard and had no nap at all. Even the base paths were artificial turf, with the only dirt areas being the batter's box, pitcher's mound and sliding pits around the bases.

As we took our places for infield practice, I could feel a certain strangeness in the air. The groundballs came faster than on real grass, and bounced higher, and our cleats stayed on top of the surface of the turf, rather than sinking into it. It was kind of like playing in a parking lot, and we all struggled with our timing.

The balls hit for outfield practice were even crazier, as a stream of water shot out from behind every grounder that rolled across the saturated outfield "grass," slowing the ball to a snail's pace. By the time we surrendered the field to Highlands; every one of our practice balls was water-logged and heavy and scrubbed bright white from rolling across the artificial turf over and over.

We trotted off the field shaking our heads. Our usual snap and precision weren't there. We struggled with footing and timing. We had always prided ourselves on intimidating our opponents with our slick fielding and professionalism even before the game had begun. But today we looked like just another high school baseball team and not the polished, regimented squad that had always represented Coach Sherman and Lakewood City High School so well.

Highlands came into the game at 18–1. We were 30–6. And although they had a higher winning percentage, we had played nearly twice as many games as they had. It was our experience that gave us the advantage. It was our repetition that made us nearly flawless on defense. But out on that artificial turf, we looked intimidated by our surroundings.

Still, as I watched the Highlands team take the field, I felt confident that we could handle them. They looked like a solid team, but they were no West Mifflin North.

"Did you hear about the busses?" Kerry asked me as I took my seat next to him on the bench. "Coach Sherman just got a call that one of our student busses broke down outside of Ambridge on the way to the game, and the second student bus is waiting with them until help arrives."

"Oh, that's just great," I moaned. "What else can go wrong?"

Just before the game started, the announcer introduced the starting lineups, and we each, in turn, ran out along the first base line and waited for the playing of the national anthem. And, although there were nearly 4,000 fans in the stands, the eighty-or-so missing students, who had been our loudest and most enthusiastic supporters all year long, left the cheering for our squad at about half the volume of the cheers for the Highland ballplayers.

It's no big deal, I said to myself. *We just have to settle down and play our game.*

But instead, the strangeness of the day just continued to grow. The crowd was still buzzing from the pre-game introductions and a roar went up as Porter unleashed his first fastball of the game. The Highlands' leadoff hitter jumped on the first pitch and smashed a hard ground ball between short and third. On our home field, I might have been able to get over and backhand the ball in the hole, but instead I froze for half a second and the ball rolled untouched into the outfield. *Where's the crack of the bat?* I bemoaned.

The roar of the crowd, as it banked and echoed throughout the major league stadium, was deafening. I had no idea that my brain had been programed to react to the sound of the bat, and even though I saw the ball coming toward the hole, without the sound, I hesitated to move toward it. *Oh, this is some crazy shit.* I lamented. *I can't hear. I have to force myself to move based solely on what I see.*

The next batter dropped a bunt down the third base line, but Phil Lombardo was charging hard and got to the ball almost immediately. "Second base," screamed Theisman from behind the plate.

That's more like it, I thought. *They try a sacrifice bunt and we turn it into a force-out at second base. That's the kind of play we make better than anyone else.*

But, as he turned to make the throw to second, Phil's right foot slipped on the artificial surface. His throw flew off target, a good four feet over Kerry's head, at second base. And the runner from first streaked toward third, as the throw bounded into center field. Instead of a man at first base and one out, Highlands had first and third occupied and no outs.

I glanced up at Jerry Delpino seated in the stands right behind the plate. His nightmare was coming true, and he had his face buried in his hands.

The next batter smacked a hard ground ball to Kerry, and we turned a much-needed double play, as the first run of the game raced home for Highlands.

That's not good, I thought to myself. *Sure, we got the double play, but so many of these championship games are pitchers' duels, that one run might be all it takes to win the game.*

Joe struck out their cleanup hitter to end the inning, and we trailed 1–0, as we came to the plate for our first at bat.

They were pitching a 17-year-old left-handed sophomore named Dave Blaylock. Apparently, he had a lengthy illness one year in grade school and was now a year behind the rest of his class. But he sure didn't throw like a sophomore. He had pinpoint control of his fastball and a big breaking ball that was sure to confound our left-handed hitters.

Of course, I was delighted to see a left hander on the mound. No need to worry about a right-handed curve ball like the one that Dewey had thrown a week earlier.

Lombardo, our first hitter, worked the count to 3–2, and then drew a lead-off walk. And Kerry followed with a perfect sacrifice bunt to get him in scoring position. Blaylock's next pitch was in the dirt and skipped away from the catcher, as Lombardo moved over to third. With one out and Phil at third base, we were fairly confident we would tie up the game, especially when Jay Farroni lifted a medium-deep fly ball to right field.

Kowalski, the Highlands' right-fielder started to back up on the ball, then came charging in when he realized he had misjudged it. Phil was our fastest baserunner, and when he tagged up at third, we all figured we had tied up the game. But Kowalski was charging hard, and his momentum added ten miles-per-hour to his throw. The ball never even touched the ground. It was a bang, bang play at the plate, but Lombardo was out. The Lakewood City fans moaned in dismay, while the Highlands' fans screamed deliriously.

The game settled down after that, and Porter set the Highlands hitters down one-two-three in the top of the second. In the bottom of the second inning, our cleanup hitter Gino Petrella stepped into the batter's box, while Porter and I picked out our bats from the bat rack.

"Where the hell is my bat?" I barked at our little nine-year-old batboy Stevie Heaton, as he scampered over from the dugout.

"I don't know, Teddy," he blurted with panic in his voice. "It's the 34-inch Hank Aaron, right?"

"Hell, yes, it's the Aaron." I squawked. "It's a Flame-Fused Louisville Slugger. There's a piece of tape at the bottom of the handle with my name on it."

Stevie dumped a second equipment bag out next to the dugout, but all that rolled out were some infield balls and our backup catcher's mask. "I can't find it, Teddy." He couldn't even bring himself to look at me.

I was coming into the game as our leading hitter, the hottest bat on the team. And Stevie had committed the cardinal sin for batboys; he hadn't protected the bat I had used all season long. Panicked, he and I scrambled from bat rack to equipment bag to back inside the dugout, but the bat was nowhere to be found.

Petrella flew out to centerfield on the third pitch on the inning, and Porter was walking into the batter's box with me on deck. The time for searching was over. Now I had to find a substitute. "Try this Kaline," Stevie offered in desperation.

I checked out the bat, a 34-inch Al Kaline autographed model. It was a birch, power-fused Louisville Slugger with a skinny handle and most of the weight in the barrel, just like I liked it. The Aaron model had a brown-grain look to it, but this Kaline was a pale, almost white in color. I swung it a couple times and liked the feel of it. But, in the back of my mind, I couldn't shake the feeling that this was no accident.

Hell, my name was on the bat, I thought as Porter took the first pitch for strike one. *Sure, it was owned by the high school and any player was allowed to use it, but when I started getting hot at the plate, no one else had dared to touch it.*

"Did someone break it in batting practice?" I questioned the batboy. "Did someone take it?"

"Teddy, I don't know." Stevie pleaded. "Who would break it and not tell you about it?"

In the back of my mind, one thought kept nagging at me: *Can this Rockland vs. Lakewood City shit possibly be a factor in this?* Certainly, there were still plenty of Lakewood students who didn't care for the Rockland kids, but would somebody actually *steal* my bat before the WPIAL Championship game? Nobody on the *team* would steal it for sure, I figured. But if someone had cracked it in batting practice on Saturday, would they have had the guts to tell me?

On the next pitch, Porter grounded weakly back to the mound for the second out.

I glanced back at Stevie one more time, as I headed for the batter's box. "It's not the bat, Teddy," he consoled, "It's the batter."

I ripped Blaylock's first pitch into centerfield for our first hit of the game. Never had I heard a sound like that before. CRRACKKK! It was like an explosion. As I rounded first base, my ears were still ringing. I knew I had caught the pitch right on the nose, and an audible gasp had gone up from the crowd and the players. Was it the acoustics from the major league stadium? Was it the brand new birch bat crushing a brand new ball? Whatever it was, it was

216

certainly a major-league-caliber hit and Blaylock shook his head in disgust, even as he tipped his hat to me standing at the base. I never worried about my lost bat the rest of the game. Still, a nagging thought raced around the back of my brain. *Would anyone have broken one of the Lakewood boys' bats and not told him about it?*

If someone from Lakewood City really was behind the missing bat, they can kiss my ass, I thought to myself. *Nothing's going to stop me today.*

Our left-handed centerfielder, Don Hicks, stepped to the plate next, but he struggled to hit Blaylock's big curveball, and eventually struck out. Still, after the swing I had put on the ball, our team was no longer intimidated by the hard-throwing left hander.

Highlands didn't score in the third or fourth inning, and we came to bat in the bottom of the fourth, still losing 1–0, just as the Lakewood student buses finally arrived at Three Rivers Stadium

Our right fielder, Jay Farroni, opened the inning with a base hit to right field. And our cleanup hitter, Gino, followed with a solid smash up the middle. It was Gino's first hit of the playoffs. Our leading RBI man all year, he had struggled in the tournament, but he was picking the perfect time to come out of his slump.

With me on deck, Porter laid down a perfect sacrifice bunt to put the runners in scoring position. As I stepped into the batter's box, the umpire chuckled, "Well, here he comes—Roberto Clemente. You know my ears are still ringing from that hit you got in the second inning." The Highlands catcher didn't speak, but he nodded his head in agreement.

The Highlands coach came out of the dugout to settle down his star pitcher and remind him of what pitch he had thrown me in my first at bat. I took the time to gaze up at our cheering section, now on their feet for the first time since their late arrival. I was disappointed to see Lorraine sitting in the middle of our senior students with Blake. They were joking and laughing and passing cups of Coca-Cola down the aisle from the vendor. *This could be the biggest at-bat of my lifetime,* I thought in disappointment, *and she's too busy to even watch.*

Blaylock's first pitch was in the dirt, and the second one was high and outside. When his third pitch also bounced in the dirt, the count hit 3–0 and I got the feeling they might be trying to pitch around me.

Coach Sherman then called time out from the third base coaches' box, and walked half-way to the plate to meet me. "If the pitch is in there, I want you swinging," he whispered. "You're our hottest hitter. Now, drive in those runs."

But, when I returned to the batter's box, their catcher was already signaling for an intentional walk on the fourth pitch. I shook my head in disgust as I trotted toward first base. The strategy made sense. I had pounded the ball in my first at bat, while left-hander Hicks had fanned on three big breaking balls. When I looked into the stands again, I could see Lorraine leaning forward to question the fans in front of her. I tried to read her lips. I can't be sure, but I think she said, "How did Teddy get on base?"

Christ, I thought, *she's not even watching me play.*

With the bases loaded, Don swung at the first curve ball but missed it by a foot. The second pitch was a called strike. And the third pitch started down the middle, but broke way outside, with Don chasing it out of the strike zone for strike three, the second out of the inning. This was going to be our best chance to take the lead, but just like in the West Mifflin game, it was now going to be up to Rick Theisman to save the day.

Theisman immediately called a timeout and walked toward Coach Sherman at third. *He wants permission to swing at the first pitch,* I thought. *Hell yes, Rick. Get in there and jump on one.*

Rick returned to the batter's box, and Blaylock's first pitch was a fastball, right down the heart of the plate. *Smack...* Rick hit a hard ground ball between short and third. Farroni scored easily, and Coach Sherman was waving wildly for Petrella to do the same.

The throw from the left fielder was headed toward home, so I never broke stride and tried my best to go from first base to third on the play. But Blaylock, who was lining up the throw to home cut-off the ball and fired to the third baseman, trying to nip me sliding into the base. If I were tagged out before Petrella crossed the plate, his run would not have counted, and I cursed myself for even trying to advance on the throw.

"Get down, Teddy," screamed Coach Sherman. "Get down!"

The pitcher was standing halfway between third and home and his throw was to the infield side of the base, so I laid out my slide as far as I could to the outfield side. My perfect hook slide got my foot in under the third base-man's tag. "Safe," screamed the third base umpire, as a roar went up from the crowd.

I was safe, I thought, *but I'm lucky I got the call. Sometimes, umpires will call the runner out just because the ball beats you to the base.*

"Atta boy, Teddy," sang Coach Sherman over the din of the crowd. Then he turned to the base umpire. "Great call, Blue. Not every umpire would have had the guts to make that call."

The tall, farm-boy-looking umpire smiled and nodded. He was the third base umpire, on the four-man crew that had been selected for the championship game. Most of our regular-season games included just two umpires, sometimes three, but never four, and the Mr. Greenjeans-look-alike probably wasn't expecting too much action at third base. But now, Phil Sherman, the winningest baseball coach in WPIAL history, is calling him "gutsy." The guy was beaming.

The newly-arrived Lakewood City cheering section went wild, and the players themselves were jumping around like we just won the game. Premature? Maybe, but if Porter kept throwing the next three innings the way he had thrown the last three; we were well on our way to a WPIAL Championship. The cheers and screams echoed and reechoed across the Three-Rivers Stadium walls and scoreboard and poured energy and excitement into every ball player. Dusting myself off at third, I felt a huge wave of pride and joy surge through me. *How could things ever be better than this?* I wondered. *How can I ever be happier than this?*

Even when Huddy grounded-out back to the mound to end the inning, I still felt pretty good, sitting on a 2–1 lead heading into the fifth.

Their next rally started innocently enough when Highlands' right-hand-hitting, left-handed pitcher led off the inning by walking on a close 3–2 pitch. He was followed by right-fielder Kowalski, who squared around to bunt. I got a little jolt of pride when I saw our infielders roll into place for the sacrifice attempt. Lombardo swept in from third, while Porter converged on the entire right portion of the inner infield. Hudson was moving to cover first, and Rolley was already in range of second base.

It was the kind of play that gave many high school teams fits, but it was the kind of execution that set Lakewood City apart from all the other programs. We had played 36 games together that season; it was and is the record for the most high school games ever played by one team in one season in any sport in school history.

We were primed and ready for this moment except, it didn't work out that way. The ball was bunted straight to Phil, who was charging hard, and grabbed the bounce cleanly just above his knees. He had a pretty good shot at getting the lead-runner at second, but after the throwing the last bunt into centerfield, Theisman called for Lombardo to just get the out at first. But when Phil tried to plant his foot to throw to first, it again slid on the artificial surface and his throw bounced wildly past Hudson covering first base. It rolled about 10 feet into the outfield grass.

Kowalski stayed at first base, while Blaylock flew all the way around to third. Instead of one out and a man at second, they had first and third and no outs. It was a big turning point, and it made all of us uneasy, this was the kind of play that usually set us above the other teams, but now we were the victims.

I glanced over at Jerry in the stands behind our dugout. He was staring out over the field at nothing in particular. *He's daydreaming,* I thought. *He's seeing himself taking the field. This is his dream; I'm living it for both of us.*

We still had the lead, but it was going to take a miracle, to get out of this mess. And then, it happened. The very next Highlands batter squared around to bunt again, but pulled back his bat. His intent was not to bunt, but to try to set up the first-and-third double steal. We pulled off this offensive play all the time, but no one, no one, ever did it to us.

They were pushing their advantage with this aggressive base running, but Theisman was no ordinary catcher and he still had plenty of tricks up his sleeve. When the pitch came through and the runner at first took off for second, Rick flew up from his catcher's stance and drew back his arm, but instead of firing through to second base, he faked his throw to second, drew back his arm again, and picked Blaylock off third base by twelve feet.

Excitement shot through our whole team. Finally, *this* is the way it should be, *us* taking advantage of their blunders. That's the way it had been all season.

We controlled the bases. We controlled the action in the infield. We were the more solid, practiced, experienced team. And Theisman had just run the third base pick-off play to perfection.

Lombardo charged at Blaylock to begin the rundown, while I swept in to cover third base behind him. We practiced rundowns all spring, even when the weather had been too bad to go outside, we practiced in the gym. Every player on the team, both infielders and outfielders, had been schooled on the proper way to run down a trapped baserunner. Everyone was involved in the play. Outfielders, pitchers, catchers, they all ran in to back each other up, and step in when the player in front of them chased the runner. We had gone the whole season, and no one, not one runner, had ever escaped a Lakewood City rundown.

Phil's first throw went to Theisman, and Rick grabbed it and started running Blaylock back towards third base, where I was now covering the bag. I expected Rick to throw to me early, so I could comfortably chase the runner down and make the tag, but instead he kept running towards Blaylock, chasing him back towards third. I didn't like him waiting so long to make the throw, but I understood what he was doing. The runner from first base had already taken second on the play. If we had to keep Blaylock in a long, multi-throw rundown, it would give the runner at second time to get to third base.

If we got this runner out, after the other runner came all the way to third, they would still have the tying run at third and only one out, but if we were able to nail Blaylock quickly, the other runner would have to stay at second base. And our chance of keeping the lead would be much better. Rick ran at Blaylock until the runner finally committed to trying to return to third.

I was a little worried that Rick might not throw to me in time to make the tag, but the throw came in plenty of time, and I swept the tag down on Blaylock's shoulder as he dove for the bag. His hand was still a good foot-and-a-half from third base, when I applied the tag. And I quickly turned my attention to the runner at second base, who had wandered about six feet off the bag. A good throw could make it close at second, but I really didn't think we had a good enough chance to get another out there.

And then I heard it, one word that would haunt my life for a long, long time. "Safe," barked the third base umpire.

"What?" I screamed in disbelief. I felt like a bolt of lightning had just shot through my entire body. I leaped into the air and spun to face him. "You *can't* blow that call," I cried. "Not now. Not in *this* game!"

In the local newspaper the next day, they published a photo of me mid-jump with my palms raised over my head, pleading for sanity. I'm more than four feet off the ground in the photo and screaming at the umpire. "Gosh!" reads the cutline under the photo, "That's probably what Lakewood City shortstop Ted Tresh is saying after Highlands' pitcher Dave Blaylock escapes a rundown in the fifth inning."

If there are three things in my life that I'm absolutely sure about, here they are: (1) Blaylock was out at third. It wasn't even close. (2) I wasn't saying "gosh" after the bad call. And (3) under any normal circumstances, there is no way I can jump four feet off the ground.

The very next Highland batter singled up the middle, scoring both runners. And we were trailing again, 3–2.

Porter retired the next three batters in order, but the damage had been done. It seemed like our well-trained, game-hardened defense was coming unglued. Coach Sherman grabbed my arm as I entered the dugout. "Did we have him, Teddy?" he shook his head in outrage and disbelief.

"Coach, I promise you. He was out by a foot and a half."

"You know, we created the monster?" he pulled me aside and whispered. "If we hadn't made such a fuss over him calling you safe last inning, he wouldn't have been so gung-ho about making another *safe* call now. I called him 'gutsy' for not making the automatic out call. Now it comes back to bite us in the ass."

We didn't score in the fifth. And when they came to bat in the sixth inning, their leadoff hitter smacked a ground ball up the middle, that I cut-off in front of second base. But incredibly, I bobbled the ball, and the runner was safe at first. Porter's disgust with our once-errorless infield was obvious. His concentration was broken, and a walk and another base-hit stretched the Highlands lead to 4–2.

I led off our half of the sixth inning by taking the first pitch for a called strike. But on the next pitch, I crushed an outside corner fastball, sending a screaming line drive right at the Highlands second baseman. Again, the crack of the bat was ear-piercing. The ball was hit so hard, that the infielder barely had time to raise his mitt. It smacked off the heel of his glove and then banged off his chest but lay on the ground right in front of him. I ran as fast and as hard as I could muster, but the throw to first beat me by half a step.

I kicked at the turf in disgust. And, as I returned to the dugout, I turned to face Blaylock. He knew I had beaten him on that pitch, but he just smiled and shrugged. "Hey, that's baseball," he chided. I was really beginning to hate the kid. We went quietly after that, and at the start of the seventh and final inning, we were still losing 4–2.

In the top of the last inning, Porter's arm looked shot. He had started the game with a sore shoulder, and now that his adrenaline was no longer pounding through his veins, he seemed to labor over every pitch. He was deflated and disgusted and expressionless as he toed the mound. He walked the first batter on four pitches. *Porter has given up,* I thought to myself. *Things are going to get ugly.*

Coach Sherman saw it too and sent Rob "The Big Baboose" Blaine out to the bullpen to warm up. After a pop-up in the infield and a strikeout, Highlands' next two batters both singled, scoring a fifth run, and sending their clean-up hitter to the plate. By now, Porter looked like a boxer who had just gone 12 rounds with Joe Frazier. He laid a punch-less fastball right down the middle of the plate and their big clean-up hitter pounded a fly ball deep to centerfield. The ball would have been a home run at any high school field we had played on all year. But this was no high school field. This was Three Rivers Stadium. And Don Hicks, who had struggled at the plate all day, spun around from his centerfield position, and sprinted straight toward the wall. He made an incredible over-the-head, Willie-Mays-type basket catch to end the inning.

"Atta baby, Atta baby," I screamed in joy, but as I turned to head off the field, I couldn't help but notice that the entire team was flat, especially Porter, who was walking slowly back to the dugout with his head down. I shot a glace into our cheering section in the stands. Everyone seemed deflated, and no matter how hard I tried, I couldn't locate Lorraine's face in the crowd. Where the hell was she now?

We came to the plate losing the game 5–2 in the bottom of the last inning.

Our number nine hitter and fellow Rockland boy, John Hudson, would lead off the inning, and I counted the number of hitters who would have to get on base for me to get another chance at the plate. It looked doubtful, I would bat seventh in the inning, and if I was going to get another at bat this season, we would have to put together one hell of a rally.

Huddy worked the count full, and then drew a walk on a pitch that was just off the outside corner. We had life. Coach Sherman immediately called time out and sent in the speedy senior Nick Martini, my backup at shortstop, to run for Hudson.

Our leadoff hitter Phil Lombardo came to the plate and immediately hit a little roller towards shortstop. Martini got a great jump off the base, so the only possible play would be at first. The infielder charged hard, and grabbed the grounder, but with Phil's speed, he looked to have a great chance of beating the throw.

The shortstop hurried his throw and bounced the ball well in front of the first baseman, who was unable to block it. The ball rolled a good fifteen feet past the base, and our runners advanced to second and third with no outs. That brought a roar from the Lakewood faithful, and our number two hitter, Kerry Rolley, to the plate. He got ahead in the count 2–0, before smashing a drive to deep left-center field. For a second, I thought the ball would go all the way to the wall, but Highlands' centerfielder Tom Stenko raced into the gap and hauled in the long fly.

Martini was tagging up at third base, and Lombardo was tagging at second. Martini scored easily, and when Stenko's throw to third bounced off Lombardo's helmet, it ricocheted up into the stands and Phil trotted home to make the score 5–4 with just one out.

In the dugout, I was starting to get excited. Just three more hitters would bat before me. With a little luck, we might just be in a position to win this game after all!

I was amazed at the never-say-die attitude of our senior ball players. Huddy, Phil, and Kerry had all battled like their entire careers were on the line, and I guess, in a way, they were.

That brought our number three hitter, Jay Farroni, another senior, to the plate. After falling behind in the count 1–2, he waged war with Blaylock, fouling off pitch after pitch and finally drawing a walk. We had the tying run on base and just one out.

Our cleanup hitter Geno Petrella stepped to the plate and smashed Blaylock's first pitch up the middle for a base hit. Now we had runners on first and second with one out. Coach Sherman immediately called time out and sent Skip Bruno out to run for Petrella. Along with me and Huddy, Skip was the only other Rockland boy on the team. And now he was in position to score the winning run in the WPIAL Championship. It was exactly what we had been hoping for. In the dugout, I was overjoyed. Porter would be our next batter and I was *on deck*. Unless Porter grounded into a double play, I would definitely get another shot at Blaylock.

The Highlands' coach now called time out and went out to try to settle down his rattled star pitcher. It looked like he might even be pulling his starter, in favor of the big right-hander he had warming up in the bullpen, but after a quick look in to see the left-handed Porter coming to the plate, he decided to stay with the left-handed Blaylock on the mound.

During the visit, I put my arm on Porter's shoulder. "It's all on us now, buddy," I told him. "All those weeks ago, when Sherman called us into his office and told us he was going to rely on us, the juniors, to pick his team up. Remember, he asked you to beat Hopewell on just 2 days' rest. And then, he moved us both up in the lineup. Since then, we've come through for this team over and over and over again. Now, we're going to win the whole damn thing for him."

I looked close for Porter's reaction, anything, a smile, a confident head nod, anything. But his face was blank. I guess he just couldn't get over how our defense had let him down. This was supposed to be *his* showcase. He was our star pitcher. The stands were full of major league scouts who were following him. He was supposed to win this game 1–0 or 2–1. Instead, he had given up five runs, and it had drained the life out of him. This rally wasn't going to change that.

He gave me a heavy sigh, "I'll do my best," he shrugged. And he stepped into the batter's box. Blaylock started him off with a big breaking ball that started down the middle, but broke way outside. Didn't matter, Joe took a big sweeping swing at the pitch and missed it by a foot and a half. He took the next fastball inside for a ball. *Blaylock's trying to set him up for another curve ball,* I thought, *trying to move him off the plate.*

The next pitch was another fastball on the inside corner, that Joe fouled off into the screen. Then with the count 1–2, he came back with the exact same curveball he had thrown for strike one. And even though it was again off the plate, Joe took his same big swing, and again, missed the ball by a foot.

I stood in disbelief, as I watched Porter walk back towards the dugout. There was no expression on his face, no grimace, and no show of emotion whatsoever. And I wondered if I could be so calm if it was me who had just struck out.

Now I stood there in the on-deck circle. It was all being left up to me. If Joe had been emotionless, I was just the opposite, a chaos of fear, excitement, and terror.

I closed my eyes and saw the faces of every coach I had ever had, and, then the faces of every Rockland boy who had ever put on a Lakewood City uniform. This was the end of it. Next year, I would be the only Rockland boy left on the team. And all the younger Rockland players, for all the years to come, would be making their mark at Beaver Falls High School. It was my chance to be immortal, my chance to leave Lakewood City with one more Championship, courtesy of the Rockland boys. I felt like I was going to jump out of my skin.

Pope Trippy II, Huddy had called me. But I felt the weight of the moment growing heavier with every step I took toward the plate.

"The right man in the right spot," shouted out Jerry's brother Randy Delpino from the dugout. "There's nobody we'd rather have up there."

"It's not the bat. It's the batter," sang little Stevie Heaton as I stepped into the batter's box.

But suddenly, I felt the strangeness of the Kaline model in my hands. I had used that Hank Aaron bat through 36 games this season. It was almost an extension of my shoulders and arms and hands. I stepped out and re-gripped the Kaline, rolling it slightly one way and then the other. The bat felt fine, but someone in this stadium had stolen my Aaron model or had broken it in practice and never let me know. I glanced into the Lakewood City cheering section. Someone out there was rooting against me. Maybe a lot of them were.

I could see Lorraine, talking, laughing. I saw her slap Blake on the shoulder and wondered what wise-ass comment had elicited that reaction.

Just two rows in front of her, I spotted Lynn Batista, the girl from my journalism class. She was sitting next to her boyfriend too, but her eyes were glued on me. I shot a quick look towards my parents. My dad was standing and clapping encouragingly, but my mom was sitting, and had her face buried in her hands. She couldn't even watch.

I stepped into the box and dug in. *Wait for a good pitch,* I told myself. *If it's right down the middle, then jump on it. If it catches the corner, just wait for a better pitch to hit.*

I steadied myself one more time, and Blaylock let the first pitch fly. The damn thing split the plate, but for some reason, I didn't swing. I froze in the batter's box. "Strike," screamed the umpire.

What the hell was that? I admonished myself. I had played thousands of organized baseball games in my life, and I had never, ever frozen at the plate. The pitch was exactly where I wanted it. *What the hell is wrong with me?*

I stepped out again, furious with myself for taking the pitch. *I should have won the game right there. He just laid it right down the middle.* And I vowed to take a big swing at the very next pitch. But Blaylock was too smart to come back with the same pitch. He threw me an off-speed curve that dropped out of the strike zone. I took a huge swing, but I was so far out in front of the pitch that I missed it by a foot.

Now, the pressure was all over me, inside, outside, every muscle in my body was twitching. Coach Sherman called time out and walked down the third base line to settle me down.

"Relax in there," he said calmly. "You've got two strikes now. You have to protect the plate. Don't let him get one past you."

My two-strike approach was nothing like my regular batting stance. I dug-in my right foot just inches off the inside of the plate, choked up on the bat, and shortened my stroke. My dream of hitting a gap shot to score both runners became very unlikely now. I could produce a line drive or hard ground ball from this short-stroke and open stance, but probably not a deep drive. Still, it had been more than a month since I last struck out, and this two-strike, contact approach was the reason.

The butterflies were still twitching in my stomach and arms, but this short swing was something I could do in my sleep. I knew I would make some kind of contact with the ball.

When Blaylock saw me crowding the plate, he decided to move me back. His next pitch came right at my left shoulder, and I dove to the ground to keep from getting hit by the pitch. That was his mistake. The brush-back pitch shot adrenaline pumping through my veins, and all the fear was gone.

If he thinks he can intimidate a Rockland boy with that inside shit, he's badly mistaken. I dusted myself off, stepped into the batter's box and dug in even closer to the plate. I almost smiled. *As if I'm worried about getting hit.* I thought. *As if I wouldn't rather get hit in the face than strikeout.*

Blaylock tried to hit the outside corner with the next pitch, but I cleanly lifted a foul ball out over the first base dugout. I had taken the corner away from him. He tried to reclaim the strike zone by coming inside again, and once again he sent me sprawling on my back for Ball Two.

This time I asked for timeout, dusted myself off, and dug in even closer to the plate. My right foot was touching the lime on the inside of the batter's box, and my elbows were practically hanging over the strike zone.

He reached back and fired an inside corner pitch that jammed me, and I hit a little roller toward third base. *Oh, no,* I screamed at myself, with first and second occupied, all the third baseman has to do is field this little grounder and step on the bag. But, as the ball rolled down the line, it slipped into foul territory. The count was still 2–2.

Blaylock didn't want to come down the middle, so he tried to get me to chase one off the outside corner. I took the pitch for Ball Three.

The count was full now, and I knew our runners would be off and moving on the pitch. That meant that Jay Farroni should score easily on almost any hit to the outfield. I looked over at Skip at first base. He could fly around the bases and would surely score the winning run if I could hit any kind of gap shot.

I wish I was taking my full swing; I shook my head in disgust. *But I have to defend the plate. I just have to make contact.*

The count was full, the runners were moving, and Blaylock fired a high pitch, down the middle, and just at the top of the strike zone. I got a good swing at it, but fouled it straight back and onto the screen directly behind the plate. *Damn it,* I thought, *in my normal stance I would have hit that ball a mile, but all scrunched up in the batter's box, I just couldn't get my arms extended.*

I looked out at Three Rivers' huge $10 million scoreboard. There was the score 5–4, and the count 3–2, and right next to it was a big photo head-shot of me that towered thirty feet in the air. And, for some reason a wave of confidence and well-being surged through me. *He can't get it past me,* I thought.

I *knew* what the next pitch would be. Blaylock didn't want to walk me. That would load the bases, and the Highlands coach would surely pull him in favor of the big right hander who had been warming up for the last twenty minutes. *If he walks me, he's gone. He has to take a chance and come right down the middle.* I knew what he was going to throw now, just like I had known that Dewey was going to throw me that curveball in the West Mifflin game a week earlier. It was just good baseball.

This is it, I told myself. *In 1962, they had carried Trippy Wyeth off the field. In 1968, it was Derrick Dawson. Now, in our very last year in Lakewood City, it will be another Rockland boy who brings a WPIAL title back to this high school.* I closed up my stance and went back to my power swing. *I know he's coming down the middle,* I thought. *If I take my best swing, we're going to win this game right here.*

"Come on," I whispered between my clenched teeth. "I've got you. Just throw that same pitch you started with."

He reared back and fired.

The funny thing about baseball is that it is *not* a science, and sometimes seventeen-year-old kids don't do what makes sense. Blaylock was feeling just as much pressure as I was. He didn't want to think anymore, he just reached back further, kicked his foot higher and threw the ball as hard as he could. The pitch seemed to come from everywhere and nowhere. His left arm flew high over his head. His follow-through sent him sprawling toward the third base line, and a hard fastball streaked toward the outside corner, and then tailed away.

In my defensive stance, I would have surely seen the ball sliding off the plate. I would have taken the pitch for Ball Four. But, in my aggressive approach, it was too late. I was already swinging, and I knew I couldn't reach the pitch.

"Strike Three," screamed the home plate ump. And the damn stadium exploded. To my ever-lasting shame, the first emotion I felt was relief. At least I was out of this pressure-cooker. At least I could breathe again.

And then, the weight of reality came crashing in. It was like gravity itself was multiplying, Two-G's, Three-G's, Five. It pushed me to my knees. I tried to stand up, but I couldn't. There were shouts and screams and cheering from the Highlands faithful, but I couldn't look up to see any of it. I couldn't lift my head from my chest, and my shoulders felt like I was carrying 500 pounds on them.

"The great part about baseball," my Uncle Jiggy used to tell me, "Is that redemption is only a pitch away."

But there were no more pitches. There was no redemption. Just the empty, empty place in the soul, that comes from a lost opportunity; an opportunity that took a whole season to build. Hell, it took a whole lifetime for me to get here. And I knew it was an opportunity that would never come again.

The next thing I felt was Coach Sherman's hand patting me on the back. "You came through for us all season, Teddy." I looked up and saw his own pain written across his face. He shook his head slowly, "We just hoped you could do it one more time." Then, he turned and headed off toward the Highlands dugout to congratulate their coach.

I tried to stand; tried to lift my chin from my chest, but I just couldn't muster the strength. Then I felt another hand on my shoulder, and an arm lifting me to my feet. I looked to my left where Huddy stood, like the mountain-of-a-man he was, slowly raising me to my feet. And then to my right, where Skip Bruno, his hand on my shoulder, was protecting me from the waves of Highlands' players and fans that were streaming onto the field. No other Lakewood player had left the dugout. They were all lost in their own disappointment.

"Of course," I whispered to myself. "Of course, it's the Rockland boys."

There was a photo published in the Lakewood City Ledger the next day. It showed the three of us, the last three Rockland boys to wear the Blue-and-White of the Wolverines, walking slowly off the field, surrounded by a sea of Highland's players. We all looked heartbroken. No other Lakewood players are in sight.

I peered into the stands, where my mom was crying on my dad's shoulder, all his attention was on her, just as it should be. I saw Lynn Batista. Her boyfriend was on his feet, chatting away, as Lynn just stood there, motionless, staring out at the field, staring at me. I hardly knew the girl, but I could read her lips. "It's okay," she was saying. And then repeated it, "It's okay."

I managed a weak smile, and then turned my attention to where Lorraine had been sitting with Blake and his group of senior friends. She was yakking away and laughing as she stood and cleared her things from her seat. Then she glanced at me, but only a glance, as if she didn't want to get caught looking my way.

Jesus, I thought. *Take a minute, will you? Take five goddamn seconds. Don't you know that the world has just changed forever?*

All the rest is a blur. I can't remember the walk to the clubhouse, the shower, the reporters, the bus ride back to Lakewood City.

The first thing I do remember is the dread. The town of Lakewood City had a parade planned for us. "Win or lose," the papers had said. But a parade was the last thing I wanted now…Now that I had just lost everything.

That too, was a blur…the people lining the streets…half cheering…half shaking their heads…the speeches on the courthouse steps…the anguish on Coach Sherman's face. Someone yells, "You'll get 'em next year," and I wince at the thought.

When I got home, my father was unsympathetic. "Shake it off," he chided me. "You have to be a man now. Why did you have to drop to one knee? Don't you know what that did to your mother?

"I'm not going to allow you to mope around this house all summer," he barked. "This was just a game. What will you do when life throws you a real problem? Don't you know what you'll have to face out there…Sickness and Heartbreak and Death? This is nothing!"

I just stared at him blankly. I could barely believe his lack of compassion. Little did I realize the truth and depth of his comments.

"Look, Ted, I know you're hurting. But sometimes God gives you disappointments like this to make you stronger; to prepare you for the real horrors of life."

I just shook my head and slipped into my room, where I pulled off my tie and sports coat. I couldn't *just shake it off*. I didn't want to go outside or see anyone.

The thoughts wouldn't leave me alone: Why did I take that first pitch? Why did I abandon my defensive stance with two strikes on me? Why didn't we get that out call at third base? Why won't God give me a do-over? He had never let me down before.

Although high school baseball was over for the year, I knew that I still had to find a way to get ready for the American Legion season. I wouldn't be playing for Lakewood City anymore. I'd be back to playing ball for Rockland, and Rockland was the reigning Beaver County Champion. That's right, just a season earlier, tiny Rockland had assembled a team that took on Beaver Falls, and Hopewell, and New Brighton and Beaver and Ambridge. And beat them all. Then went up against Lakewood City, the Lawrence County Champions, and eliminated them from the American Legion District playoffs.

Would Lakewood City High School really miss the contributions of the Rockland players? Of course, they would. It was the end of an era. And I had had a chance to end it in style. But I blew my chance. Now my confidence was shot.

I stumbled around the house for the next few days. I didn't really want to see anyone; didn't want to face the questions or hear the excuses that well-intentioned friends would make for me.

A few days later, the American Legion season began, and I was a shadow of what I had been. I had hit nearly .400 during the high school season, but now I struggled at the plate. My timing was off. I was thinking too much, instead of just swinging. I was barely able to stay above .250.

Confidence is a funny thing. When you have it, you don't even know you have it. But, when you lose it, every part of your life is affected.

In the first two weeks after the championship, I tried to call Lorraine three times. Each time, I would pick up the phone, but just couldn't get myself to dial the number. Didn't she look away when I searched for her in the stands? Didn't she just stroll out of Three Rivers Stadium while my life was imploding?

And that note she wrote in my yearbook; I thought it was a love note. But now when I read it over, it just sounded like a sweet goodbye. My depression colored everything I heard or saw or felt. And everything was gray. Maybe it wasn't really that she saw me any differently; but I saw myself differently. And I couldn't imagine that the girl of my dreams was ever going to be with me now. I thought I was beaten, and until I could disprove that thought, I *was* beaten.

Every night I had the same nightmare: waiting for that last pitch; the sudden surge of confidence; the ball moving away; the swing; Lorraine's back as she walked away. I could see Blake laughing and chatting like nothing had happened. I could see their heads disappear into the stadium tunnel. And poof… she was gone forever.

And the waking hours were no better than the sleeping. For the first three days, I woke up thinking that the championship game was still ahead of me. And then, the reality would hit, and my grief would come roaring back.

I was in mourning. I didn't really want to see my friends or teammates. On the third day, I managed to walk down to Uncle Joe's drug store for a cherry Coke. He had always been my baseball mentor, my advisor, my personal coach, but even he lowered his head when I walked in off the street. He looked like someone with something to say but couldn't bring himself to say it.

Finally, he put my Cherry Coke down on the counter and cleared his throat. "I know that I taught you guys the importance of teamwork," he started, "And hard work and sacrifice. I know that I taught you to love the game. And I'm proud of that. But there's something else you need to know about baseball. Something you've probably already figured out for yourself."

"What's that?" I shrugged.

He stared me right in the eyes and spoke slowly and deliberately. "Losing hurts worse than winning feels good."

LOST IN THE FOG

"Jesus, Dad," Gene shook his head slowly. "I know you were upset, but I hope you didn't let a baseball game ruin your summer for you."

"Well, confidence affects everything, Champ," I lamented. "When you're cocky and you win, everyone's your friend. When you're cocky and you lose, your detractors are everywhere. I could feel the loss of respect every time I left the house. I could see it in their eyes.

"But, you know, maybe it wasn't really in their eyes. Maybe it was all inside my head. My confidence was gone. It colored everything I felt. It colored everything I saw. The world probably hadn't changed. I had changed. But, at the time, I couldn't see it.

"I needed someone to bring me back to reality. I needed my girl, but Lorraine wasn't really my girl. She was someone else's girl. And I would daydream about the conversations that she was probably having with Blake."

"I'm sorry Lakewood lost," he would probably say, "But I'm glad it was Ted Tresh who struck out to end it. That arrogant bastard didn't deserve to be the hero."

And what would Lorraine say to that? Would she be the kind of girl who would jump to my defense? Hell, no.

"Jan's not that kind either," Gene sighed. "She never has been. And she's even worse than Lorraine. It's not just that she doesn't defend me. It's that *she's* the one who is putting me down; the insults, the attacks on my pride."

"Well, I don't think Lorraine ever openly insulted me." I said, eyeing up the vodka and orange juice again. It had been about thirty hours since I got up for work on Friday, but I could see this birthday was far from over. The effect of the coffee and alcohol had kept me rambling for the last twelve hours, no use changing the recipe now.

"But some girls do show their interest that way. Remember, I told you about Rosie. She feigned indifference about me all through grade school and high school, but ten years later, I meet her for coffee and she tells me that she always loved me. I adored her! But she kept up this wall, this defense. It couldn't be penetrated. Sure, a defense, I guess that's what it was, a way to keep herself from getting hurt."

"Maybe that's what Jan's doing, Dad," Gene sighed. "I know deep down, she loves me, but her mocking and teasing are too much to take."

"Much like Rosie," I pounded the table for effect. "Years later she said she was in love, but you would never know it from her actions."

"I thought you said that you gave up on Rosie a year earlier?" Gene said. "Did you still have feelings for her?"

"I'll always have feelings for Rosie," I chuckled. "But I really *had* given up on her. And then, the next opportunity came knocking at my door."

ALMOST ROSIE

I t had been the worst week of my life. I was walking around in a daze, brooding, practically home-bound, not wanting to go anywhere, except maybe my next American Legion game, where I might get some feeling of redemption, where I might prove to myself that I was still a ballplayer. But everything was off somehow, my timing, my cockiness, my confidence. How long would this feeling last? Would it ever go away?

Finally, one Thursday afternoon, there was a knock at my door. When I opened it, there stood my longtime crush Rosie Williamson and six other Rockland girls. They were carrying softballs and gloves and bats. "What the hell is this?" I laughed out loud.

After all, this was 1971. Very few girls played softball. As far as I know, there were no organized girls' leagues in all of Beaver County. Except for a few of the neighborhood tomboys, most girls had never touched a bat in their lives. And this group was no exception. The ball gloves were borrowed. The bats were too big for them, and the three girls who wore baseball caps had them tilted to the side to pull their hair back. They looked cute. Almost all Rockland girls were cute, and I couldn't help but smile. "To what do I owe this unexpected pleasure?"

Rosie spoke first. "Have you heard about the big Rockland Centennial celebration in July?" She asked. "Well, they asked us to be part of it."

"And do what?" I chuckled. "I thought it was just a big banquet in the church hall." It was the first time I had smiled since the championship game.

"Earlier in the day, they want to have an Old-timers' softball game," she laughed, "Just the mothers against the daughters."

I thought about the *mothers* she was referring to. Skip Bruno's mother was a true athlete and Lou Petrella's mom could hit a ball as far as any man in town. These women were children of the Great Depression, and my guess was, they had been out there on the ballfields and backyards going toe-to-toe with every boy in the neighborhood their entire childhood.

"They'll kill you," I sighed. "Do you know what you're getting yourselves into?"

"That's why we need you," pleaded a skinny blonde, who was still standing on the steps of my front porch. It was Skip's sister Betty Ann. I had seen her swing a bat and throw the ball a few times. She wasn't too bad. But the rest of them, including Rosie and her sister Colleen, were hopeless.

"Well, what can I do?" I asked.

"We want you to *coach* us," Rosie chirped up. "It's the only chance we have."

"Why me?" I shook my head.

"You're the best high-school ballplayer in town," Rosie toyed. "Who else would we ask?" Her bright blue eyes sparkled like sunlight off the ripples in a pond. "Besides, it will be fun."

Is she flirting with me? I wondered. I had given up on Rosie years ago, but there was something about the way she was looking at me; something like admiration.

My image in Lakewood City had been badly damaged, but I realized, here in Rockland, I was still a big deal. It was exactly what I needed to get me out of my funk. "Okay," I sighed, "I'll do it."

"When can you start?" giggled Betty Ann.

"Well, it looks like you brought your equipment. We may as well get started now."

"Are we going to the ballfield?" chimed in Connie Martini excitedly.

"I think we better start right here," I said, as I led them into my backyard. "I don't think you're ready for a full-size field. Let's just see if you can catch a ball."

Half of them didn't even carry a mitt. "Wait here," I instructed. And I went around to the cellar door under my back porch. Inside my cellar, I found five or six old baseball gloves that my brother Nelson and I had outgrown, plus a couple Little League bats that might be easier for them to swing.

"Try these on," I barked, trying to assume the role of head coach as I strode out into my side yard under our giant oak trees. "Let's just see you play some catch."

They were terrible. Connie wore a right-handed glove on the wrong hand, and Rosie could throw the ball a little, but very rarely could she catch one that was thrown to her. "What a circus," I grunted in mock disgust. But Rosie just laughed and laughed.

I couldn't take my eyes off her. *You know, she could be exactly what I need to get me out of this funk,* I pondered, *and maybe even forget about Lorraine. Why not? It wouldn't be like I was using her,* I rationalized. *I had never lied to Rosie about my feelings for her. I liked her way before I ever liked Lorraine. I just gave up on her. And I never completely got over her. Maybe I owed it to myself, and to her, to see if there was still anything between us.*

After about an hour of hands-on instruction, the girls were actually able to carry on a game of catch without the ball bouncing all over the place. Maybe we wouldn't be humiliated as badly as I thought.

"That's enough for today," I told them. "Tomorrow, we go to the real baseball field."

"I'll find you a left hander's glove," I smiled at Connie. "And I want you all to contact any Rockland girls you know. We only have seven players and we're going to need at least four or five more. Start thinking about what position you might want to play. I'll see you all at six o'clock tomorrow at the field."

"Ummm, can we make it five o'clock?" Rosie offered softly. "We're all going to the Chippewa Carnival tomorrow night, and we need to leave by 7:30."

"Okay," I replied. "See you at five o'clock at the ballfield." *The Chippewa Carnival?* I thought to myself, *that might just be the perfect place to re-ignite with Rosie.*

Fifteen Rockland girls showed up at the ball field the next night, but only two of them could make an accurate throw to first base, Betty Ann Bruno and Mary Jo Carselle. At first, I had Betty Ann at third base and Mary Jo at short-stop. But there was another problem; they were also the only two girls on the team who could be counted on to *catch* the ball. So, eventually, I had to move Betty Ann to first base. If the Mothers team hit ground balls to short or first, we might have a chance of getting someone out. If they hit it anywhere else, we were in trouble.

Infield practice was a monkey circus, with balls flying all over the field. Batting practice was even worse. We had only four or five girls who could hit the ball out of the infield, and at least five or six others who never hit the ball at all. They literally swung and missed *every pitch*. It could have made for an incredibly boring evening, but Rosie's laughter kept everyone loose. I guess, she alone saw the ridiculousness of the situation, and she alone made it fun to be on that team.

"Alright," I barked, trying to act serious in the face of absurdity. "Let's try a little rundown practice." I placed one fielder at second base with a ball in her hand and one fielder at third, with a *runner* between them. "Let's see if we can get anybody out." We couldn't.

Most throws were wild. Even the good throws were bouncing off their gloves and rolling around the infield. Eventually, we got to the point where the fielders could get the runner out about fifty percent of the time. "I guess that's good enough for today," I shouted. "Does anyone know what time it is?"

"It's 6:30," Rosie giggled, "And we need to leave for the Carnival at 7:30."

I called them all into the dugout for a little pep talk. "We're improving," I deadpanned. "That's about all I can say."

"I think we looked pretty good," chirped Connie Martini from the end of the bench.

"Well, ignorance is bliss," I replied. And they all burst out laughing again. "Let's get together again in three days, right back here. In the meantime, I want you all to buy a rubber ball and practice bouncing it off the wall and catching it."

"I already know I *can't* catch it," smiled Rosie's sister Colleen sarcastically.

I just shook my head. "In your case, just see if you can hit the wall." And all the girls giggled like I was Rodney Dangerfield.

As I packed up the equipment, Rosie came over and gave me a hug. "Thanks for doing this," she offered. "You know, we're leaving for the carnival at 7:30. Why don't you come with us?" Rosie had just turned sixteen the month before, and she never looked more beautiful than she did at that moment.

"We already have about twenty kids going," Colleen interrupted, "And only three drivers. I don't think we can fit any more."

Rosie still had her hands on my shoulders. "Do you think your dad will let you have the car tonight?" She pleaded. "I'll ride with you."

It was Friday night and, unbeknownst to Rosie, I already had permission to take the Thunderbird for the evening. "I'll ask him," I replied. "But I still need to go home and change. And look at this," I said pulling off my sweaty ball cap. "I need to wash my hair."

"Just get changed," Rosie replied. "My mom has a little beauty shop in the basement. Come up a little early and I'll wash your hair for you."

Whoa, I thought, *Rosie washing my hair, hands-on contact. That's a pretty good start to any evening.*

As I walked back up the street to my house, I tried to get it all in perspective. I was pretty sure Rosie was flirting with me. But she had flirted with me so many times before and I had nothing to show for it. When I was fourteen, she was *almost* my girlfriend, but had broken it off after just twelve hours. She was *almost* the first girl I kissed, but every time I got close, she laughed and turned away.

"Almost Rosie," I said out loud. "That's what I should call her, because every time it looks like we might be together, something goes wrong.

"Hell," I said finally, "What have I got to lose? She's the only one who can get my mind off that damn championship game, and she's the only one who has a chance to make me forget Lorraine."

When I arrived at Rosie's house, I could see how things were shaping up. My buddy Jerry Delpino was one of the drivers. Of course, he was dating Colleen, so I kind of expected him to be there. He had his dad's navy-blue Maverick. They could probably squeeze five or six kids in there.

Across the street was Willie Gacik's 1939 Gray Buick, the one that his great aunt had left to him. It was round on the edges and looked like something that your great grandfather would be driving, but Willie rolled around in it like the king of the road. "After all," he used to remind us, "It's not my dad's car; it's mine."

I was glad to see Willie. I knew that in another week he would be gone for the summer, just like he was every summer. Willie was one of the only kids in town whose parents were divorced. Nine months of the year, he stayed with his dad in Rockland, but in the summer, he headed to Long Island to spend three months with his mom and her second family. I thought maybe he had already flown out to New York. But he was going to drive his car out this year and wasn't leaving for another week. Anyway, we could probably get six more kids in the Buick. I wondered who the third driver was.

I stepped inside to room-after-room of kids, all excited, all engaged, all anxious to get going. It was my first real social gathering since the championship game, but everything felt comfortable. Jerry was sitting in the master easy chair with Colleen on his lap. Gacik and our buddy Anthony Caruso were chatting-up a group of four or five Rockland girls, most of them sophomores, who went to Beaver Falls High School. And standing right in the middle, with her back to me, was Rosie.

I could hear her addictive high-pitch laugh over anything else in the room. "Am I late?" I announced myself, and was met with the greetings and good-natured groans from fifteen-or-so of my closest friends. It felt good to be back in my element.

"Well," said Rosie, spinning around to meet me. "Let's see what I have to work with." I was a little worried that she would forget all about her promise to wash my hair, but here she was running her fingers through it, like Michelangelo sizing up a lump of clay.

"Are you sure we have time for this?" I mumbled, looking right into her eyes. She glanced into mine for a second and smiled, and then went right back to scrutinizing my curls and waves.

"We have to wait until Collen's friend Linda and her cousin get here anyway," Rosie sighed, "Linda's our fourth driver. So, there's plenty of time." She looked me in the eyes again, "Alright, follow me," she ordered. And I fell in step behind her through the narrow hallways and down the steps into her semi-finished basement.

I was more-than-acquainted with that basement. In seventh and eighth grades, after the roller rink closed down, the kids of Rockland used to alternate houses every week and host dance parties. Sometimes it would be near somebody's birthday or a holiday, but any reason was a good reason for a party, and whenever it was Rosie's or Colleen's turn to host, the party was right here. I had probably slow danced with Rosie in every inch of that semi-finished basement over the years. I remember once when we were dancing to "Everyone's Gone to the Moon." We were standing right next to that big gas furnace near the window, and when the music ended, we just stood there in the silence, holding each other for a good ten seconds. *This is it,* I remember thinking. And I moved in for a kiss. But, by now, everyone's eyes were on us, and she just laughed that high-pitched laugh of hers, and turned away.

"Almost Rosie, indeed," I chuckled to myself.

The basement hadn't changed at all. In one corner, was her mom's "Beauty Salon." It was really just a large porcelain sink with a rest for the back of your neck. A short hose was connected to the faucet with a sprayer-nozzle at the end of it. There were two kinds of shampoo on the ledge of the sink, *Johnson's Baby Shampoo* and *Prell.* I pointed to the transparent-green bottle and took my seat.

"Close your eyes," whispered Rosie, as I sat back on the reclining chair, and lowered the back of my neck into the head rest. And then she turned on the warm water and started running it through my hair. I wasn't exactly sure what all this meant, but I knew it was not going to be an ordinary evening.

Gacik and a few other kids had followed the action downstairs, and started howling, "Get a room, you two." Neither of us really knew what that meant, but his comment threw us into the spotlight.

This is usually when Rosie goes for the laugh and hangs me out to dry, I thought. But instead she leaned in closer and whispered, "Has that kid always been jealous of you?"

"Always," I laughed, as she poured the thick transparent-green Prell over my forehead and across my washed-back hair. Then she slowly started massaging the mounds of shampoo bubbles into my scalp. There were still some snide remarks being made by Willie and Anthony, but I didn't really hear them. I was thinking how long I had waited for this night with Rosie. I had the car. She was riding with me. I was seventeen and she was sixteen. And it was all starting like this. *Could she get me to forget the disappointment of the championship game?* This was a good start. *Could she get me to forget Lorraine?* Lorraine Who? My focus was back on Rosie.

I opened my eyes and she was leaning over me, all I saw was that little beauty mark at the very place where her skin ends and her bra begins. But I didn't call her "*Almost Rosie*" for nothing. At that very instant, she pulled my hair forward and my long, soapy bangs flopped into my wide-open eyes.

"Oh shit," I screamed, in pain, but trying to disguise it. "Shit," I laughed. "You really got me." But I couldn't laugh it off. This shit was Prell, practically clear, green lye! They used to run commercials where a pearl would slowly sink to the bottom of a Prell bottle. It was supposed to show how luxurious it was. But Prell had no conditioners, no softeners. It was just green liquid soap. And the pain in my eye was excruciating.

"I've got to wash this out," I said stumbling back to my feet and pulling the nozzle head out of her hand, and then I started spraying the mounds of shampoo out of my eyes. You would have thought I just shot her.

"I didn't do anything," Rosie scoffed.

Now, everyone's laughing.

"I didn't do anything. I told you to keep your eyes shut. It's your fault."

"You're right, you're right." I agreed, trying to recapture the moment. But this was *Almost Rosie* and the moment, as always, was gone. Kids were laughing. And she was insulted that I'd made a spectacle of her. She felt like she was under attack and, real or imagined, I had put her under a microscope. For Rosie, there was no bigger crime. Whatever might have been rekindling was gone.

She stormed up the basement stairs with me in close pursuit. "Rosie, wait," I called after her. I had a towel in my hands and was desperately trying to wipe away the stinging shampoo. I could barely see through my watering eyes, and I missed the first step completely, stumbling into the banister. This set off another round of laughter and cat calls from our friends, exactly the kinds of comments that Rosie avoided at all costs.

Back upstairs in her living room, I finally cornered Rosie. "C'mon," I pleaded. "This was just an accident. It's funny if you think about it."

"You always have to ruin everything," she barked. "Everything's a joke to you."

"This isn't a joke. I didn't want this to happen. I'm in real pain here," I rambled. But nothing I said seemed to get through to her. Rosie had been embarrassed.

"Why were your eyes open?" her question hung in the air for long time.

What could I say to that? Whatever romantic feelings that were in the air, were gone. I could feel the change immediately. It would take days, even weeks, to overcome what had just happened. I'd have to start all over again. An old feeling rushed over me, an old familiar pain, a deep, profound disappointment, the loss of something that never was.

Almost Rosie, the thought echoed through my brain. And, for some reason, I saw myself back at Three Rivers, swinging and missing, turning to the crowd and watching them slowly disappear into nothing.

"Let's get the hell out of here," I said in disgust. My tone with Rosie was anything but romantic now. As always, she had turned on me. And, as always, I was determined to show her that I didn't care.

"We can't leave yet," Rosie scolded. "We have to wait for Colleen's friend Linda and her cousin to get here. Linda's going to be our fourth driver."

"Great," I nodded sarcastically.

I didn't know much about this Linda girl. I just knew she was a senior at Lakewood who had moved to Lakewood City back in October from someplace near Chicago. I guess she had a hard time making friends with the senior girls from Lakewood, but the junior girls from Rockland had accepted her right away. That wasn't surprising. Rockland girls were known for two things at Lakewood High School: being beautiful and being kind to everyone.

Anyway, Colleen and Molly and Patty had taken Linda under their wings right away. They sat with her at lunch. They walked with her in the halls. They took her to ballgames. Every time that Spring when I'd look up from my shortstop position to find the Rockland girls in the stands, Linda was right in the middle of them.

"Here she is now." Rosie grumbled, as she grabbed me by the shoulder and spun me around to see the door. "Now we can all get out of here."

Linda was kind of cute, blond, but really tiny. She was only about five feet tall and weighed maybe ninety pounds. I probably hadn't said ten words to the girl in my life, but she was always smiling, and seemed friendly enough.

"Hi, everybody," she chirped. "I hope we didn't keep you waiting."

Rosie and I were standing across the hall from the doorway when, suddenly, a hush fell over the room and rolled over us like an ocean wave. "I want to introduce you to my cousin Carrie Ann Rayburn," Linda announced. "Carrie Ann is from Georgia, but she's visiting me for two weeks. So, I hope you'll be as kind to her as you are to me."

Whoa…a jolt went through me. This girl was gorgeous. I mean Hollywood gorgeous, about 5'8" with big blue eyes, perfectly fit in a cute blue jumper with long, light-brown hair and streaks of blonde. "The sun did it," she would tell me later.

How can she be related to Linda? I thought. *Linda looks like a child compared to her.*

All my buddies had jumped to attention by now. Jerry sat up in the easy chair so fast that Colleen almost fell out of his lap.

"Carrie Ann is Class of '72, just like you," Linda told Willie, as he reached out to shake her hand.

"Have you got a ride to the carnival, Carrie Ann?" Gacik asked, wasting no time. "I have my own Buick outside. No curfew."

"You mean the gray one?" She answered with a long southern question mark at the end of her sentence. "I thought my grandma was visiting."

The whole room cracked up. Even Willie was laughing, and I could hear Linda making her way across the room introducing her cousin as she went.

I pretended not to notice, tried one last time, to turn my concentration on Rosie. "Look," I whispered. "We were really getting along tonight. Ever since you said you were going to the carnival, I was hoping that this would be our night."

"Well, you blew that didn't you?" She was still in attack mode.

"Hey." I was grabbing at straws now. "How about if we go downstairs and you finish getting the suds out of my hair?"

I still had the towel wrapped around my neck, and I tried to hand it to her, but she just pushed it away.

"Do it yourself." She directed the words at me, but it was like she was announcing them to the whole room, just another public put down.

Linda's cousin was still making her way across the room, and I could hear her long southern drawl getting closer. Just for a second, I glanced up at her, but Rosie jumped on the glance. "I know you want to meet her," Rosie chided. "You're looking at her. You're always looking at everybody."

"I'm sure her dance card's full," I scoffed, looking around the room. The southern girl was so glamourous that she looked out of place. She was like a model or a Miss Georgia contestant. And, although they were all gathering around her, it was very unlikely that any guy in the room had any kind of a romantic shot at this all-star.

"I'm not concerned with her," I said slowly and deliberately. "Tonight is *our* chance."

But Rosie went on like she didn't even hear me. And she got louder with each sentence. "Go ahead. Go talk to her. I know you want to."

By now, five or six kids in our immediate area could hear every word we were saying. "This is our night," I reminded her. "It has nothing to do with some stranger."

"I never said it was *our* night," she mocked. "You can do whatever you want to do." And then, one final dig... "What's the matter? Is she out of your league?" She nearly shouted it into the room.

Of course, the girl *was* out of my league. She was out of all our leagues. She was like Babe Ruth at an American Legion game. But, I couldn't say that to Rosie.

I could feel everyone's eyes burning a hole into the back of my head. This was vintage Rosie behavior, just like a year earlier, when she challenged me to pick up the phone and get a date to the picnic, now she was challenging me to approach some knockout southern belle right in front of the whole Rockland gang.

I dropped my head for a second, and then felt a surge of anger shoot through me. I felt the towel around my neck and used it to wipe the excess water from my forehead, and then leaned in close to Rosie's ear. "*No one* is out of my league, honey," I boasted. But we both knew I was full of shit.

And, just like that, I went from the frying pan into the fire. I could feel a burning sensation cross my face. "You know, I really needed you on my side this time," I told her with the resolve of a man heading to the gallows.

That's how I finally said goodbye to Rosie. I can still hear the echo of those words. But I didn't even have time to dwell on it. I just had time enough to spin around and face this final humiliation she had thrown me into.

So many feelings were rushing through me at the same time; the old betrayal from Rosie; her constant need to bring me down a peg; my pent-up depression from the championship game; the anger that all that brought with it. It all crashed down on me now.

Of course, it was the anger, not courage that made me approach the girl.

"Hi," she said, as soon as I got within earshot. "I'm Carrie Ann Rayburn. I'm from Georgia, but I'm staying with my cousin Linda for a couple weeks."

"Hi," I answered. "I'm Ted Tresh."

"Oh, I *know* who you are," she gushed. "You're Teddy Tresh, the baseball player."

"Well, God bless you, Carrie Ann," I smiled. "No one has called me that in weeks."

"Oh, Linda told me about that too," she said softly, her voice taking a mock-serious tone. "The star shortstop that was always smiling and nice to everyone. But then he struck out in the championship game, and now he's always sad."

I didn't know what to say. "I really don't know your cousin that well," I stammered.

"Well, she knows you," Carrie Ann laughed, drawing out the final "*ooooooou*" the way Southern girls sometimes do. "She has all your game clippings, and a newspaper picture of you hung on her bedroom door."

"Really?" I smiled.

Carrie Ann was rolling now, and she grew more animated with every word. "And I told her 'you mean that big, strapping, good-looking boy is depressed? Well, we really can't have that, can we?'"

I was still in shock that this glamorous young woman was even in the same room with us. So, her comments were much more than unexpected. But I knew a come-on line when I heard one. "Well, what are we going to do about that?" I asked, with mock concern.

"You know," she smiled. "I came here with my cousin, and she's driving to the carnival, but if you want, I can tell her that I'm riding up there with you instead. Then I can tell you all about it."

You could have knocked me over with a feather. "Wow, Carrie Ann," I said. "That was out of nowhere."

"Not really," she winked. "I came here to meet *you*."

I glanced around the room. Every eye was on us. Five or six kids had heard Rosie's challenge and expected me to fall flat on my face. But this was a slam-dunk. I looked over at Rosie again. She hadn't heard any of the conversation and was still expecting me to crawl back with my tail between my legs. Instead, she watched Carrie Ann put her hand on my wet shoulder.

"Ummmmm…I still have some suds in my hair," I said, pulling the towel off my neck and offering it to Carrie Ann.

"Come on," she smiled. "I'll rinse it out for you."

When we got to the porcelain wash basin in the basement, there were still two bottles of shampoo sitting there, the shiny-green Prell and the golden bottle of Johnson's Baby Shampoo, which I picked up and examined. *Almost Rosie*, I muttered to myself. *If I would have picked the Baby Shampoo, it might have been our night.*

Carrie Ann looked at the bottle over my shoulder as she leaned me back into the salon chair and turned on the warm water. "No more tears," she read out loud. "Sounds like good advice."

WALK AWAY

"So," Gene yawns, "Your little Rosie was exactly like my Jan is now. Her defense mechanism was to attack first before she can get hurt."

"To the point of the ridiculous," I answered. "She knew I wouldn't just stand there and be insulted, be rejected by her over and over and over again. But she did it anyway. It was like she couldn't help herself."

"Maybe you were reading her wrong," Gene offered. "Maybe she didn't care about you as much as you thought she did?"

"That's what I thought for years." I shook my head slowly. "I was convinced that it was all just a mirage; that I was seeing something in Rosie's eyes that wasn't really there.

"But remember I told you that ten years later, I ran into her on the street? We ducked into a restaurant to grab a cup of coffee. Then, all of a sudden, she got dead serious and said, 'You know, I always loved you.'

"'Loved me?' I couldn't believe my ears. 'I thought you hated me. What about the insults? What about the name calling? What about all the times I asked you to be my girlfriend and you blew me off?'

"'I was just testing you,' she smiled, as she slowly shook her head in regret. 'Why didn't you fight for me? Why did you stop trying?'"

"'Fight *for* you?' I grimaced. 'I was too busy fighting *with* you.'"

"Rosie just lowered her head. 'It was just a little girl's defense mechanism. It was my way to protect my heart from disappointment.'"

"'But, I kept telling you how much I cared about you.' I countered."

"'Well, I guess I never believed you,' shrugged Rosie. 'I was just protecting myself.'"

"Now, *I* got dead serious. 'Well, that was *some* defense mechanism, Rosie. It was impenetrable.' Those were the last words I ever said to her."

"That's exactly what Jan is doing to me!" Gene barked, jumping to his feet for emphasis. "She's afraid of being hurt. Maybe you made a mistake with Rosie. Maybe, if you kept trying, you would have ended up with her, just like she said. Would that have been so bad?"

"Look, Gene," I answered. "I *loved* Rosie. I'll always love Rosie. But she had *never* stuck by me, even once. What would have happened when we got older, and we had *real* problems? Financial problems? Illness? Problems with the kids? What would have happened if it was just me and her against the world? Would she have backed me or berated me? Would she have been looking out for the team, or would she have just kept protecting herself?"

"It *might* have worked out, Dad," Gene nodded. "Maybe she would have changed. Maybe you walked away from the love of your life."

"Is that what you're afraid of, Gene, that you might be walking away from the love of your life?"

"Of course, that's what I'm afraid of," Gene dropped his head in disgust. "Maybe I'd be making a big mistake to let her go."

I waited for him to lift his head, and then looked him straight in the eye. "All these '*mights*,' Champ, all these '*maybes*.' It doesn't have to be that way. You *can* be sure. Look, when you first meet a girl, you play all these dating games for a few weeks or a few months. But eventually, you've got to be a *team*. Eventually, you've got to know that she'll stand with you no matter how many times you get knocked down. Can you honestly say that you think Jan will do that for you?"

Gene just sat there in silence for a full two minutes. "So, that was it with Rosie?" he asked finally. "You never thought about her after that?"

"Oh, I thought about her all the time," I laughed. "She became my lesson of what *not* to do. She tried to make herself seem unattainable and, no matter how much I liked her, I really believed that she *was* unattainable. In fact, I gave up on Rosie about ten different times, but that day was the *last* time.

"I shouldn't have even been thinking of Rosie that day anyway. By now, I had Lorraine on my mind twenty-four hours a day. It was just youthful pride that made me take one more shot at Rosie; just my own defenses against disappointment and loss. I was depressed about baseball and disappointed about Lorraine. I needed something to get my mind off my problems. I need to stop obsessing about that damn Championship game. And I needed to forget about the girl that turned her back on me and strolled out of Three Rivers Stadium at the worst moment of my life.

"Fortunately, the prescription I needed was standing right in front of me."

"That's right," Gene laughed. "What happened with Carrie Ann? But wait, if you had feelings for Lorraine and you had feelings for Rosie, then why would you want to get mixed up with some beautiful southern girl? Weren't you mixed up enough?"

"I guess I was," I shrugged. "But, I was also just a teenage kid, and I thought, *what can it hurt? I won't get serious about her. She's only going to be here for two weeks. Can it really hurt anything if I let her chase my blues away for a little while?*

"She was exactly what I needed, an ego boost, a pick-me-up, a victory in the middle of all this losing. She could be my summer romance, a distraction when I needed one the most, a way out of this unending funk. How could anyone get hurt?"

"But someone did get hurt, didn't they?" Gene smiled.

"I learned a lot of lessons that summer," I told him. "The biggest one was learning when to give up on a dream, learning when to walk away."

"Okay," Gene smiled. "Tell me what happened with Carrie Ann."

No More Tears

When Carrie Ann and I walked back up the cellar stairs, everybody was waiting to leave for the Chippewa Carnival. "C'mon, you two," barked Willie. "It's time to get going. Carrie Ann, are you driving up with me?"

"Oh, I'm so sorry," she replied. "Teddy has already asked me to drive with him."

I glanced over at Rosie. No emotion at all showed on her face. It was like she couldn't possibly have cared less that she had just been replaced in my front seat. "Who cares which car we go in?" she shrugged. "Let's just get going."

"Can you wait just two minutes?" cooed Carrie Ann. "I have to use the little girl's room."

Rosie just rolled her eyes, but everyone else started heading out to the cars, while I waited in the doorway for Carrie Ann. As her cousin Linda walked past me, she whispered, "Can I see you in private for a minute?"

We stepped out into Rosie's front yard, maybe ten feet away from the rest of the kids. "Listen, Teddy," she sighed, "The last time I saw Carrie Ann was two years ago when I went to visit her in Georgia. Back then she was just my tomboy cousin. We used to call her *Toughie*, because she was just as tough as any boy in her neighborhood. She could climb trees and ride bikes and mow the lawn. She could hit a baseball a mile and wore blue jeans every day.

"Then, two days ago, she shows up at my house for a vacation looking like *this*, with her round hips and curves, and streaks of blonde in her hair. She always had those big blue eyes, but now she wears makeup on them, and she looks like a damn model. I couldn't believe it.

"Anyway, Teddy, I don't think she has any idea how beautiful she is. When I try to tell her, she just laughs at me. And then she saw that newspaper photo of you on my bedroom door and asked who you were. I told her that you were the shortstop on our high school baseball team. I told her how well you played and how everyone liked you, and then I told her about the game at Three Rivers, and how sad you were after that. She said, 'I'll bet I could make him happy.' And then she laughed.

"I told her that she probably could. 'You're exactly the kind of girl he likes.'"

"Whoa," I whispered, "She's exactly the kind of girl *everyone* likes."

"Yeah, but, I still haven't gotten used to the idea," Linda laughed, "I still think of her as that tomboy. Anyway, promise me you'll be nice to her. I mean, I know you're nice to everyone, but promise me you won't, you know, take advantage of her."

"Of course I won't," I replied. "Look, Linda, she's only in town for two weeks. What can happen?"

"Just promise me," she answered.

"Okay," I laughed. "I promise that I won't take advantage of your cousin."

"And you won't hurt her?"

"Of course I won't."

When we all piled into the four cars, Carrie Ann jumped into the long couch-style front seat of the T-Bird and moved all the way over, until she was practically on my lap. *No big deal*, I thought. *She knows we have to get three people in the front seat to fit everyone in the car.*

Rosie never said a word. She just climbed into the back seat with a couple other Rockland girls.

When we got to the carnival, Carrie Ann never left my side. We broke away from the rest of the group and strolled around the grounds, laughing and chatting like we had known each other for years. I spent three bucks trying to win her a stuffed animal by knocking over six milk bottles, but no matter how hard I hit the damn things, at least one always remained standing. I started moaning that the bottles were filled with cement, or maybe they had magnets in the bottom. But Carrie Ann just laughed and laughed. And every time I would lose, she would wrap her arms around my right arm and squeeze my biceps with both hands. "Aww, poor baby, won't those bad bottles fall down for you."

"Let's share a cotton candy," she urged, pulling me away from the milk bottles before I lost all my yard work money to that stupid game. But after latching onto my arm, she never let go of it again.

I could feel my old confidence coming back. She laughed at every joke I told, and only had eyes for me all night. Chippewa was near the Beaver Falls school district, and later in the evening, we ran into three Beaver Falls High School ballplayers in the crowd, including their shortstop Ricky Mangerie, who had always been a personal rival of mine. Instead of giving me the business over our loss at Three Rivers, they all seemed to commiserate over it. Our two victories over Beaver Falls had helped us win the Section 6 Championship, so I guess they really didn't have anything to gloat about. But it was more than that. It was Carrie Ann on my arm. How could they not respect that? They were grinning like the Cheshire Cat from the moment they saw her. Who wouldn't? She was breathtaking.

"Listen," I said when we were finally alone again. "I'm really having a good time, but I have to be home by 11:00 tonight. I'm re-taking my S.A.T.'s tomorrow at Beaver Falls High School, and I have to get enough sleep."

"Well, isn't that a coincidence," she smiled. "I knew I'd be up here visiting my cousin this month, so I signed up to take my S.A.T. test there too."

"Really?" I couldn't believe my luck. "Would you like me to pick you up? We can drive in together?"

"It's a date," she chirped up, even before I could finish the question. And she wrapped her arms around my biceps even tighter."

After a couple hours on the carnival grounds, we started walking back to the car. "Don't get me wrong," Carrie Ann was saying, "I love this James Dean thing you're doing. You know, the misunderstood loner bit. It's sexy. But, somehow, it just doesn't fit you. I mean, poor baby, everyone worships him, but that's not enough. What's it going to take to make you happy?"

I stopped dead in my tracks, spun her around and kissed her. A good one too, it was soft and wet and lasted for about ten seconds. Then we parted and I stared into those big blue eyes for a beat or two and went right back in for another thirty seconds. In that moment, I felt all my troubles melt away. *This is going to be a great two weeks,* I thought to myself.

After gathering together all the kids who had ridden out with us and piling back into the car, I glanced over at Carrie Ann's sweet, smiling face beside me. *I don't even have to worry that I'm leading her on,* I thought. *Sure, I still have feelings for Lorraine, but this girl will be gone in two weeks. I don't have to worry about breaking her heart, because I can't disappoint her. She will be leaving <u>me</u>.*

On the way home, Rosie, who was seated in the back seat of the T-Bird, asked Carrie Ann, "So, what are you going to do for the rest of your two weeks in Lakewood City?"

"Keep dating Teddy, if he keeps asking me," she answered.

I looked up into the rearview mirror for a reaction from Rosie; to see if there was any sign of disappointment or anger or any other kind of emotion in her face. But there was none. Her defenses were impenetrable, as always.

Meanwhile, Carrie Ann was just what the doctor ordered. I had no fear of commitment, because she was only going to be in town for two weeks. I had no worries about ruining my chances with Lorraine, because, the fact was, she was spending her last months with Blake before he shipped out to West Point.

Now, I could let Lorraine say goodbye to him without agonizing over everything they were saying, everything they were probably doing. Instead of sitting home feeling sorry for myself, I was going to be having the summer of my life with the most beautiful girl I had ever seen.

There were no worries with Carrie Ann, no implications for the future. It was just fun. I saw her every other day. I took her out for burgers on Thursday night and to a beach picnic at Lake Arthur all day Saturday with a whole group of Lakewood and Rockland kids. On Monday night, we headed out to Spotlight 88 Drive-In Theater for a double feature. We saw almost none of it.

We were pretty physical for how short a time we had dated; kissing and nibbling and grabbing each other; first in the front seat, then in the back. It was non-stop, but after an hour or so, I decided to take my chances at sliding my hand up under her blouse. I felt a little guilty, because I had assured her cousin that I wouldn't take advantage of her, but if she really wanted to be closer, well, I had to know.

"Teddy," she sighed, grabbing my wrist and pulling my hand out from under her frilly, yellow top. "Now what would you think of a girl who let you do that on the third date?"

"I would think, *what a wonderful girl*," I laughed. "But it's okay. I mean, I understand. I don't mind. That is, I *mind*. But I don't mind, mind."

Carrie Ann was laying on top of me in the back seat of the T-Bird, as beautiful a sight as I had ever seen. "You mean you still want to date me..." she whispered.

"That's exactly what I mean." I answered. And I meant it.

After every night out, we always headed back to her aunt's house, where Linda and her mom would hang out with us until about 11 pm, then head off to bed, leaving me and Carrie Ann alone on the couch until midnight, when I had to head home.

We would roll around on that couch for about a half hour each night, and then spend another twenty minutes at the door, saying goodnight. I knew my parameters: No boobs, no butt, no hands in her pants, but other than that, we got pretty intense.

Every day I felt more like my old self, happy, confident, and even cocky sometimes. Her make-out restrictions were fine with me. Because, otherwise, we were all over each other from the time I picked her up until the time I drove off. It was almost embarrassing to have this beautiful young woman grabbing my arm, kissing my neck, and rubbing herself up against me every time we went anywhere, embarrassing, but ego-inflating.

After the first couple dates, I realized that I hadn't thought about that damn championship game in four days. That was a miracle! I wanted to see her all the time. If we were only going to have two weeks, I would make sure they were eventful weeks.

I never even mentioned Lorraine to her because it didn't matter. My best shot with Lorraine would be coming up in September, after Blake had gone off to college. There was no reason for me to hold back with Carrie Ann. She wouldn't be around long enough for me to disappoint her. We were inseparable.

Of course, we were from two different worlds, and we had a few small disagreements from time to time. One night, on our way home from J & T's Custard Stand, a news report came on the car radio. The announcer reported,

"Because of fears about run-away inflation, President Nixon today signed an executive order mandating a nationwide wage/price freeze. With few exceptions, all wages will be frozen at current levels and the price of consumer goods may not be raised without federal approval. The president has given no timetable for how long the freeze may last."

"What?" I screamed. "That's impossible."

Carrie Ann had no idea what I was talking about. She either hadn't heard the report or didn't understand it.

"Nixon's calling for a wage/price freeze," I told her. "That can't possibly work."

"Why not?" she laughed, "If wages and prices stay the same, there can't be any inflation. I think the president is a genius."

Of course, our backgrounds were light years apart. Most Western Pennsylvanians were steelworkers and life-long Democrats. So, anything Nixon suggested was suspicious. Truth is, steelworkers and their unions just didn't trust conservatives. Her family, fairly well-to-do and from the Deep South, was, quite possibly, just the opposite.

"A freeze can't work," I told her. "The economy is based on supply and demand. You'll either have too much stuff, and nobody to buy it, or you'll have too little stuff, and there will be shortages everywhere."

And that wasn't the only social argument we had. One night we again drove out to J&T Custard Stand for the Flavor of the Week, and on the way home I told her that I was worried about getting drafted in the next year. I again blamed Nixon. "If John or Robert Kennedy had lived, the government wouldn't still be shipping us off to Vietnam," I speculated.

"My family didn't really care for the Kennedys," she replied.

Didn't really care for the Kennedys? I couldn't comprehend that idea. In my family, the Kennedys were like saints. My grandmother had JFK's portrait on her bedroom wall, right up there next to DaVinci's Last Supper.

"They just tried to help out regular people," I argued. "And they got murdered for it. I think they were the last leaders I trusted."

"I think people determine the kind of life they're going to live themselves," she said, not sensing the rising irritation in my voice. "And I think that politicians don't really make much difference in our lives."

"So, you don't think it matters who's president?" my voice was getting a little sour.

"Not really," she answered, but this time she seemed to notice that an argument was brewing. "I don't think Robert Kennedy would have been any better than Nixon."

I was slurping down a chocolate malted milk shake, and practically choked on the comment. I really didn't want to spend the next week arguing politics with Carrie Ann. So, I decided to count to ten. As always, that turned out to be a pretty good decision.

"I'm not really very political," she offered finally, in her long, slow southern drawl. "I'm sure you could convince me of anything if you tried."

I looked over at her smiling face and big blue eyes and softly streaked brown hair, and I forgot all about presidential politics.

"Her politics? Who gives a shit about her politics?" Willie Gacik laughed out loud the next night, as the boys and I cruised around in his big old Buick one last time before he left for his mother's house in Long Island.

"I wouldn't even care if we spoke the same language," smirked Jerry from the back seat. And we all burst out laughing.

I was glad I got to spend this last night with my boys before Willie left town. The four of us, me, Willie, Jerry, and Anthony, had become virtual legends of the junior class just three months before, when we all went out for a drive on a Friday night in February and just kept driving. One minute, we were just cruising and bullshitting in my grandfather's car, and the next minute we were on the Pennsylvania Turnpike, heading to Long Island, just because Gacik said he had some friends out there that we should meet.

We didn't come back until Monday! Of course, our parents freaked out when we called them from the road, but I was able to convince my somewhat stern father that I was calling to let him know where I was, which is a lot better than *not* letting him know.

"I'll accept whatever punishment you have for me when I get home," I told him from a phone booth outside of Breezewood. "I just wanted to make sure you didn't worry." He bought it. I was never punished at all. In fact, all our parents were very understanding, and the school principal himself just gave us a slap on the wrist, two days of detention for missing school on Monday.

It was well worth it. When we got back to school on Tuesday, everybody in the school knew our names. We were the juniors who *ran away to Long Island for the weekend;* you don't get any cooler than that. Gacik took photos during the whole trip, and a week after we got back, we put on a slide show at my Cousin Connie's house. There wasn't an open seat in the place.

Plus, the trip gave the four of us a chance to bond over adventures and jokes and stories about girls. These guys were my sounding board now, and they were all on board with this Carrie Ann thing.

"If she's all over you," Willie laughed again. "Why in the world would you waste your time talking about Vietnam?"

"It's a little like dating a kitten," I admitted.

"And who doesn't want to date a kitten?" chirped Caruso from the back seat, and Gacik laughed so hard, he almost drove off the road.

It all ended in disaster, of course. While I had been enjoying fourteen days of bliss, I had also been planning my new courting strategy with Lorraine once we returned for our senior year. Thanks to Carrie Ann, my confidence was soaring and, with Blake soon leaving for college, I could take my time getting close to Lorraine again. No need to rush. I was pretty sure of her feelings for me and even surer of my feelings for her. Everything was falling into place.

On the last day of Carrie Ann's visit to Pennsylvania, I stopped to pick her up. The plan was to take a ride over to Ewing Park, pull into a vacant picnic shelter and say our goodbyes there. Her parents had just arrived from Georgia the night before. And I saw their gleaming gold Cadillac outside when I arrived.

She greeted me at the door with a kiss, the kind of kiss you give someone special when your parents are standing ten feet away. She introduced her mom and dad by their first and last names, but I called them Mr. and Mrs. Rayburn. No use getting too familiar with folks I would probably never see again. After a short exchange, we left her parents behind and walked out onto her aunt's front porch.

"How about if we take a ride down to the park," I suggested. But, before I could say another word, Carrie Ann surprised me with "*good news.*"

She had stayed up all night negotiating with her aunt and her mom and dad. "They said I could live with my aunt this year," She laughed.

"What?" I shouted in disbelief.

"I'm coming to Lakewood City High School for my senior year," she gushed. Then teased, "That is, if you want me to." She stood there in expectation, waiting for me to grab her and hug her, and maybe lift her off her feet. But instead, I stood there in shock and numbness. She had every right to expect that all I wanted was to spend the next ten months together.

Instead, I stammered, "You'll miss your senior year, all your friends in Georgia. I can't ask you to…"

But she cut me off. "You didn't ask," she smiled. "I'm offering."

She was still waiting for the big hug and kiss to seal the deal. And, when I hesitated, she smiled knowingly. "Oh, I get it," she whispered. "You think I'm a prude." It was something only a Southern girl would say back in 1971. And she looked so cute while she was saying it. "I'm no prude," she winked. "I just didn't want you to think I was easy. I just wanted to make sure this was real, and now I know. It *is* real."

I closed my eyes tight.

"You *do* think I'm a prude," she laughed. "You think I won't let you touch me."

She was way off base. That wasn't why I hesitated. I hesitated because I had a plan. Because I was ready for one last push, one last big effort to reclaim Lorraine; to fall in love with her; to get her to fall in love with me. Up until this moment, I never even realized that I was using Carrie Ann, using her to get over my depression, using her to restore my pride, using her to get me ready for the girl I really wanted, the one I really loved.

"I know you tried to get more intimate that first night at the drive-in theater, and I said 'no,' but you never really tried again," she prattled on.

I was metaphorically back-pedaling now, "Well, *no* means *no*, right?" I was stumbling through my words.

"Sometimes it means *not yet*," she smiled coyly.

I looked at her again, a long, hard look. She was damned near perfect, sweet and beautiful. Her lips were red and moist; her eyes were like big blue diamonds. Why was I hesitating? Why wasn't I sweeping her up in my arms and telling her that I was thrilled, thrilled that she was rearranging her life to come to my school, to be my girl? What was wrong with me?

It was one of those major crossroads we all have in life. But I couldn't take another step until I was sure about my future with Lorraine. My life was going nowhere until this whole Lorraine situation was resolved, one way or another.

"I can't, Carrie Ann." I could barely believe the words that coming out of my own mouth. "I can't let you change your life for me. Not, until…" But I couldn't bring myself to say the words.

"Until what?" she said, loosening her grip on me for the first time. "Until what?" she repeated.

I dropped my head. I couldn't even look at her. "I have unfinished business," I sighed.

"You mean someone else?" Her voice was rising now, and the smile ran away from her face. "You never said there was someone else!"

"Because I thought there was time to deal with it later," I offered. But I wasn't even convincing myself.

"Later?" she was almost shouting now. "Like…after I was gone?"

"I guess," I said, shaking my head slowly. "Maybe in a year or two, who knows?"

"A year or two? Oh, Teddy, I could never go through this again. I thought we were like Romeo and Juliet, like one of the great legendary love stories. Imagine Juliet finding out she was second fiddle."

I dropped my head again. I couldn't even look her in the eyes.

"Teddy," she said finally, as she backed away. "Don't ever do this to anybody else; it hurts too much." She opened the door to her aunt's house, and she was gone.

I could still hear her final words as I drove away, the sound of her voice. I could still see her sweet face, her vivid blue eyes. How could I have hurt her like that?

I tried to imagine the conversation that was going on behind the door of her aunt's house at that very moment, the shame, the disappointment, the heartbreak. And it was my fault. I did this to her. What kind of an asshole was I?

I can never let this happen again, I vowed. *When school starts up in the fall, this thing with Lorraine begins for real or ends forever.*

And, for the first time in two weeks, I felt a painful vision rushing back into my brain. I closed my eyes and flashed back to Three Rivers Stadium. I step into the batter's box. The perfect pitch is on its way. I freeze.

"Goodbye, Carrie Ann," I whisper to myself. "Goodbye."

TIME TO GROW UP

"I can't believe it, Dad." Gene shook his head slowly. "Carrie Ann sounds perfect, perfect. What were you thinking?" Lunchtime had drifted into an early-winter afternoon by now. But the sky was so blue, and the day was so bright, that the December sun lit up our backyard like mid-July.

I stared out our rear picture window and shook my head at the insane beauty of the scene. It had been a day-and-a-half since either of us had had any rest, but the urgency of the conversation kept our minds swirling and our eyes wide open. "I *wasn't* thinking," I said finally. "When I answered her, I was shocked at my own words.

"I had grown accustomed to the fact that Carrie Ann was going to be a two-week diversion; this wonderful two-week party that would make me happy for a while, but when it was over, wouldn't have any real effect on my life. The idea of her staying with me had never entered my mind. If I had had time to think about it rationally, I might have convinced myself to forget about Lorraine, to start fresh with this blue-eyed knockout of a girl that I barely knew.

"But I didn't think about it rationally. I didn't have time to weigh the pros and cons and make a reasonable decision. Instead, my subconscious took over, and my subconscious was *not* ready to give up on Lorraine. I could barely think straight, and alarms were going off in my head. I wasn't ready for that. I wasn't ready for a commitment to anyone else. Hell, if I said 'Yes. Move to Lakewood for the next year,' it would have been like a marriage proposal. My entire life, as I knew it, would have been gone."

"But, Dad," Gene scoffed. "Weren't you taking things too seriously? These were just teenage romances. Didn't you know there would be plenty of chances to get things right? "Don't we always get more opportunities?"

I smiled and shook my head slowly, "You mean a little angel that drops into your life at the wrong time? I think everybody gets one or two of those. That's what regret is all about. The world is full of things you're missing when you're in a screwed-up relationship. That's the lesson, Gene."

He stood up and stared out the window. "So, you think that Jan is keeping me from something else; some life that I really should be living?"

"Look, Gene, here's what I'm sure about: I was so blinded by my desire to be with Lorraine, that I pushed aside this *dream* girl. Not that a relationship with Carrie Ann was sure to last forever, but at least it was a *live* dream. It needed to be pursued. But instead, I thought about all the work I had put into Lorraine, over so much time. I had to finish it, one way or another."

"Wasn't it time to put that aside?" Gene scolded. "She had been going steady with some other dude for over a year by that time. You can't keep thinking about where you *were*; sometimes you have to think about where you are; about where you might be going."

I didn't answer right away. I let my son's words linger in the air for a minute or two. He was giving himself advice and didn't even realize it.

"And where are *you* going, Gene? Where are you *right* now?"

He shook his head slowly and sighed, "Well, I guess I've got a girl, a woman I mean, that puts me down incessantly. Then, tells me that she loves me, whenever I try to walk away."

"So, what are *you* missing out on, while you're busy playing this game with Jan?" I asked finally. "I think you already know the answer. You're missing your *life*. You're missing your opportunity at a real, healthy relationship."

"That's just it, Dad," he responded. "How do I know if a relationship is *worth* saving? I don't have a crystal ball and neither do you."

"Well," I smiled. "Believe it or not, when we were in college, my cousin Tony and I actually came up with a way to determine whether a relationship is worth saving. And, I can show it to you *on paper*."

"On paper?" Gene laughed out loud. "You mean like a system or a score?"

"Kind of," I smiled. "It's an index."

Gene stood up in disgust. "Oh, right, your famous Cripple Creek Index. I was wondering when we'd get back to that," he sighed. "Listen, Dad, I don't need an index to tell me how I feel about Jan."

"But maybe you need an index to tell you how she feels about you." I paused for a moment, trying to let that possibility be planted in his brain. But, before I could say another word, Gene's cell phone belted out the first few cords of "I'm Still Alive," his special ring tone for Jan, and it seemed to suck all the air right out of the room.

"I guess she's recovered from our last argument. I guess she's done giving me the silent treatment," Gene sighed as flipped up the screen on his phone. "I knew it was too good to last."

"Hello," he started, but before he could say another word, a shrill barrage of accusations started pouring out of the earpiece. I couldn't quite make out the words, but the message was pretty clear, Gene's earlier assertion about waiting until tomorrow to fly back to Florida was not going to go unchallenged.

He got up from the table and headed out toward the front porch again, but this time he held the phone away from his ear, giving the impression that he not only didn't appreciate the volume of Jan's comments, but he didn't think it was important that he heard every word either.

"Well, that's some improvement," I muttered to myself, as the voice on the phone drifted down the hall and out the door.

I got up and poured myself another screwdriver, then mixed one for my son. This wasn't going to be an easy sales pitch.

After about ten minutes, Gene wandered back into the house with his phone in his pocket.

"Well, how did that go?" I asked with a shake of my head.

"About like I expected," Gene answered. "She's demanding I get on a plane today. And, no matter what I said, she just kept whining that if I loved her, nothing was more important than flying to Miami right now to work things out. I said my plane ticket was for tomorrow, and she'd just have to wait. But she wouldn't listen, and she absolutely refused to hang up."

"How'd you resolve it? I wondered.

"Finally, I just shouted over her," Gene shrugged. I said, "I came home for my Dad's birthday, and I won't be back until tomorrow. If you want to meet my plane, fine. If not, I'll take a cab back to campus. Then, I just hung up on her."

I didn't say a word, but he could tell I was proud of him. "You know, Champ, what you really need to do is…"

But Gene wasn't looking for advice at that moment. "I *know* what I need to do, Dad." He barked.

Silence filled the kitchen again, as Gene made his way across the room and drained half his screwdriver in one gulp.

"Tell me about what happened when Carrie Ann left town," he said, finally. "Did you bounce back from your depression?" After his outburst, I was just glad Gene wanted to get back to our original conversation.

"I just hung out with my boys," I nodded, "Jerry and Willie and Anthony. I leaned on them more, and more, and they kept my mind off Lorraine and whatever she was doing to say goodbye to Blake before he left for college."

"I thought you said Willie was leaving for Long Island for the summer?"

"That's right," I answered. I was impressed that he had actually been listening that closely. "But, before he did, he invited us to drive or hitchhike out to New York to spend a week with him out there and meet all his summertime friends.

"I was interested right away. It would certainly keep me from obsessing about Lorraine and grieving over Carrie Ann for the next two months. Anthony loved the idea too, but Jerry just laughed and said that his parents would never go for it. They were still a little pissed off about our unexpected excursion in February.

"I was sure it would be me and Anthony heading back to Long Island this summer, but when it became obvious that no one would lend us a car for the trip, and our only option was to hitchhike 300 miles, Anthony's parents refused to allow him to go.

"But the idea wasn't dead. After weeks of bragging about our next trip, the idea had caught the attention of another buddy of ours, Jimmy Cartwright.

"Jimmy was the president of our junior class, and his family was pretty well-to-do. But he was kind of a wild child. And his older brother had already done a lot of stupid shit, so he assured me that he could convince his parents to let him go.

"Still, I was surprised when I heard, for sure, that Jimmy's parents had given him the green light to hitchhike to Long Island. Now, it was my turn. How was I going to get my parents to approve this adventure?

"You know, Gene," I explained. "Hitchhiking wasn't considered as dangerous in 1971 as it is today. I'm sure there were plenty of lunatics and sexual deviants around back then too, but we rarely heard about them on TV or in the papers. If some teenager got grabbed off a highway in Texas, we didn't hear a word about it in Pennsylvania. Maybe it wasn't safe to hitchhike back then, either, but we thought it was. When I was fifteen years-old, that's how my buddies and I got around everywhere. I had probably hitched a ride from Rockland to Lakewood City a hundred times by then; and from Rockland to Beaver Falls too. It just wasn't a big deal."

"But this wasn't a five-mile ride, Dad," Gene reminded me. "This was 300 miles across three states; maybe even overnight."

"Well, sure," I agreed, "Safety was still a concern, but in the early Seventies, a lot of kids were doing it. Anyway, my father was the only one who could give me permission for an excursion like that, but he was tough and stern, and I thought my only chance was to get my mother on my side. Then we could both work on him together."

"Really," Gene smiled in disbelief. "Somehow you got Grandma, *my* Grandma, to agree to let you hitchhike across Pennsylvania, New Jersey and New York? That's amazing!"

"It *would* have been amazing," I nodded in agreement. "But it didn't happen. Instead, she absolutely refused. She said it was far too dangerous, and she would never allow a child of hers to do something so reckless. It looked like the idea was dead.

"When I broke the news to Jimmy, he was really disappointed. 'You know it wasn't easy for me to get permission either,' he told me, 'It took a long heart-to-heart talk with my dad before he agreed to let me go. But, you know, I think in the end, he was kind of proud of me.'

"I had never thought of that, Gene." I told my son. "That maybe, no matter how tough and stern my father was, that maybe he would be the one to know when it was time for me to grow up; time for me to be a man.

"So, I told Jimmy that I'd give it one more try. That, in spite of my mother's fears and protests, I would take the argument, man-to-man, directly to my dictatorial father. I prepared some pretty good points for the discussion. But I still figured my odds were maybe one-in-ten of pulling it off."

"I never met Grandpa," Gene shook his head slowly. "But from what you've told me about him, I don't see how he would ever let you take that trip, especially when Grandma had already said no."

"He knew some things about life that Grandma didn't know, Champ. Things I didn't know either. He knew how bitterly hard life could be. During the Great Depression, he had been one of seven children of a disabled railroad worker. His family had nothing. They lived day-to-day, meal-to-meal. Then, at 18, Uncle Sam drafted him right out of high school and sent him off to fight in World War II.

"What did I know about struggles like that? What did I know about survival? Hell, just six weeks earlier, he had seen me drop to my knees at Three Rivers Stadium. I had to be helped back to my feet by my teammates. I couldn't pick myself up off the ground, and for what, a baseball game? No, even though I was seventeen, he knew I had a lot of growing up to do."

"Don't tell me he said okay," Gene scoffed. "Hitchhiking all over the country for a week or two? I don't believe he'd let you go."

"Well, at first he said 'no way;' that it was too dangerous, that there were all kind of lunatics out there on the roads waiting to prey on teenage boys. That there were drugged-out freaks out there, who shouldn't even be behind a steering wheel.

"But I promised that we wouldn't get in a car with anyone we suspected was on drugs, or anyone that looked like a pervert. 'Besides,' I told him. 'I'm six feet tall, and I'm an athlete. And Jimmy is captain of the wrestling team and weighs 185 pounds. Who's going to mess with us? Plus, he's president of the Junior Class. Who could be a more responsible travel companion than that?'

"To my surprise, it looked like Grandpa was at least *considering* my point of view," I told Gene. "But, when it came to child rearing, he had never overruled my mother, and she had never overruled him."

"'I can't let you go, Ted,' he told me finally. 'Your mother thinks that it's too dangerous. And it probably *is* too dangerous. It's just not worth the risk.'

"'Dangerous?' I countered. 'I'm almost eighteen. When you were eighteen, the army had you trampling through the jungles of the Philippines, looking for Japanese guerilla fighters. This doesn't compare to that, not even close.'

"He dropped his head for a second, and I waited. At that moment, I could feel something different in the room. Something I had never felt from my father before. Was it love? No, I always knew that my father loved me. Even when he was whacking me with a belt for lying or stealing or cursing, I always knew that he loved me. But this feeling was different. It hung in the air, and in that moment of silence, I felt it. It was respect. My father respected me.

"'Okay,' he said finally. 'You can go. I just wish you hadn't asked your mother first.'"

"That night, as I lay on my bed, I could hear them arguing in the next bedroom. 'He's too young and it's too dangerous,' my mother wailed.

"'He has to face his fears,' my father countered. 'He has to be courageous. We have to let him become a man.'

"'He's too young!' my mom sobbed out loud. 'He's just a kid. Something terrible could happen to him. And it would be *our* fault. *We* would be the irresponsible ones. Could you live with that?'

"'Sooner or later, he has to learn to stand up on his own,' my dad spoke softly, but firmly. 'He needs self-confidence. We won't always be here to take care of him. Bad things are going to happen in his life. He has to be ready to face them.'

"If only he knew how prophetic those words would be."

"So, they gave you permission to hitchhike across three states?" Gene shook his head in disbelief.

"When I finally drifted off to sleep that night, they were still arguing," I nodded. "But two days later, Jimmy Cartwright and I were standing at the Cranberry entrance ramp to the Pennsylvania Turnpike with our thumbs out and holding signs that just said 'EAST.'"

"Well, you're here," Gene laughed, "So, I guess you survived."

"It was the adventure of a lifetime, Champ." I smiled at the memory. "We met one character after another. We got our first ride right away, and then spent the next eight hours at the Monroeville Exit outside Pittsburgh, waiting for somebody else to pick us up. After that, we figured we didn't have time to get all the way to Long Island in one day. So, we took out a marker and changed our sign to say 'Philly.'

"My sister, your Aunt Sandy, lived in Philadelphia, and we figured if we got that far on the first day, we could stay at her place, and finish the trip the next day. The strategy worked. Almost as soon as we held up our new sign, some big, 300-pound businessman in a station wagon picked us up and took us all the way across Pennsylvania. He looked like he hadn't done a push-up in his life, but he claimed to be a former semi-pro quarterback for some football team in Buffalo. He told us all his old stories about road trips and locker room pranks, about touchdown passes and about his career-ending injury.

"*Everybody has had their disappointments,* I thought. *Everybody's had their great victories and heart-breaking losses.* Jimmy and I ate up every word. We let Semi-Pro Quarterback re-live his glory days. We sighed and nodded at his disappointments. The hours flew by.

"It was dusk when he finally dropped us off at the Valley Forge Exit outside of Philadelphia. I called Aunt Sandy and she drove up the Schuylkill Expressway to pick us up.

"After a good night's sleep at her apartment, she and her boyfriend, Ken, took us to the entrance of the New Jersey Turnpike early the next morning. Almost immediately, we got a ride from a van full of long-haired, music-loving hippies. They were heading to New York City to see the *Harrison Concert*. The Beatles had just broken up a year earlier, and this was going to be George Harrison's first live concert without John and Paul. Young people all over the country were buzzing about the concert at Madison Square Garden, starring the former Beatle, plus Ravi Shankar, Bob Dylan, Billy Preston, Leon Russell and Eric Clapton.

"It was the biggest two-day musical event since Woodstock, and was later called *the Concert for Bangladesh*, a South Asian country, that was not only embroiled in a war for independence from Pakistan, but was also hit by two years of drought and was collapsing under the weight of a starving popula-tion. It was the first Benefit concert, a world-wide phenomenon, and we felt like we now had some connection to it.

"When we first hopped into the back of the van, I was worried, because the air was full of smoke, which I figured *had* to be marijuana. 'You better let us off up here,' I told a blurry-eyed hipster, who called himself *Blaze*. 'No offense, but I promised my folks that I wouldn't get in a car with a driver who was high.'

"'He ain't high,' Blaze assured us. 'That's Gary. He's our designated driver. That's the only reason we brought his sorry ass along.'

"They were a great bunch of guys and seemed genuinely concerned about the starving children in Bangladesh," I told Gene. "And the lesson I learned that day was that you don't judge a book by its cover."

"Outside New York City, we got our last ride from some athletic-looking, thirty-ish guy who claimed to be a U.S. Olympic Javelin Coach. We believed him. Why not? He was cool as hell, and took us all the way to Freeport, Long Island, where Willie was waiting to greet us."

"Sounds like a great trip," Gene marveled, "I guess your mom and dad didn't have to worry about you after all. How'd you make out on Long Island?"

"We spent ten days, there," I answered. We met twenty-five or so new kids, people we didn't know at all, people who were completely different from us, and we flourished from the experience. There was one girl who sang and played guitar, and we would sit in her bedroom for hours listening to her entertain us. I felt like I had met Joni Mitchell. There was one dude who worked at a Country Club all summer and would bring back leftover appe-tizers. We ate like kings every night and hung out at Jones Beach every day.

"Sure, it was an adventure. It was an experience, but it was much more than that for me. Every day, I could feel my confidence coming back.

"Jimmy and I had had comfortable, enjoyable conversations with Semi-Pro Quarterback, and Olympic Javelin Coach. We fit right in with a van-full of Hippies. We even thrived with a whole new gang of New York high school kids. They were complete strangers, and they all seemed to like us. Hell, they all seemed to love us.

"Carrie Ann had helped me get over my depression, but this trip was giving me back my self-confidence. It was exactly what I needed, exactly *when* I needed it. I was still extremely disappointed that I had struck out at the championship game at Three Rivers, but I wasn't going to let that own me. I wasn't going to let that moment define me. Cocky, self-assured Teddy Tresh was back. And I was never going to lose him again."

"So, you were ready for the big showdown with Lorraine," Gene laughed. "How'd that work out?"

"Well, I went back to school looking for a decision, looking for answers. But sometimes answers are hard to come by, and sometimes the truth is very hard to recognize."

"Tell me about it," Gene smirked. "Tell me the secret. That's some insight I could really use."

40

GRABBING AT SHADOWS

I had only seen Lorraine once or twice the whole summer, once at a ballgame in Ewing Park and once at the Lakewood City Summer Festival. Both times she was with a group of kids from the Class of '71. She was loud and happy and clinging to Blake's arm like a showgirl with Sinatra. Both times I caught her eye, but only for a moment. She'd glance, then glance again, then turn away, like a guilty cat with its paw in the fishbowl.

Finally, September rolled around. On the first day of classes in our senior year, we were again in the same homeroom. I came straight through the doorway and made a beeline across the room and sat at the desk right next to her. "I hear you had a big Summer," Lorraine chirped, with a mixture of sarcasm and teasing.

"You mean thumbing to New York?" I answered. "Yeah, it was quite an adventure."

"Oh, I heard your summer was *full* of adventure."

I was pretty sure that was a reference to Carrie Ann. News travels fast in a little town like Lakewood, but I decided to play dumb. If Lorraine wasn't going to make a direct reference to her, I certainly wasn't going to offer any new information about the girl from Georgia. Breaking someone's heart is nothing to discuss just to make small talk. And I felt I owed it to Carrie Ann not to trivialize our weeks together. I kind of let the conversation end at that point, as we listened to Mrs. Byers, our new homeroom teacher, lay out the rules for the new school year. We had heard it all before, of course. "You can sit anywhere you want for now, but I reserve the right to move you around if I think you're disruptive to the other students," Mrs. Byers sang in her always-cheerful voice.

Lorraine looked away for a moment or two, and then pulled out a full sheet of notebook paper, wrote something on it and folded in over three times. As soon as the home room teacher turned to write some instructions on the green "black board," she handed the note across the aisle to me. I opened it slowly with one eye on Mrs. Byers. "I need to talk to you. Can you meet me at lunch?" the note proclaimed.

Now it begins, I thought. "It's a date," I whispered back to her.

The whole month of September was a roller coaster ride. We would have long, meaningful telephone calls about love gone wrong. We would both bemoan our regrets over things we had done or failed to do. But, when it came right down to it, nothing really changed. Lorraine still wore Blake's class ring every day, and in public, all she would do was talk about him and how much she missed him.

She was like two different people, one who would exchange private notes and whisper flirtations in homeroom, the other one who refused to be seen with me in the hallways and preferred to walk to classes surrounded by an entourage of girlfriends.

"Are you going to the dance tonight?" I asked her on the first Friday afternoon of the school year.

At Lakewood High School, we had dances every Friday night in the Old Gym, sponsored by the Dance Club, of which I was Treasurer. The dances were not only the highlight of the week for students, but were a big money-maker for the club. The Dance Club probably had the biggest budget in the school, including the senior class treasury itself.

"Sure, I'm going," Lorraine said, with an enticing smile.

"Can I pick you up?" I paused to read her reaction. "How's eight o'clock?"

"Maybe, I should just meet you there," she sighed without hesitation.

Wow, I thought. *She always gives me just enough to keep me hanging on. She doesn't want anyone to think it's a date, but she did promise to meet me there. How can I be pissed off about that?*

But I *was* pissed off. I hated that I couldn't really get close to her, that she just kept me grabbing at shadows. I hated that she never really followed up on the promises she seemed to be making last Spring when she wrote in my yearbook about how much she cared, about how if either of us would have had the courage to say *I love you*, we would have probably stayed together. Wasn't that some kind of commitment? Wasn't that some kind of promise of better days to come?

Oh, sure, we had our moments at the dances. We were cheek to cheek dancing to the Delphonics' *La, La, Means I Love You* and *Just My Imagination* by the Temptations. When we held each other close on the dance floor, it really felt like she would never let go. But, when the music stopped, she'd just return to her entourage, and the next Monday in homeroom, it was like it never happened. I was starting over every week. I never made any progress.

By the third weekend in September, I was feeling neglected. My pride just wouldn't let me keep chasing her around like this.

On Thursday afternoon after school, I was hanging with some Rockland boys outside the drugstore in town, when an old baseball teammate from the Class of 1970 drove up. It was Billy Conti. Billy was in his sophomore year at Gulf Coast Junior College in Florida, but had gotten suspended from the baseball team there. He was back home now, planning his future and looking for a little excitement to motivate him.

"I'm heading up to Greenville tomorrow night to visit my brother at Thiel; any of you guys want to ride up with me?"

My head perked up right away. "We're going to a Frat party," he smiled, "Music, beer and college girls. And we ain't coming home until Saturday."

Everybody roared with approval, but only Willie Gacik, Johnny Hudson and I thought we could pull it off and get our parents' permission. "I'll try to go," I promised.

"You gotta go," countered Gacik. "It's sorority girls, for Chrissakes. You know what that means?"

I really *didn't* know what it meant, but it sounded cool as hell. "What about the school dance?" I hesitated. "Lorraine expects me to be there."

"Are you kidding me?" Gacik countered. "When are you gonna wise up? You're wasting your life chasing that skirt around, and for what?"

The next night at eight o'clock, I heard the blast of Conti's car horn outside my house on Fourth Avenue in Rockland. Hudson and Gacik were already in the car, smiling like the cat that ate the canary. "Are you packed?" laughed Billy, as he waved his toothbrush out the window. I actually had packed a gym bag with some fresh clothes, but I dropped it by the door and fished out my toothbrush and toothpaste. *Apparently, we were travelling light tonight.*

"No drinking!" my mother shouted after me as I jumped in the backseat. "You promised."

But when I got in the car, I could already see a brown bag on Johnny's lap. "No problem," I mouthed the words through the back window as we drove away.

Before we even left Rockland, Johnny handed me the bottle. "It's Iron City," he laughed, "The good stuff." Iron City was a local brew that tasted like athlete's foot smelled.

"No thanks," I waived him off. I had promised my mother and dad that I wouldn't drink on this trip. And if I was going to break that promise, it would have to be at a party with some sorority girl on my lap, not on the ninety-minute ride up to Thiel College. Besides, I hated the taste of beer, especially Iron City.

I was relieved to see the Billy wasn't drinking either. "No, I'm driving," he waved off Huddy. "But Sammy's frat has a whole keg waiting for us on campus. No use getting shit-faced before we even get there."

"More for us," laughed Johnny as he passed the bottle up to Willie in the front seat.

"So, how the hell did you get tossed out of Gulf Coast already?" I questioned Conti.

Billy had graduated in 1970 and was the starting third baseman of the Lakewood City High School team that year. He had a nice scholarship to play ball for Gulf Coast Junior College, and I had heard he was doing well down there.

"It's Corso's fault," he barked in disgust. Brian Corso had been the starting shortstop on that 1970 team in Lakewood, and I backed him up during my sophomore year. He and Billy had both gone to Gulf Coast to play ball.

"Brian's girlfriend was going to Georgia Tech," Billy continued. "We had four days off between our spring games and the start of our conference games. And he wanted to jump in his old Chevy and drive from Florida to Georgia just to see her for a couple days. What could I do? I couldn't let him go alone. Besides, they had been battling on the phone for weeks, and Brian thought she might be messing around with one of those Tech dudes."

I could see where this was leading. "You mean he didn't tell her he was coming?" I gasped.

"Yep, and it was just as bad as it sounds," Billy shook his head in disgust. "We couldn't find her in her dorm, so we waited in the car outside until morning. Along about 9 a.m. she comes strolling up the sidewalk arm-in-arm with some greasy-haired, pimple-faced hippy. Well, you know what a hothead Brian is. He jumps out of the car and starts swinging. It took me and three campus security guards to pull him off the guy. They took him straight to jail. He spent a week locked up; while I tried everything I could to get him out.

"He begged me not to call the coach or even his parents. But finally, I had to call my dad, who flew down to Atlanta and bailed him out. By the time we got back to Gulf Coast, we had missed two conference games. They tossed us both off the team. My dad went ape-shit, screaming at the dean and the head coach, but it was too little, too late. And my college baseball career was over."

"God damned women," Huddy barked from the backseat. He was already beginning to slur his words. "They'll be the end of you. That's for sure."

I bit my tongue and avoided saying the obvious; this was more Corso's fault than the fault of some small town co-ed who was on her own for the very first time. "See," scolded Billy, "That's what I'm talking about, Teddy. You can't go throwing your life away on some girl."

"It can be a shit-show, that's for sure," I told Billy. "Well, I feel bad for Brian, but a lot worse for you. I mean, it wasn't even your shit-show."

There had been three Rockland boys that started for the 1970 Lakewood team, Billy Conti, my cousin Tony DeVito, and Derrick Dawson, the ace of the pitching staff. Tony was at Duquesne University in Pittsburgh. Dawson had been drafted by the Detroit Tigers and was working his way up through their farm system, pitching for their Denver affiliate for some guy named Jim Leyland.

We Rockland ball players were a pretty tightly-knit group, and it hurt to know that one of us had been cheated out of his college playing days. "I'm going to go back to school in the spring," Conti assured us; "Maybe Beaver County Community College. I hear they're building a nice program with a lot of local ballplayers," he chuckled, but you could hear the disappointment in his voice.

Johnny Hudson had just finished his high school career, playing first base with me on that Lakewood City High School team that had just lost the Championship game at Three Rivers Stadium. He was working at the B&W Steel Mill now. "I might head to Community College in the spring to play some ball too," he announced. "Imagine that, me and you starring at CCBC."

"You know, you're the last one, Teddy," Billy sighed from behind the steering column. "Skip and Huddy are gone, and you'll be the only Rockland boy playing for Lakewood next year."

"We could have gone out in style," Huddy shook his head in disappointment. "Me at first base and you at shortstop; we could have given them something to remember us by."

"Even Skip," I added, "He was running at first when I fanned to end the game. If I hit a gap shot and he scores from first, we win the game. They would have carried us both off the field. *The Last of the Rockland Boys,*" I groaned. "Imagine that."

We all sat there in silence for a minute or two, but it seemed like an hour. "Pass me that bottle," I said finally. "Let's get this frickin' party started."

We met up with Sammy Conti outside his frat house just before ten p.m. He was standing with a half-dozen fraternity brothers, all dressed up in jeans and a dress shirt with the sleeves unbuttoned. *That must be the style on college campuses,* I thought. And that's the outfit Gacik and I wore every day of high school for the rest of the year.

The mixer was cool. It was at the Sorority House for Lambda-Lambda-Lambda, and of course, Billy's brother and his buddies called the sisters "the Lambs." They were a lot different from the high school girls I knew, more confident, and self-assured and intellectual; well, intellectual for a bunch of half-drunken college students I guess.

Billy and Huddy dove right in, confronting Lamb after Lamb after Lamb with their Rockland boy charm. Within five minutes, they were both on the dance floor swaying to *Ooo, Baby, Baby* with the first woman who smiled at them.

Gacik and I hung back by the keg, sipping down some flat Iron City Beer, and trying to get our courage up. "I wonder how old this beer is," Willie moaned, spitting some back in his cup. "It tastes like piss."

"Just drink it," I laughed. "And maybe you'll have the balls to talk to one of these women."

"Me?" he countered, "You act like you've never seen a female before."

"What's the use?" I shook my head. "I'm going nowhere until I get this Lorraine shit sorted out."

"For Chrissakes, will you forget about that chick for ten minutes? You're in a room full of sorority girls. Get out there and be a man!" Willie chided.

"Look at the blonde by the punch bowl, the one dancing with that skinny, red-haired girl," he smirked. "She's exactly your type."

"You like her? Go ahead and make your move," I suggested. "I'll tell you what. I'll be your wing man."

"You mean I get Brigitte Bardot and you'll take Little Orphan Annie?" he gasped. "What if she blows me off?"

"She won't," I assured him. "She won't want to ruin things for her freckled-faced friend."

The ploy worked to perfection. The sweet blonde had her head on Gacik's shoulder all night long, while I was as friendly as I could be without misleading her friend. Turns out Belinda, the redhead was a very sweet girl, and we had fun just dancing and bullshitting about everything from the differences between high school and college parties, to why beer from a keg is always flat.

When we got back to the frat house, Billy, Huddy and Will all had girls' phone numbers which they waved in the faces of all the fraternity brothers. "Those probably aren't even their real numbers," goaded Sammy. "That's an old college-girl trick."

"Sour grapes," countered Billy. "You're just jealous that we waltzed in here and conquered the Lambs in one night."

Sammy tossed each of us a ragged pillow with no pillowcase and a shabby blanket, and we spread out on the hard floor with nothing but a thread-bare, thirty-year-old carpet for cushioning. My three beer-saturated buddies passed out right away, but I tossed and turned all night long. The rock-hard floors and the nagging thought of Lorraine, and the effect she was having on my life, kept me twisting and buzzing until sunrise.

When we piled back into the Cutlass the next morning, my buddies were acting like rock stars, but I was dead tired. The only thing keeping me awake was a driving determination to confront Lorraine, and get this relationship defined, one way or another.

Billy dropped me off at my house about 11 a.m., Saturday morning, and I headed straight for my father sitting at the kitchen table sipping his second or third cup of coffee. "I need the car for about an hour, Dad," I announced. "It's important."

Normally, he would have questioned me like the Nazis at Nuremberg, but something in the tone of my voice stopped him. And he just reached into his pocket and tossed me the keys. I only stopped long enough to make a quick phone call to Lorraine's house. Of course, her mother answered.

"Lorraine, it's for you," she announced. "It's that boy from Rockland. What does he want?"

"I need to talk to you," I proclaimed, when she got to the phone. "It can't wait."

"I was just about to walk over to Margie's house," Lorraine answered. She seemed a little taken aback by the urgency in my voice.

"Great," I told her. "I'll meet you on the way."

Fifteen minutes later, I pulled down Todd Avenue and onto 7th Street, when I saw Lorraine tripping down the sidewalk toward Margie's house. I pulled over immediately and hopped out of the Thunderbird. "Hi, there," I smiled confidently at Lorraine. I felt like a preacher when he gets the calling; inspired, driven, ready to testify.

She froze in her tracks as I walked toward her. She was smiling, but before she could say a word, I greeted her with a kiss. It was only a moment or two, but as she pulled away, her eyes darted up and down the street, looking for witnesses and hoping she wouldn't see any. She needn't have worried. We were the only souls on the street this bright Saturday morning.

"You're not going to make this easy, are you?" I shrugged in disappointment.

"We're right on my street," Lorraine replied nervously. "What did you expect? What if my sister or brothers saw us? What if my mother did?

"What if she did?" I spoke calmly and firmly. "Would that be the end of the world?"

"Not for you," she scolded. "But she'd make my life a living hell. Why do you always have to be so selfish? Why do you only think about yourself?"

"I'm not thinking about myself." I tried to stay calm and cool. I was here to speak my mind; not to get drawn into some divergent argument. "I'm thinking about us."

"I'm not going to fight with you," she smiled, trying her best to fend off this conversation; to steer it away from the topic she wasn't prepared to face. Again, her eyes swung east and west, north and south. And then she stepped in so close I could feel the heat of her breath on my neck. She kissed me, soft and slow and tenderly. And I almost forgot what I wanted to say.

"I'm glad you don't want to fight," I whispered. "Because you know what happens when we argue? Sometimes I win. Sometimes you win. But *we* always lose.

"We've been dancing around this for months now," I continued, "Ever since you wrote that note in my yearbook."

"Teddy," she interrupted, "That message was about regrets; about what might have been. I wasn't making any promises for the future."

"I get that." I had both hands on her shoulders, as I spoke softly, clearly, deliberately so that there would be no chance of miscommunication. "You said that we could have, *should have*, been together, if only either one of us had had the courage to say *I love you.*"

"But we always let our pride get in the way," she sighed, diverting her eyes for a second or two, "Yes, I said that."

"Well, I was up all night thinking about it." I was still holding her by the shoulders, but took a half step to the right, so that I was back in her direct field of vision. "And I've decided I'm ready. I don't want anybody else. I don't need anybody else." I waited a moment or two, until I was sure her eyes were locked up in mine. "I *love* you, Lorraine."

Now, her gaze dropped to her feet, and she sighed in uncertainty and disbelief. "Look," I said, "I've never said that to any girl...ever."

She just stood there in silence, staring at the ground.

"Say something," I pleaded. "Say anything."

I could feel a warm September wind kicking up around us. And, in the distance, I could see one of those little dust storms swirling up the street like a small tornado. It was headed straight for us. "Tell me what you're thinking," I prompted her.

We could both feel the moment closing in on us. "I want you to completely understand where we are." I was still holding her in my arms. "Make no mistake, Lorraine. This is it."

"This is what?" she asked finally. "What am I supposed to do? You know how I feel about you, but I just can't change my life like that." And she snapped her fingers. "What about this?" she said, holding up her left hand with Blake's class ring shining in the noonday sun. "What would my friends say? What would my mother say?"

"Your *mother*?" I gasped, "What's she got to do with it?"

"She'd be so upset," Lorraine shook her head in despair. "She'd be so disappointed in me. And she would *hate* you."

"She *already* hates me," I scoffed.

"And that's no way to start a relationship," she interrupted. "She needs time to get to know you better. And I need time to figure out what I really want."

"Time?" I asked incredulously. "This has been going on for a year and a half. I'm out of time.

"*This* is the moment," I proclaimed emphatically. "This is what we've been waiting for."

Just then the little dust devil that had been swirling up the street reached us. I pulled her close and we both closed our eyes to ward off the stinging bits of street cinders. It passed in just four or five seconds, but we both stood there in that embrace for another twenty seconds, knowing our next words could change everything.

"Teddy, I'm not ready," she said finally. "I'm with somebody else. Maybe it's just too late for us."

"Too late?" My tone began to rise now. "You're sixteen years old. How can it be too late?"

"I just need time to think," she responded. "I can't do this right now. I'm not ready. What did you expect to happen? Did you think you could just come over here and say you love me, and it would just change my life?"

I could feel all my excitement being drained from my body. I was disappointed and disgusted, and suddenly, the fatigue from my sleepless night hit me in a wave of despair. "Well, that's what I *hoped* would happen. But I guess I didn't really *expect* it to happen."

I shook my head slowly, and deliberately. "*This* is what I expected to happen, exactly this."

I backed up a step or two and tried to look into her eyes. My mind was flooded with visions. I could see Amy Maroni's face, kissing her goodnight after all those dates. We must have gone out twenty or thirty times in the last year. And I never took it seriously. Sure, she had a "boyfriend," but there was something special between us, and I had ignored it because I was so obsessed with Lorraine. And Winnie, already a woman…We had a chemistry that I knew very little about, except that I longed to be with her every minute. But she could see me carrying that flame, that torch, that burning compulsion to return to Lorraine, and she just wouldn't take it anymore. Who could blame her?

And Carrie Ann…For Chrissakes…Carrie Ann, my dream girl, who I decided was just going to be a summer fling, who I used as a diversion until I got another chance with Lorraine. How stupid was I?

We stood there in silence for a long time. "I give up," I whispered finally. "I quit."

"What's that mean?" she shrugged. "You can't give up on us anymore than I can."

I didn't say another word. I just turned and started walking back towards my car. "Teddy," she called after me. "I don't believe you. I don't believe you can change your feelings just like that."

"All that work," I shook my head in disgust and sadness, "Over so much time." My eyes fell to the pavement, as I turned and walked slowly towards the T-Bird.

When I reached the driver's side door, I looked back at her. "I want you to understand something," I told her, "If I had two lives, I would use one of them to chase you around forever. I would try everything I knew to get you back. I would try and try and try to win your love, and I would never, ever give up. But I only have one life, and seventeen years of it are gone already."

"You're mad at me, aren't you?" she called in desperation.

"No," I replied, as I stepped into the car. "I'm not mad."

While driving back to Rockland, I could feel the weariness starting to overtake me, and some other emotion that I couldn't quite put my finger on. Sure, there was some pain there, and a lot of disappointment and sadness. There was something else too, something that resembled relief.

Back in school on Monday, I was determined to keep Lorraine off my mind. It felt good to be light and free, and I looked at every attractive girl in the hallways as a new possibility. I bumped into Willie, who was still flying high from our trip to Thiel College. "Hey, man, thanks for the assist Friday night." He grinned. "That *wingman* stuff really works!"

"Maybe you can return the favor sometime," I laughed. "This time you get Little Orphan Annie, and I get Bridgett Bardot."

"What about your girlfriend?" Gacik rolled his eyes. "Don't tell me you've finally wised up and gave up on the princess of Lakewood High?"

"I talked it all out with Lorraine on Saturday. I'm done, buddy," I pledged. "I'm pulling my hat out of the ring. I've taken enough abuse for one lifetime. Those days are gone."

"I'll believe it when I see it," he scoffed, as he turned down the hall towards second period gym.

I don't blame him, I thought as I stepped into Mr. Ionelli's Advanced Journalism Class. *But, it's a new day.*

The class was full of familiar faces. Almost without exception, these were the same students who had filled my Introduction to Journalism class from the year before. But, this school year, besides tests and research and reports, we would also be charged with publishing the monthly school newspaper, *The Lakewood Echo.* We had all contributed articles to the school paper in previous years, but this year, we would design the paper, make the writing and photography assignments, and edit, sell and distribute it. The room was full of good writers and reporters, the best communicators in the school.

From the back of the class, one face beamed above all the others. It was Lynn Batista, the 5-foot 1-inch Italian knockout. When I say *beamed*, I mean just that. She looked like an angel, and I swear, in that instant, I could hear a choir singing somewhere overhead. She was like this dear friend who I hadn't seen in a long time, even though I had barely ever spoken to her. It was like I was seeing a lifelong friend for the first time in years. Then, in a flash, I remembered the last time I saw her. It was right after the worst moment of my life. I had just swung and missed the last pitch of the WPIAL Championship game and was hanging my head in shame. When I finally had the strength to look up into the crowd, all the Lakewood fans had already turned their backs and headed towards the exits. My father had his arm around my mother as he led her down the exit ramp. I searched for Lorraine, but she was already over the disappointment of the moment, and had joined her entourage of new friends, led by her boyfriend Blake Bianchi and his senior class cronies.

But, as my eyes kept searching the seats, I had seen Lynn holding onto the railing of the box seats, and staring out onto the field, as her own boyfriend was tugging at her sleeve. I remembered how she seemed concerned, even though she didn't know me that well, just a caring person who recognized suffering when she saw it. *What a sweet girl,* I had thought that day. *What a sweet girl,* I was thinking right now.

Of course, the problem then was the same as the problem now. She *had* a boyfriend, and not just any boyfriend, but Denny Nowitzki, a kid who was universally loved by the whole school. He was the link between the straights and the freaks. He was a friend to the nerds and the cool kids, the greasers and jocks. Everybody that knew him thought he was a great guy. Hell, I even liked the kid myself. It didn't even matter that he was two years older than Lynn and had graduated with the Class of 1971. She was still wearing his class ring, and they seemed like the happiest couple in Lakewood City.

I walked straight to the back of the Journalism class and sat down right next to her. "Hey, Lynn," I whispered. "I want to thank you."

She looked a little puzzled. "For what?" she smiled.

"For giving a shit," I answered with all sincerity. She just smiled and nodded her head, and I could tell she knew exactly what I was talking about.

I couldn't get my mind off her all day. And, as the Rockland students loaded back into the bus after school, I confided in Willie and Lonnie, "I wish I could find a girl like Lynn Batista."

"Forget it," they barked in unison. "That's Denny Nowitzki's girl," Lonnie continued. "You could never break them up, and even if you did, everyone would hate you for it."

I just sighed. I knew it was a lost cause, but it felt good to be thinking of somebody besides Lorraine for once. *I guess I'm making some progress,* I smiled to myself. *At least that's something.*

As the days and weeks went on, I did my best to be unemotional around Lorraine. I would always greet her with a smile and pleasant conversation, but our usual flirtatious banter was gone. "What are you doing this weekend?" she said nonchalantly one Friday afternoon.

"I'm not sure," I smiled. "Gacik and Dillon want to head over to the Beaver Falls-New Brighton game tonight. Willie has his eye on some Beaver Falls Majorette, and I'm thinking of tagging along."

"What's the matter," she teased, "Aren't Lakewood girls good enough for you now?"

"Too high maintenance," I laughed, "Thought I'd try something different."

"There's a surprise," she answered, without an ounce of sarcasm in her voice. But the irony came through anyway.

She can feel the difference, I supposed. *She knows that things have changed. I wonder if she even cares.*

Back in Journalism class, I started talking with Lynn Batista almost every day. She was sweet and smiling and easy to talk to. I knew this was going nowhere, but I looked forward to those three classes per week that we had together. Of course, every day after school, there was Denny waiting for her outside the Commons area. They'd hug and laugh and walk off together to who knows where? And every day, as I climbed on the bus back to Rockland, I would glance out the window for a moment or two. *Why can't I find a girl like that?*

Finally, one day in early October, I met Lynn in the hallway after eighth period, and our conversation led back to her home room, where she grabbed a few books, and then we walked together down the stairs, through the Commons Area and out the side doors of the school. "Well, it was great talking with you," I smiled. "Where's your boyfriend?"

"We're fighting," she shrugged. "I suppose we'll work it out, but it's been going on for weeks with no end in sight."

"Do you want to talk about it?" I asked with as much concern as I could muster. "You can tell me anything."

"I don't think that's a good idea," she answered with a smile. "That wouldn't really be fair to him."

Even when they're fighting, she stays loyal, I thought as I strolled away. *Why can't I find a girl like that?*

I boarded the bus again, but this time, when I looked out the window, Lynn was still standing there watching me. I shot her a quick smile and wave. She just nodded and watched until the school bus rolled out of sight. *Okay, that's got to mean something,* I thought.

"What's up, Rockland boy?" came a familiar voice from the aisle beside me. It was Molly Bellinski. "Is this seat taken?" She laughed as she squeezed in next to me. Over the years, we had become old friends, the kind of childhood friends that you can't lose, and you never forget. The fact that she had been my girlfriend when we were ten years old was a non-factor now. We were just a couple of kids who had grown up together in the same small town, who shared a simpler, more innocent time.

"Is that your newest prospect?" She nodded towards Lynn as we pulled away.

"Naw," I said. "She *has* a boyfriend. I kind of like her though. She's sweet and smart and funny, and loyal to one guy, come hell or high water. Actually," I paused for a second. "She kind of reminds me of you."

"I'm just glad you're over Lorraine Donatelli," Molly confided. "It hurt to watch you chase her around month after month. I think she really liked you, but she was never going to leave Blake. She just liked you hanging around."

"Jesus," I moaned. "Does the whole school know my business?"

"We're Rockland kids," she smiled. "We have to watch out for each other." And she reached down on the seat and put her hand on mine. There was nothing romantic about it, nothing sexual; just one old friend caring about another old friend.

I closed my eyes, and I could still see Lynn watching the bus pull away. And that final vision of her stayed on my mind all the way home.

As my daily interactions with Lorraine got more and more formal, my Journalism Class conversations with Lynn got more and more personal. Turns out her conflicts with her boyfriend were more serious than I first expected. "You know he has a lot of freaky friends," she confided in me one day after class. "And that's okay. They're all nice kids. But it's the pot smoking that really bothers me. We used to spend almost all our time together, and every once in a while he would go out and party with his friends. And I didn't care. But now he's smoking almost every day. He even shows up at my house high. When I tell him to cool it, he agrees with me and everything is okay again.

"Then he comes to my door the next day with blood-shot eyes and chomping on two sticks of gum. And he pulls out the Visine every ten minutes. He denies being stoned, but I'm not blind. He slurs his speech and laughs at things that aren't funny."

"Well, a lot of kids smoke pot," I answered, pretending to defend Denny.

"I know," she nodded. "And there's nothing wrong with that. If he wants to party with his friends sometimes, that's fine. But it's not for me. I don't want to be around it, and I can't even talk to him, because, when I try, he lies to me."

"Well, it's not a good situation. That's for sure." I agreed. "You're a straight-A student, and your dad is a teacher here. He'd be pretty disappointed if you were ever in a car with Denny and you both got busted. But he's a good guy, Lynn. People like him, the jocks, the freaks, the greasers, they all like Denny Nowitzki."

"I like him too," Lynn sighed. "I'm just not sure he's the guy for me."

After that we talked every day, in the halls, during Journalism class, anytime we saw each other; nothing serious, just some mild flirtations and lots of smiles. I even opened up to her, putting aside my cocky personality and phony confidence long enough to admit to my battles with depression and insecurity.

I had always thought that I had to project strength in order to gain a girl's respect. But, instead of losing respect for me, she seemed more and more drawn to the person I really was.

In late September, we were assigned to co-edit the October *Lakewood Echo*. That meant a lot of one-on-one time planning the issue, assigning stories and photographers, writing headlines, and editing the rest of the staff's copy. The talk flowed easily and naturally, and it was a relief to be with someone who liked the real me; not the arrogant persona I had worked so hard to project. We were constantly complimenting each other's journalism skills. From there it wasn't long before the compliments got much more personal.

"Gee, you're gorgeous," I told her after some joke I cracked about Lakewood's winless football team made her laugh out loud. "And you're smart. And you're funny. Just the kind of girl everyone wants to meet.

"But you know what," I told her as I took her by her left hand. "You'd look a hell of a lot better if you weren't wearing this ring." It was a bold move on my part, and I felt a little foolish for exposing my feelings like that, but I was tired of sniffing around other guys' girlfriends. And I kind of expected that comment to put a stop to whatever it was we were pretending to be.

Lynn didn't respond at all, and when class was over, she walked down the hallway alone.

The very next day, right after lunch, we had to present the unedited *dummy* version of next month's *Lakewood Echo* to our teacher and advisor, Mr. Ionelli, for his approval. Lynn was already waiting in his office when I arrived. And she smiled broadly when I came into the room. "Do you have the front-page layout?" I whispered to her as Mr. Ionelli cleared his desk.

"Here it is," she said, extending her hand and offering me a tan folder containing about five or six light blue layout pages.

"Thanks," I replied quickly. But she just kept smiling at me expectantly, like she knew the punchline of some private joke. And her left hand still lingered in the air between us for an extra moment or two. Then I saw it or, I guess, I *didn't* see it. Denny Nowitzki's class ring was *gone*.

We both sat there, formally reviewing the newspaper with our advisor. Mechanically and methodically defending our choices for the most relevant stories, our front-page preferences and the shots we would need from Bruce David, the staff photographer. I could hear myself talking, responding, and even cracking a joke now and then. But my mind was a million miles away.

As soon as we were back in the hallway, the real conversation resumed. "It's gone," I exclaimed. "Denny's ring is gone. Did you break up because of me, because of what I said yesterday?"

"Not exactly," she smiled. "But your timing was pretty good; I've been having a lot of doubts lately. He's been smoking pot regularly, and now he's trying acid."

"You mean LSD?" I responded. "When did that shit hit Lakewood?"

"It's been around town for a couple years now, I guess." Lynn shook her head slowly. "I told him to do whatever he wants to do when he's with his friends, but I didn't want it around me. And then I started thinking, *maybe it's him I don't want around me.*"

"So...what now?" I asked as earnestly as possible.

"Well, I'm still going to see him, I guess," she smiled. "But I'm not *going steady* with him anymore." And she waved her empty ring finger in the air.

"I'll take that as an invitation," I smiled.

After that, we talked almost every day, not only in class, but on the phone. And our conversations grew longer and more personal week by week. And, for once, I kept my bravado in check.

I talked openly about my fear of getting drafted into the army. The Supreme Court had just ruled that college deferments were unconstitutional, so the fact that I was headed for college could no longer delay the draft for four years. They could take me right out of school any time they wanted. And although the Vietnam Conflict seemed to be winding down, there was still plenty of time to get sucked into that crazy war.

I opened up to her about my loss of confidence after the game at Three Rivers and about how I wondered if I would ever really get over it. I didn't even worry that exposing so much weakness would drive her away, because it seemed to do just the opposite. The more I opened up, the closer we got.

Of course, she wasn't my girlfriend, and she still had Denny Nowitzki soap operas occasionally, but when we were together, it was pretty obvious she liked me.

On our first date, I drove her out to the Pittsburgh Airport to watch the planes take off. It was fun and budget-friendly, and we had our first kiss on the observation deck, while an endless procession of jets flew into the darkened skies, and thousands of passengers zoomed off to embrace their futures. And, before I knew it, we were discussing our futures, our dreams.

On the next Friday, I met Lynn at the high school dance, and slow-danced for the first time to Chicago's *Colour My World*. That would become *our song* for the rest of our lives.

But it wasn't all smooth sailing for me and Lynn. Just moments after our first dance, one of her old girlfriends raced into the Old Gym and whispered excitedly and anxiously in her ear.

Then, she pulled me aside. "I'm sorry," she said. "I have to go."

"Go? Go where?"

"Denny is having a bad trip," she said, dropping her head. "He's in really bad shape. He's out in Sully's car right now drinking milk."

"Milk?" I smirked. "What's milk going to do?"

"He's trying to come down from whatever chemical he took. He's asking for me. I *have* to go."

"If you have to go, then go," I nodded rigidly.

"Thank you," she said, forcing a smile to her face. "You know I don't *want* to go, right?"

"I guess," I shrugged.

Then she put her arms around my neck and kissed me tenderly. And I stood there with my own thoughts as she walked out of the gym and into the cool autumn air with her old girlfriends clamoring around her.

Well, I thought, *I don't like that he's using bad behavior to manipulate her. But they've been inseparable for the past twelve months, and I have to admire her loyalty.* And, in spite of myself, I couldn't help but thinking, *I wish I had a girl like that.*

The next Monday morning, in school, Lynn was waiting at my locker.

We dated, without commitment, for the next month or so. But, all the while, I was still dealing with the remnants of my feelings for Lorraine. That reached its peak one last time in early October.

For the second year in a row, I had been asked to coach our class' Powder Puff team. It was kind of a big deal.

Every year, the Senior Class girls would play an indoor two-hand-tag football game against the Junior Class girls in the gym. It was a grudge match if there ever was one, preceded by weeks of good-natured barbs on morning announcements, bad-mouthing posters hung on the classroom walls, and trash-talking female ballplayers exchanging abusive insults in the hallways between every period. It was fun but, to us, it had a serious side. When we were juniors, we battled the senior girls to a 0–0 tie at halftime, then grabbed the lead on a 40-yard bomb early in the third quarter, which was called back for offside. We ended up losing the game 19–6 to the bigger, more athletic seniors, but the junior girls on the team never forgave the teacher/official that called the dubious penalty. The guy had been the most popular teacher in the school for years, but for months after that, our entire class refused to speak to him.

This year, we would be the bigger, tougher seniors. And we were expected to win the game. I called a few practices, and the team was much better and more experienced than the junior girls. And, of course, as the coach, I got to spend some quality time with Lorraine. Like other years, the trash talking in the hallways was as intense as ever, and the senior girls looked at me as a team leader to guide them through this battle.

That wasn't lost on Lorraine, and our mild flirtations became more intense as the game drew near. In the meantime, Lynn and I were walking the halls of Lakewood after every class, and although she was still seeing Denny once or twice a week, our classmates around the school began to see us as a couple.

When the Saturday night of the big Powder Puff game finally arrived, there was a real *junior vs. senior* vibe going through the gym and the crowd. I don't really remember the details of the game, but we beat the junior girls pretty badly. On one play, late in the game, I called for a screen pass to our left flat. I grabbed JoAnn Martinelli, our right guard, and told her, "Just bump their left tackle then get down field and block Lynn Batista, their safety. We might just be able to break this one for a touchdown."

The play worked to perfection, our running back hauled in the short pass, with no one but Lynn standing between her and the goal line. I don't think Lynn ever saw JoAnn coming, and she certainly wasn't expecting to get knocked over in a two-hand-touch indoor girl's football game. JoAnn's block sent her flying across gym floor and landing on her outstretched hand. The play went for an easy touchdown, and left Lynn grabbing her wrist and moaning in pain. I felt bad that she got walloped like that, but she stayed in the game, so I figured she must be alright.

After the lopsided game, we had a victory party scheduled and Lorraine asked me to drive her to the off-campus church hall where the party was being held. For weeks now, I had given up on Lorraine, but I guess I decided to follow this flirtation one last time.

Driving across town with Lorraine was a strange trip, we didn't speak much, but she immediately slid across the long front seat of the T-Bird until she was almost in my lap. I put my hand on top of hers and glided along the darkened back streets of Lakewood City with just my left hand on the steering wheel. The church hall was less than five minutes from the gym, but as we pulled to the curb Lorraine whispered, "I think we need to talk." I stared at her for what seemed like a long time, but was really only four or five seconds. "Not here," she whispered. And I swung the T-Bird back out onto the road.

We cruised in silence, my right hand still locked in hers, to nowhere in particular. Finally, we rolled by her house on Todd Avenue and turned right onto the Seventh Street Extension. "Stop here," she sighed.

In this part of town, all the houses were on the avenues, the dissecting streets were just dark houseless, one-lane roads to connect one avenue to another. It was the exact spot where three weeks earlier I had located her on her way to Margie's house, the place I confronted her about our feelings, the place I had told her that I loved her. We pulled to the side of the road, and I immediately pulled her close enough for a long, soft kiss. I wasn't sure what was about to happen; what she was about to say, so I held the kiss for a long time. Maybe it was good news coming, maybe it was bad, but for right now, I just wanted to hold onto the moment a little longer. Something was about to change, and I knew it. So, I tried to communicate my emotions through that kiss, and she responded exactly how I hoped she would. They say that actions speak louder than words. But what she said next made me realize that sometimes her words could speak louder than her actions.

She touched my face and looked me straight in the eyes. "Teddy," she sighed again. "This isn't going to change anything."

Okay, I thought, *We NEED to address that. But not right now. If she wanted to communicate physically first, I was sure we could work through the commitment part at a later date.*

For the next 20 minutes we spoke very little, but communicated a lot. We were parked just blocks from her home, so nobody was getting too bold. But she held on like she wanted the moment to last forever.

A half hour later, I was dropping her off at home instead of taking her back to the party. "Don't give up on me." She smiled, as she slid back across the front seat of the T-Bird and out the door. She never looked back on her way into the house. And when the door closed behind her, I again was left with more questions than answers.

No commitment, the thought struck me now. *I'm still going back to pretending none of this happened on Monday. What had she said, "Don't give up on me?" That's a promise for the future,* I reasoned, *but doesn't really say a damn thing about right now.*

When I finally pulled into the winners' party, Willie Gacik was walking out of the party with our Rockland pal Bo Dillon in tow.

"Hey, Coach," Willie laughed. "Where you been? This party's winding down; we're driving over to the junior's post-game party to console the losers."

He was thinking of the four or five eligible junior girls he had been exchanging glances with since the new high school year started shaking into place in September, and he was eager to see where those might lead. Although Lorraine's words were still ringing in my ears, "This doesn't change anything, Teddy," my first thought was about *Lynn Batista,* about how we had confided in each other, about the honesty and transparency of our feelings.

"I'll follow you over there," I said, stepping back into my car. It felt good to be full of adventure again, full of excitement for the future. All this halfway stuff with Amy Maroni and Winnie and Carrie Ann, what had it gotten me; nothing but regrets and hurt feelings and wasted time? There was no commitment; Lorraine had made that clear. I was a free agent. It was time to start acting like it.

We walked into the Losers Party and were met with a good-natured chorus of boos. Louie Palmieri, the coach of the Junior Girls team, was hosting the party at his parents' house and made his way over to shake my hand. "Good game, Coach," he smiled. "Where did you get those *bruisers* from, a women's prison?"

"We have some pretty big girls," I agreed. "I just came over to make sure nobody got hurt too bad."

"You better talk to Lynn Batista," Louie laughed. "She thinks her wrist is broken, but she's not letting it keep her from having a good time."

I looked across the room. Lynn was sitting on a couch pillow in the middle of the living room surrounded by teammates, with more than a few of the Junior Class bloodhounds sniffing around and giving her advice on how to care for her injury.

I got here just in time, I thought to myself. The word about Lynn's breakup with Denny had spread throughout the school by now. And the young lions were positioning themselves to lay their claim to her. My time to act was right now.

"Lynn," I shouted across the room. "How's that wrist?"

"Go home, Coach," barked Randy Delpino from the end of the couch. And the chorus of boos grew a little louder. "We don't need your sympathy."

Randy was my best friend Jerry's brother. We were friends, so I just smiled at the comment.

"I have a bone to pick with you," shouted Lynn, as she made her way across the carpet and straight toward the doorway, where I was still standing. "Did you send JoAnn Martinelli to knock me down?"

"Of course not," I smiled. "I sent our guard to block your safety. She just happened to be our guard, and you just happened to be your safety. I didn't realize she was going to pop you like that. I'd say 'I'm sorry,' but we did score a touchdown on the play."

"Look at my wrist," she barked in mock anger. It was wrapped in an ace bandage but flopped around like a dead fish when she tried to move it. "I'll have to go to the Emergency Room tomorrow to get it X-rayed, and if it's broken, you're in real trouble."

"Maybe we better get it checked out right now," I offered. "C'mon, I'll drive you to the emergency room." Now, every head in the room turned to follow the conversation. "Where's your jacket? I'll grab it for you," I continued. And, as I wrapped it around her shoulders, she turned and kissed me.

I was laying claim to Lynn, and everyone at the party knew it.

"I'll meet you back at your place in Rockland," called Willie, as we headed out the door, "If it's not too late."

An hour and a half later, I was driving Lynn home. She *did* have a hairline fracture of her left radius, and the doctor had wrapped it up tightly in a new Ace Bandage, although no cast would be needed. She pretended to be mad at me for calling that pass play, but mostly, I could see she was enamored with the way I had come to her rescue. And, when we got to her door, I gave her one long kiss and embrace before her mom appeared in the doorway, and we had to explain the entire incident over again.

"I'll call you tomorrow," I said as I returned to my dad's car, "To see how you're doing."

"You better," she warned, with a confident smile on her face.

I pulled the T-Bird into my driveway in Rockland just a few minutes later. Little did I know that in just a few short hours, all hell would break loose...

REALITY CHECK

Gene popped up from his kitchen chair. For hours now, he had been listening intently as I droned on about my teenage angst, my confusion, and my conflicts. But now he recognized that this father-and-son conversation was about to hit a new level. "What do you mean, 'All hell broke loose?'" he laughed nervously. "It seems like everything was already changing pretty fast."

"That was the night my father died," I blurted out. "Everything else disappeared. Loss…Loss and Survival became my main concerns after that."

"How did it happen?" Gene leaned forward now.

"When I got home from taking Lynn to the emergency room that night, Willie was already waiting in my living room with my Dad watching Chiller Theater. It was a weekly home-town horror show hosted by Pittsburgh's own Chilly Billy Cardille. He had a stage full of ridiculous characters like *Terminal Stare* and *Stefan the Castle Prankster*. And he would air two classic horror films every Saturday Night, starting at 11:30 pm. Tonight, it was George Romero's *Night of the Living Dead*, which had been filmed in nearby Zelienople.

'Shhhhhhhhhh' they both greeted me as I entered the living room. There was a groundskeeper for the cemetery on the screen, locking the gate at night. There was a shadow moving through the long weeds and brush; then a shot of an open tomb, then two open tombs. I sat down on the floor and got caught up in the movie.

'How'd things go with Lynn?' Willie whispered when the next commercial break finally arrived.

'Great,' I said, 'I'll tell you all about it tomorrow. But it's been a long evening. I've had it for tonight. I'm going to bed.' And I started up the stairs towards my room.

'Don't forget to say your prayers...' my father barked out.

"*How embarrassing*, I thought, rolling my eyes, *my Dad still treats me like a little kid.* I saw Willie's eyes light up, like he was going bust out laughing, but he just winked at me instead.

"My dad saw everything. He heard everything. Nothing got past him. 'On your knees,' he added loudly.

"It bugged me a little that my dad would embarrass me in front of my friend, but I can't say he didn't practice what he preached. Every night before he got under the covers, he would drop to his knees and talk to God for fifteen or twenty minutes. He did his best to make sure that I did the same. But this was the last time he would make that decision for me. Starting tomorrow, I was on my own.

'Good Night, Dude,' Gacik chirped after me. His own house was right across the railroad tracks from mine. So, he was practically home.

"Obviously, me going to bed wasn't going to make him miss the end of *Night of the Living Dead*. I watched from the stairway, as they both got a sour look on their faces when some zombie's arm got slammed in the doorway and fell into the room, still clutching at the legs of a family trying to barricade themselves inside.

"*Hilarious*, I thought, *Frickin' Hilarious.*

"The next morning, I woke to a note on my nightstand, 'Daddy had trouble with bleeding ulcers last night. We're at the Emergency Room. Get Nelson and Sophie off to CCD Classes (you too). See you after church. ~ Love, Mom'

"I thought I had heard moaning in the middle of the night, but I didn't worry too much about it, because my dad's ulcers woke him up many nights. He would always take a big gulp from his bottle of Maalox and pray to God until the pain subsided, then go to sleep.

"I guess this time was worse. Apparently, the chest and abdominal pains grew more and more severe, and no amount of Maalox could change that.

"When they got to the hospital, they had to wait hours for Dr. Freemont, who was covering for our family doctor. The asshole had decided to go to 8 o'clock mass before heading to the emergency room to examine my dad. By the time he got there the nurse was barking, 'This man is having a heart attack.' Dr. Freemont immediately admitted my dad to the Cardiac Care Unit. While they were preparing to transport him, from the E.R., he turned to my mom. 'I never thought it was my heart,' he confided. She looked down at her feet and shook her head. When she looked up again, he was gone."

"Jesus Christ," Gene blurted out now. "How old was he?"

"He was 45," I replied. "And, except for the ulcers, he was never sick a day in his life."

"Grandma must have been heartbroken," Gene whispered, lowering his head. "What happened to your family? How did you handle it?"

"We were *all* heartbroken," I sighed. "We all went over to Uncle Joe's house and mourned; me, your Aunt Sophie and Uncle Nelson, Uncle Joe, Aunt Betty, my cousin Tony and all his brothers and sisters. Nobody knew what to do. So, we just sat there and sobbed. I cried for three hours.

"Finally, Uncle Joe grabbed me by the shoulders. 'I know you're just 17,' he said, 'but you're the man of the house now.'

"Everything from the last four months came roaring back to me. It all made sense now: The deep disappointment of the Championship game; the struggle to regain my self-esteem; the hopelessness of the Lorraine situation; the hitchhiking trek to Long Island. I looked at all of it through a different lens now. I was a kid, but I needed to grow up.

"What had my dad told my mom in July, as she lay in bed crying about me hitchhiking to New York?

'Sooner or later, he has to learn to stand up on his own. He needs self-confidence. We won't always be here to take care of him. Bad things are going to happen in his life. He has to be ready to face them.'

"He knew. Somehow, he knew. And all those strangers I met along the way, and all Willie's friends on Long Island; hadn't I approached them all with confidence? Hadn't I held my own with Olympic Javelin Coach, with Semi-Pro Quarterback, with the van full of hippies headed to the Bangladesh Concert? Wasn't I fearless?

"And what had he told me after the game at Three Rivers? 'You can't be sobbing over a baseball game,' he scolded me; 'Don't you know what that did to your mother?'

"A few seconds later, the phone rang at Uncle Joe's house. 'It's the funeral home,' my cousin Tony announced solemnly. 'They want to know if Aunt Bella can come up to make the final arrangements.'"

'Ohhhhhh,' my mom moaned loudly at the very thought of it.

"'Tell them I'm coming instead,' I announced, as I stood up and wiped the final tears from my eyes. I pulled out my handkerchief and blew my nose, took a deep breath, and headed for the door.

"'I'll go with you,' Tony added confidently.

"We drove up to the funeral home in silence. I was 17 and Tony was 18, but our childhood was over, and ready or not, the torch was being passed to our generation."

Out of the blue, Gene's cell phone blasted out Eddie Vedder singing *I'm Still Alive*. It was Jan, once again, bursting into our conversation, thrusting her way into Gene's life, trying to control his judgement, trying to dampen any influence I might still have over my son.

"I guess you better grab that," I told Gene, trying my best to hide my disappointment. He just reached out and hit the *Decline* button.

"Tell me about grandma and your brother and sisters," Gene coaxed. "Tell me about *my* mom. Did she help you to move on?"

I just smiled and nodded my approval. "Over the next few days, your mom really stepped up, Gene. She wasn't even officially my girlfriend, but there she was, standing next to me at the wake, serving refreshments to the friends and relatives back at my house, comforting my mother every time she started sobbing. She called every day and had her dad drive her to Rockland every evening.

"On Wednesday, the final night of visitation, I spotted my Grandma Tresh, sitting near the casket. She wasn't sobbing, but her face was covered with tears. 'Our Rock of Gibraltar is gone,' she sighed. 'You have to be the man of the family now. I know you're ready.'

"Lorraine made an appearance at the funeral home too. She hugged me and told me how sorry she was. She had come to Rockland with three or four of my other classmates, but as my friends tried to comfort me, I could sense my resolution start to waiver. My new-found maturity was slipping away. And I could feel the tears welling up in my eyes.

"'Stay with my mom,' I whispered to Lynn. Then I walked evenly and deliberately towards the door, across the covered porch and out into the cool October evening. The tears were rolling now, and I kept my face turned away from the mourners who had stepped out for a breath of fresh air and watched me from the patio with concern."

"'Wait, Teddy,' I could hear Lorraine's voice behind me as I slowly strode down the sidewalk away from the funeral home.

"I was kind of surprised that she had followed me out. 'I don't want anyone to see me crying like a baby,' I whispered without turning around. 'I have to be a man now.'

"'You don't have to hide anything from me,' she sighed, stepping in front of me and blocking my path. 'Not from me.'

"The weight of the last four days caught up to me then and, in spite of myself, I started sobbing. I put my arms around Lorraine and cried on her shoulder.

"When I finally came back to into the room, Lynn was still standing next to my Mom, still comforting her in my absence. My emotions were everywhere. My loyalties were twisted and confused. But I couldn't be concerned with that now. I had to handle my responsibilities. I had to be strong for my mother, for my grandmother, for my family.

"I certainly had relationship issues to resolve, Gene, but they were no longer my main concern. Everything had changed overnight, and I needed to find my new reality. All the patterns I had followed for years were gone.

"In the weeks and months that followed, I had to constantly console my grieving mother and help her manage our new lives. She had never even paid a bill before that, never even balanced a checkbook. My Dad had done all that.

"Thankfully, he left us a decent sized insurance settlement, but it wouldn't last forever. What would happen when it ran out? And I had always planned on college after high school. Who was going to pay for that? It was a lot for a 17-year-old kid to absorb.

"No matter how strange things became; no matter how quickly I could mature; life kept coming at me. There were still tests to study for, term papers to write, day-to-day assignments to complete. And nothing was coming easily. I couldn't get to sleep at night. I had to drag myself out of bed every morning.

When I tried to study, I couldn't concentrate on my books. I had to read the same lessons over and over. I didn't flunk any courses, but my grades slipped badly.

"Lynn—I mean your mom—met my bus every morning and we talked on the phone every night, and we got closer and closer. Meanwhile, Lorraine became more and more of a mystery to me. I would see her every day, but our conversations were always cryptic and confusing.

"A couple weeks later, Lorraine was elected Homecoming Queen, and that was a *big* deal in Lakewood City. Most high schools have a small homecoming celebration and save the big celebration for the prom, with a queen and her court and a big coronation. But Lakewood had no prom court or queen. The homecoming court was the only game in town, and the homecoming queen was at the top of the food chain. Lorraine's life just seemed to get brighter and brighter.

"She picked a nice, harmless kid to escort her to the homecoming dance, someone who Blake, who was off at West Point, wouldn't be jealous or upset about.

"I was at the homecoming dance with Lynn, and we sat on the bleachers of the Old Gym watching the court and their escorts slow dance the ceremonial coronation waltz. But, as soon as it ended, the DJ announced, 'By special request of our homecoming queen, she'd like to ask Ted Tresh to come to Center Court.'

"I looked over at your mom. 'Go ahead,' she said. 'I'm not worried.'

"As I approached the middle of the dance floor, the sound system eased into the first few bars of *Love on a Two-Way Street*. It was our song, mine and Lorraine's. She walked straight into my arms, and we slowly started moving to the music. She wrapped her arms around me like she would never let go. And, I have to admit, I did the same. We were the only ones on the dance floor, and three-hundred students and alumni watched us embrace and sway and whisper into each other's ears.

"'So, you picked our song?' I sighed, 'Why?'

"'Because I wanted to hold you,' she said. 'And I wanted to explain.'

"'Go ahead,' I smiled, 'explain.'

"'This song, it's not just a love song. It means something different now. The *two-way street?* That's the road from Lakewood to New Castle, to Troggio's Restaurant, the road where I fell in love with you. I literally found love on a two-way street. Then the next line, *And lost it on a lonely highway.'*

"I pulled back and stared her right in the eye."

"'That's the highway from Rockland to Beaver Falls. The highway you took to pick up your date, the one you lied to me about.'

"'That girl didn't mean anything to me.' I gasped. 'I was just mad at you for refusing to be my girlfriend; for talking to Blake on the phone every night. I was hurt and I was trying to get back at you.'

"'Well, I never forgot it.' She had tears in her eyes now. 'I never trusted you after that. But I always, always thought we'd get back together. Then Blake and I started getting serious, and I didn't want to risk that. I didn't want to lose him. I didn't want to take that chance.'

"'Are you saying that you can *never* trust me again?' I shook my head in disbelief. 'Because of that night, that girl? I hardly even knew her.'

"The song was winding down, now, and there was still so much to say."

"'I'm having a little party at my house after the dance. It's just for the homecoming court and their escorts, but I want you to come. We really need to talk.'

"I made my way back to Lynn—I mean, your mom," I told Gene, who had gotten up from the table and started pacing around the living room.

"'Well, I'm glad you remembered she was there.' Gene scoffed. 'If I wasn't your son, I would really have to wonder how this all turned out.'

I laughed out loud. "Sure, we all know how it turned out now," I told him. But, at the time, I was completely confused. I had spent so much time chasing Lorraine around. And when I finally decided to move on, she didn't want me to move on.

"The only one who wasn't confused was your mom," I smiled. "When I told her about the late-night party, she just said, 'I think you *should* go.'"

"When I asked her why, she said, 'I'm not afraid of Lorraine Donatelli. The sooner you see what she's doing to you, the better.'

"'What's she doing to me?' I asked her.

"'You're a smart boy.' She replied. 'You'll figure it out.'"

"What did you figure out, Dad?" Gene laughed.

It had been more than twelve hours since my son had come through the door and asked for advice, and more than thirty hours since either of us had had any sleep, but this was no time to worry about sleep. This was the most significant father-and-son conversation of our lives.

I got up and poured yet another screwdriver.

"Well, here's what I had to figure out," I told him. "I had to understand why Lorraine only seemed to express her feelings when she was caught up in the moment, when she couldn't help herself. Why did she hide her feelings for me? Lynn never hid her feelings.

"Lynn stood by me no matter what the circumstances, not just when I was at my best, not just when I was the center of attention.

"How much of it was my fault? Maybe it was my own loss of self-confidence that Lorraine was sensing. I really *had* changed.

"Confidence is a funny thing. When you have it, you think you'll always have it. And when you lose it, you think it's gone for good. Did my failure at the championship game change the way she looked at me? Maybe it didn't change the way she saw me. Maybe it just changed the way I saw myself.

"Maybe her mom was right. Maybe I was just some kid from Rockland, the last Rockland ballplayer. It could have meant a lot if I was the school hero. But it didn't mean shit to her mother, and maybe now it didn't mean anything to Lorraine herself.

"The only time she really showed her feelings, was when she thought she was going to lose me."

"That's it," screamed Gene. "That's Jan. She doesn't really want me; she just doesn't want to lose me. But, why?"

"Or maybe she *does* want you, but not the negative feedback she gets from her friends. Maybe she's a crowd pleaser. Maybe she's afraid that her friends will turn their backs on her if she really *teams up* with you?"

"Tell me something," Gene seemed on the verge of an epiphany. "If Lorraine was your girlfriend, would she have been elected Homecoming Queen?"

I paused for a long time now. I really had to think about that. "No," I said finally. "I was still the outsider, the kid from Rockland. There was no way they wanted me anywhere near their princess, and if she was my girl, there was no way they elect her homecoming queen. Maybe if I had won that championship for the school; maybe they all would have accepted me then. But that didn't happen. I struck out at the worst possible moment. I was nobody special, just some kid from Rockland."

"Did she *like* being Homecoming Queen?" Gene looked at me knowingly.

"I guess she did."

"You know, Dad. Maybe you're lucky you didn't hit that baseball out of Three Rivers Stadium."

"You may be right," I sighed.

"I bet now you're glad you struck out."

"Well," I paused. "I wouldn't go that far…"

THE INDEX

S o, I went back to Lorraine's for the party, waited for her to find a minute to get away from the crowd, waited to be alone with her. She was the center of attention. She smiled and nodded and accepted everyone's praises and tributes. It went on for hours, until one by one they started departing for home. Of course, I outlasted them all. It was just past midnight when the final guest had finally walked out her door.

"I guess I'll say goodnight, now," I told Lorraine as I made my way across the floor.

"Good night," chirped her mother, relieved that I was finally leaving. Her older sister Angela was standing next to her mom, and she smiled at me sympathetically. Angela was four or five years older than us, and every bit as beautiful as her sister. I had always felt that Lorraine had confided in her about her feelings, and I considered Angela something of an ally.

"Wait a minute," Lorraine sighed, grabbing my hand as I passed her. "I'll walk you out."

"You can't go out this late," her mother barked from the living room.

"We'll be right on the porch," answered Lorraine, mustering all her courage. "I'll just be a minute."

Her mom started to object, but Angela led her into the kitchen and out of sight.

"Thanks for coming back," Lorraine smiled as we stood on the porch alone.

"Well, her majesty summoned," I smiled. "What else could I do?"

"Listen, Teddy. I want you to know that I still have feelings for you. I might even love you. But it's so hard. Everything is set. It feels like it's too late."

"How can it be too late?" I looked down at her. "We're kids, not even eighteen."

"Maybe if things change," she stammered. "Maybe there's a chance. Just don't quit on us. Maybe…"

"I can't live on maybes," I interrupted. "Not anymore. I've found someone special, *really* special. And there aren't any maybes with her. I don't know if it will last, but it's real right now, and I'm going to see where it's headed. I have to."

"Teddy," she sighed again. "This is real too." And she stepped forward and kissed me, long and soft and tender.

I'm not sure how long the kiss lasted, but we didn't stop until we heard her mom tapping on the front door window.

"I have to go," she said, shaking her head in frustration, and she bolted back into the house.

Back in class on Monday, we exchanged glances four or five times, but she kept her distance, especially when we were in a crowd of classmates. I started thinking of her as waiting for an opportunity, a chance to escape into the darkness again. And, although that sounds romantic, exciting even, I couldn't get away from the thought that I was only seventeen years old, why did I need to escape at all?

Meanwhile, Lynn and I were walking the halls of Lakewood High, hand-in-hand every day and talking on the phone for hours every night. Some of her friends, especially the ones who just loved Denny Nowitzki, didn't like me at all, and put me down every chance they got. Lynn wouldn't hear of it. If her old friends persisted in insulting me, she dropped them like she was tossing out worn-out shoes.

We were together more and more each day, and whenever the subject of Lorraine came up, Lynn would just laugh confidently, "I think I need to save you from yourself," she'd say. Her self-confidence was enthralling.

A couple weeks after homecoming, my cousin Tony, who was now a college sophomore, gave me a call at home. "Hey, cousin," he chirped into the phone. "I was just calling to see how you're holding up."

"Pretty good," I told him. "Things are getting back to normal in school; girl problems, but what else is new? The worst part is my mom," I continued. "She cries herself to sleep every night. And nothing I do cheers her up. She's taking so much Valium that when she's not crying; she just walks around the house in a daze."

"You need to get away for a weekend," he said evenly but sternly. "Can Nelson and Sophie stay home with her for a couple days?"

"I guess so," I shrugged. "But I hate to let my mom think I'm abandoning her."

"You have to start living your life again," he answered. "Come down to Duquesne on Friday. I'll introduce you to the baseball coach on Saturday afternoon. I know he's interested in recruiting you. Plus, on Friday night, there's a Fraternity mixer. I'll introduce you to some college girls."

"That's all I need," I laughed sarcastically.

"Then forget about the college girls. We used to talk all the time and we haven't had a real conversation since your father died."

"I'll talk to my mom about it," I confided. "I don't think she'll mind, especially if I'm meeting the baseball coach. With my dad gone, I'm probably going to need some kind of scholarship next year."

"It's settled then," he said finally.

I was kind of amazed at how much Tony had matured since leaving for college. He really was becoming a man, not just taking responsibility for his own future, but being concerned about mine as well.

I get the feeling that this weekend might be a life-changer, I thought as I hung up the phone.

Early Friday evening, I hopped into my dad's silver T-Bird and headed down the Expressway toward Duquesne. It was about eight o'clock when I knocked on Tony's dorm room door. His roommate, Joe Gramich, sat around bullshitting with us for about half-an-hour, then left to go pick up his date. "I'll see you guys at the mixer," he called as he made his way down the hallway toward the elevator.

"Who's the sorority tonight?" I asked Tony as he came back in the room and sat down next to his turntable and sound system and shuffled through a couple dozen vinyl albums.

"The Zetas," he chuckled. "They're kind of stuck-up, but super sweet. Now, *I* have a steady girlfriend back home, but I'm sure *you* can find something to occupy your time."

"No, thanks," I barked out in mock disgust. "I have enough woman problems to last a lifetime."

"No such thing," he smirked. "I thought you were crazy about that girl you brought to the funeral home. Christ, you had her holding your mother's hand all night and running around serving sandwiches to the family back at your house. That seems pretty serious."

"That's Lynn," I told him, "And I really like her, but I'm just not ready to give up on Lorraine."

Tony rolled his eyes. "You can't be serious. You've been chasing that chick around for years. Why would you still be wasting your time on her?"

"Last week, she told me she *might be* in love with me. Besides, she's the new homecoming queen. Of course, I'm interested."

"Come here," Tony motioned from his dorm room window. "Look down there."

I gazed down at the long, green Duquesne University Common, filled with undergrads and co-eds.

"Do you know how many small-town princesses and homecoming queens are down there? Plenty; this is the real world, man.

"Sure, you were a big-time high school shortstop last year, you led your team in hitting, but next year you're going to be competing with twenty other All-Section infielders and guys who led their high school team in batting. Do you think you'll just waltz into a Division I baseball program and be a starter? No.

"It's the same with the women," he was raving now. "They were all popular in high school. They were all sweet and shiny and everybody liked them. It's time to grow up, man. You have to look through your own eyes. You have to decide what's really important to you. And it has nothing to do with popularity."

"Yeah?" I laughed nervously at the revelation. "What *does* it have to do with?"

"Well," Tony smiled, as he headed back to his stack of vinyl 33 rpm albums. "Me and Gramich and some of the Frat brothers have a theory about that."

"I'm all ears," I laughed. "If it's good enough for the Alpha Sigs, it's good enough for me."

"It's kind of an index," he smiled. "It helped me make a decision on Mary Theresa and you know how good she's been for me."

"So, what's this index about? How does it work?

"Here, listen to this," Tony seemed excited, as he shuffled through the albums until he found one called *The Last Waltz* by The Band. "This group used to play back up for Bob Dylan. He always referred to them as 'The Band' and when they went out on their own; I guess the name just stuck. I'm sure you've heard of them. They have a hit song out called *The Weight*. Here, I'll play it for you first.

The needle crackled through the scratches from the song being overplayed on the vinyl record. "*I pulled in to Nazareth, was feelin' about half past dead,*" it began.

I liked their sound. It was kind of a raw country-folk ballad, not unlike the sound of Dylan himself.

"*I just needed some place where I could lay my head.*"

"I like them," I said to Tony after a few minutes, as *The Weight* eased into its final line: "*Take a load off Fanny, Take a load for free. Take a load off Fanny, And (and) you put the load right on me.*"

"But what does it have to do with picking the right girl?"

"That's not the index song," he chuckled, picking up the needle and carefully placing it back on a different track. "Here it is. Listen."

"*When I get off this mountain, you know where I want to go...*"

I leaned forward from the edge of his dorm bed and tried to make out every word.

"Here, listen to this part," Tony interrupted a few seconds later.

"*Up on Cripple Creek she sends me.*

If I spring a leak, she mends me."

"They're talking about the perfect woman," Tony whispered, "Listen."

"*I don't have to speak, she defends me.*

A drunkard's dream if I ever did see one."

"Don't worry about that last line," Tony waved his hand. "He's just talking about hitting *rock bottom*. I mean, we're all the *drunkard* sometime."

The song went on for a while. The singer tells a story about taking his girl to the racetrack, something Tony and I could identify with. When the singer wins big money betting on his horse, he gives his girlfriend half. But she tears it up and throws it in his face, "*Just for a laugh.*"

"So, this girl's not after him for his money or what he can give her. She just loves him the way he is.

"She's the perfect woman: She loves him. She stands by him. She defends him." Tony pronounced finally. "I mean, have you *ever* had a girl like that?"

I thought about it for a long ten or fifteen seconds. "Well, I know this sounds ridiculous," I smiled, but yeah, I had a girl like that once."

"Who?" Tony scoffed.

"Well," I hesitated. "It was Molly Bellinski."

"Your girlfriend back in Rockland?" he laughed out loud. "You're talking about your girlfriend from when you were ten years old?

"That's bullshit," he continued. "I'm talking about real love. The kind you have with a real woman, not some kid stuff."

"No," I said, "You're talking about what makes a girlfriend *real*. You're saying it's someone who stands by you. *If I spring a leak, she mends me.* That's someone who knows when you're hurting and tries to make you feel better. Molly *always* did that. If I had a terrible baseball game, she always told me how good I was. If I was sick from school one day, she left brownies on my desk the next day. If I screwed up once in a while, and danced with another girl behind her back, she didn't lose trust in me. She always forgave me. She tried to make things better. She always looked forward, not backwards.

"And the next line, *I don't have to speak, she defends me.* That's how she always was. If some kid teased her about being my girlfriend, she never denied it. She never got embarrassed. She'd just say 'so?' That's not an easy thing for a ten-year-old girl to do. She always, always stuck up for me!"

Tony just shook his head. "I'm not just talking about some little-girl crush. I'm taking about real love, real loyalty."

"I get that," I answered. "But she was my first girlfriend, my introduction into the female psyche. I didn't know there could be any other kind. I thought they would *all* stick by me. I thought loyalty was a given. Molly just *ingrained in me* that that's how a real girlfriend acted.

"So, when Rosie Williamson was embarrassed that her friends were teasing her about liking me, it never occurred to me that she was just worried about getting hurt. And, when Lorraine refused to defend me against the negative comments her mother or her friends were making about me, I never imagined that she was just trying to protect herself from ridicule. All I knew was that a real girlfriend shouldn't act that way. I knew that was wrong. I never realized *why* I knew that was wrong until now. I had the memory of the perfect little girlfriend deep-rooted in my mind. I was *conditioned* to know who was reliable and who wasn't; conditioned since I was ten years old, to know what was real and what was fake.

"Play that part of the song again," I urged.

"I don't have to," Tony chuckled, "I have it memorized.

"*Up on Cripple Creek she sends me.* Gramich and I always thought that meant; *is she someone I'm compatible with? Is she someone I'm really attracted to?* If the girl in the song is a 100 index, how did little Molly compare to that?"

"Well, that's not fair," I answered. "She was only ten years old. I had barely even touched her. But I'll tell you something, I was crazy about her. I was crazy about how it felt to have a girlfriend. She was someone I always *loved* to see; and someone who was always happy to see me. So, if I had to put an index number on my attraction to her, I'd give her a 100 index."

"Impossible," said Tony. "You can't have a 100 attraction index for a ten-year-old girl."

"Too bad," I laughed. "Every time I saw her face, I smiled. And every time I smiled at her, she smiled right back…every time!"

Tony just rolled his eyes again. "Agree to disagree," he chuckled. "But the next line, *If I spring a leak, she mends me?*"

I just shrugged. "I already told you about building up my self-esteem after a bad baseball game. I told you about the brownies she left on my desk when I was sick"

"What about any girl *since* you were a kid?"

"Hell no," I answered. "Not Rosie for sure; I told her a hundred times how much I liked her, and all she did was insult me. I don't even know why she hung around. I'd give her about a 50 index against 100 for the girl in the song."

"And Molly?" he sighed.

"100 for sure," I answered.

"And the last one, *I don't have to speak, she defends me?*"

"100 again," I laughed, "Even if it was just us vs. everybody else."

"I can remember being in the batter's box in Rockland with two strikes on me, and some kid from my class, Joe Novak I think it was, was standing behind the backstop next to Molly. 'He's going to fan,' Novak was chirping at her. 'Your boyfriend is going to strike out.'

"Molly just laughed at him. 'Do you think I care if he hits or strikes out?' she asked him. 'I care because he cares, but to me, it doesn't matter at all.'"

"Jesus," Tony shook his head in wonder. "Your ten-year-old girlfriend *was* the perfect girl."

"Lucky for me," I laughed. "She taught me what to look for...what a real girlfriend should be."

"Okay, okay," he said finally. "Now the ten-million-dollar question. What about Lorraine and Lynn?

"Wait a minute, hold on," Tony was getting more excited, more animated, now. "Let me grab a piece of paper and pen." He flipped open a composition notebook, and at the top of the page he wrote *Lorraine* at the top left of the page and *Lynn* at the top right.

"So, the girl in the song is the perfect girl. Her index is 100. How attracted are you to Lorraine, what's her number?"

"100," I blurted without a second's hesitation. "She's absolutely beautiful. I'm very attracted to her."

"Okay," Tony smiled, "And how about Lynn?"

"Also 100," I reported.

"Really?" Tony rolled his eyes. "You're grading too easy."

"No. I'm not," I corrected him. "They're both fantastic. Lorraine is more popular of course, but when I really look with my own eyes, Lynn is a knockout too. I'm just as attracted to her as I am to Lorraine. In fact, Lynn and I have a lot more chemistry."

"Is that what the kids are calling it these days?" Tony smirked, "Chemistry?"

"Hey, when we're together, we're like *glued together*. She's actually put *hair* on my chest." I pulled down the collar of my jersey to reveal a few dozen new hairs.

"Oh, Christ," Tony chided. "I don't want to see that shit."

"Well, it wasn't there six weeks ago," I laughed.

313

"Okay, okay," he smiled. And he wrote a *100* under both their names.

"Here's the next line: *If I spring a leak, she mends me.* That's a big one.

"Well," I answered. "I'm never really sure about Lorraine. I mean, when we lost that championship game last June, I really needed her. Sure, she had a boyfriend, but she could have reached out to me somehow. I didn't hear a word from her for three months.

"Then again, when my dad died, she chased me down 3rd Avenue, outside the funeral home. She told me how much she cared about me, and that was sweet."

"What's her index?" Tony coaxed, pen in hand.

"Ummm, 65, I guess."

"And Lynn?" Tony continued.

"Well, she stayed right next to my mom all night at the funeral home; and, helped her make sandwiches when we got back to my house.

"She calls every day, just to share her day, and to see how I'm doing," I nodded.

"Since my dad died, I've had a hard time getting up in the morning, and I've missed a lot of school. I'm not sure if I'm really sick, or just feeling down. But if I take a sick day, she brings me chicken soup that night."

"Just like Molly?" Tony wondered.

"A lot like Molly," I laughed, "But in a more grown-up way."

"So, what's her number?"

"100," I shrugged.

Tony smiled. "I knew you were going to say that."

"Okay, the last line, *I don't have to speak, she defends me.* The girl in the song is a 100. What's Lorraine?"

"Well, sometimes she does. I've overheard her telling people that I'm smart or sweet or a good ballplayer, or whatever. But, if they disagree, she doesn't rock the boat. She just lets it go. So, no, she doesn't *always* defend me.

"Like, last season. We went up to Hopewell, and I was playing some of the best shortstop of my life. And in the bottom of the seventh, we were up by one run and, with one out; I booted an easy ground ball. I felt like hell. We *had* to win that game. And I had just made an error that would put that win at risk.

And, out of nowhere, I hear Lorraine screaming from the bleachers, 'Come on, Teddy. What are you *doing* out there?'

"I stared right at her in the bleachers and shook my head. Man, was I pissed off."

"Did you win the game?" Tony smiled.

"The next batter grounded back to the mound, and we turned an easy game-ending double-play," I laughed. "But I never really forgave her for that."

"And Lynn?"

"Well, she has no problem openly defending me if someone *really* puts me down," I confided. "And if it's just a minor criticism, she'll say, 'That's not how I see him at all.' But she makes a mental note that this friend is expendable, if it comes to that."

"So," Tony said, "What's the number?"

"50 for Lorraine," I shrugged, "100 for Lynn."

"Man, this isn't even close, Teddy." Tony shook his head slowly. "What are you thinking of?"

"All that work," I whispered, "Over so much time." I held my thumb and my index finger about a half-inch apart. "And I'm this close."

"Be careful what you wish for, cousin," Tony warned. "Look at this: *Lorraine—215, Lynn—300.*"

"Does that score really mean anything?" I wondered out loud.

"You just agreed that the girl in the song was the perfect girl," Tony reminded me, holding up his score sheet.

I looked down at the index numbers.

For a moment, I saw Lorraine's eyes staring up at me at the Y-Teens Dance; felt that kiss in the darkened hallway outside the cafeteria, where we were slow dancing all alone.

Then, I remembered the twinge of pain I got over and over again, watching her turn her back on me in public, giving me a parting glance, if anything; trying to make sure no one was watching.

I closed my eyes for a second, and felt Lynn in my arms, looking in my eyes, oblivious to the world around us.

"It's not really close, is it?" I told Tony, as a rush of well-being poured across my face and down my spine.

"*Up on Cripple Creek, she sends me,*" I spoke each word slowly and deliberately, "*If I spring a leak, she mends me.*"

Tony joined in on the next line, "*I don't have to speak, she defends me.*"

Then he continued loudly on his own, speaking right over me, "A Rockland Boy's dream if I ever did see one," he said finally.

"I know you always felt bad about the break-up with Molly," Tony smirked. "But that was kid stuff. You're not ten anymore, and if you lose Lynn, well, you're just stupid.

"Besides," he added, circling the *300* on his note pad, "Where else are you going to find a girl like that?

"When little Molly was your girlfriend, you didn't have any other point of reference. You just thought that all girlfriends would be loyal and steady and devoted. Now you know better. Now you know that all girlfriends are not equal."

I don't remember much about the rest of the night. The mixer was okay, I guess. There were some pretty Zetas dancing around, but I barely talked to them. Of course, the beer in the keg was flat and warm. I nursed one glass of Iron City all night.

The next day, I got to meet Rich Spencer, the Duquesne Head Baseball coach. He told me he'd be watching my progress in class and on the field, and he handed me a Duquesne University application with the words *FEE WAIVED* stamped at the top and his signature underneath it. "Get this application in by the end of November," he suggested. "We only have three scholarships remaining for next year, and I can't hold them long."

"Have you taken the SAT's?" he questioned. I nodded yes. "What was your score?"

"Twelve twenty," I replied.

"That should be fine," he smiled and shook my hand.

On the drive home, my head was spinning. The real world was closing in. I had a month to submit my applications and decide on a school. I had to look into student grants and financial aid. I had to shake off my depression and get my grades back where they belonged. I had to get off my ass and start working on my future.

I knew one thing. I didn't have time for chasing around some girl who was afraid to be seen with me. I was ready for someone steadfast, and loving and beautiful. There really was no comparison.

I drove through Rockland and straight to Lynn's house in Lakewood City. When she came to the door, she smiled, "How was your trip to Duquesne?"

"Very enlightening," I told her. And I pulled my class ring off my finger. "Will you wear my ring?" I asked. "I want you to be my girl."

"It's about time," she smiled, and she threw her arms around my neck. Her embrace and her confidence were intoxicating.

43

ALTERNATE REALITIES

Gene was up and staring out the picture window at our front yard with downtown Lakewood City in the distance. He seemed to be taking in the whole scene, while focusing on nothing at all. The bright winter day, the mighty, but leafless maples and oaks surging toward the sky, the occasional car or truck winding past our hilltop-house on Beechwood Boulevard, the time-less sun itself; he took it all in as one would a painting, not a changing scene of moving parts, but a singular impression of life as a whole, his life.

"You know, Dad," he began, "I never think about the lasting effects of the choices I make. I just live day to day, handling each situation, each decision as if it had no real consequence on the rest of my life. But it does; doesn't it?"

I walked over and stood beside him. "Well, Champ," I offered. "Your life goes rambling along. A lot of it you can't control, but every now and then, yes, you have to grab it by the horns, and force it into the right direction. You're not just along for the ride. You're the driver.

"Do you want to compare Jan to the Cripple Creek Index?" I asked gently, "Do you want to see how she stacks up to the perfect woman?"

"I don't have to," he shrugged. "I already know.

"She doesn't mend me. She abandons me. She doesn't defend me. She joins in the attack. And when I'm at rock bottom, she throws the first shovelful of dirt on top of me.

"But what about how I feel about her? I really love her in a way. I forgive all her shortcomings, hoping things will change."

"We all do that," I nodded. "But for how long? How long do you let your emotions keep you from doing what you know is best for you?"

"Tell me something," Gene turned to face me now. "Are you ever sorry about giving up on Lorraine or Rosie? I mean, will I be sorry later if I let Jan go now?"

"Wow," I blurted out. "As Tony used to say, 'That's the million-dollar question, isn't it?' And the answer is *yes*, you *will* be sorry sometimes. Those feelings, those emotions, they never really go away. You'll always miss Jan, and to some degree, you'll always love her."

"How do you know when to give up, Dad? How do you know when to move on?"

"This is going to sound strange, Gene, but have you ever heard the term *Multiverse*?" I asked him. "Have you ever studied it in philosophy class or sociology or even physics?"

"I kind of remember hearing about it," He replied. "It has something to do with alternate realities, right?"

"Some scientists believe each decision we make, each second of our lives, stretches out into a million different universes. And there's a different version of you living out each of those lives. Maybe in thirty percent of those lives, I'm still with Lorraine. And, maybe in another twenty percent, I'm married to Rosie. So, do I think that my Lorraine-lives and my Rosie-lives are happy? Sure, most are probably very happy and maybe we're even still in love. There are a million different successful lives we might live. And, if that's all true, God bless them. I'm not jealous of them. I hope they are supremely happy and satisfied. I hope they have smooth sailing for eternity.

"But for all practical purposes, all we know about is one life, one reality. And we need to buckle our seatbelts, because it's a bumpy ride. There are a million pains and disappointments even the best of those lives will contain. So, who is the woman most likely to help you through the pain? Who is the partner to fight by your side?

"Remember, our last two years living in Boston? Remember the hell that we went through?"

"How could I forget," Gene dropped his head into his hands at the memory.

"When I caught those high school seniors bullying your sister outside the school auditorium? One of them was holding her hands behind her back and two more were rubbing poster paint on her face and in her hair. I completely lost it, and just started beating the hell out of them. It took nearly a year to beat those assault charges in court; and another eighteen months battling those civil cases.

"I had put everything we had at risk, our futures, our fortune, our peace of mind. But did you ever once hear your mother blame me for our troubles? Did she ever say, 'Why didn't you let the police and school officials handle those punks? Why did you have to put everything at risk?'

"No, she never said it. We handled it as a team. She never second guessed me. She never moaned and complained that I had put all her dreams at risk. We swam or sunk together, as one.

"Would Lorraine or Rosie have stuck by me like that: Maybe, maybe not? Would Jan have stuck by your side through thick and thin, without ever blaming you? Not a chance in hell!"

"It's just hard to let go of the dream," Gene whispered, never raising his head from his hands.

"And while you're hanging onto this dream, the *real* girl of your dreams might be out there waiting for you. And she will never hurt you and will always be on your side."

Now, Gene's defense mechanisms kicked in, "So, you don't miss them? You never miss Lorraine or Rosie?"

"Of course I miss them, Gene. But were they the right woman to go through life with?

"Just listen to The Band's simple message again: *Up on Cripple Creek she sends me. If I spring a leak, she mends me.* That's loyalty, Gene. That's what you need to get through life. For a man and his wife, it's loyalty that's the most important thing. Does she stand by you right now? If she doesn't now, she never will!

"*I don't have to speak, she defends me.* Jesus, Gene, that's the kind of girl you want to go through life with. Not just someone who *sends* you, but someone who *goes with* you every step of the way. Sure, you need someone you're crazy about, but you also need someone you can depend on."

"But this *feels* like love, Dad. How can I tell the difference between momentary love and the real thing?"

Now, I stood right next to him, looking out the same window at the same timeless picture of an always changing world. "Let's take a step back," I urged him. "There are always ways to tell the real thing from the illusion. Did I ever tell you the story of my last home run at Beaver Falls?"

"Really, Dad, another baseball story?" Gene walked across the room and sat down on the couch in disgust.

"Give it a chance," I smiled. "It points out all the differences between real love and the illusion."

"Here we go again," sighed Gene. But there was a hint of a smile on his face.

"HE STINKS"

By spring it was just us, me and Lynn. We were together every single day, and we spent another two hours a day talking on the phone. For my benefit, Lynn had become an avid baseball fan. She studied the game. She asked questions about strategy and umpire rulings and situational decisions. She made it her business to understand the game inside and out. We reviewed my scholarship and grant offers together and she helped me research each school from an athletic and academic perspective.

In high school baseball, there are many advantages to having a great junior season. Colleges can scout you, just like they do with football or basketball players. They can review film and interview coaches. If you wait and don't excel until your senior year, it's too late. By the time March and April and May roll around, nearly all the scholarships are gone.

As my senior season started, I had offers from four schools, including Penn in the Ivy League and Division I Duquesne, where Tony was already starring in centerfield.

But, was I the same player as the year before? How much effect was there from my Championship game washout, and the depression from my father's death?

Things didn't look too good early in the season. I was still hitting the ball well, but was blowing up all over the infield, fielding errors, throwing errors, and my range had narrowed by half-a-foot in either direction. With the depression over my father's death, I had stayed secluded inside with Lynn all winter (who wouldn't), and I came back out of shape. I wasn't really sure what was wrong. I had never been out of shape in my life. I didn't realize that all those exciting nights on the couch with Lynn, and all the fried dough and Rice Crispy Squares that her mother had been feeding us were messing with my muscle tone and stamina.

In previous winters, I had always played some intramural basketball and pick-up games of hockey. I was outside, most of the time, and I just played for fun, but I didn't realize that those activities were keeping me in shape for baseball. Now, I limped into the spring season out-of-shape and overweight.

But, as the season went on, I got better and better. Against weaker competition, we came out of the pre-section portion of our schedule at 5–1. But when the real section games started, we were just 2–2, and in danger of dropping out of the title chase completely. This was terrible news in Lakewood City. We had won section championships for five-straight years, and after going all the way to Three Rivers Stadium in 1971, we were favored to do so again.

Now, we were heading into Beaver Falls, and both teams were 2–2, and fighting for their lives. And the responsibility for saving the season had been placed squarely on the shoulders of the returning starters from the previous season, me, Porter and our star catcher Rick Theisman. With me being the very last Rockland boy to play baseball for Lakewood City, it was an unexpected honor to be voted co-captain of the team, along with Joe. That had never happened before, a Rockland boy voted co-captain. Better late than never, I guess.

The task of climbing back into the section race was a big one. We would be starting our ace, Joe Porter, the 1971 MVP of Section 5, one of the toughest sections in the state. Beaver Falls was throwing their star right-hander, Kenny Stringfield, who was semi-famous. He was the first African American starting quarterback in the history of Beaver Falls High School, one of the toughest football programs in Pennsylvania. Their previous QBs included Joe Namath, who led them to the Pennsylvania State Championship in 1960.

The match-up of Porter vs. Stringfield packed the place. I looked up into the stands after infield practice. It seemed like every girl I had ever dated was in the crowd. Lorraine was there with her entourage, and Lynn, of course, wearing my Letter Jacket and Class Ring. Plus, Rosie Williamson was there chanting and cheering for Beaver Falls. So was Sherry Sanders, the Beaver Falls major-ette who had asked me to the Band Dinner-Dance on that fateful night back in 1970, when I lied to Lorraine.

There were even two Beaver Falls girls that Rosie herself had introduced to me over the past couple years, in an attempt to prove that she couldn't care less who I dated. "I did that to test you," she would tell me ten years later over a cup of coffee. I had dated each of them very briefly, but here they were today, both cheering for their Beaver Falls Tigers.

The game also drew big numbers of pro and college scouts, who were there to watch Porter. Unfortunately, Joe was nursing an aching shoulder from a *coaching blunder* just a week earlier.

"What's he got, Rick?" I asked Theisman as they concluded their pre-game warm-ups.

"Not much," shrugged Rick, as he shook his head in disappointment.

We were both blaming the coaching staff for Joe's suddenly ailing shoulder.

Our legendary coach Phil Sherman had not returned this season over some political battle on the school board that had re-classified the longtime High School Guidance Counselor as an administrator, instead of a teacher. And only teachers were allowed to be coaches under the current school code. Only Lakewood City could screw up a good thing like Phil Sherman and his twelve Section titles.

Mr. Sherman was replaced by his assistant Bill Childress, who was woefully inadequate to take over the powerhouse team. He was shy and backward and seemed very uncertain of himself. He certainly did not command the respect of his ballplayers. And we all second-guessed his strategy and knowledge of the game. The very fact that we were just 5–1 in the non-section games was another slam on the new coach. Just a year before we were 17–1 in those early season games. We had worked out all the kinks and bad habits over that long eigh-teen game pre-season. But Coach Childress had only scheduled six pre-season games, not nearly enough for the team to jell and mature.

Just two weeks before this Beaver Falls game, Porter was supposed to start our section opener against Hopewell, our top rival for the section title. We had finished just one game ahead of Hopewell in 1971, and they had come right back with another strong team. The day of the Hopewell game was overcast, and showers began to fall in the early afternoon. Both teams were at the Lakewood Stadium, dressed and ready to go, when the umpires finally declared the condition of the field unplayable.

We had all packed up our duffle bags and were ready to take the bus back to the school locker room, when three pro scouts, who were there to report on Joe Porter, approached our coach. Although the field was wet, the rain had abated finally, and they asked if they could possibly see Porter throw warmups with Rick Theisman for a while. And Coach Childress gladly agreed to the demonstration.

They all took out their pens and pads and radar guns as Joe and Rick searched for a dry spot in the outfield and marked off the 60-feet, 6-inches between the mound and home plate. I grabbed my old buddy Jerry Delpino, who had finally recovered from the severely shattered leg that had scratched his junior year and was now our starting third baseman. "C'mon man," I tugged at his sleeve. "I gotta see this."

We followed Porter and Theisman and Coach Childress and the small band of scouts out into the outfield to watch the show. There was no real mound, and Joe took a good ten minutes digging himself a dry, grassless area in the outfield to throw from. But, once he started throwing, it was easy to see what the excitement was all about. Joe's fastball just exploded as it smacked into Rick's mitt over and over again, bang, bang, bang. I had never seen Porter throw so hard.

"Jesus Christ," remarked Jerry. "How long can he throw that hard?"

The answer, apparently, was *not* for the half-hour, that Coach Childress allowed him to entertain the scouts.

Three days later, before the makeup game against Hopewell, Porter couldn't lift his hand above his head. His left shoulder was aching. He had to be replaced by our big farm boy sophomore pitcher Mike Bronson. Bronson had talent but was no match for the steady bats of the Hopewell nine. The loss had started us on the downward spiral leading to this must-win game against Beaver Falls.

"It was just stupid coaching," Theisman had suggested after the workout. "No high school kid can throw that hard for that long. And he didn't even have a pitching rubber to push off of.

"And you can't blame Porter," I added. "Who isn't going to throw their hardest for scouts and radar machines? He had to think about his future."

It only added to our distrust of Coach Childress and his baseball expertise. And his new assistant coach wasn't much better. Jeff Donofrio was only about five or six years older than the players. He had been a pretty good left-handed pitcher for Lakewood City in his playing days, so he knew the game. But he had no idea how to coach teenage boys.

When I was having my fielding problems earlier in the year, he would send me out to shortstop during batting practice and, from the third base-line, he hit me shot after shot, the hardest ground balls I had ever seen. Instead of considering that I might need some more conditioning, he decided to punish me with an artillery of bad hops and searing line drives, as if that was going to bring back my finesse in the infield.

Of course, I was a Rockland boy, and could never be intimidated by the speed of a baseball. I never backed away from a single shot, but, by the end of practice, my shins and arms and chest were covered in bruises. What made matters worse, was that the coach was engaged to Lorraine's gorgeous sister Angela. And he seemed to be making an example of me. I'm not sure why, but the guy never seemed to give me a break. He'd put me down constantly in the dugout, and even told the local sports reporters that I was overrated.

Everybody has a right to their opinion, I guess. So, I didn't take him too seriously. It was Coach Childress who called the shots. And I was his all-section shortstop and leading hitter, so I didn't waste time paying undue attention to Assistant Coach Donofrio's stinging comments.

I was the starting shortstop, whether the new assistant coach liked it or not. But I knew he was not a fan of mine.

When we finished infield practice at Beaver Falls, and after Theisman had given me the bad news about Porter's arm, I looked up into the stands again, searching for Lynn's supportive smile. She was all bundled up for the early-spring game. I remember the chilly weather, the puddles around the dugout, the college and professional coaches and scouts, the buzz from the stands and the chattering of the radio announcers.

326

It was Porter, the section MVP who had shut out mighty West Mifflin North and led us to Three Rivers Stadium, versus Stringfield, the quarterback/pitcher from Beaver Falls with his blazing fastball. Scouts were everywhere and so were their radar guns and binoculars.

My cousin Tony had driven in from Pittsburgh for the Friday afternoon game with Rich Spencer, the Duquesne University baseball coach, in tow. I thought about how cool it would be to team up with Tony again next year. There was no doubt about it. With the exception of last year's WPIAL Championship, this was going to be the biggest game of my life. I saw my brother Nelson in the stands. Despite attending Beaver Falls High School, he was sitting on the Lakewood side of the bleachers. He was going with 100% family and 0% school loyalty. And I could hear him chiding and prodding some of his cocky classmates.

During my first at bat, I could hear Rosie barking "he stinks," over and over again, and I had to back out of the batters' box for a moment to stare at her in disbelief. I understood that she went to Beaver Falls now and wanted to root for her Tigers. But I'm a frickin' Rockland boy. I've known her all my life. I used to think she walked on water.

Rosie could feel my eyes on her, as well as the eyes of all the Rockland fans, who now rooted for Beaver Falls. "I love to get on that kid," she jokingly apologized to everyone around her. But, the Rockland fans, who had rooted for me since I was eight years old, knew she was going too far.

"I was just trying to get your attention," She would tell me ten years later.

Lorraine sat with her group of friends who had all taken the student bus to the game. She cheered when they cheered. She chanted when they chanted. From all outward appearances, I was just some Lakewood ballplayer she used to know. Maybe it was better that way.

I ended the first inning by lining out to shortstop. It was no hit, but I pounded the ball.

For his part, Joe Porter looked sharp in the first, and then pitched his way out of trouble in the second. But, by the third inning, his shoulder was throbbing; he had trouble throwing strikes and gave up three runs. I remember thinking that this may have been his greatest game, because he never stopped battling, even though he was throwing every single pitch in pain.

In the top of the fourth, we finally broke through and got Stringfield. With runners at first and second and two outs, Joe hit a towering double to right-centerfield, and both runners scored. I followed that with a ringing base hit up the middle to score Joe and tie the game.

Standing at first base, I could hear Rosie squirming in the Beaver Falls cheering section. "Lucky," she shouted, "Nothing but luck."

Is this how Rockland switches their loyalty to Beaver Falls? I wondered, *without any respect for history, without any regard for those of us who went before?* And I felt a twinge of sadness for my hometown, the town I loved. All my childhood heroes had been Rockland boys. All my pride was caught up in playing like they did. But now, Rockland students were being bussed to Beaver Falls. Forty years of Rockland tradition was nowhere to be found.

On the Lakewood side I could see Lynn cupping her hands around her mouth to be heard. "Way to go, Ted Tresh," she shouted over the crowd. "Big hit, big hit, Ted Tresh. Woo, that's our Shortstop. Way to go, Number Eleven."

I had to smile. It seemed like such a cute thing to root like that, by using my full name so often, by using my number and position. It was a little embarrassing, but *my mother used to do the same thing,* I remembered.

Lorraine was cheering too, cheering that we had tied the score. And, when I glanced over at her, she winked at me, all the way out at first base. I had to laugh. *I guess I'm still her secret star,* I thought.

In the bottom of the fourth, Beaver Falls got the go-ahead run, when Porter's shoulder finally gave way; a walk, a hit and a hit batsman loaded the bases with nobody out. Coach Childress made his way to the mound, and thanked Joe for his efforts, then sent him out to play center field and brought in our big farm-boy sophomore Mike Bronson.

Our number two pitcher Donnie Martini had just thrown seven innings in a 3–2 loss to Ambridge the day before, and Bronson was the only one left who could throw hard enough to stop Beaver Falls. Sure, he was a big kid, but was he ready for this?

Their first batter was Sammy Bellissimo, a left-handed-hitting Rockland boy. Sammy was a junior and was the first of the Rockland boys to star for Beaver Falls. We had played all-star games and backyard pickup games together in

Rockland for years. He was the kind of prized player that can change a team; the beginning of a new chapter of Rockland baseball. Sammy drove Bronson's first pitch to deep right-center field. The ball was deep enough to go over the short left field fence, but the right field wall was 400-feet away, and Joe Porter, now in centerfield, ran hard enough to track it down. The runner on third tagged up and scored easily. And Porter, with his ailing left arm, could barely manage to get his throw to the relay man, so the runners on first and second also tagged and moved up on the bases.

The next batter tried to drop down a bunt to squeeze the runner home from third, but popped the ball up. Jerry ran hard from his third base position and dove to catch it in the air, a tremendous play. With two outs, Beaver Falls still had runners at second and third with a one-run lead.

Now, Bronson faced their clean-up hitter, catcher Paul Burlingham, who ripped a ground ball up the middle. I ranged far to my left and grabbed the ball behind second base, then fired a strike to first to nail Burlingham.

"Is that *our* shortstop?" Coach Donofrio laughed mockingly from the Lakewood dugout. Even at my finest hour, this bastard was going to use the occasion to put me down. I ignored his comment, so he said it again, "Was that *our* shortstop?" Everyone in the place could see that Porter and Delpino and I had just saved the game. *What's wrong with that asshole?* I thought as we trotted off the field, still trailing by just one run.

In the top of the sixth inning, we got two runners on base with just one out. Then Theisman singled to tie the game. With runners on first and second, Jerry Delpino hit a little roller in front of the plate. It was as good as a bunt, and Stringfield charged in, scooped up the ball and threw Jerry out at first.

Now, I came to the plate with runners on second and third and two outs with the score still tied. The fact was that I had been a pain in Beaver Falls' ass since I was ten years old. In Little League, I was the ten-year-old starting second baseman when little Rockland had knocked off mighty Beaver Falls twice to win the New Castle Little League Tournament. In high school, my Lakewood City teams had topped the Tigers three times when I was a reserve as a freshman and sophomore and twice more last year, when I was our starting junior shortstop.

They *should have* been afraid of me.

The smart baseball play was to walk me intentionally; to pitch around our best hitter and load the bases to set up a force out at any base. When Beaver Falls Coach Joe Shantz called time out and went to the mound, I was sure that was the move they were going to make.

But this was Stringfield's spotlight, and he wasn't going to give it up without a fight. He strutted around the mound and stomped his feet and complained and argued. Our on-deck batter was Terry Mahoney, our left-handed right fielder. And Stringfield, who was right-handed, barked that he would rather face a right hander than a left hander. It was bullshit of course; I was our clean-up batter and leading hitter. But, Stringfield loved the confrontation, the drama. He wanted to show everyone just how good he was. "Put him on," screamed Sammy Bellissimo from right field. But when Coach Shantz returned to the dugout, there was Stringfield, still on the mound, staring me down as I stepped into the batter's box.

I can't believe this prima-donna is going to overrule his coach, I thought. "Throw to him, Kenny," screamed Rosie from the Beaver Falls cheering section. "He stinks!"

I can still feel the excitement, the fear and anger and the power of teenage angst pulsing through veins. The first pitch was a ball outside. "Come on, Teddy, you're due," pleaded Lorraine from our student section.

Am I due? I scoffed; *I just tied-up this game twenty minutes ago.* I appreciated that she was rooting for me, but her comment left the impression that I hadn't been playing well.

"Come on, Ted Tresh," called Lynn, drawing everyone's attention to the matchup even more. "They *want* to pitch to you. Do it again. Make them pay."

"He stinks!" retorted Rosie one last time as Stringfield went into his windup. His next fastball was belt high and right down the middle.

Now, Beaver Falls had a short left field fence, just 290 feet away, due to the Babcock & Wilcox Steel Company's scrap-iron yard and rail line right behind the left field wall that sometimes (as now) was occupied by a working crane, pulled by a diesel engine. From the batter's box I could see the fence, and then the tracks, then the piles of scrap iron and coke to feed the furnaces.

The sound of the wooden bat contacting the ball was as sweet and sharp as any crack-of-the-bat I had ever heard. The ball was still climbing when it cleared the fence, then the crane, then the mountain of scrap steel behind it.

It was the farthest I had ever hit a baseball and was my biggest moment as a Lakewood City Wolverine. The Lakewood side of the bleachers erupted, while the six or seven Rockland fans, sitting on the Beaver Falls side, stood and applauded politely. Sammy Bellissimo trotted half-way in from right field and shouted, "Nice hit, Teddy," as he shook his head in disgust. But his hometown pride, his Rockland pride, showed through. It was a kind of farewell to the old and hello to the new, an acknowledgement that we were brothers, no matter what high school they bussed us to.

When I reached second base, I looked up at Rosie. She was half smiling, but she stuck her tongue out at me, and I just shook my head. Lorraine, for her part, was bouncing up and down with her girlfriends, but I didn't pay too much attention. I was searching for Lynn, as I rounded third base.

"Way to go, Ted Tresh," she rang out like a bell. "That's number 11," she shouted as if someone had just asked the question (although no one had). "That's Ted Tresh."

As I closed in on home plate, I heard her call my name three or four more times, and always my full name. I smiled, but felt a little bit embarrassed. *Why my full name?* I tried to look her straight in the eyes, although she was almost obscured by radar guns and radio broadcast lines. And then, it hit me.

Holy shit, I thought, *she has herself positioned among scouts and announcers and Tony and the Duquesne coach. She keeps repeating my name so THEY know it; so the scouts write it down; so the radio announcers say it. She's not just jumping up and down shouting 'Yay.' She's supporting me; supporting us, the team; not the Lakewood City Wolverines, but the team of Lynn and Ted.*

The Tigers scratched for one run in the bottom of the sixth, and another in the seventh. But it wasn't enough. And we drove out of Beaver Falls with a hard fought 8–7 victory.

THE TEAM

"That's what you need from a serious girlfriend, Gene," I jumped to my feet for emphasis, "Loyalty to you, loyalty to the team, to what you are together. Not someone who's always worried about herself or how she appears to others.

"Someone who says, 'damn the torpedoes;' someone who takes a chance on you, without reservations. If it blows up, it blows up. But she's willing to take that chance. Sure, it's a gamble, but she doesn't hedge. She dives in. She's willing to actually give you her all, especially when she knows that you are willing to give her *your* all. It's a mutual effort, Gene. It's a *team* effort.

"That's what love is, Champ; not this halfway game that Jan is playing."

A silence hung over the room, as my words reverberated off the walls and out across the front yard, off the mighty, but leafless, oaks and maples, off the buildings and streets and rail road tracks of downtown Lakewood City, off the clouds and sky and the timeless sun itself.

Gene rose slowly from his easy chair. "Excuse me," he whispered, as he made his way down the hall and into his bedroom to place another phone call.

Lynn walked in from the kitchen. "Well," she said "You two have been up for 32 hours. I hope you got something accomplished."

"It's hard to say," I sighed. "I don't want to make his decisions for him. Then, if he regrets it later, it becomes my fault. I just wanted him to understand that all girlfriends are not the same; that some will make their stand *with* you, not jump ship every time you falter.

"It looks like this Jan is his first real love, and I don't want to be the one who tells him to give up on that."

Lynn walked across the room and wrapped her arms around me. Just eight years earlier, we had gone through twenty-four months of hell back in Boston, but instead of dividing us; it had made us closer than ever.

I held her hand and moved across the floor to the living room couch, sitting silently and looking out the picture window for what seemed like a long, long time.

Finally, Gene emerged. "Jan is moving to Los Angeles," he announced solemnly. "She just kept saying that if I really loved her, I'd fly back right now to save our relationship."

"That's ridiculous," said Lynn evenly.

"She really didn't want to leave," Gene offered. "If I had just kept insisting on her waiting until tomorrow, she would have agreed. But, first, I had to pay. She wanted me to repeat over and over that she was the most important thing in my life; to assure her and reassure her. And I just wasn't in the mood for that."

"What did you do?"

"Well, she had been talking to her mother all day," Gene replied. "And her mother has a short fuse, especially when it comes to me. She told Jan to quit complaining and come home to California. She told her that I wasn't worth all this trouble; that she really didn't need to get a bachelor's degree in fashion; that she could learn more just working at her mother's design house.

"And, I don't know, maybe she can," Gene continued, "But she's never really going to be independent that way. She's never really going to find out how good she can be, if she has any real talent, or if she's just sailing along on her mother's coattails."

"Did you tell her that?" I wondered.

"I've told her that a hundred times," Gene said in disgust. "I just didn't feel like trying anymore. I told her that maybe she was right, maybe it was better if she *did* go back home."

"Then what?"

"Complete silence," Gene shook his head again, "For at least ten minutes; just the sound of her sobbing.

"Then she said she hated me; that I was a bum, just like her mother said I was; that I would never find another girl like her."

"What now?" I asked, trying to hide my relief.

"I guess I'll call her back later. I can't really leave things like that," Gene sighed.

"But not now. The coffee? The booze? The lack of sleep? I need to get some rest to think clearly. I'll call her when I get up. I have no idea what I'm going to say."

Gene turned and headed down the hallway, stopping at the door to his bedroom. "I'll tell you one thing," he admitted. "I miss her already."

Lynn reached out and put her hand on my shoulder. "You need some sleep too," she breathed. "Why don't you take a nap? I'll get you up for dinner."

I could hardly keep my eyes open as I walked off to my bedroom. So many issues we had discussed; so many of life's problems still hanging in the air. But as my head hit the pillow, I was thinking of no one but Lynn. How strange.

46

STAND BY ME

Lynn woke me up about 6:00 pm. Gene was already awake and reading "A Separate Peace" for an American Literature book report that was due in a few days.

"Hey, Sleeping Beauty," Lynn sang out, as she entered the room. "Time to rise and shine. I'm hungry and I don't feel like cooking. How about if you and your son go pick up some fish sandwiches at Hazel Manor?"

"Sure," I said, as I tried to wipe the cobwebs from my brain. I walked slowly across the hall to look in on Gene. "How are you feeling?

"Okay, I guess" he sighed. "I'm a little sad, but the more I think about Jan moving back to California, the more I feel like a 120-pound weight has been lifted off my shoulders. I wasn't expecting that."

We pulled into the Hazel Manor Restaurant about 6:30, ordered three fish sandwiches to go, and sat down at the bar to wait for our order. We had barely settled into our seats, when I heard a vaguely familiar voice order "Double Rum and Coke."

I looked up at the end of the bar, and there sat my old nemesis, Coach Donofrio. From what I had heard he was still teaching History at the high school and had even taught Gene for a few years. I really harbored no ill will toward him anymore. While I was in college, I used to come home in the summers and play ball for the Lakewood City North County League team for three or four seasons. Jeff was in his late twenties by then and was the top pitcher for our team. So, as teammates, we had buried the hatchet long ago.

"Unbelievable, Jeff," I sang out, "We were just talking about you.

"And I'll bet I know what you were saying," he chuckled as he moved over to sit beside us.

As he got closer, I noticed that the years had not been kind to Coach Donofrio. He looked weary and sad and defeated. "What did your dad tell you about me?" He asked, as he shook Gene's hand and sat down next to him.

"That you gave him a hard time," laughed Gene.

"Well, he was the best hitter on the team," the old coach admitted, "but he was cocky, and I thought I should teach him some humility."

"He also told me that you married the most beautiful girl in town," Gene continued.

"And paid the price for it," Coach Donofrio interjected immediately.

"Jeff, I'm surprised that didn't last," I told him. "She seemed almost perfect. And you two seemed so in love."

An odd silence filled the air for five or ten seconds. Then I coughed and added, "You know, I used to be in love with her sister."

"Oh, I knew that," he grinned. "The whole family knew. But you never had a chance.

"Her mother absolutely worshipped Blake Bianchi. With his lawyer father and his doctor uncle, she thought he was the only one good enough for her daughter. She would belittle you constantly to Lorraine. But, I knew what she was really doing; she was really complaining about me to Angela. *I* was just this small-town ballplayer. *I* was the one with no future. When she insulted you, she was really insulting *me*.

"So, I did my best to join in; to put you down; to show her that we were *not* alike. I'm sorry I gave you such a hard time when I was coaching. I knew the truth; we were exactly the same. Plus, I was *just* a teacher, not nearly good enough for Angela."

"Did she actually *say* that?" I wondered out loud.

"Teddy," Coach Donofrio stopped and looked me straight in the eye. "She said it every single day."

"But Lorraine and *Blake*? That was another story. Blake could do no wrong— great family ties and an army officer to boot? She called him the finest man she ever met.

"You dodged a bullet, Teddy," he interjected. "Believe me.

"You just can't have a lasting relationship with a woman, when every day you have to hear that you're not good enough for her.

"We were *so* in love at first. I was sure that would be enough to hold us together, but little by little, it all slipped away. It wore me down, Ted. I couldn't sleep at night. I worried all the time. I wondered if maybe I *was* a failure.

"Poor Angela, she was caught in the crossfire, and it eventually pulled us apart."

I glanced over at Gene. He was riveted to every word Jeff was saying.

"Of course, it was the self-fulfilling prophecy," he stated matter-of-factly, lowering his head into his drink. "The fights got worse and worse and one day, she just left. And I didn't have the strength to win her back."

He could see the quizzical look on my face, and the unasked question that hung in the air like heavy fog.

"Sure, the same thing would have happened to you, Ted," he announced finally. "The old lady didn't want you anywhere near her daughter. She wouldn't even call you by your name. She always referred to you as *that Rockland boy.*

"I know you probably think she hated you, but she really didn't. It's just that she couldn't brag about you like she could with Blake. She wanted to be able to go to the beauty shop and tell all her friends that her beautiful daughter was dating a lawyer's son; a Bianchi. She wanted her brothers and sisters-in-law to admire her.

"Believe it or not, the old lady was an Italian beauty herself when she was young. But, she got married at an early age, and then started cranking out babies. She had seven kids! She didn't have time for her own life. She lived vicariously through her daughters. You and I? Well, we just didn't fit into her plans. She was the kind of mother-in-law that could really wear you down.

"And look what you got instead!" he exclaimed, "The Batistas: with old Gene Batista, a high school social studies teacher for forty years, and the finest gentleman I've ever met; and his wonderful wife Martha, maybe the sweetest woman on earth.

"I *know* they supported you. Gene used to brag about you in the teachers' lounge; how hard you two worked; how well you treated his daughter. Gene and Martha—they both *love* you. Do you know what my life would have been like if I had that kind of support?" Coach Donofrio got up slowly now and walked back to the end of the bar, deep in thought.

Gene just looked at me in understanding and relief, as the bartender handed over our takeout order.

As we walked out the door, I glanced back at Jeff Donofrio. He was only six years older than me, but he looked so drained and feeble, as if life itself was just oozing out of him and draining into his double rum and coke.

When we got back to the car, Gene smirked, "you asked Mr. Donofrio to be here, didn't you?'

"No Champ," I answered, "It was just a coincidence. But I think sometimes God plays a part in every coincidence.

"I hope you understand, now, how lucky I was to find your Mom when I did," I spoke evenly and paused for effect after every word.

"And how lucky you were to have a small-town girlfriend?" Gene nodded, "Who stuck by you through thick and thin?"

"Well," I agreed, "Molly was the one who taught me, at age ten, what loyalty was; what a real girlfriend, a real teammate was. And that ideal stuck with me for the rest of my life."

I turned the key in the ignition and fastened my seatbelt. "So, tell me, Gene. Did you get anything out of our marathon discussion last night?"

Gene laughed, "Yeah, Dad. Thanks. You probably saved me from ten or twenty years of misery."

A feeling of well-being filled the car as Gene leaned over and switched on the radio to the Youngstown Oldies station just in time to hear the first bars of John Lennon singing his cover of an old Ben E. King classic.

When the night has come, and the land is dark, and the moon is the only light we'll see...

"Are you kidding me?" gasped Gene. "Is that another coincidence?"

"The Lord moves in mysterious ways," I laughed, as the radio sang on: *No, I won't be afraid. No, I won't be afraid, just as long as you stand by me.*

Now we both joined in the singing, "*So darlin' darlin' stand by me. Oh, now, stand by me.*"

And, as the car weaved its way across the Fifth Street Bridge, we could see in the distance, the cold, full Moon rising slowly over the Old Clock Tower of Lakewood High School. It was huge and bright and full of promise.

"Look at that!" Gene gasped in awe.

I just smiled and nodded and kept on singing.

ABOUT THE AUTHOR

ED PRENCE grew up in the tiny town of Koppel, Pennsylvania. An amateur baseball player, Ed played for a powerhouse high school team in nearby Ellwood City, and then became a Division I shortstop at Duquesne University of the Atlantic 10 Conference.

He trained for a career in Journalism at Duquesne, but made the leap into advertising sales, where he quickly became one of the leading media accountant executives in the northeast. In 2010 he retired from Comcast Spotlight in Pittsburgh, having authored over 1000 radio and television commercials. He won the prestigious Telly Award in 2000 for his work in Pittsburgh market advertising.

Now retired, Ed has turned his talents back to his first love—creative writing. In *The Last of the Rockland Boys*, his second novel, the author draws upon his experiences as a life-long amateur player and his boyhood growing up in a small western-Pennsylvania steel town, where baseball was everything.

Ed's first novel, *The Last Perfect Summer*, was the winner of the 2014 Independent Book Publishers Association's Benjamin Franklin Silver Award for the Best Historical Fiction of 2013, and also won Pittsburgh Authors' TAZ Award as the Best General Fiction in the Pittsburgh market.

Ed makes his home on Clearwater Beach, Florida, and also in Ellwood City, Pennsylvania.

Made in the USA
Middletown, DE
08 October 2022